JUST ONCE

D1506764

H O V A V   H E T H

Translation from Hebrew by Daniella Zamir

May 2009

ISBN: 1539831531
ISBN 13: 9781539831532

CHAPTER 1

Men manage statistics in their heads: how many women did I sleep with, how old was I when I first had sex, how many girlfriends have I had? And for some reason, these men, or at least many of them, attach great significance to these internal stats, so the data sometimes undergoes touch-ups and updates: a light make-out session is added to the list of full blown sex, a girl you dated for a week without even touching her suddenly turns into an ex-girlfriend, and despite the fact that this internal deceit is carried out with complete self-awareness, it still provides some odd form of comfort.

And these stats, they're meaningless, if you get what I'm saying. Take for example two men, Mister A and Mister B. Mister A met his wife, the love of his life, when he was sixteen. A's wife is a real goddess, smart and charming, beautiful and hot, any sane man would want her, and A would never cheat on her. Even after twenty years of marriage, the sex is still great. B, on the other hand, never experienced a relationship with a woman. He goes to hookers. His first time was with a hooker, and his last time will be with a hooker as well. He never seduced a woman, never pleased a woman, has no clue how to touch a woman because he never got feedback, he was never with a woman who actually wanted him. And when the lives of both these men are summed up, under the category of how many women you've slept with, A will have one woman. B will have maybe a thousand, maybe even more, it's all a question of money. But it will be A who chalked up a great sex life, and B who actually didn't know a thing. You could say that he died a virgin.

"But don't you think B still has some advantage? It must be exciting meeting a different hooker every time, even if you don't know anything. And A, even if the sex is great, don't tell me that after twenty years he still feels with his wife that excitement of being with someone for the first time. And besides, how does he know it's so great if he has no basis for comparison? After all, he's never been with anyone but his wife!"

"Fine, I'm not trying to convince you to marry the first woman you meet."

"And are you so certain that a man can't please a hooker? Didn't you see Pretty Woman?"

"Forget about it, if that even happens, it's one in a million. After all, if a woman wanted you, she wouldn't take money, right? And Richard Gere is hardly an example, Mister B is no Richard Gere. If he was such a stud, he wouldn't have become a permanent John."

These strange dialogues took place in Eyal's head for one simple reason: Eyal was Mister A. Actually, his condition was slightly worse than Mister A's, because he met his wife, the only woman he had ever slept with, at the age of twenty-one, after the army. He was obviously intelligent enough to know that these nagging voices in his head pointed to a certain problem. Perhaps not a huge problem, but a problem nonetheless. These stats bothered him. At thirty-four he looked great. He was the VP of marketing at a startup, a smart and successful man, and he knew that if he tried his luck in the meat market, he would be a big hit. He didn't have to guess. He got a lot of looks, innuendoes, even straight-out propositions. But he loved his wife Galit fiercely, his marriage was wonderful, they had a three-year-old son and a girl on the way. Divorcing Galit obviously never crossed his mind, and cheating on her seemed like a horrible idea. All in good time, he told himself. If I screw up my wonderful family life at thirty-four, it won't make me twenty again. And still, this hiccup in his resume bothered him. So what to do?

"Gin, are you getting out of the shower?" Galit started calling him Gin the first day they met because he was a virgin. Eyal warned her that she could expect an execution if she ever told anyone the source of the nickname. Many friends asked Eyal where the nickname came from and he answered with a shrug—Ask Galit.

"Come on already, Gin, you've been in there for almost half an hour." That happened to him a lot, musings in the shower, overstaying his welcome in the shower, what about the water level in the Sea of Galilee, what will become of the kid, you can't get anything done like this.

"Gin?"

Now her voice reached him from a distance of about two centimeters. He turned off the water, opened his eyes and the glass door of the shower.

"You're so sexy when you're angry." It was the truth, she was always sexy, she had wide hips, a narrow waist and heavy breasts, but when she had that murderous look in her eyes there was something completely captivating about her. She was two years older than him, immigrated from Romania when she was six and still spoke the language with her parents. Smack in the center of her royal back was a tattoo of a Rubik's Cube, the famous Hungarian invention, and when Eyal asked her why not a Romanian symbol, she said that she had wanted a tattoo of mamaliga but no one knew how to draw it. She had a long and oval face, looked a little like Nadia Comaneci, only that her eyes were narrower and more beautiful. She had straight, shoulder-length hair that was almost always gathered in a short and sweet fan-shaped braid. A quiet and steady voice reflected her inner-peacefulness. In times of crisis people would listen to Galit even though she didn't have a loud voice at all, and almost never yelled. The few times she did throw a fit and screamed, the effect was harrowing.

"Goddammit, Eyal, you're pissing me off with those comments."

"Yes, yes, you're right. Very bad comment, I take it back."

"Come on, get out of there already and help me, I'm five months pregnant, remember?"

"Yes, coming out."

He looked at the shower's steam-covered glass doors. They had bought this shower when they renovated the apartment four years ago. They wanted a comfortable and elegant bathroom. The old bathroom had nearly ancient tiles, over twenty years old, the same age as the building, and the shower was 30 x 30 inches. With his broad shoulders, Eyal could barely soap himself in there.

"Gin, what's up with you today?"

"I'm coming, I'm coming."

What will it be like when they have two kids? Can he really go through with it today? He knew this was his opportunity, a work meeting in Haifa until midnight, maybe even past midnight, it was entirely plausible that he stay overnight and return in the morning, he would have done it even without his cheating scheme, and she understood, understood completely, what sane five-month-pregnant woman with a three-year-old would want to risk losing her husband in a car accident?

"Good God, Gin, what's going on with you today, you're all over the place!"

"What?" He looked in her direction. His towel was lying on the mat like a used rag, and the shampoo bottle had fallen from the shower rack, slowly spilling its contents on the floor. "For fuck's sake. Don't clean it up, the garbage squad is on it!"

"Like I had any intention of doing that. Do you realize it's already twenty to eight?"

"Yikes, Daniel isn't even up yet, is he? I have to leave in three minutes if I'm going to drop him off at kindergarten and make it to Fugu on time."

CHAPTER 2

Fugu Ltd. was a high-tech company with the most ridiculous name in the industry. Max, the entrepreneur, had given Eyal a whole lecture about fugu, the deadly Japanese fish that with the right touch can be made into a divine delicacy—just like a startup that is likely to end up in the brimming garbage can of failed startups, but with the right management can turn into a giant success and make all of its executives millionaires. Eyal thought it was all hooey and that Max just went for a cool name. The employees, not without a certain amount of affection, called the company Puffer. Fugu Ltd. developed software that analyzed the human voice. Based on a recording of the speaker, the software was supposed to identify whether the person was telling the truth or lying, whether he was under pressure, content, suffering, and so on. There had already been attempts to develop similar software, but Max's algorithms were revolutionary and way ahead of the competition. The applications were obviously endless, from recording your rival in a negotiation in order to identify his weaknesses and to see if he's trying to pull one over on you, to police interrogations and countless other possibilities. The company was located on the fourth floor of an elegant five-story glass building in the high-tech district of Herzliya Pituach, north of Tel Aviv. Twenty-five employees worked at Fugu Ltd., and more than a fine delicacy, the company now resembled the dangerous creation of a sloppy cook. The money was quickly running out—the market only starting to recover from the collapse of the subprime bubble, and investors thought long and hard before signing checks, if they signed them at all.

Eyal had already gone through one round in the startup industry, which grew to terrifying dimensions before the 2000 crash of the internet bubble. The company was called Cream, after the legendary band that released only one record. Perhaps naming the company after a band that broke up so quickly because there wasn't a room in the world that could contain all of its members' egos at the same time had been a poor choice. The company's business was—big surprise—the internet. And as befitting a company with such a pretentious name, it indeed had to do with rock 'n' roll, enabling people to meet online and create music together. The company's intention wasn't to actually produce records, but its intentions were nonetheless professional. A drummer from Brazil could collaborate with a guitar player from England and an Italian singer, each adding their part through the company's rather diverse platform, without using their original instruments. You could create a pretty decent sketch, a type of mission statement that would subsequently be performed with other instruments, the instruments of the real world. This was long before revolutions that brought down regimes sprang from the internet. The idea that musicians from different corners of the planet would meet in the virtual world and found a hit band was riveting. There were rumors about big names in the rock 'n' roll world who had invested in the company, even though no official announcements about the matter were ever released, rumors about Elton John and Peter Hammill. What was certain and official was the fact that at its peak, the company was valued at approximately two hundred million dollars, which meant that in theory, at the age of twenty-five, Eyal was worth about a million dollars. He also had a salary that came close to his current one, and a Mazda Lantis like every other good little high-tech employee of that period. Eyal worked in the business development department back then, still yet to reach a VP position, merely one of three employees who were subordinate to the strategy and business development VP. He had an office on the fortieth floor of the Azrieli Circular Tower, where the company had rented an entire floor for an insane amount of money, which obviously contributed to the company's early demise.

Eyal and the two other junior business developers would often have coffee together in the office, even whisky if it was late enough in the day, gaze at the mesmerizing view of the incessant traffic on the Ayalon highway and of the Ramat Gan Towers, and dream about big business and even bigger money. His colleagues, who were single, also dreamed about the super models this money would certainly attract. It was an insane period, a time in which Israeli entrepreneurs who received offers of two hundred million dollars for a company that would fail less than a year later, refused on the grounds that less than a billion dollars wasn't real money. Ziv, the company's CEO, a brilliant thirty-year-old who had served in the military's elite security research and development unit, liked gathering his "special staff officers"—as he liked to call them—to discuss all sorts of theories. Theories about the development of the internet, theories about how to motivate people to march the company into the future, political theories—everything was discussed with the utmost seriousness and the belief that every word uttered there on the fortieth floor was of actual significance in the world. Soon we are going to witness a new Middle East, without borders, Shimon Peres's Middle East, he said about two months prior to the colossal failure of Camp David. You don't know what amazing economies are developing in the Persian Gulf, mountains of money just waiting for projects. Obviously, most of this money will go to the Arab countries, which are also picking up quickly, the large Arab countries are the China of the small oil emirates, but we can also grab a cut if we're smart. I see joint projects funded by Qatar or Dubai and carried out in Egypt, there will be some huge opportunities here, no doubt. I'm already looking into the possibility of founding a small company that will represent our interests in Dubai. Everyone nodded enthusiastically. Many stories were woven around him, in the manner that stories are told of legendary fighters or great leaders. It was said that he had a perfect memory, that he remembered every word exchanged in every business meeting. That he had an iron bladder that allowed him to sit for hours and even entire days (for instance, in those endless meetings with the Chinese or the Japanese) in the conference room without getting up once. There were even some who talked about telepathic abilities that enabled him to know, for instance, what he should say to investors who injected tens of millions of dollars into the company and led to its inflated value. There were obviously rumors about sexual prowess. Ziv was rather ugly, but everybody was sure that he was having an affair with his beautiful secretary. Whenever he shut the door behind him and the secretary was nowhere to be seen, even if everyone knew she hadn't come to work that day or that she had gone out for lunch, a temporary rumor would spread about wild sex taking place inside his room. There was even a rather ugly rumor of the kind that only spreads in predominantly male work environments; it was said that he gave a go at every new female hire. Not in the sense of forcing himself on them, but that they just fell at his feet. It wasn't completely clear if people actually believed these rumors, but it was obvious to everyone that Ziv operated in a different world, a world of superheroes in which the rules simply didn't apply. He operates outside the sphere of mere humans—was a favorite expression of the VP of business development, and on the fortieth floor of the Azrieli Towers, with the billions looking closer than ever, it sounded very intelligent.

In 2000, Cream Ltd. had about a hundred employees, thirty of whom worked in the company's U.S. branch. Traveling to the U.S. and to Europe, the company employees always flew business class, and in Israel, they wined and dined clients and potential investors in Tel Aviv's most expensive restaurants, luxury establishments that quickly closed after the crash. Money was spent like water. There were people who cautioned about the company's crazy burn rate, and some even joked about it. The problem was that no one took the warnings, or the jokes, seriously. Everyone was convinced they had entered a world in which there were neither mistakes nor failures. It was obvious to them that the billions were just around the corner (no one even dared to entertain the notion of an exit worth less than a billion dollars). Three months after the Second Intifada broke out, most of the company employees, including Eyal, received their termination notices. The money that had poured out of the company like a surging river simply ran out. The revenues were so negligible that no one actually new the exact shameful figures, and the investors weren't willing to put another penny in the company. The ten employees who remained on the payroll moved into a shabby building that looked a bit like one of the local auto repair shops. The company lasted six more months of slow demise until it finally closed down. Eyal remained in contact with Ziv for a few years, meeting with him once in the house Ziv had managed to buy in one of the posh Tel Aviv neighborhoods before the business went belly up—the best investment he had ever made. Ziv was already heading a new company that developed financial software to help companies analyze their business performances in various segments, for instance, regional segments, analyzing the true profitability of a region as opposed to the one presented in the profit and loss accounting statements. As far as Eyal could tell, the new company wouldn't amount to much. The post-Cream Ziv seemed a little like a soldier suffering from PTSD. He talked a lot about the need to keep things in perspective, about losing his humility and with it, all connection to reality. He seemed like a man who had lost all his self-confidence. When Eyal looked at him he recalled all those crazy rumors dating back to the glory days in Azrieli Towers. The contrast between those rumors and the broken man now sitting in front of him was perhaps the starkest illustration of the complete absurdity of everything they had taken for granted before the crash.

They were sitting in the elegant conference room around an oval wooden table facing a giant tinted glass window. They used to joke that they had a great ocean view from that window, because on an especially clear day you could see a few inches of the sea between two distant buildings. Everyone was present in the meeting.

Mandy—at fifty years old, Mandy the CEO was nearly twenty years older than Eyal. He was a smart and pedantic person, but had yet to lead a startup to an exit or any kind of substantial success. The money was running out, and with adversaries among the investors as well as among the company employees, he was under a significant amount of pressure. His adversaries claimed he was simply desperate.

Max—the anarchist entrepreneur who now held the position of VP of Research and Development, he had invented the company's technology, and knew it better than anyone. It was obvious that no one would buy the company without Max. On the other hand, he was an extremely messy person, all over the place. An attempt had been made in the past to switch him to CTO—a chief technical manager who deals with complex technological problems, but doesn't manage the R&D employees. But Max did more or less whatever he could to impede the work of the miserable VP of R&D who was brought in in his place, and eventually he was reappointed to his VP position, which he filled rather poorly.

Eyal—in his position as VP of marketing, Eyal somehow had the knack of getting along with everyone.

Boaz—as the COO who made too many mistakes, Max believed he was on the way out.

Yonit—the hot finance manager—at such an early state of the company's life she wasn't entitled yet to the position of CFO, but everyone appreciated her and was sure that she would get the job if and when the company reached a size that would justify such a position. Appreciated or not, as often happens with attractive women, malicious and mostly bogus rumors were spread about her. At least half of the company if not more was sure that Yonit and Eyal were having an affair. This was obviously not true, but Eyal had stopped denying it a long time ago since commenting at all only made things worse, and one has to admit that there was something nice about automatically being suspected of having an affair with the most attractive woman in the office. Many whispered behind her back that she had received her stock options after providing not entirely professional services to Jeff Elroy, the Sheringham board representative. Sheringham was Fugu's largest investor, and even though it had yet to hold fifty percent of the shares, it in fact controlled the company. These rumors obviously stemmed, at least in part, from Jeff's dubious reputation. Jeff Elroy had been married for at least three decades, and he loved talking about his unyielding love for his wife and about their romantic luxury vacations around the globe. Every so often photos of him standing next to gorgeous women at various events were published in the gossip columns. But the cameras never caught more than a hug or peck on the cheek, and Eyal didn't know if there was any truth to the rumors about him. At any rate, if couldn't be pleasant for his wife.

"Okay, gentlemen, let's start. Yonit and I will be flying to the States in three days to close this round and the deal with Citi, I hope. I believe the money from the fundraising will come in two weeks tops."

One of the reasons for the rumors surrounding Yonit was her frequent fundraising trips abroad. A finance manager in such a small company isn't usually involved to this extent in fundraising rounds. But she had a pleasant personality, she was intelligent and spoke excellent English, and no one thought her presence in such meetings could do any harm.

"Why are you even going to New York? Isn't it enough to meet Elroy here?" Max asked, and everyone knew the answer. Because the deal wasn't closed yet, and it was another one of Sheringham's ways to pressure them, to squeeze a little more out of them. Mandy ignored the question.

Sheringham already owned forty percent of the company, and in the next round they would get their hands on more. This irritated Max, the anarchist entrepreneur. The company's first CEO who was replaced by Mandy was Itzik, Max's childhood friend and his partner in founding the company. Itzik was much better than Mandy at fundraising. There was something about his presence that was lively and theatrical compared to Mandy's stiffness. Itzik brought Sheringham on board and then Sheringham got rid of him because he was as sloppy as Max, a far cry from CEO material.

"Max, the material I'm waiting for will be ready by tomorrow, right?"

"It'll be ready, don't worry. How much oxygen do we have left?"

"We're going to get capital that will carry us for an entire year."

"I mean before we get the new round."

"Two months."

"What can I say, great bargaining position. If they don't give us money now we'll have to shut down. I'm surprised they're not demanding a hundred percent of the company."

"Itzik, this is hardly constructive right now."

"My name is Max. If Itzik was here he would have brought in more investors long before we were standing with a gun to our head."

Mandy was visibly contemplating whether to punch Max. He decided against it.

"Calm down, Max. In a few days we'll know if we have an agreement with Citibank. If all goes well it will generate more revenue."

Eyal had managed to sell to someone at Citibank the idea that Fugu's technology could help them improve their credit portfolio. The idea was simple: Fugu's software would analyze the customer's conversation with the credit manager. If the analysis suggested the person asking for credit wasn't reliable, it was an indication they shouldn't extend him credit.

"How much are they going to invest?"

"It's not a done deal yet. But think how much money this company can make if a major bank like Citi integrates our technology into their credit system. There are a lot of banks out there, this could be a game changer."

"From your mouth to God's ears," Max said in a slightly reconciled tone.

"Eyal, you're going to Haifa to meet with the Japanese today?"

"Yes." And then I'm going to cheat on my wife, what do you have to say about that? How strange it felt.

"What do these Japanese want anyway?" Max asked.

"They're NICE's competitors. They develop systems that police use to analyze the dispatchers' voice traffic. They think they can use our technology to sort calls according to the level of urgency."

"Most stressed out first served?"

"Something like that."

"So basically it's a system that gives priority to geeks?"

"So it's definitely in everyone's interest here to close the deal," Yonit said and laughed. It was almost a tradition, hot Yonit complaining about the geekfest that was her workplace, excluding the divine Eyal, of course. It was all done in good spirit and it didn't really bother anyone, expect maybe for Mandy, who had a bit of a complex in that specific area.

"Ha ha, so witty."

"Indeed. So why isn't Max coming with you?"

"Yeah, why?"

"Because Max has his work cut out for him with all the material he has to prepare for you, and it's just a first impression kind of meeting, it'll be fine." Eyal panicked for a moment, and maybe deep down he was even hoping that a last-minute addition of Max to his meeting would foil his illicit scheme, but it didn't happen.

"Of course it'll be fine. Okay, I wanted to talk a bit about your subordinates' coffee breaks, or rather, work breaks between coffee. If things go on like this, we'll have to consider firing people…"

This was a known sign that there wasn't really anything left to talk about until the results of the upcoming round of fundraising became clear. Even the deal with Citibank wouldn't help them if the investors decided not to stand behind the company. But why not talk about coffee breaks? Surely as important a subject as any.

"Who even drinks the coffee here anymore?" Max said, and everyone laughed. One of the few good things Itzik had done as CEO was to arrange for the delivery of fresh bags of coffee beans from Colombia and other coffee superpowers to the kitchenette each morning, and there was even a state-of-the-art coffee grinder. One of the first things Mandy did as CEO was move the company to Tasters' Choice. Max also claimed that this detrimental act was the single significant change Mandy had made. Max never forgave them for getting rid of Itzik, and he obviously viewed the new CEO as one of the major culprits in this crime. Max had told Eyal what happened in the board meeting in which Itzik was informed of his termination. Jeff Elroy, Chairman of the Sheringham board, was the main speaker.

"In conclusion, we are very grateful, Itzik, for your contribution to—"

"You can't fire me! This is my company, I founded it!" Itzik was a tall, lanky man with straight black hair pulled into a long braid. He had angular features, oddly high and pointy cheekbones and a small hook nose that looked a little like the beak of an Angry Bird. Eyal always thought that he looked like a strange combination of a computer geek and a hoodlum. More than once he told Max that Itzik didn't look like a CEO.

"There's a majority on the board, darling…"

"I brought in all the investors, I brought *you*, without me this company would be worthless!"

"Listen to me, boy wonder, the fact that you brought in investors doesn't mean you can run a company! You're sloppy, you can't even put together a proper presentation. The document you prepared on corporate strategy was the most infantile thing I've even seen from a company manager. You're no CEO. If I was the one interviewing you, you wouldn't have gotten any kind of managerial position here. It's way out of your league, get it?"

It was at that point that Itzik lost his temper.

"Fuck you!" he pounded on the table, "I have no idea what you want from me, you fucking piece of—" Max held Itzik back, keeping him from leaping across the table.

"I want you to quietly leave my company and go do whatever it is that you know how to do, maybe become a barista."

"This isn't your company, it's my company!" Itzik yelled at him. His expression was that of a man eager to murder.

"If you were worth something as a CEO, you would have realized long ago that this isn't your company, you don't even know the agreements made with your investors." At this point Max was forced to restrain Itzik and drag him out of the room, as it was becoming increasingly clear that he was on a direct path to physical violence, and Max knew that Jeff could knock him out with one blow.

The following day, Eyal received an invitation to join Jeff for lunch. They ate at Raphael, the posh restaurant in the hotel district near the beach. They dined in the private room, which could seat at least ten, even though they were only three—Eyal, Jeff, and his pretty assistant, Tali.

Jeff was an impressive man. He was in his early fifties, tall and broad-shouldered. He had thick gray hair, piercing brown eyes, and he wore dark suits that hugged his athletic body. He ran at least one marathon a year. He sat in front of Eyal with a fat cigar in one hand and a glass of whisky in the other. Each year, he abstained from cigars and whisky for the three months that preceded the marathon. In what was perhaps his most famous photo, he was standing at the finish line in sweaty sports clothes, a wide smile plastered on his face and a bottle of Jack Daniel's in his right hand. He told them war stories from his days as a young investor, while Tali looked at him with visible adoration.

The sommelier came with the wine bottle.

"An excellent choice as always, Mister Elroy."

Eyal hoped they couldn't see how nauseous the shameful flattery had made him.

"Thank you, thank you. You know that it's the best boutique winery in the country, in my opinion. Henry, the owner of the winery, invites me and the missus once a month for a steak and wine dinner. We can easily empty five bottles between us. I drink at least two myself."

"Judging by the price of this bottle, I think Fugu is in the wrong business. Maybe we should start developing a system to analyze wines."

"A system to analyze wine. That's an interesting idea, Eyal. If you bring me that kind of technology I'd be happy to invest."

"I'd have to consult Max. I have no idea how to develop something like that."

Jess sniffed his wine while twirling the glass.

"Mmmm, this wine has the distinct aroma of citrus, truly excellent."

Eyal loved wine, but he was always suspicious of those types of statements. When he sniffed wine, all he could smell was wine.

"You mentioned Max, which is actually the subject I wanted to talk to you about. Eyal, you don't know me that well yet, somehow we haven't had the opportunity to really talk." There was a slight remnant of an American accent in his speech, almost unnoticeable.

"Yes."

"But I've certainly been following your work. I think you're very important to the company."

"Really? I'm trying to think of even one useful thing I've done for the company so far and I can't really think of any. I can't believe I just said that. I'm going to stop giving myself bad PR now."

"It's fine," Jeff said and laughed. "I like your modesty. And what I like even more is the fact that you're calm, and you can calm others. I want you to make Max calm down."

"Max told me what happened in the board meeting. Couldn't you have just fired the man and leave it at that? Itzik is a sensitive matter for Max."

"You're right. I spoke a little too much, although I can assure you that every word was true. The company couldn't afford one more day with Itzik."

"Are you so sure that Mandy, the new CEO, will deliver the goods?"

"Trust me, if Jeff found him he'll deliver," Tali said with complete seriousness. She probably felt the urge to contribute something to the conversation. Eyal knew he was guilty of chauvinistic thoughts, and that there was no shortage of gorgeous girls with a good head on their shoulders. His wife Galit was an excellent example, and so was Yonit, the finance manager. But he still couldn't help thinking that Tali's professional skills weren't necessarily Jeff's primary consideration when deciding to hire her. Jeff was just surrounded by so many gorgeous women, and it didn't stand to reason that all female venture capital experts looked like supermodels.

"It's fine, Tali. Eyal's doubts are certainly understandable. Mandy is without question better than Itzik, but whether he'll deliver? We'll have to wait and see. If he turns out to be a disappointment, we'll replace him as well, after a respectable period, of course. We have to give him a fair chance. It doesn't matter. If we can get back to the issue I wanted to discuss with you—I'm simply trying to make you realize that the situation is critical. Max has to get it into his head that the company is literally on the verge of shutting down. Max is a genius, no doubt. The company wouldn't be worth much without him. But he's just as disorganized as his friend."

"You want to bump Max too?"

"I still want him to be the CTO and handle the complicated technological problems, but I want him to let a professional manager run the day-to-day operations of the development staff. I haven't told him yet because I'm afraid it might overload his nervous system. I want you to talk to him, calm him down and make him see that this is in his best interest as well, since he hates managing people, right? Of course I'm right. And on the other hand, there's no one better than him at solving technological problems. I want you to explain these things to him urgently. Tell him that he needs to work with the new CEO as well as with the new head of research and development."

Eyal knew that Jeff was basically right. Itzik was a catastrophe. Max was brilliant and essential, but he was no manager. And he really was the person who had to make Max calm down, there was no one else who could do it. But there was something infuriating about Jeff's smugness. Itzik was a hothead, and Eyal could have easily imagined him trying to kill Jeff with all that dashing self-confidence he spread around him.

"I also want to tell you that if Max doesn't pull himself together, we'll have to consider suing him personally."

"I really think you're exaggerating, Jeff, you can't just skin a man alive every time he disagrees with you. We're all human beings, sometimes a person doesn't do exactly what you want, but that's life, right?"

Eyal immediately started thinking about the countless stories he had heard about all the agonies high tech people had suffered at the hands of venture capitalists. High tech companies simply couldn't do without the venture capital industry. Eyal knew that very well. But while venture capitalists had earned the reputation of villains who cared only about money, technology people like Max were known as visionaries who pursued justice.

"You're wrong! Look, Eyal, I understand this upsets you. But I represent the partners at Sheringham, people who don't exactly like losing money, as you probably know. Max and Itzik approached us a year and a half ago with a very impressive presentation that convinced us to invest a lot of money in the company. So Max can't exactly sulk right now. There are a lot of things that can bring down a company, sometimes even bad luck can ruin a great idea. But what can't happen is the founder, the engineer behind the company's technology, deciding that he's giving us the silent treatment. It's simply unacceptable, do you understand me? I won't take it, under any circumstance, and if you intend to become a serious businessman, and you do have what it takes, Eyal, then you must understand this," Jeff said. He gave Eyal a meaningful look, stuck his fork into a big chunk of steak and devoured it. Eyal felt that he was quickly losing his appetite.

"If I tell Max what you're asking me to tell him, you can forget about him. Sue him or don't sue him, you'll never see him again, maybe only in court."

"You're right. I don't want you to tell Max what I said. I told you this only so you'd realize how important it is to get Max back on track as soon as possible. Approach it with composure. You already have the experience, Eyal, you've already experienced a startup collapse, you know a company can't afford a month of soul searching. There's never time for that. Talk to Max, today. Get him back on the straight and narrow. I trust you."

Eyal left the meeting feeling slightly confused. He actually agreed with much of what Jeff had said. But Jeff annoyed the hell out of him, and Eyal was envisioning scenarios in which he and Max waged an all-out-war against the evil money man. But with time Eyal learned that there was nothing truly bad about Jeff. Even his flattery of Eyal was genuine, he actually appreciated him. Jeff viewed every company in which Sheringam invested solely through the eyes of his partners at the venture capital firm. Nothing else interested him. He was as cool as a cucumber. If he believed that an employee at a company he invested in was harming it, he would get rid of him without a shred of mercy. It wasn't meanness. It was simply a cold judgment call, void of any sentiments. Although in hindsight, the cold judgment calls Jeff had made at the time weren't particularly successful. Max tormented the new VP of R&D until the latter had to quit—within less than two months. And Mandy, well, he was no maverick.

Eyal met with Jeff on several other occasions. Sometimes he caught him in the middle of a consultation: young entrepreneurs used to call him because he was considered a kind of guru in his field, and he talked to them with great courteousness, listened attentively to their problems and devoted long moments to them. But sometimes Eyal felt like warning them after their conversations with their guru. To tell them not to get confused, because despite the kind approach, if Jeff invests in them they better not mess up, because if they do, nice Jeff will disappear and they'll discover Jeff the shark, the snake, the merciless businessman.

CHAPTER 3

At about six o'clock in the evening, Eyal had finished with his tasks and was ready for his fateful trip to Haifa. There was something slightly embarrassing about meeting with Japanese clients; it always made him self-conscious about how stupid the name of his company was, a little like meeting with a Japanese company called gefilte fish. Eyal was very interested in Japan. His honeymoon with Galit was a three-month trip to the country, and meetings with Japanese businessmen always made him a bit nostalgic, as if through them he could recreate that magical period. Now it only contributed to his guilt, and he struggled to focus on the preparations for the meeting. All he could think about was what was going to take place after it. He sat behind his elegant large desk and remembered how proud he felt when they had moved into the new offices two years ago, how optimistic everyone was, and how quickly things go down the crapper sometimes. He was starting to have déjà vus from the good old times at Cream. Who knew, maybe there was hope for Fugu yet. He made a last phone call to Galit, asked her once again if it was okay to spend the night in Haifa, and again asked himself why he was even asking her. There was nothing out of the ordinary about a night in Haifa. He was acting suspiciously and he knew it. Eyal took his laptop and a small projector. He got into his Mazda 3—which came with his contract—where a white dress shirt and a suit were waiting for him. Adhering to a strict dress code was always advisable when meeting with Japanese, even in the middle of an Israeli heatwave. He started the car, turned onto the highway and began making his way to

Haifa. He never thought of Haifa as an especially exciting place, but today he felt as though he was on the way to sin city Las Vegas.

Eyal arrived at the hotel at eleven-thirty at night, exhausted and cranky. He kept experiencing troubling flashbacks from the meeting with the Japanese. The Japanese VP of marketing, Mr. Hiroshi, wanted him to provide explanations about certain technical issues that were simply outside Eyal's area of expertise. He was very concerned about the technical feasibility of integrating Fugu's technology into Japanese products. Eyal, who had spent most of his prep time mapping out a collaboration between the two companies, tried to explain that there had never been a problem integrating Fugu's technology into the products of any company, but Mr. Hiroshi insisted, and Eyal didn't have a feel for whether his answers had satisfied him. When parting ways, he had no idea whether it had been a good, decent, or completely catastrophic meeting. He had also drunk much more than he should have, and was in urgent need of a cup of coffee. He checked into the hotel and inspected the room, which was somewhat disappointing. The wall-to-wall carpet was slightly frayed, and while the TV was connected to cable, the set itself was an outdated model. The remote worked only after banging it several times against the table. The wall paper in the bathroom was peeling in every corner. This room wasn't the ideal setting for his adventure, but it would have to do. Eyal took out his laptop, turned it on and connected to the internet. He wasn't sure how to go about it. He had never searched for sex services online. But actually, he thought—what was the rush? He had the whole night ahead of him, and needed a cup of coffee anyway. He thought about making himself one with the old kettle and cheap instant coffee in the room, but then decided to go down to the lobby, have a proper cappuccino and relax before diving into business. The room's grim décor already indicated that the experience in the hotel lobby wasn't going to be that of flashy hobnobbing with jetsetters, and of course, it was already very late. There was only one other man in the lobby, a businessman who every now and then whispered something in German into his cellphone while sipping beer. The cappuccino wasn't very good. The foam was too thin, the coffee itself of mediocre quality, and yet Eyal relished every sip. It was as if the fatigue had disappeared, every muscle in his body was alert, the adrenaline was flowing and he felt his entire being brimming with energy and ready for what would happen next. He took a small sip, twirled the spoon in the cup, licked it as if it was slathered with fine chocolate mousse, leaned back comfortably in the aging blue armchair, and took another sip. It was the longest cappuccino he had ever had, but every good thing must come to an end. Eyal noticed that for some reason he was trying to delay the inevitable. Maybe just one more cappuccino? He couldn't remember ever having enjoyed a cup of coffee this much. In fact, the cappuccino was so good that he thought maybe he should just settle for it, quit while he was ahead and go home—to the only woman he had ever loved. But Eyal knew that every nerve in his body was committed to this experience, and it was time to go back up to his room and carry out his little experiment before dawn broke. He ordered a double espresso and downed it in one gulp, because the effect of the cappuccino had worn off a minute after he finished it and he still needed something to get him through the night.

Back in front of the computer, he logged into Google, typed 'escort services' and 'Israel,' and waited. According to the flood of results, one could buy a lot of love online. Eyal stared at the myriad of names. Some were porn sites that he had already visited, to his embarrassment, and which apparently also advertised that type of service. Other sites were for proper escort agencies. Eyal chose an agency called 'Natasha,' even though there was something kind of yucky about the name, some racist undertone. Apparently all the girls on the site were from Russia and the neighboring countries, and they all had the same name—Natasha. Ha ha, very funny. Every Natasha had a personal ID number. Obviously all the Natashas were incredibly sexy. Under each photo was a short text, such as: Natasha is a sexy, voluptuous woman. She immigrated to Israel only recently and already wants to show all Israeli men a good time. Terrific. Eyal didn't like the site. There was something about it that was just too…

slutty, perhaps? Big surprise indeed. The misspellings didn't make him feel better, either. And there was another small problem—the service was only available in the Tel Aviv Metropolitan area. After two more sites that were also less than thrilling (and also limited to the Tel Aviv area), Eyal decided to add the word 'Haifa' to his search. The results weren't exciting. Apparently in Haifa there was a lot less activity of that nature. What to do...? Eyal deleted the word Haifa and tried again, hoping to find some Tel Aviv-based agency that provided country-wide services. It would probably cost a fortune, but what did it matter now? Of course it mattered! The fact that he was going to cheat on Galit, the love of his life, his better half, the mother of his child and the most important person in his life suddenly struck him with force. How had he managed to repress this trifle fact until now? If Galit found out she'd never forgive him, she'd murder him. Being married to a strong, independent woman had its advantages and disadvantages. And what about him? Was he at peace with his decision? Of course not! But—Enough, he thought. He was going to do it and that was that, one fuck to wipe away the disgrace of being a man who had only had sex with one woman. And that way he'd also have perspective, right? It would actually be a step toward strengthening his relationship with Galit, he thought, scoffing at the silly notion. And it wasn't that he had any doubts about how wonderful and amazing Galit was, but now he'd know for sure. What pathetic excuses, what an asshole he was being. Enough!

Oh, here was an interesting website: www.satan_maison.co.il. Looks interesting, a combination of French and English. Or maybe Satan was a universal word? And the initials, SM—a name that certainly pointed to some level of sophistication. THE SITE FOR THE MAN WHO WANTS TO BE FUCKED! the site announced in a fiery red font. Eyal knew he was certainly not that kind of man, but he still entered the site, just out of curiosity. There were ten women there, and the first one was named Esty. In each of her photos she wore black leather, highly revealing outfits, some of which even exposed her pubes. In one of the photos she was holding a chain that was wrapped around the neck of a man on all fours, while her open palm was ready to spank his bare behind. No, this was certainly not what he was looking for. It was already half past midnight and Eyal was starting to question whether his grandiose plan was going to amount to anything. He reviewed a few other sites, which all seemed to him… Seemed what, actually? What exactly was he expecting? He wasn't sure, but for some reason he was expecting something cool and special, and the only thing that came close to fitting that criteria was a woman who wanted to put him on a leash and turn him into her pet. Hmm. Here's another site that looks interesting: www.filthyrich.co.il. Could it be a mistake? A website that wasn't supposed to appear in his search results? Eyal entered the site, which declared: This website is unsuitable for men who are either under the age of 21 or poor. Register to our website only if you do not belong to the aforementioned categories. There was something about the eloquent phrasing that appealed to him, as opposed to the sloppy writing and the ridiculous misspellings of the other websites. He clicked 'enter,' and the following text appeared: All details that appear on this website, excluding the names of the girls, are completely accurate. The photos are real, but the women's faces have been pixelated in order to protect their privacy. We guarantee that all women on the website are first-rate beauties. Our women may only be reserved for an entire night (or a shorter period, but the price is the same). We provide countrywide services, and the price is the same for all regions—NIS 10,000+ travel expenses.

Ten thousand? Wow! Could he even afford it? For just one time, he certainly could. On paper Eyal was pretty well-off, his stocks at Fugu were worth about half a million dollars, but Eyal knew how very theoretical that half a mill was; he had already seen a theoretical million vanish in the blink of an eye. In cash he had a few hundred thousand shekels. But he would have to lie! What a joke. He was about to sleep with a prostitute, and was worrying about having to lie about the expense. He was concerned that such a large sum would get him caught, and obviously, there was another element of betrayal in such a large expense for such a sleazy act—it was her money as much as it was his. And let's say that for the sake of mending this historical injustice, he put aside moral considerations—how would he explain the expense? Eyal had foreseen this problem and come with 2,000 shekels in cash. It never crossed his mind that he would need ten thousand. He could say he wasn't paying attention and accidently typed in the huge amount that just slipped out of the ATM! Could an ATM even discharge such amounts by accident? Maybe. After all, he did have two platinum cards. All these contemplations about the lies he would tell Galit made him feel nauseous, dirty. It was odd—the idea of sleeping with a prostitute left him feeling relatively indifferent, while all the lying about the money made the guilt surface. Eyal noticed that at the bottom of the screen, underneath the promising text, was a banner with flashing musical notes. He turned on the volume and the sound of ethereal violins emerged from the computer. No doubt, he had reached the icing on the virtual prostitution cake. Eyal clicked on the next page—another elegant display of twelve photos of women, also accompanied by classical music. In every photo, the women had their faces turned so that they couldn't be recognized. They all wore fancy evening gowns, but some revealed just enough to prove their sexiness. Oh! There was no limit to the refinement. It was surprising that these people had decided to open an escort agency. It seemed as though a boutique hotel would have been more appropriate to such a display of good taste, or perhaps a shop specializing in rare books. Eyal clicked on Orit's page. There were five photos and a short text. She wasn't naked in any of the photos, but in one of them she was posing in elegant lace lingerie, looking directly at the camera. Or at least that's what Eyal thought. He couldn't be sure, since her face was pixelated. She had very short, spiked blond hair, and almost unnaturally pale skin. She was full-figured, a stunning body with large round breasts that peeked out of a beautiful low-cut evening dress in one of the photos.

Orit is a real Scandinavian! Since emigrating from Finland to Israel four years ago, Orit has been studying Hebrew, and already speaks the language (if not perfectly). She is fluent in English and of course, Finnish. Orit is a professional chess player, and in her homeland she had reached the quarterfinals in the national championship! If you'd like to play chess with Orit before you get down to business, she'd love to! She is also an excellent swimmer (two kilometers every day in four different styles!), she loves travelling, mountain climbing, rappelling, and she even practices transcendental meditation! And in case you were wondering, she's one hundred percent natural—yes, even that lovely pair!

Remember: all the details that appear on this page are one hundred percent accurate. Why, you are probably asking yourself, would such an amazing girl come all the way from Finland for us? The answer: five thousand shekels a night (we charge half) plus tips, and bear in mind that our customers are big tippers!

It was certainly impressive. Eyal didn't know if he could believe every detail, but something felt genuine about the relatively modest text, which even admitted to certain trifling flaws like her imperfect command of Hebrew. And obviously, Orit looked amazing. And yet, even though her face was concealed, it seemed to him that there was something aggressive about this girl. Maybe it was the haircut and the heavy, somewhat masculine chin that stood out despite the pixelation. Eyal left Orit's page and entered the page of a girl named… Natalia, what else?

He liked Natalia from the first moment. Her frame was narrower than Orit's. She had a vase-like figure, a round and wonderfully voluptuous bottom, and a small waist; her breasts were smaller than Orit's but beautiful. Or at least they looked beautiful in the photos with the cleavages and bras, since there were no nude pictures. She had dark, long thick hair that cascaded into small waves at the end. Truly magnificent. Her skin tone was darker than Orit's, healthier.

Natalia is a true Muscovite; she is as sophisticated and refined a woman as you would expect from someone born and raised in the remarkable city of Moscow. She studied English literature at the University of Moscow and speaks flawless English with just a touch of an endearing accent (Wow, Eyal thought, they really brought in the writers). Natalia has a natural talent for languages, and she speaks fine Hebrew as well as Italian. One look at her long fingers and any musician would immediately see the potential—Natalia is an excellent pianist, who has been playing for more than fifteen years, and has even performed several times. And if we may add—those delicate fingers are talented in other areas as well!

A site that is entirely understated, wonderful! At the bottom of Natalia's page appeared the fixed statement: Everything is true. You don't believe such a classy girl would be selling herself like this? The answer, five thousand shekels plus tips. Obviously, the refined website didn't use those exact words. 'Selling herself' was phrased simply as 'choosing to work with us.'

Eyal knew his mind was made up. Natalia was the one, and he was going to do it! He picked up the hotel phone and after a few rings, a woman with a very pleasant voice answered. Nice. He had no desire to talk to thuggish pimps, even if he was fairly certain those were exactly the types behind the lovely operation.

"Good evening."

Okay, and what now?

"Sir, may I help you?"

"Yes, I, huh… I saw on the internet…" Good grief, what an idiot!

"Yes, I understand. Has Sir read all the details, including the price of our service?"

"Yes!"

"Okay, may I ask where you are presently located?"

"In Haifa. Is that okay?"

"No problem at all. That will be an additional four hundred shekels."

"Four hundred?"

"Yes. Traveling expenses, back and forth. Gas is expensive nowadays, you know."

So be it. It wasn't so bad.

"Okay."

"Do you have any sexual preferences that might help me direct you, or perhaps you already know who you are interested in?"

"Yes, Natalia."

"Ah, you have fine taste, if I may say. But I'm not sure she's available at the moment, let me see. Please hold."

Eyal waited a long, nerve-racking moment, in which he scrolled through the pages of other girls, even though he had no doubt that Natalia was the one for him.

"You're a lucky man. Natalia is available tonight."

"Popular girl, I guess?"

"She certainly is."

"Great."

"So we're good to go? It will cost you ten thousand four hundred shekels. Natalia will be at your place in about an hour and a half, and she'll stay the night. Until what hour exactly will be up to her, but if you two click, you might even want to have breakfast together, who knows. We won't interfere."

"Okay."

"What's your name?"

"Huuuh…"

"We just need a name. Any name will do."

"Oh. Yossi." What an idiot!

"Okay, Yossi. So our guy will arrive in fifteen minutes at… wherever it is that you are. His name is Yermi and you have nothing to worry about, he's very nice and discreet. You're at a hotel?"

"Yes."

"Okay. Yermi has two roles. He'll have to meet you in person to see that you check out, and then he'll give the final confirmation for the deal. He'll also collect a two-thousand- shekel advance. Is this okay?"

"Sure. Although I was actually hoping I wouldn't have to meet anyone besides the girl."

"I understand you, but it's necessary. We're sending you one of our girls, and we make sure you're a decent character. Besides, you're committing to a substantial sum of money here. But don't worry, if we didn't take good care of our clients, we would have been out of business by now."

Eyal knew that her promise should be taken with a grain of salt. If they were such angels, they would have opened a charity fund for the needy and not an escort service.

"Yossi?"

"Excuse me?"

"That's your name, to remind you."

"Yes, yes, that's fine. You can send Yermi."

"Wonderful. Where exactly are you?"

Eyal gave her the name and address of the hotel.

"Wait, you said he'll be here in fifteen minutes?"

"Yes, Yermi is our guy in the north. You have nothing to worry about."

"Okay." Wow, must be quite an organization. It was a little bit scary.

"Okay, Yossi, so we've settled everything. I hope you'll be pleased. In fact, since we're talking about Natalia, I can congratulate you. You're about to experience the best night of your life, honest to god."

"Good. Just one more thing, are you sure they won't give her any problems entering the hotel?"

"You don't have to take care of anything, don't worry. After Yermi gives us the confirmation, you just wait patiently and Natalia will knock on your door, okay?"

"Great."

"Good night, Yossi."

"Good night."

"Sweet dreams…"

Wow! He did it! So what now? Should he cancel? Eyal felt like a man who had decided to commit a terrible crime but could still back out. One of the things life had taught him was that as long as the deed wasn't done, you were allowed to change your mind. Telling someone you were going to jump off the roof didn't mean you had to follow through. But he knew he wasn't going to back out. About fifteen minutes later, the receptionist rang. A deliveryman with documents was waiting for him downstairs. Eyal's heart raced like crazy, his mouth was dry, he felt the same as he did during his first stakeout in Lebanon. This was insane! Was he really going to go through with it? Yes! He went down to the lobby, where he was greeted by a large man with a respectable appearance. He looked nothing like a thug. He doubted Yermi was his real name, since the man in front of him was obviously from the Russian Commonwealth. He had probably served in Afghanistan and escaped captivity after killing his captors. Although this guy was probably still in preschool during that war.

"Should we sit here for a moment?"

"Okay."

They sat down and Yermi gave Eyal a large brown envelope filled with papers.

"It's nothing, the papers are blank, this is just a cover story, okay? Just sign here. It doesn't have to be your real signature."

Eyal signed and noted to himself with satisfaction that they were in fact protecting his privacy much better than he would have. He was so nervous, he probably would have given his real signature had they asked for it.

"You have the money?"

"Yes." Eyal took out the two thousand shekels from his pocket and buried the bills in Yermi's large hand. Yermi quickly counted them.

"Okay."

"So, now what?"

"Now you wait in your room and Natalia will arrive. You gave our manager the room number, right?"

"Yes," Eyal replied and smiled. "So am I okay? You approve?"

"You're more than okay. You don't look like someone who needs to pay girls. Natalia will be pleased."

"Great."

"Goodbye, Yossi."

"What?"

"Yossi. That's your name, forgot?"

"Yossi, of course!"

"Well, have a good night, and believe me, it's going to be a very, very good one." They had probably been awarded most polite escort agency of 2009.

"Great, good night to you too."

Eyal smiled and so did Yermi. All in all, the atmosphere was very amicable. But of course, he had no proof of payment. There were no receipts in this business. Was it possible that he had just been charged two thousand shekels and would never hear from them again? He almost wished that was the case. Eyal went to the ATM to withdraw another eight thousand four hundred shekels. How much could he withdraw with one platinum card? He tried five thousand, and it worked. He withdrew another three thousand four hundred with the other card, watching his filthy little lie grow. Then he withdrew another thousand. You have to tip at least ten percent, right? Insane!

Eyal went back up to his room and opened the envelope. All the papers inside were indeed blank. What to do now? He had at least an hour to burn, maybe even more. He went to check the minibar. There were several tiny bottles of alcohol inside, a few snacks, Pringles, nuts, etc. He took out a small bottle of whisky and poured the contents into a glass. He turned on the television, flipped to CNN, took a small sip and watched the reports about the situation in Iraq and Afghanistan. Another thirty casualties. But on such a night of celebration, who cared. He took pleasure in his whisky, savoring each sip like a person on death row. Even though he made sure to take small, measured sips, one for every news report, he inevitably ended up with an empty glass. He considered opening the vodka bottle, but decided against it. Too much alcohol could screw up his plans. An hour passed and Natalia still hadn't arrived. Maybe it really was a scam, two thousand shekels down the drain. The level of tension and excitement steadily rose until it completely took over him, making all other feelings disappear; Eyal no longer knew what he preferred—being the victim of a silly scam or cheating on his wife. The window of his hotel room overlooked the main street, and he now paced back and forth like a caged lion, from the window to the bathroom to take another leak, and back again. Nervous like a virgin before her first fuck, he thought with ridicule. Another twenty minutes passed until he saw a taxi pulling up to the hotel. A girl got out of the car and was quickly swallowed into the hotel entrance. Eyal's heart suddenly produced a series of fast, irregular beats. He took a few deep breaths and stabilized his pulse, thinking: This is crazy, I'll end up getting a heart attack over of this. Would he even be able to perform in his condition?

Long, nerve-racking moments passed until he finally heard the knocks on the door. Eyal approached the door carefully, as if a predator was waiting on the other side. He opened the door and Natalia stood in front of him. Wow, was this girl gorgeous! Her mocha-colored skin was flawless, without an ounce of makeup apart from maybe a little lipstick. Her eyes were green, and the dark brown hair flowing down her shoulders shone with the faintest auburn tint. On heels, she was slightly taller than him. Her eyes radiated intelligence, or perhaps just infinite self-confidence. She was so beautiful, he could barely look at her.

"Can I come in?"

"Yes, of course, forgive me, I know this will sound corny but you're just the most beautiful woman I've ever seen, I apologize."

"There's certainly no need to apologize. So, you're Yossi?"

"Indeed, Yossi, that's me."

She removed her long coat, revealing a tight red dress wrapped around a perfect body. There was nothing slutty about the dress, he noted to himself. One of those dresses that end just an inch above the knee.

"Where should I put this?"

"Huuuh… Feel at home, there's a closet behind the door, it's perfectly fine."

After she hung up her coat, she approached him. Eyal was overwhelmed, none of it felt real. Was he really going to sleep with this bombshell?

"What would you like to do now? It's already the middle of the night so I guess you don't want to go out, but we have time if you want. Of course, we'd need to drive at least twenty minutes to—"

"No, no," he interrupted her, "I don't want to go out."

"Sure, so I'll just take shower, if that's okay." She wrapped her arm around his waist, drew closer to him and lightly brushed his cheek. "You look pretty shocked, if you don't mind me saying. Don't worry, everything will be okay."

"Okay, if you say so, I'm willing to believe you," Eyal said, and thought that he must truly be in a state of shock if he kept uttering these stupid sentences.

"Do you want the money now?"

"It's fine, honey. There's no rush. I have a good eye for people, and you don't seem like the type who's looking for trouble."

"Okay."

Natalia entered the bathroom, and Eyal sat down and continued to watch CNN. He waited for maybe ten minutes. The moment Natalia stepped out of the bathroom, a towel wrapped around her perfect body, the banal truth of it all suddenly struck Eyal. In the daily dialogues in his head it was always obvious, but today, for some reason, this truth had eluded him, until now. Natalia was a prostitute, and prostitutes don't actually want their clients, period! They do it for the money. Theoretically, the idea of squeezing that magnificent bottom and those perfect breasts and licking her from head to toe, swallowing all that beauty, was very tempting indeed. But how could you do all those things to a girl who doesn't even want you? It was obscene! If he had swept her off her feet, if she had arrived of her own free will, for him alone and not for his money, well, that would have been wonderful. And Natalia was probably a great actress, one who could convince any man that she was actually into him. But Eyal wasn't that stupid. And it wasn't a prudish pretense, he truly no longer wanted a Natalia who didn't want him, and there was no other kind of Natalia out there. His body responded accordingly. His cock, which had stood to attention all night like an eager soldier, was now completely soft. Eyal decided he had to abort the mission, the sooner the better. Any way he looked at it, it was utter insanity to cheat on Galit. But to cheat on her when he didn't even want to and wouldn't even enjoy it—that was already a war crime. He felt bad for Natalia, as if he was about to hurt her feelings. Ridiculous! She wouldn't exactly be devastated. Oh well, he could look at it as a tuition fee or tax for his stupidity. What he certainly didn't need on top of the fine was to cheat on Galit just to justify the expense.

"Is everything okay, Yossi? You don't seem so shocked anymore, but now you look kind of down!" she said with the loveliest smile. This girl truly was something special, and the website didn't exaggerate, her Hebrew was perfect!

"Do you really speak Italian?"

"Yes, my husband is Italian."

"Your husband?" Incredible.

She blurted out something in Italian in response, a few curse words or maybe a prayer. Eyal didn't understand a single word, but he had no doubt they were in Italian.

"Can I sit next to you, on the bed?" she asked. It was funny, like a boy asking a girl if he could hold her hand.

"Sure," he said and smiled. She took off her towel, and for some reason there was nothing awkward about her nudity. Maybe because of the remarkable perfection of it. She put on underwear and a bra and sat down beside him. Now they were both leaning against the headrest.

"May I ask what a married woman is doing in this... profession?"

"I could return the question."

"It's not the same. For me this is a one-time thing, not a profession."

"You're right, and I even believe you, despite the fact that most men tell me it's their first time and then give me a list of requests that was obviously formed over years, after hundreds of these kinds of sessions."

"Yermi, your delivery guy, told me that I don't look like someone who needs to pay for sex."

"It has nothing to do with that. Some men look amazing and are just addicted to it, I'm not sure exactly to what, it's complicated. Some men need someone to control them or rough them up, and that's hard to find without paying. Some think regular women are saints, and until you've paid them and turned them into prostitutes, you can't touch them. Those are usually the most fucked up. And for some it's just a fantasy, and in fantasies there really are no rules."

"I see you have a PhD on the subject."

"Pretty much. And what about you, what's your story? What are you doing here?"

"Me?"

"You." Natalia paused, and then took her identity card out of her purse. She covered part of the card with her hand, and showed him only her first name.

"Maria, see? That's my real name."

Eyal looked closer, and there was no doubt about it. Maria. She also let him see her photo.

"Are you Jewish?"

"Not really, my dad was Jewish."

"So how come you decided to tell me your real name?"

"Just seems to me that for some reason you're not in the mood for fucking, so we can at least spend the night having an interesting conversation. What do you say?"

It was amazing how smart she was.

"Do you tell your real name to all the clients who don't want to fuck you?"

"You're first in both categories. Actually, that's not entirely accurate. Some clients know ahead of the session that they're not interested in fucking. Some are impotent, some just want to talk all night, and some want to have things done to them, they want to be demeaned or just be bossed around, stuff like that."

"So what now? Am I supposed to tell you my real name?"

"Whatever you feel like. You don't have to. You don't have to tell me anything. We can just sit here completely silent all night, or I can leave, if you want."

Eyal didn't want her to leave. He knew at least that much. But he didn't have his next move in mind either. He just continued to speak.

"Eyal, my name is Eyal."

"Nice to meet you, Eyal."

"Nice to meet you, Maria." They shook hands. It felt nice.

"You're married." She wasn't asking, she was declaring.

"How did you know?"

"I could give you a lot of baloney about female intuition, but you're wearing a wedding ring..."

"Oh."

Silence spread throughout the room.

"So are you going to tell me something about yourself, other than the fact that you're married and your name is Eyal?"

"Hmmm." Dilemma. He actually really wanted to tell her things, to talk to her. But what could he tell her? There were things he simply wasn't supposed to say. But he also didn't want to stretch out the silence and kill the fragile sense of intimacy created.

"Maybe you could go first, tell me a little about yourself? I don't know, maybe after what I say you won't want to speak to me anymore. I just need to know what I'm allowed to say and what I'm not, on the wife's part, and…"

"No problem, what do you want to know?"

"You mentioned that you're married and your husband's Italian? That would be a good start, if you feel like it, of course."

"Okay. My husband was one of my first clients."

Eyal laughed. "Maybe I'm just too naïve, but every other sentence of yours manages to blow me away."

"It's actually a pretty common story, a prostitute marrying a client."

"And continuing to work?"

"Well, maybe that's less common. We have an agreement. My husband is an Italian businessman from Florence. He's very rich, he deals with real estate, among other things. He's twenty-five years older than me."

"How old are you?"

"Twenty-six. And you?"

"Thirty-four."

"My husband is one of those Italians who looks good in a suit, just because they know how to dress. But he's really fat, and underneath the suit it isn't a pretty sight. He's also impotent, on a certain level."

"What does that mean?"

"Well, he can get it up, and he can certainly squirt in all directions, just not the right one. When it comes to sex, his self-confidence is pretty much non-existent. I don't know what it was like in the past, maybe he was better, but that's where he's at now. He's been with maybe a thousand women, but his sexual stamina is more like a fourteen-year-old's, not entirely competent."

Eyal laughed. "You married Mister B!"

"Pardon me?"

"I'll explain later, okay? First finish your story, it's interesting."

"Okay, but I'm taking a mental note that you owe me an explanation about this Mister B thing. Anyway, my husband and I never had sex, not in the full sense of the word. The first time we met, he explained to me that he wanted me to do things to him, to lead and be the dominant one, and he wouldn't do anything. And that's how it's been ever since. I caress him, I hit him, I massage him with my body and give him blowjobs and jerk him off, using every part of my body that isn't my pussy. And that's what our sex life has been like for over two years now, if you can call it a sex life."

"And he doesn't give you hand jobs, doesn't go down on you…?"

"I told you, his self-confidence in that area is zilch. He just doesn't believe he could make a woman come. I look like some kind of unattainable goddess to him. Some men view me that way, I suppose. Well, I know, actually. For him, the idea that he could please me in bed seems entirely implausible, the way climbing Everest would seem to you, or something like that. I have to admit that this arrangement is pretty comfortable for me. I have no desire for him to give me hand jobs or go down on me. The first time I met him, he was here for business. We have a lot of clients who come abroad for business purposes and want to have a little *good time*. He took me to an insanely expensive restaurant, the seafood place at the port, you probably know it. He ordered us a bottle of French Champagne that cost like two thousand shekels, and two bottles of wine, plus dessert wines, and just a crazy amount of food. The owner came to greet us personally. I don't think he had ever made so much money from one couple."

"And you drank all that wine?"

"Mostly my husband did. His capacity is endless. Afterwards we took a stroll on the promenade. Then we went to some bar, and then to another restaurant that's open all night. I was completely full and only drank a little, but he, well, there's truly no limit to his ability to stuff his face. He told me about himself, about his businesses, about his love of Italian opera and beautiful women, and about everything else the good life has to offer. At that point he didn't tell me anything about his slightly strange sexual taste. He said he'd be staying in Tel Aviv for a week and wanted to meet me every day, and that he didn't want me to meet with any other client during that period. Which was no problem, because we don't schedule more than one client a day anyway. And that was it. Apart from a handshake at the beginning and a kiss on the cheek at night, he didn't touch me. And apart from the ten thousand shekels he paid, from which I get to keep half, he also gave me a ten thousand shekel tip."

"Wow."

"That's nothing, Eyal. You can make endless amounts of money from sex, it's just a fact. I'm not saying that I've made the best choices in life so far, but at least financially, there's nothing that can come close to it."

"Start working for a startup, you'd get stock options."

"They wouldn't hire me."

"Have you tried?"

"Stop bullshitting me."

"You're only twenty-six, you can still learn, especially now with all that money you have."

"You've already decided you want to fix me?"

"What?"

"Come on, give me a break. I actually kind of like you, so far. Don't screw it up now by trying to straighten me out, like ninety percent of my clients who want to fix my life because they feel guilty for supposedly taking advantage of me. I say supposedly, because I'm the one taking advantage of them."

"Sorry, you're right, I'm talking nonsense. Continue with your story," Eyal said, but wondered if her description of who was taking advantage of whom was accurate.

"Okay. We spent two more nights that were nearly identical to the first. Without any real physical contact, with a lot of alcohol, food and endless conversation. I speak Italian, as I mentioned. I studied it back in Russia and I'm good at picking up languages. On the third night, after tips that amounted to... forty thousand shekels, I think, I started feeling a bit sorry for him, so I asked if there was anything else he wanted to do besides sit in bars and restaurants and talk. He said there were things he wanted to do, but we would talk about it the next time. I was a little bit concerned, I have to say, even though he made the impression of a decent guy, even impressive, but somehow still a little bit pathetic. But I thought to myself that if it takes this guy three days to tell me what he likes, he must have some serious perversions. And in that case, had I known beforehand, I would have probably passed him on to someone else. I'm willing to do all kind of things. I'm good at taking control, for instance. A man that wants a dominant woman would enjoy himself with me. But if he wants a real dominatrix, I'd pass him on to one of the two dommes we have in the agency. Spanking men and making them lick the floor isn't my thing. I also like being fucked, I have no problem with that, I don't have to be the dominant one, but if someone wants a slave, again, I'll just pass him on to someone else, because I'm just not into that. We even have a girl who's willing to do animals, god help us…"

"It's interesting that these specialties aren't mentioned on the website."

"True. The owners of the agency are certainly clever people, and that's their way of branding the agency as a respectable establishment that caters to the upper class. But you were asked if you have certain preferences, right?"

"Yes."

"So, anyway, on the fourth date he picked me up in a stretch limo. I sat next to him in the back, and I was pretty worried about what was going to happen. But my precious husband has a gentle soul, and there's no reason to fear him. He explained to me more or less what I explained to you, about what he wanted. It was obviously a bit more complicated, because for such a big shot businessman, asking a woman for such things isn't easy, but I managed to get it out of him and I had no problem with his requests. It was even convenient. I don't usually enjoy sex with clients, and with him, such a fat, older man I was convinced I wouldn't enjoy it. So I was pleased with what he wanted. Then we went to a restaurant again, but this time, after the restaurant we went back to his apartment—the guy has at least two apartments in every country where he has business. And there, well, I pretty much told you how it goes with him."

"So he was satisfied? Obviously he was, he married you."

"Exactly. At first we made an agreement that whenever he's in Israel I'm his, and he pays me and the agency for all the days he spends here, even for the days he doesn't need me. And after about a year, he popped the question. Since he's Italian, and apparently Italians are almost obligated to propose in a romantic way, he arranged for a helicopter that took us to the desert. And there, in an extremely charming spot, a romantic table with candles waited for us, along with an entire staff that prepared amazing dishes, and a trio of two violinists and a cellist."

"Incredible."

"A little pathetic, actually. He really is in love with me, I don't doubt it, but he knows I don't love him, and as far as I was concerned, well, I might be exaggerating, and maybe there was something magical about it, I guess, but it was mostly just creepy."

"Why creepy? Well, I guess you're right... There's something a bit crazy about it all."

"Yes, but there's also something else here. Things you notice about a person after getting to know him better. Back then it just seemed weird that there were three musicians, and the food was served on three plates, you know, small, medium and large set on top of each other, and three knives and three forks. And there were even three tables. One for us, one for the wines and beverages, and one for breads and the rest of the food."

"He likes the number three?"

"He more than likes it, he's obsessed with it. Did you see that movie with Jack Nicholson, 'As Good as It Gets'? The one where Nicholson avoids stepping on the sidewalk cracks, or has to walk only in a diagonal line? So it's a similar disorder. Nothing too serious, just another aspect of his weirdness, that's all. But once you start noticing it, it's pretty irritating."

"Wow, when I asked you to tell me about your Italian husband, I never thought I'd get so many details."

"You're right, I got carried away. But to be honest, it's just because you're cute and I like you, that's all. Would you believe a pretty girl like me can actually get really lonely? I think you're kind of like a psychologist to me, believe me, these are things I haven't told anyone. And it does feel good. Maybe I'll pay you," she said and laughed.

"But, and you'll have to forgive me for nagging, why? Why do you have to live like this? You're so beautiful and also intelligent, if I may add. You should have let millions of worthy suitors fight over you!" And why, he suddenly thought, had he waited until he was twenty-one to have sex for the first time, despite the endless opportunities he had? People, he realized, willingly enter stupid traps that screw up their lives for no good reason.

"I don't know. You're right. But maybe it's not too late for me, right?" she asked.

Eyal suddenly thought that if he was single, he would have been the one to save her, to end her misery. It was a painful thought, and it also made him feel horrible about what he was doing to Galit. How could these thoughts even cross his mind?

"You're young. Of course it's not too late."

"Yeah… The thing is, when you make a pact with the devil, it's not so easy to break it. Enough. Now tell me who Mister B is."

"Okay. Mister B is…" Eyal did his best to explain the internal dialogues in his head.

"So you're Mister A." Again, that confidence. She didn't ask, she simply knew.

"Yes."

"You're completely Mister A? You met your wife when you were sixteen and haven't been with anyone else?"

"Worse. I met my wife when I was twenty-one, and haven't been with anyone else, neither before nor after."

"Are you serious? Do you have any idea how good-looking you are? Even if you went outside now, just to wander the streets of Haifa in the middle of the night, without entering a bar or anything, just on the street, you'd manage to get laid. Like, you're *that* hot. A real catch. I really hope your wife is a catch, too."

"She truly is."

"Then today's the today I'm supposed to liberate you of... of Mister A's status?"

"Yup. I didn't want to have a real affair because that can really mess up a person's life, and I love my wife, I love her so, so much, I don't want lies to come between us. And I certainly can't just start going to bars to find sex. So I thought that maybe like this, with someone I paid, I could solve the matter with a relatively small lie, one that wouldn't completely ruin my life. The only problem is... it was only after I met you that I realized you can't solve my problem."

"Why?"

"Because... because it's a paradox. I need someone who wants me, someone who doesn't charge for it. But someone who really wanted me and didn't take money is a woman who could get me into a lot of trouble. There's no way out."

"But I can you solve your problem, I think. I really don't want to get you into trouble, but I do want you, I really do. I've wanted you from the moment you opened the door."

"That's nice of you to say, but it's also a bit hard to believe."

"Why? You just don't know how cute you are."

"Maybe, but there's the matter of money. Eventually I'd know you did it because you got five thousand shekels and a big tip out of it. You do understand that after that kind of payment it'd be difficult to believe you actually want me, right? It doesn't matter, it's nice just talking, why ruin it?"

"Can I touch you?"

"One touch of yours and all men surrender, huh?"

She caressed his cheek and gently kissed him on the lips. It felt good, even exciting, and Eyal knew he was no longer indifferent, his body was once again ready for action. But he couldn't be bought just like that with a kiss. He wasn't a child anymore.

"Can I make a small suggestion?" she asked.

"Sure, what?"

"What if I removed the obstacle, took the money off the table? I don't want the money, I'll do it for free."

"Yeah? And what about the agency? You'd go back and explain to them that the client was just really bummed out by the money issue, so you decided to let it go, and they'll just understand? I don't think that would work."

"I'd pay out of my own pocket. All they need to see is another three grand, since you've already paid two, right? So I'll pay them the three grand out of my own pocket, and give you back the two you've already paid. What do say?"

"You're going to pay five thousand shekels to sleep with me?"

"But I won't tip you. I hope you'll be able to forgive me."

He laughed. "Why is it so difficult for me to believe you?" he said, but he was no longer sure what he believed and what he didn't.

"Probably because you don't know how rich I am. After the wedding, my husband bought me a three-bedroom apartment that was, let's just say pretty expensive, and then he put three million dollars into my bank account. That was after a negotiation. He offered a million, I wanted five, we settled for three."

"How romantic."

"I also get twenty thousand dollars a month for bills and regular daily expenses. And don't forget that I still make pretty good money as a prostitute."

"And the tax authorities, they aren't interested in where all that money of yours comes from?"

"He's my husband, honey. He can give me a billion dollars and the tax authorities won't care. About the rest... believe it or not, we actually declare some of our earnings from the agency. And there's also a kind of 'arrangement,' a certain angle we work. But that shouldn't interest you."

"So why didn't you just quit your job? Do you have some kind of contract with the agency? I guess they're the kind of people you wouldn't want to get into trouble with, huh?"

"It's not that at all. I'm free as a bird. It's just, I don't want to suddenly find myself dependent on him, and the only way I know how to make the kind of money that can compete with the amounts he gives me is... well, you know."

"I guess you have to meet with a lot of clients a month to compete with him."

"Not at all. My last client was two weeks ago. He booked me for an entire week. You have no idea how much money men spend on me. On the other girls as well. You'll probably find it hard to believe, but sometimes a girl can make more in one month from tips and gifts than the entire agency itself makes."

"And you're comfortable with accepting all those gifts?"

"Not always. I have pretty good instincts. It took time, but I learned. I once had a client who booked me for two solid weeks. During that time he spent half a million shekels on me, including the money that went to the agency, the most expensive suite in Tel Aviv for the entire two weeks, gifts and jewelry. Afterwards we learned that he got in over his head with loans. He had a wife and two daughters, and loan sharks were threatening to break his bones."

"Wow, what an idiot."

"Yes, and believe it or not, we helped him out. I gave him back some of his money, and my boss talked to the loan sharks and they agreed to build him a more or less humane payment plan. And I've since learned my lesson—try to be only with the truly rich."

"I'm not rich."

"I already told you, I don't want your money." This time Maria didn't ask, she simply drew closer to him and kissed him. She started to unbuckle his belt, and with that any kind of potential negotiation had ended. Eyal knew he was going to sleep with her. The only thing that could have stopped him was if Galit herself appeared at the door, and then it probably would have ended with divorce. But even this thought did nothing to hamper the incredible desire that had taken over him.

"Just lie down and relax, sweetheart, I'll do everything." Eyal followed her orders, and Maria gently lowered his pants with one hand while the other found its way into his underwear. It was crazy, he was going to explode. She took off his underwear and his cock bounced out.

"Wow, you have an amazing cock, if you don't mind me saying."

"Really?" What else was there to say? Maria licked his cock and his balls a little, and Eyal was afraid he was about to come. Then she put a condom on him. Lucky. He was so nervous he completely forgot about it. What an idiot. But Eyal didn't have much time to think about his idiocy. Maria mounted him and skewered herself on his cock, as Galit used to say. What a shitty lover, Eyal thought—I'm not doing anything. Maria started moving on top of him and quietly moaning. Her hand stroked his stomach and suddenly pinched his nipple, and Eyal could no longer control himself.

"Can you stop for a moment? I'm just afraid that…"

"It's okay, honey, you can come, I intend to fuck you at least five times tonight."

"That's a bit over-optimistic. I don't think I'm physically able."

"You just wait and see. With me you'll be able."

Eyal looked at Maria. She was sitting on top of him, with a straight back, beautiful and smiling. She was a vision, beauty that defied words. Suddenly she leaned forward and kissed him. In the midst of the passionate kiss, she started swaying above him again, gently. It was real intimacy. There could not have been a greater betrayal of Galit, he thought with disgust; and yet, it didn't change anything.

"Do to me whatever you do to your wife," she whispered in his ear. Was she a mind-reader?

"Here, suck my nipple. No biting." She laughed and placed one of his hands on her other breast. Eyal suddenly found himself slightly irritated. He wanted to show her he wasn't a child. He was a strong man; he pulled himself up onto his knees with her on his thighs, and she moaned.

"You want to change positions?"

"Yes."

"You want to fuck me from behind?"

"Yes." He pulled his cock out of her, placed her with her knees on the floor and her stomach on the bed and penetrated her from behind. He cupped her breasts and Maria groaned. Eyal continued to thrust his hips with force, looking at her beautiful ass pressed against him and caressing it. He was stunned by the fact that he hadn't come yet, since he couldn't remember ever being this aroused before, except maybe when he and Galit had sex for the first time. Maria's moans grew louder and louder until they finally came at the same moment, and it was amazing. But a mere second after it was over, Eyal felt a wave of deep self-loathing that struck him un-expectedly and ruthlessly—the same feeling that was familiar to so many men and was new to Eyal, who had never before cheated on or even just lied to a woman. What an idiot, what was he doing here instead of being with his wife and young son? And what if he had just caught something? If Galit found a wart on his cock one day, it would be the end of him! Not to mention the possibility of infecting Galit and their unborn baby! But he had used a condom, so he couldn't have caught anything. On the other hand, they did have oral sex without the condom. Not for long, and the risk there was smaller, but there was still a risk. Eyal had researched quite a few websites related to sexually transmitted diseases before embarking on this operation, since it was something that troubled him, and one of the conclusions he had reached was that oral sex, despite the lower risk, was safest with a condom. He had to take a shower! The idea was ridiculous, of course. If he did catch something, a shower wouldn't help—he wasn't that stupid. And yet, he couldn't resist the urge to wash himself, and that was exactly what he did. He caressed Maria, who was now lying on her back, and said he would be back in a minute. He went to the bathroom, stepped into the shower and turned the water on. He scrubbed himself with a bar of soap from head to toe perhaps three times, maybe even more, since he kept imagining there was an area he had somehow forgotten to scrub. Suddenly he remembered that she had sucked his nipple, and a strange notion crossed his mind. Milk emerges from the nipple, right? So maybe saliva could find its way in. Maria sucked his nipple like there was no tomorrow. Could she have scraped him? Eyal examined his nipple thoroughly, and it didn't seem like there were any scratches there, but now he started to scrub his nipples vigorously, and then his cock and balls once again, just in case.

Eyal turned off the faucet. He stood quietly in the shower and tried to figure out what he was feeling. He had never felt so confused, that was for sure. He hated himself with conviction, and wanted to erase this cursed day from history. And now Maria was waiting for him in the room and he could already feel a small sense of excitement developing in his lower stomach. What a fucking asshole, what a piece of garbage! Galit once told him that she felt a little sorry for men, because it wasn't their fault that God had created them as slaves to that pathetic little piece of flesh of theirs. And yet, there was no room for doubt—if Galit found out about this, she wouldn't feel sorry for him. There would be no mercy.

When he came out of the bathroom, Maria was still lying on her back. She was holding her legs up in the air, and looking at him.

"It's never a good sign when a man feels the need to take a forty-minute shower after sleeping with me."

"Forty minutes? Really?"

"Swear to God. Are you okay?"

"Yes. Just a little fit of guilt, that's all."

"Trust me, you'll get over it quicker than you think. And you don't have to worry, I don't have any STDs or anything else. Nothing you can pass on to your wife, okay? I get tested once a month. I actually got tested a week ago. And I always use a condom, always. In fact, I'm less of a risk than any random girl you'd meet at a bar, so you can relax."

"Cool." The girl was truly a mind-reader, no doubt about that. And it did have a calming effect on him. At least a little.

"What's that? What are you doing?"

"Oh, just exercises to release the stomach muscles."

"Sorry, I didn't know I made your stomach cramp."

"It's okay, I'm ready for a few more cramps. Come, sit next to me, I won't eat you," Maria said. She straightened out her legs and leaned back against the headrest.

Eyal lay down beside her. "You… you can't be trusted."

"Indeed," she said and smiled.

They were silent for a few minutes, and then Maria said, "Now it's your turn."

"Pardon me?"

"To tell me something. I told you about my husband. Now tell me how a stud like you could stay a virgin until twenty-one and have sex with only one woman. Well, until now."

"Hmmm."

"You don't have to tell me, only if you want to."

"Well…" Eyal said, and then shared with her his somewhat tragic story.

When Eyal was sixteen, he had his first serious girlfriend. Ranit. By then he had already dated girls and made out with them in dark movie theaters and other corners that hormonal teenagers favor for such activities, but Ranit was his first true love. She was a tall, beautiful girl with a permanent smile on her face and long light-brown hair that was so thick it almost looked like a wig, lending her the appearance of a religious Orthodox woman, which for some reason was a turn-on for Eyal. There were other somewhat Orthodox-looking things about her, like the long skirts that wrapped her tight, beautiful body, and only made her more attractive. And her family was on the verge of fully embracing Orthodoxy. They were already observing some of the rituals, but back then, they still didn't observe the Sabbath, and the boys didn't wear kipas. They hadn't gone all the way yet. Eyal had a lot of conversations with Arieh, Ranit's father, about faith and embracing religion. Sometimes it seemed to Eyal as though Arieh felt the need to apologize to him. For what, he still didn't know.

"I don't think God wants to cause us pain," Arieh would say while sawing another board that would become a closet or a table. Arieh was an amateur carpenter.

"Faith has to be something good that brings joy, not separation and division. And so, even if we decide to fully embrace the Orthodox religion, and we become religious according to the conventional definition, we wouldn't cut off our relationships with our family and friends. I'd still continue to play basketball with the guys. I want religion to add good things to our life, not to detract anything."

At that stage, Arieh already lay phylacteries every morning, went to synagogue every Saturday, and the family kept two sets of dishes in the kitchen, one for meat and one for dairy. But they weren't completely kosher yet. This state of affairs had certain implications for Eyal and Ranit's relationship. She wouldn't sleep with him, and wouldn't even take off her shirt. At first nothing was directly stated. They would sit in some corner, hugging and kissing passionately, and Eyal's hand would wander over Ranit's clothes. But she wouldn't let him touch her breasts, even over her sweater. Other strategic zones were obviously off limits. After a few months, Eyal decided it was time to talk.

"Ranit?" he asked with a concerned voice, and wasn't sure how to proceed. But Ranit was a clever girl.

"That's it? You've had enough? I know what's bothering you, but I still don't feel ready. Some people do wait until they're married, you know."

Eyal looked into her intelligent, stubborn eyes, and for the first time, he wasn't sure if he found them sexy and appealing, or prudish and irritating.

"We're sixteen and a half. I don't think there's any chance we'd get married until we're at least twenty-one. I love you, but I don't think I can wait that long, can you understand that?" he said with desperation, the kind that only a horny sixteen-year-old that doesn't know if he'll ever get laid could feel.

"Can you wait until we're eighteen?"

"You want to get married at eighteen?"

"No, but you'd be going to the army then, and we would do it before you enlist."

"Do *it*?"

"Come on, you know."

"You mean sex, right?" Eyal felt embarrassed, as though he was negotiating the draft of an agreement.

"Yes."

"Why then? Is there any biblical verse that says you have to have sex before enlisting? That if I die in battle I shouldn't die a virgin?"

"I don't know, maybe you're right, but it doesn't matter. It's just the way I feel. Can you live with it?"

Eyal agreed to live with it. Why? Even he didn't know. He didn't know what he meant exactly when he told her he loved her, but he said it, and Eyal's word was his bond. He really wanted to add a condition to the agreement—that she wouldn't tell anyone he was still a virgin. But he was too embarrassed. He couldn't ask her to lie to her friends. For his part, Eyal never told anyone that he had sex with Ranit, but he also never denied it. Since he was one of the hottest guys in his class, no one doubted that they were having sex like all other couples. There were also rumors about other girls in school, and Eyal never bothered to deny them either. He decided to present a façade of mystery. And of course, there were always propositions. A lot of the girls in his class wanted him. The best looking girls. To this very day, at thirty-four years of age, the thought of all those hot sixteen-year-olds he had rejected, just because he was waiting, in vain, to fuck Ranit, haunted him. There were some real goddesses in his class. Ranit was a goddess too, but there were a few that weren't as holy. There was Lina, a smart girl who majored in physics with him. Lina whose breasts defied the rules of gravitation. They usually pierced the eyes of tormented boys through thin fabrics. And she wanted Eyal, there was no doubt about it. She didn't hint, she said. And there was the petite yet wonderfully voluptuous Lily who had the most enchanting laughter, and was always grilling him about the state of his relationship with Ranit. And there was the hot Sharon, who was five centimeters taller than Eyal, with hair so blond it was almost white, and a frozen expression that gazed at all the boys with contempt, and yet one time, in a chance encounter, she had asked if he wanted to come to her house to listen to the new album of some sophisticated jazz band, and Eyal refused in a panic. And there were others. Many others. And with his stupid pride, he rejected them all. Because Eyal had to be the moral one, the one who always stood up to defend the weaker kids from the bullies, the one who was always there to help. The perfect sucker.

Eyal and Ranit's relationship supposedly carried on in the same manner. They continued to meet with friends and project the same phony solidarity of 'us against the world,' continued to go to movies and cafes, continued with their 'over-the-clothes' make-out sessions as usual. But for Eyal's part, the passion was gone. As if they were a bored couple that had been married for a million years. At a certain point he even stopped getting hard, because it was obvious that it wouldn't go anywhere.

And then, a month before he was enlisted, Ranit's entire family, headed by Arieh, made the final move, the formal, full embrace of Orthodoxy. Ranit informed him, not without pain, that she would have to find a religious boyfriend. Arieh apologized to him. Eyal was afraid that out of sheer awkwardness Arieh might kneel before him. Eyal wondered if he even knew what he was apologizing for. Three years ago, when Eyal was thirty-one, right after Daniel was born, he ran into Arieh at a convention. Arieh was an accountant, and the convention focused on the analysis of companies' financial reports. Eyal decided to attend even though it wasn't within the scope of his responsibilities at the company. It was a very pleasant meeting, and Arieh was very impressed by the remarkable young man Eyal had become. Eyal noted to himself that Arieh had indeed kept his word. He was the same Arieh, just with a kipa. The same positive attitude to people, secular as well as complete strangers, and apart from the kipa and the physical signs of aging, his appearance and demeanor had remained the same. He truly didn't want their conversion to Orthodoxy to hurt anyone. But it had certainly hurt Eyal. At eighteen, his virginity suddenly became a real burden. And it was because he was so handsome, and everyone was sure he was such a stud, that his lack of experience was shameful and hopeless in his eyes. Sometimes he suspected that Ranit was the one who had led the family toward religion, only so she could get out of her contractual agreement with Eyal. And maybe that was all nonsense, but it didn't change the outcome. Eyal could have found a new girlfriend in a split second, all he had to do was pick up the phone and call one of the many goddesses who wanted him. But he was shell-shocked. He did what he would expect someone as moral as himself to do—to consider the matter with seriousness and only after a cooling down period, return to the flesh market. The cooling down period lingered into boot camp. Eyal was enlisted to the paratroopers brigade. There was a lot of mud and very little time spent at home, which meant very few occasions to meet girls. And yet there were opportunities. He had a lot of friends in the unit, and they went on trips to Eilat together during their leaves, danced together, met girls together, got invited to all kinds of parties—pool parties and rooftop parties and beach parties—and there was a lot of fooling around with girls, but in some mysterious way, without understanding how, he still managed to finish his military service not only without a girlfriend, but without having sex even once. Suddenly he found himself with sexual anxiety, he wasn't sure where it came from, but he feared the moment a girl would see how unexperienced he was. He used every excuse to postpone the moment. And to his great frustration, everybody was jealous of him, they were sure he was a free spirit, a stud who wasn't willing to settle down with one girl and who spent his time fucking all of them.

In the paratroopers unit it was obvious that anyone who could get into the officer's course went, and no one doubted that Eyal was cut from the right cloth. To this day Eyal couldn't remember which maneuvers he employed to duck that fate, because he knew he didn't want to serve even one more day beyond the three mandatory years. He felt as though the military was suffocating him, preventing him, for some reason he couldn't figure out, from attending a party in which he was actually supposed to be the center of attention. Once completing his service, he didn't wait, he didn't even go straight to work in order to save money for his big post-army trip—he borrowed from his parents because he was running out of patience. He wanted to get out of the country as soon as possible and meet that Norwegian or German woman who would put him out of his miserable virginity. Two days after his discharge, he returned to the central processing base to return his equipment and from there he drove straight to the airport, waiting for the plane that would take him to Bangkok, and from there to Laos. It was in Laos, in a small but famous tourist town named Luang Prabang, on the banks of the Mekong, that he met his wife, Galit.

"Wow, what a waste, you could have gotten so much more action. But actually, not really, it's all just white noise. True love and family are all that matter, the rest is bullshit."

"I'm happy you approve."

It was strange. Until now he had only told this story to his wife. Galit and Maria, a fine pair. He thought about telling her that, and decided against it.

"Can you rub my back?"

Eyal massaged her back, and it rather quickly led to heavy petting and Maria's hyper-sexy moans, which of course led in turn to another round of sex, followed by yet another thorough shower, more conversation, and more sex. At about seven in the morning, after the two of them slept for barely an hour, Maria took a shower and kissed him goodbye, leaving Eyal alone and very confus

CHAPTER 4

Eyal left the room and went down to the lobby to check out of the hotel. The receptionist was very cute; a blonde, nearly as tall as him, maybe forty years old. She didn't seem like a receptionist—possibly one of the recent casualties of the high-tech industry? Many were getting laid off these past few years. She still had the body of a young woman and a very beautiful face, although he could see quite a few wrinkles down the cheeks and on the forehead. She narrowed her beautiful eyes at him in a way that accentuated the tiny lines around them, and Eyal was almost convinced that if he only offered, she would have abandoned her post and followed him to his room. Or was he just imagining things? The experience with Maria might have clouded his judgment. Eyal obviously didn't invite her to his room. He was about to pay the bill, and suddenly remembered that the room included breakfast. He asked to leave his bag with her at reception, and went to eat.

It was a typical Israeli hotel breakfast, not bad, but not great; chopped salad, several kinds of Israeli cheeses, salted fish, nice bread, muffins and horrendous coffee. Apart from a few foreign businessmen, there was an Israeli family, parents in their mid-forties and two daughters. The older one looked sixteen, and was incredibly cute.

"Did anyone ever tell you that you eat too much salted fish?"

Eyal was standing next to the buffet. He looked at his plate and found a surprisingly large pile of salted mackerel on it. He was extremely tired, and his mind raced restlessly between thoughts of Maria, whom he would probably never meet again, and the hot receptionist he would probably see in fifteen minutes; and it aroused him a little, which in turn led to horrible, truly insufferable guilt.

"It's… Yes, I always had a penchant for salted fish."

"Maybe you just like that nice thing that reminds you of salted fish?"

"What thing? I didn't know there was something nicer than salted fish."

"Like, smell-wise? Do you want me to spell it out for you?" she said, bursting into laughter; and Eyal finally understood. Only a night ago he wouldn't have understood. Galit had almost no smell at all down there. Maria's was much stronger.

"No, no need for that. And I think it's probably better that we restrict our conversation to salted fish."

"Really? Why?"

"It's just such a broad subject, so fascinating. I wouldn't want us to digress before we explored every aspect of it."

"That's not a good reason, and you're starting to repeat yourself."

Eyal looked around him and saw that the girl's parents were out of earshot.

"Well, there are other reasons. Mostly I'd like to avoid being punched by your dad."

"I doubt he could punch you, you look pretty strong."

"And that's because I make sure to eat a lot of salted fish. So now I'm going to go to my table and finish this plate."

As Eyal walked to his table and the girl to her family's table, she looked at him with a teasing smile and swayed her hips. She had a very nice butt. Eyal sat down and found himself with a plate piled with salted mackerel and a buttered roll. He drank two cups of coffee along with two banana muffins, and on the way out of the dining area the girl blew him a kiss, right in front of her enraged father. Eyal smiled and walked away. When he met the receptionist again, he no longer had any doubts. She gave him a teasing look and brushed his hand, as if by accident, when handing him his bag. Eyal was now fully convinced he could have had her that very night if he actually wanted to, and it excited him. Enough! He quickly left the hotel, checked his bag to make sure the wad of cash was still there, including the two grand Maria had left for him under the pillow, and walked toward his car, anxious but flooded with adrenaline. About a minute after he started the car, his cell phone rang and he nearly lurched from his seat. Eyal looked at it with panic, expecting to see Maria's number, or heaven forbid, the agency's, but it was Max's name flashing on the screen.

"What's up, Max?"

"What's wrong, Eyal? Haven't slept well?"

"I spent the night in Haifa. The meeting ran late and I was tired. I slept terribly."

"Well, I just wanted to tell you it looks like we're going to do business with Citibank."

"You're serious?" That was good news. Eyal was in a pretty shitty mood and absolutely terrified about meeting Galit. He had a nearly mystical belief in Galit; was it possible that his omnipotent wife could miss the signs? And then he gets this great news, which can really change everything, and it managed to pull him out of his obsessive thoughts, his remorse and his fear of what would happen next.

"That's incredible, Max. I really hoped it would happen, I have to say…"

"Calm down, Mandy just got a positive email about it, that's it, it's not a done deal yet. But it looks like next week they're going to sign something, at least some term sheet or something like that, so I just wanted to make your morning a bit nicer. Mandy puts on a good show, but you were the one who brought in the deal, no one else."

"Thank you, how very kind of you. We'll talk when I get to Fugu, okay? I'm driving."

"Sure, Eyal, drive safe."

That night with Galit, after the time he had spent with Maria, was a passionate one. Eyal hadn't felt so horny and full of vigor with his wife in a long time, and Galit even mentioned that she thought his cock had somehow grown recently. It was funny, but also slightly disturbing. Only after she fell asleep, the thought about having caught something suddenly struck him again. Maybe he had infected his wife and his unborn daughter, Eyal thought, and spent the entire night tossing and turning, with horrible nightmares. Nightmares about Galit falling out of bed and miscarrying, a tiny baby flailing on the floor, and Eyal knowing he had to save her, he had to call the doctor but he didn't know the phone number—every attempt at dialing the number eventually led to the wrong person. He finally woke up covered with sweat. It was a bad night. At breakfast he sat with bleary, sleep-deprived eyes and looked at Galit, who was so pleased with his performance at night that she slept better than ever. That morning she also displayed an uncharacteristic lack of insight, and was sure that he too had slept well.

"How's our baby doing?" he asked.

"I don't want a baby," Daniel said while sitting in his chair, moping around and making a general mess.

"Why don't you want a baby? How do you even know you don't want her, you haven't even seen her yet."

"I don't want one!"

"Well, you have no choice."

Daniel started crying.

"Well done, Gin."

"Sorry. Come to daddy. Do you want daddy, Daniel?"

"I want mommy," he continued to whimper. Galit picked him up and held him in her arms.

"Everything's okay, my little sweetheart," she said to Daniel, and then turned to Eyal. "The baby's fine, why? You look a bit worried."

"It's nothing, just a bad dream."

CHAPTER 5

Immediately after Maria left the hotel, she called her friend Anna.

"Anushka, I have a problem."

"It's seven in the morning, must be an urgent one. Can't it wait a little?" Anna had returned home at five in the morning from a date with a client, and was planning to sleep at least until noon.

"No, I'm in Haifa, I can be at yours in about an hour, I hope. Is that okay?"

"Yes, of course it's okay. I didn't sleep at all last night, but for you, Masha, you know I'd do anything."

Maria obviously never had any trouble hailing a taxi. Taxi drivers were always pulling over next to her, hoping she might need their services. She could even get special rates for long rides, which was how the taxi driver from Haifa, who was planning on spending the day in his hometown, found himself headed to Ramat Aviv, where Anna had rented an apartment.

When Eyal stepped into the shower the first time, Maria did what had become second nature for her, and one of the agency's demands. She went through his bag, took out the important cards—driver's license and resident ID card, as well as credit cards—and photographed them with her cellphone. In fact, any one of these cards would have been enough. The credit cards could provide her bosses with the client's identity as much as his ID card could, but the requirement was for the maximum amount of information. Not even once had a client been careful enough not to leave some form of identification lying around. If they locked their briefcases, they usually kept something in the pocket of their pants. Clients were usually too excited and nervous to calculate their steps with the necessary caution. All the girls in the agency became experts in the matter, and usually, a mere moment after going through their things and taking photos, they could lie back in bed as if nothing had happened.

Maria didn't consider herself a bad person. In her building, she always said hello and good morning to her neighbors, she took care of a cat she had found after a motorcyclist ran it over and broke its hind legs—and quickly fled the scene of the accident—and she even donated to charities. But her job had made her sense of morality flexible, and there were always excuses to be found; the clients were assholes, they deserved it. It wasn't very difficult to find justifications that would enable her to continue doing her job and sleep well at night. After all, her very job as a prostitute forced her to hone her repression skills. She knew that the information she passed on to her bosses was occasionally used to hurt their clients, her clients. To blackmail them. Despite her bosses' attempts to compartmentalize their organization, the girls more or less knew what they did with the information. Every client underwent a thorough investigation that documented his assets, his weak spots—which were usually simply the fact that he was a married man cheating on his wife—and all of his interests. If they didn't catch a big fish, they would just drop him back into the ocean, unperturbed. An agency that screwed all of its clients wouldn't last very long. But every now and the girls would hear rumors about a very rich man who had paid a lot of money or passed along inside information, or helped the organization in some other way, after having been told that if he didn't, his wife would receive very detailed information about his actions.

After Maria left the hotel, one thing was clear to her: she wasn't going to pass on Eyal's information to her bosses. It was the first time she truly cared about a client. More than cared, she was in actual pain. Her entire body ached from the sense of missed opportunity. She suddenly felt what she was losing. She should have been married to Eyal. Instead, she had given up too soon, choosing big, easy money. But there was at least one thing she wasn't going to do. She wasn't going to betray him. But how would she go about it? If she told her bosses that she simply couldn't find the documents this time, that Eyal had been more careful than all the other clients, it would just raise their suspicions. She had an idea, more or less. After sending the documents, the girls were supposed to get rid of the files. But not everyone did that. No one was sure exactly why, but they felt it gave them some kind of power over their bosses. Maria and Anna trusted each other completely. She knew that Anna also kept the files. Together, they had information on about a hundred clients. All they had to do was find someone who looked enough like Eyal, and send his data instead of Eyal's. It was important that the client they chose resemble Eyal, because the boss always sent a representative to check out the client, and she couldn't afford to be suspected of foul play. And yet, she knew she was putting herself at risk. The receptionist who receives the calls might remember, for instance, that it was a first-timer. It was very easy to distinguish between those who had already used their services and those who weren't familiar with the procedure. There was no doubt about it, she was risking herself. And she almost felt good about it. Maybe it was a way to atone for her long list of sins.

Anna made them both coffee with her sophisticated espresso machine, and they sat together with their cellphones, reviewing their different clients in an attempt to find one who resembled Eyal.

"Here, he looks kind of like him, doesn't he?"

"Anna, are your eyes up your ass? You think *he* looks like Eyal? How can you compare? I remember him. He looked like a body builder and had such a tiny dick that when I took off his underwear I almost felt sorry for him. Two hundred pounds of muscle and half an ounce of cock."

"Yeah, those types have a problem," Anna agreed. "Girls look at them and are sure they're carrying a baseball bat down there. Should I make us more coffee?"

"Definitely."

Anna came back with two more cappuccinos, and continued to go through Maria's phone, after failing to find suitable candidates on her own.

"Here, what about this one?"

"Him? Oh my god, you're crazy. He looks like Eyal??"

"Oh, honey, you're in love! Falling for a client, I can't believe it. What a cliché."

Maria's first instinct was to deny, of course. But then she thought for a moment and said, "Are you jealous?"

"Actually, a bit." Neither Anna nor Maria were lesbians, but their relationship was very physical, and they even had sex every now and then.

"You won't believe it. I even didn't take money from him."

"What?! Babe, you're really getting yourself into trouble here."

"I'm not getting into trouble, I'm going to pay for him myself."

"But why? Was he that good?"

"He was a terrific fuck, but that's not what this is about. Listen to this," Maria said, and told Anna everything that happened between them.

"Wow. What can I say? So you're really willing to put your neck on the line for him, huh? You know you're taking a risk here. Even the fact you haven't passed on the documents yet is a risk."

"I did it once for a day or two in the past, and nothing ever happened."

"Maybe, maybe not. You can't really know. They might have checked. Which is why it's not enough to send the data of an old client and hope they won't notice. You have to be ready for the possibility that they'll suspect something, that they'll investigate."

"What should I do?"

"There's the hotel registration. If they decide to investigate, the first thing they'll probably do is go to the hotel, to see if the client's name you gave them is registered. We have to check if Eyal registered at the hotel under his real name. He might have used an alias. Remember they usually use their real names, because in respectable hotels, trying to register under a fake name is a real headache. You have to provide identification. After that we'd have to enter the name of our bogus client into the hotel's computer, instead of Eyal's name. I don't think it will be that difficult. We'll just have to extort one of the hotel employees."

"And what if Eyal used a credit card?"

"So?"

"So they'll check with the credit card company."

"I don't know, we'll leave that to this guy I know, Eddie, to organize. I hope he'll tell the hotel clerk how to change the details in the best possible way to protect Eyal."

"And what if they call the client?"

"Which client? The one we choose?"

"Yes, what if they call and ask him, 'were you at the hotel that day?'"

"You really think they'd do that? Look, Masha, you want to protect Eyal, right?"

"Yes."

"Then I think changing the registration information at the hotel is the best we can do. We have to hope that if they get a little suspicious, they'll check with the hotel and find out that you gave them the right name, and back off. I told you, if you get the feeling they know something, take your legs and run."

"Assuming I'll still have legs."

"Are you sure you want to do this?"

"Yes." Maria knew that even this moral act of hers had an immoral aspect, trying to set up and extort a man she didn't even know, a man that might have a wife and kids. She could only hope that nothing bad would happen to him. And what if her good friend Anna got into trouble? But the possibility of passing on Eyal's information to her bosses for them to use against him was unbearable. She was willing to do almost anything to keep that from happening.

"My guy, Eddie, he might be able to do it. And you'll have to seduce some clerk, someone Eddie will choose. It has to be tonight. And we'll have to blackmail him. Make him change the hotel registration."

"Are you sure we can arrange all that today?"

"I'm not sure, we have to ask Eddie, but there's a good chance he'll be able to do it. The guy's the best there is."

"The best what, human garbage?"

"And what do you think we are, the finest Champagne?"

"We actually do drink a lot of Champagne."

"Yeah, the Champagne of human garbage. Say, Masha, are you sure you're willing to do all this for this Eyal dude?"

"You sound like a broken record. Yes, yes. I want to do it."

"Okay, back to work then. We have to find the right client. Let's go over them one by one, and remember, he doesn't have to be the huge stud Eyal is, he just has to resemble him enough in his passport photo."

Anna called Eddie and spoke to him for about two brief moments.

"Okay, he'll let us know by the evening if we can do it. You obviously have to call the agency and let them know you're not working today. And you have to be ready to dirty your hands tonight. It'll cost ten thousand dollars."

"No problem."

Eddie was a real pro, and despite the small window of time, he managed to find a shift manager who was married and likely able to make the necessary change in the registry. His name was Hezi, and his shift was over at six. Hezi was a nice guy, intelligent, a candidate for promotion to the head of his department. He was in his mid-thirties, slightly balding and starting to grow a belly. He was no model, but he wasn't especially ugly either. He was a decent family man who had never cheated on his wife. But nothing could have prepared him for Maria's kind of seductions, no one to warn him. That afternoon, Maria took a taxi to Haifa. She waited outside the hotel for Eddie's signal. And when it came, she advanced toward the hotel entrance at the very same moment that Hezi was about to exit, and when he walked through the door, she bumped into him with a rehearsed clumsiness.

"Look where you're going! I almost think you bumped into me on purpose," he said angrily.

While Maria indeed worked as a prostitute, she was certainly a classy girl and knew how to dress in a manner that made her look both modest and provocative at the same time. A skirt that ended right above the knees and a pair of tall boots always did the trick.

"I'm so sorry, really, I didn't mean to, I'm sorry."

She bent over to pick up the papers that fell out of her bag as if by accident. Between the papers were a pair of tickets to a football match between Maccabi Haifa and Hapoel Be'er Sheva that was to take place that night at eight—the best seats in the house. Eddie had arranged the papers in her bag by color so that the tickets would stand out. Hezi was a huge Maccabi Haifa fan. It took him a few moments to realize what a gorgeous, hot woman Maria was. It wasn't every day that a girl like that bumped into you, and actually seemed apologetic about it.

"Forgive me, I'm sorry for yelling at you." He leaned over to help her gather the papers.

"It's fine, really. You don't have to."

"No, no, allow me. So, you're a Maccabi Haifa fan?"

As part of Maria's preparations for the mission, she had undergone a crash course on the history of Maccabi Haifa F.C. over the past decade, mainly learning about the current players and their rank in the league and in Europe.

"I am, but it seems that unfortunately this is one game I won't be seeing."

"Really? Why?"

"I was supposed to go with my friend Vika, but she stood me up, and now I don't have any way of getting there even if I wanted to. And anyway, watching a game alone is no fun. Are you a Maccabi Haifa fan too?"

"Believe me, Maccabi Haifa has been my favorite thing in the world pretty much since I was born."

"Then you can have these tickets if you want, you might still make it there. Consider it compensation for nearly knocking you over."

"Are you serious? I don't know, I don't think it would feel right."

"Take them, really. I can't do anything with them. But you don't have to, whatever you feel like. I'd just feel bad wasting two perfectly good tickets." They had reached a delicate spot. They weren't sure what Hezi would do. What if he turned down her offer? What if he suspected Maria? And it was also possible that he had other plans, plans he couldn't cancel. And of course, he could always take the tickets and go with a friend. But Hezi turned out to be a real gentleman.

"Would you like to go together? Don't think I'm trying to flirt with you or anything, it just wouldn't feel right any other way. The car's parked right here, getting there won't be a problem."

"Are you serious? I'd love to, but are you sure you can just drop everything and come watch the match with me?"

"I have to check, I'm going to make a quick phone call." Hezi felt bad about lying to his wife in front of Maria. While crossing the street to make the call to his wife, he tried to decide which lie would be better. He could say he was going to hang out with his friends, but that could get his friends as well as him into trouble. Maybe an urgent work meeting? But then his wife might call the hotel and find out there was no meeting. What could he tell her? The doubts started to gnaw at him. But he was on a roll. The beautiful Maria was standing a few feet away, looking at him with anticipation, and he explained to his wife that he had just received an unexpected opportunity, an interview at a luxury hotel. He said he'd be home late. He further told his wife that she was obviously not to say anything about it under any circumstances. If news reached his bosses, he might lose his current job, and no one was promising him the new one. Hezi was both proud of his unexpected cunningness as well as incredibly ashamed of it, whereas Maria contemplated how easy it was to manipulate men. They both enjoyed the game. Maccabi Haifa won two-nil. After the game Maria suggested a quick drink as a way of thanking him for the ride. Hezi started to get excited—could this night possibly summon sex with this goddess? Hezi was not the least bit suspicious of Maria. After all, she didn't want anything from him, right? She didn't want his help at all. Even going to the game together had been his idea! Hezi saw the jealous looks he received from the men around him, and it gave him great pleasure. But suddenly he started feeling anxious that the TV cameras might take a close-up of Maria, and in turn, a close-down on his marriage. He also panicked at the possibility of acquaintances seeing him with Maria. But it didn't happen. A worried phone call from his wife made his heart drop to his stomach. He explained to her that he had to wait a long time for the interview, and they were just now calling him in, so it wasn't a good time to talk. He went with Maria to a nice little bar, where they downed a drink and returned to the car fairly quickly. In the car, it turned out that Maria could no longer restrain her desire. Eddie was close enough to the car to take photos as well as to help Maria in case of an emergency. Once Hezi came, he was pretty eager to get rid of Maria. The sex itself was completely horrible. It had been ten years since Hezi slept with anyone who wasn't his wife; he was nervous and too aroused, and came almost a minute after Maria put a condom on him. Immediately after he came, he felt dirty and regretted cheating on his wife. And of course, he was also embarrassed about his poor performance. He was a mess. A minute after Maria left the car, while he was trying to eliminate the evidence by putting things back in order and spraying deodorant to conceal the smell, Eddie opened the car door and sat next to him. Eddie was a big, tough man, and he knew there was no chance that Hezi was going to fight him. And indeed, Hezi just started crying.

"Listen to me closely, Hezi. I don't want to hurt you."

It took Hezi about five whole minutes to calm down and stop crying.

"Are you listening to me?"

"Yes," Hezi replied with a choked voice, on the verge of bursting into tears again.

"Okay. All we want from you is to change the registration details of a client who checked into your hotel last night, that's all. I know you can do it, and I want to see you do it. If you won't, your wife will be getting very incriminating photos of you. Think about your kids. You only have to change the registration details of one client. There's a chance that some not very nice people will come to ask you about this registration. All you have to say is that there was nothing special about it and that you can't remember all your customers anyway. That's all. And if you do what I'm telling you to, you'll never hear from me or the girl again. Simple as that. You follow?"

Hezi followed, and Hezi also changed the registration details.

CHAPTER 6

There was something rather disheartening about how steady and predictable life could be. And it's not that nothing had changed in Eyal's world. Three years ago their daughter Meital was born, healthy and adorable, and the pace at which Daniel had grown into a little six-year-old man truly amazed him. But it was his job—which was supposed to be the truly exciting refuge from his satisfying, yet somewhat exhausting family life—that had become a real war of attrition. According to the stereotype, working at a startup was supposed to be a stressful yet challenging and fascinating life—late-night meetings in which everyone is full of energy because everything is just so interesting, and before long they can already feel the exit and the millions pouring in. But Fugu had long ago turned into a ship on the perpetual verge of capsizing, and they had to keep emptying out the water twenty-four hours a day. It was astonishing how many times a company could reach the exact same spot, money running out, endless discussions with the investors that kept the ship afloat with small breaths of air every time instead of actually giving them the oxygen they needed.

Eyal had reached a saturation point with Fugu, and had they told him the company was shutting down tomorrow, he would have sighed with relief. He was sitting in front of his beautiful wife, feeding Meital, while Daniel ran around making a ruckus.

"Gin, what are you thinking about so seriously?"

"That I just don't feel like going into the office today."

"I won't ask you again why you don't simply quit just so I can hear you say you're waiting for the exit."

"If I'd been one of your patients you'd have probably told me to leave a long time ago, huh? It's only your husband you won't treat."

"I don't tell my patients what to do, dummy. I only try to make them realize what it is they actually want from themselves. But I can tell you that it's a shame you spend most of your time at a place you're so tired of. You could get a lot more out of a new place which you were actually excited about, don't you think? But let's just drop it, we keep finding ourselves in the same spot, that exit that's been *just around the corner* for the past five years already."

Even now, after sixteen years together, there was something about Galit's intelligent gaze and her pleasant yet authoritative voice that Eyal found hard to resist. Maybe if she told him to quit, he would simply do it. Was it possible that he was waiting for her to tell him what to do?

"You do have a point, it's just that we've already had a few *almosts*, and it really could happen, maybe even next year, in some unexpected way."

"Yes, I'm sorry if I sound sarcastic. Don't you think I also want the millions from the exit? I do genuinely hope it happens. I'm getting tired of being a therapist only to rich people and corporate businessmen. The day after the exit I'd be able to finally mix it up a bit."

"That's it? You'd say bye-bye to all the rich people? Soulless high-tech people! You'd throw them down the stairs!"

Galit stuck her tongue out at him and Meital burst into laughter.

"I obviously can't do that, Gin. You can't abandon patients. But treatments do end sometimes, people don't go to their psychologist forever, and at that point I'd stop taking on new patients and make time for community work. I'd reduce my consultation hours, that's for sure. The big corporations can survive without me."

"I think you can start doing that now, it's not such a big deal."

"I'm a bit worried. Anyway, you don't have to think about my bourgeois guilt. I just hope that if Fugu becomes a hopeless business, you'll be able to recognize it in time... Never mind... Boy, I'm starting to repeat myself."

"I'm not worried about your bourgeois guilt, I just sometimes think your efforts are a bit wasted."

"Is that really what you think about my job?"

"No, that's not what I meant. I mean that in my opinion, you should be running a high-tech company. If you had replaced Mandy we would be in a much better position now."

There was a reason Galit had become a psychologist. She was excellent at reading people, and certainly much better than Mandy.

"Okay. Apart from the fact that I don't know anything about high-tech, it's a great idea."

She returned to her newspaper, and Eyal returned to Meital, who started grumbling about being neglected. A tennis ball landed on her plate, and she burst into tears.

"Daniel, how many times have I told you..."

"I'll take care of it." Galit stood up, pulled a scary face and started chasing Daniel, who ran away giggling hysterically.

"Stop it, Mom!"

"Then sit quietly and eat. Now is not the time for football."

"I don't want to... stop it, Mom."

Galit sat down with Daniel on her lap.

"What are you reading there with such interest?"

"A sad story."

"Well, there's no shortage of those."

"What sad story, Mom?"

"It's a story about a chicken that can't lay eggs." Galit turned the cover toward him, but all Eyal could see were the words 'woman' and 'murder.'

"What's it about, another murder suicide?"

"My dear husband, you're an ass." Daniel giggled.

"What's a burger suicide, Mommy?"

"Dad will explain it."

"Dad, you explain it?"

"It's complicated, I have to think for a moment." But he didn't even have the energy to think, and Daniel ran off to watch TV.

"Some girl who was suspected of being a prostitute was murdered in her luxury apartment in north Tel Aviv," Galit whispered to him.

"Really? Can I see?" Eyal tried to sip his coffee, but for some reason it spurted onto his face, staining his shirt.

"Urgh." He leaped up to clean the damage.

"What's the rush?" Galit laughed. "What's wrong? Wait, there's even a picture, she was actually a pretty girl."

"Who wants to look at pictures? Who could be prettier than you? Who?"

"Ah, I've taught you well."

The first thing Eyal saw when he walked into the office was Jeff Elroy, Sheringham's representative, who passed by him in the hallway without even acknowledging his existence. Eyal noted the distinctively unfriendly expression on Jeff's face, and wondered what happened. The mere fact of Jeff's unscheduled presence was out of the ordinary. Jeff was chairman of the board, but outside board meetings at Fugu, they would usually meet him at Sheringham's offices or the various posh restaurants in which Jeff loved to conduct meetings. If he had bothered to drag himself all the way here, then either there was an exit on the table, or, more likely—judging by his expression, a nuclear war. Eyal entered the conference room, slightly tardy, a habit of late, and Mandy gave him a weird look. It was the kind of look men gave him when they were sure he had fucked a woman they had the hots for, when he had never even touched her. Eyal suddenly noticed that Mandy was turning grayish from one day to the next. Fugu was taking its toll on him. His hair was turning gray, even his skin looked ashen. Eyal was sure that only a couple of years ago, Mandy's face had a lot more color to it. But his tired eyes kept piercing Eyal with that same angry, admonishing look.

"Whatever happened, Mandy, it wasn't me."

"And what exactly happened, Eyal?"

"You tell me. Judging by your look, I must have been a very bad boy."

"No, Eyal. I'm just looking at you because you're so handsome."

"Ahh."

"I assume you've already noticed that Jeff was here, right? So let's drop the stupid remarks. Behave like a serious human being, for god's sake."

What a tight-ass, god. Mandy was acting as if Jeff was sitting right there with them when the guy had already left. Eyal took a small sip of his coffee. He'd been drinking too much coffee recently, and he knew that after this cup there would be another, because he was just so damn tired and the day hadn't even begun. Mandy was still staring at him.

"Do you have any special connections in Italy, Eyal?"

"Connections in Italy? Oh, you mean the Medicis." Eyal noted that he indeed was talking way too much nonsense.

"Who are the Medicis?" Boaz asked.

"The largest venture capital firm in the world, about five hundred years ago," Max said and laughed.

"What?"

"They were an Italian family who, among other things, founded the largest bank in Europe in the fifteenth century. So if you wanted to found a startup in the fifteenth century, those were the guys you'd go to. Apart from that, they were also kings, popes..."

"So not musicians, I gather," Mandy said. Max was a huge fan of classical music, but Mandy claimed that his displays of knowledge were primarily intended to demonstrate contempt of his surroundings.

"They also supported many musicians, Mandy, but I'll spare you the lecture since you're so busy leading Fugu to such impressive achievements."

Eyal saw that Mandy already wanted to punch Max.

"Let's drop the Medicis for now. You asked me if I have connections in Italy, Mandy, and I have no idea what you're talking about, so why don't you just tell us?"

"You're going to Italy today."

"Are you serious? Today? When's the flight?" Eyal started thinking about all the promises he made to Galit that he wouldn't be able to keep.

She wanted to go out with friends that night, and now she would have to cancel. Maybe they could come over to their house… But Eyal knew he was in for a major fit.

"You have time, don't worry. We'll wrap up the meeting, you'll go home to kiss your beautiful wife, grab a few clothes, and then off to the airport for two days in Milan."

"You're all looking at me as if I just won the lottery, but I don't even want to go to Italy. Why aren't you going, if I may ask?"

"Because they want you. That's the weird thing about it."

"Just like that? On such short notice?"

"Sort of. We've been in contact with them for a few days. They mostly spoke to Max, because they wanted to check the technology. But it doesn't matter, the request that you travel to Italy to meet them today only came this morning. Look, you're obviously not going to sign anything there, we just have to see what they're offering…"

"I don't even know who *they* are yet."

"Fondo Lombardia, a pretty serious fund that already has investments in Israel."

"I've heard of the Lombardia League."

"That's a political party, the one that wants to separate the rich north from the poor south, it has nothing to do with the fund."

"Yes, thank you for that, Max. Yonit here will give you the portfolio, some general background about the fund. I don't know why it's so urgent for them that you, out of everyone here, meet with them, but I suppose we have nothing to lose, right? Go, speak to them, explain to the dignified businessmen that if they really want to close a deal they'll have to speak with me and with Sheringham, although they're supposed to be serious people, so they probably know that already. Come back and report."

Jesus, the man was falling apart. Jeff must have really rattled his cage. It was obvious deals weren't signed without talking to the CEO, everybody knew that. The fact that Mandy bothered to mention it just showed how weak and insecure he felt. He was so transparent. Mandy could never lead them to an exit, Eyal suddenly thought in despair, and then another thought crossed his mind: was it possible that they no longer needed to talk to Mandy before closing a deal?

"Where am I going exactly? Milan, you said?"

"Yes, you're flying to Milan, and they'll pick you up at the airport. From what I understood, you're going to meet their big boss."

"You don't say. And who's their big boss?"

"His name is Simone Donadoni."

"Donadoni? Like the footballer?"

"Exactly."

"Do you know him?" It was a little odd, though not impossible. Such senior venture capitalists weren't usually anonymous.

"I haven't even seen a photo of him, a real mystery man, I guess. But you have nothing to worry about, it's a serious fund. They want our most updated data, so you should talk to Max, right?"

"Stop by my place on the way to the airport, okay?"

"Max, I hate this mess."

"It'll be fine, don't worry."

But Eyal worried.

"What exactly do they want? What updated data are you talking about?"

"They want some add-on to the software, Eyal."

"That you don't have here?"

"That I only have at home."

The man was all over the map.

"Can't we transfer it from your computer or something? We are a high-tech company, aren't we?"

"Believe me, if I could, I would. Come by, it'll be great."

"Fine. You at least have coffee?"

"Yup, better coffee than the shit you drink here."

"Okay." Suddenly he felt there was something actually cheerful and refreshing about a day of traveling and excitement instead of the usual monotony he had to look forward to.

"Now, about the GE deal…"

Eyal looked at Mandy fearfully; had another deal gone down the crapper? It was undoubtedly the best deal Eyal had brought to Fugu to date. The cream of the crop. General Electric's healthcare products division was exploring the possibility of using Fugu's technology as a diagnostic aid. The doctor would talk to the patient, the software would analyze the patient's voice and then offer the doctor relevant diagnostic possibilities. The technology was still in its infancy, and they needed to bring a doctor to the company in order to develop it, if they wanted GE to sign.

"How much are they going to give us?" Max asked.

"Half a million dollars, to start with. Then two million, based on milestones. But think how much money this company could make if GE incorporates our technology in their products," Yonit answered. It's amazing that they still hadn't learned to decipher the nuances in Mandy's speech.

"Yes, so. I regret to inform you that it isn't going to happen."

"What? Another screwed deal?! God, I can't believe it."

"Calm down, Max," Mandy said.

"Don't tell me to calm down! Do you want to remind me of a single good move you've made since you got here? Every deal Eyal or anyone else brings in just crashes, how is that possible?"

Eyal thought Max was pushing it. That was no way to talk to the CEO. But obviously, he was also right. Apart from the deals that fell through with the banks, there was also the deal with the Japanese; the relationship with them had begun on that bitter, reckless day three years ago during which Eyal met with Maria, and the proposed deal collapsed the previous year for some unknown reason. And there were the initial contacts with Samsung, which wasn't interested in determining the speaker's credibility, but mostly wanted his diction analyses in multiple languages for a human voice activated system. And there were some other small deals that failed to materialize. In recent years, Fugu had become, more than anything else, a manufacturer of failed deals, and it was a wonder the company still existed at all.

"What happened, if I may ask? Weren't you supposed to go with Yonit next week to close? I thought it was a done deal already," Eyal said.

"I myself still don't know. They had some internal meeting that we weren't even aware about, and Michael, the man we were working with over there, wasn't even at the meeting when they decided to shut it down. There was nothing we could have done."

"Mandy, it's your job to know who to speak with and who to close deals with. You're absolutely clueless."

"Max, will you shut up?" Mandy roared.

"This is Citibank all over again, the exact same bullshit."

"Max!" Mandy yelled and pounded his fist on the table. He was on verge of physical violence.

"Max, let it go. Maybe something will come out of this Italy thing. Let's go to your place, I still have a plane to catch today."

"Fine." Max was trying to simmer down, but it was clear that he was still very upset. Eyal opened the door and let Max out of the conference room first. He was afraid that if he let Max close the door behind them, he would break it.

They were inside the elevator on the way down, and Eyal saw that Max was looking for something or someone to punch.

"Max, you know I love you, but you have to relax. I'm not sure that screaming at Mandy about it being the same shit with Citibank was an especially constructive move."

Max smiled. "Maybe you're right, but it's driving me crazy. I'm actually getting déjà vu about the fucking deal with Citibank, you know? You remember what Citibank told that idiot, the excuse they gave him for cancelling the deal?"

"It was a long time ago, Max. What does it matter now?"

"It matters. What did they say?"

"That it was too futuristic?"

"Exactly. And what did you say to me back then?"

"That it wasn't futuristic. It's not like anyone thought they were actually going to rely only on our software to extend credit. The idea was that if there was any indication of unreliability, they would continue to screen the client more thoroughly, that's all. What's so futuristic about that?"

"Yes. Well. It's a shame there was no one to explain it back then to Citibank's decision-makers."

"That was over two and a half years ago, Max, why dwell on it now?"

"Because it keeps happening again and again. I give this fucking company the best ideas I've ever had, and they don't go anywhere because our business people are worthless."

"I'm sorry, Max. What can I say?"

"It's not you, Eyal, you brought the deals for Citi, HSBC after that, then GE, and they all fell through. You did good. More than good. It's Mandy who's supposed to actually close the deals, and he doesn't understand anything. It's fucking horrible! I'm telling you, he has to be replaced, now! I'm sure that if it were you negotiating with GE we'd have a deal by now."

"Maybe."

"We've become a wasteland, we can't grow anything. I'm telling you, they should have never fired Itzik. I let them throw my best friend to the dogs for this asshole. Now the company's gone down the toilet and so has the friendship."

"Let's try to focus on what we can still work on, like the Italians, for instance. We're meeting at yours?"

"Yes. And I apologize, Eyal. I've been in contact with the Italians for the past few days without telling you. Only Mandy and I knew about it, even the portfolio you got from Yonit, she only put it together this morning. They threatened that if we breach confidentiality there wouldn't be a deal."

"It's fine, Max, I understand. And try to relax, driving when you're nervous like this isn't the best idea."

"Don't worry."

CHAPTER 7

"Eyal? What are you waiting for? Come in!" he heard Max's voice behind the door. Eyal opened the door and looked at the garbage site that was Max's apartment. He was astonished, but quickly thought he had no reason to be surprised. For the past few years, Eyal and Max had occasionally gone out for drinks. Max was often a guest at their house, and always came bearing generous gifts. But they were never invited to his house. Max was a devout believer in the myth that any serious technology entrepreneur should also be a messy anarchist. He had enough money to have moved into a lavish house long ago, and even if he didn't want to move, he certainly had the money to hire a maid. But he continued to live like a slob. The first time Max made serious money from technology was over ten years ago, in his early twenties, as befitting a tech genius. He developed a game with a battle spacecraft that kind of resembled the X-wing fighter from Star Wars. The spacecraft flew inside a tunnel that looked a little like the tunnels on the Death Star, and destroyed all types of threats, like enemy spacecrafts and monsters. It wasn't a new concept, not in the least. But it was very cool, and the thing that was especially successful about it was Max's algorithms, which gaming companies bought and were still paying him royalties for. The game itself wasn't a big hit, which deeply disappointed Max. Eyal didn't know how much money Max made from the game, but he was a millionaire by now, and the royalties kept coming in. Eyal estimated Max's fortune at ten million dollars, tops. If he had more, he would have funded Fugu himself instead of turning to the venture capital funds he hated.

"Sorry, Galit, honey. I've never been here before, I didn't know where I was bringing you to."

"You brought Galit?" Max asked with horror. On his way to Max, Eyal had called Galit, and it turned out she could make herself available to him for a few hours.

Max looked at them and smiled.

"So you've really never been here before, huh?"

"You never invited me, and now I know why. This is very impressive, did you do the decorating yourself?"

"The cat contributed a large part of the work," Max said and laughed. Eyal liked Max a lot, but this apartment highlighted the fact that Max wasn't a manager; he couldn't manage his own life, he couldn't even manage his cat, and he certainly shouldn't have been managing an R&D department, or any department in any company.

"Come on, stop staring and come in already. You'll have to forgive me, Galit, if I'd known your idiot husband was bringing you I would have just torched the place."

"It's not too late for that, just give us a head start to run and save ourselves."

"You know, Max, if one of your investors saw this place, I think it would be the end of our company."

"Well, the way Mandy's running things, the end is close anyway. And on the other hand, the apartment represents my creative side, and without that there would have never been a company to start with, right?"

"This place is indeed an example of extreme creativity. If we ever go public with Fugu, I'll demand that photos of the apartment be included in the company's prospectus."

"I'll include your mother in the prospectus."

"Great idea. We can bring her over for the photo-shoot. You'll make coffee and I'll supply the snacks."

Max laughed.

"Tell me, Max, this is how he is at work every day? How can you bear all of his nonsense?"

"Interesting question, Galit, I was just about to ask you the same thing."

"Oh, I promise you that at home he's much more restrained." Galit laughed and hugged Eyal from behind.

"Oh yes, my wife, restrain me, I love it!" Galit's touch always drove Eyal crazy. He felt her breasts against his back, and was dying to say adios to the Italians as well as to Fugu and go home with her.

"Excuse me, go back to your car if you can't control yourselves."

"Maybe we should go to the car?"

"Shut up, Gin."

"See? She's restraining me again. Galit, just think that this is the very reason everyone at Fugu thinks I'm an idiot, all this restraining at home makes all the nonsense come out at work."

Eyal lifted one leg and stepped over the threshold to a spot where the garbage level seemed lower.

"Just follow me, babe, and it'll be fine."

"Yes, sir! What happened, why is Max so angry at Mandy?"

"Another deal gone down the crapper. General Electric."

"Really? Wow, that's a shame."

"Yup."

One step at a time, he tried to pave a path for him and Galit through the piles of garbage that covered the floor. A pot with old leftovers of chicken was placed on a chair whose legs had disappeared inside the sea of garbage. Calypso, his crazy cat, was standing on the pot, sniffing it.

"God, Max, this is disgusting."

"You're right, sorry, bro." He took the pot, emptied its contents into the overflowing garbage can in the kitchen, and placed it on top of the towering pile of dirty dishes in the sink. A drumstick slipped onto the floor. Calypso leaped at the piece of chicken and batted at it with his paw.

"Much better," Galit said and laughed. Max hugged her and kissed her on the cheek.

"Galit, you're more beautiful every time I see you."

"So you're saying she wasn't so beautiful the last time you saw her?" Eyal had always suspected Max of being a little jealous of him.

"Stop talking nonsense and learn a little European charm, Gin."

"I swear I'll never forgive him, Galit. You don't do something like that. If he had given me just a little notice, I would have cleaned."

"Forget about it, Max, it would have taken you two months to clean this place up. I'd go with your first idea, burn everything."

"It's okay, Max, I actually like it. There's something about it that's very, uh…"

"Rancid?" Eyal suggested.

Classical music was playing in the background. Eyal didn't understand anything about classical music, but it was easy to notice the outstanding sound quality. Four very impressive speakers were hanging in each corner of the ceiling.

Max placed a dented old pot with water on his filthy electric stove and dropped a few spoonfuls of coffee inside.

"I'll make us some proper Arabic coffee with cardamom. Here, let's sit."

Max cleared a dirty plate from the couch and set it on a pile of newspapers, books and a few empty cans of cat food. The coffee started boiling and he added a little sugar.

"Say, Max, what is this we're listening to? It's beautiful."

"It's Tchaikovsky's Fourth, I hope you don't have anything against Tchaikovsky."

"I'm unequivocally against Tchaikovsky."

"Oh god, Gin, would you shut your trap already?"

"Yes, certainly, you're right."

Max laughed.

"Why would you think we'd have anything against Tchaikovsky, Max?" Galit asked.

"Oh, it's just an old family argument. My sister Romi thinks he's too shallow. Once the radio started playing classical music, and I mean classical in the broad sense of the word, not from the classical era, and the music became accessible to the masses, Tchaikovsky instantly became very popular. His music was also used in the soundtracks of a lot of Hollywood movies. The critics claimed that it just proved how shallow and hysterical his music is, but I think that's bullshit. He became so popular simply because he's so good. And that, by the way, is a very common opinion. My sister mostly likes German composers."

"Tchaikovsky versus Beethoven? That's what your family argues about? It's embarrassing how cultured you Russian immigrants are. At our house the arguments are usually about Hapoel versus Maccabi football clubs. Or politics, at the most."

"You emigrated from Romania, right?" Max asked Galit.

"Yes, but I was just a little girl. And even in Romania there's more soccer than culture. Ever heard of Hagi?"

"Not really. So who do you support, Galit, Hapoel or Maccabi?"

"Me? Who does the hot one with the blue eyes and the long braid play for, Gin?"

"Him, he's in the workplace league, Hapoel Firefighters."

"Well, no big surprise there. Max, I guess if you're looking for culture you should have stayed in Russia."

"God no. I'd never go back to Russia. Although there is indeed a lot of culture there."

"You should know, babe, I've learned a lot from Max's lectures."

"Like what?"

"Oh, endless things. The guy's a walking encyclopedia. Operating Photoshop, theories about the origins of the universe, and of course, a lot about classical music, which, as you can see, hasn't made me more knowledgeable on the subject."

"What's that guitar, Max? Doesn't seem classical at all."

Max's electric guitar was leaning against the wall, in what seemed like a square meter of organized cleanliness.

"You don't know? When Max was seventeen, he left his parents' house and founded a band with his friends, The Marmites. They used to perform in pubs for pennies."

"A regular Bruce Springsteen, huh?"

"Don't insult the Boss," Max said. "We just used to do it for the kicks. Here's the coffee. There's also some really good chocolate." Max poured the coffee into old, chipped glasses.

"The coffee's delicious, Max. So is the chocolate."

"Told you."

"You look troubled, Max, what's wrong?"

"Oh, a lot of things, and you know them all. Mandy is destroying the company. And these new investors from Italy, I just don't know what to make of it. Never mind, I want to show you something."

Max disappeared into the hall behind piles of garbage and returned with something that looked like a simple old Nokia phone.

"What is that?"

"This is the realization of Fugu in hardware. It records people and then gives you an estimation of the credibility level of what they said."

"Seriously? Where did this project come from, I never heard a thing about it. Does it have to do with that project Boaz screwed up back then? I find it very worrisome that no one tells me anything."

"Clam down, Eyal, no one knows about this project because it's my project. I funded it from my own pocket."

"Why? It's based on Fugu's patents, isn't it? If you try doing anything with it, they'll sue your ass."

"Let's say I'm thinking about the day after. If the company collapses, I'll buy the patents and move on. Maybe. Don't you want to hear a little bit about this device?"

"Why did you install it in a cellphone? So you can take it out in a meeting and no one will suspect anything?"

"That's one reason, Galit. But also because it is actually a phone. You can talk to someone and the software will analyze the conversation. Or you can record whoever's in the room with you, and the software will analyze that."

Eyal took the phone and examined it.

"Beautiful. It's so small, how did you do it? I remember that in the project we did at Fugu it was ten times the size."

"Yes. Among other things, it only works with two languages at the same time. You can upload any two languages you want at a time. Part of the problem back then was that we needed a big hard disk for the massive database of all the languages. Now it sits on a very small and compact flash. And also, our first try was a few years ago. The technology's better today, the minimization has advanced."

"Cool. And does it work?"

"Of course, but it's not the final version yet."

"A polygraph in a cellphone? That's so cool, a real James Bond gadget."

"Here, I'll show you, Galit. I'll press here, and it will record you. Say any lie, and then wait five seconds, and say something true."

"Okay. I have a hundred million dollars in the bank," Galit said and waited five seconds before continuing. "My name is Galit."

"Great, now watch this. You see this graph? It's divided into three parts. During the first part, you spoke for about six seconds. The level of credibility it attributes to you is forty-seven percent. Then you paused for five seconds. Then you spoke for another three seconds, during which the level of credibility rose to ninety-three percent."

"Wow, that's pretty amazing. But why forty-seven percent? That's almost fifty percent, is that even any indication of a lie?"

"Come on, Eyal, demonstrate your technological expertise, mister VP of marketing."

"You're trying to embarrass me in front of my wife? Okay, it goes like this. The lie you told was a lie you don't care about, it doesn't matter in this particular context if you have a hundred million dollars or not. It's what Max would call an uncharged statement. If you had told the same lie to a tycoon who wanted to sell you his mansion for twenty million dollars, your lie would have become very relevant, and it would have manifested in your pulse, your blood pressure and other things the polygraph checks, much more than in a meaningless lie. The same goes for your speech analyzed by Max's software, and then your credibility would have dropped to something around ten or twenty percent."

"Wow. Nice, I learned something new."

"VP or no VP?"

"And there's a hidden USB port here, you see? You can transfer these files to a bigger computer and perform more serious analyses that you can't on this phone."

"Max, that's so cool!"

Eyal's cellphone rang.

"Hello? Yes. At the Dan Accadia Hotel in Herzliya? Really? Of course, I'll be there... Okay... You sound a bit under the weather, Jessica, do you have a cold? Don't worry... Yes, I have enough time, I'll make it. Bye."

"I heard you say Jessica, are you going to meet with Jeff?"

"Apparently. I don't know why it has to be now, it's strange, earlier he passed by me at the office and didn't even look at me, and now he wants to meet. Well, I guess it's not that strange before meeting a potential buyer, right? Okay, are you giving me the disc with the software updates?"

"Yes, sure, it's all here on the USB. You need to go already?"

"Yeah, after that phone call, we have to get going. Driving to Herzliya again and then back to Tel Aviv..."

I'll take a taxi, Gin, you don't have to drive me."

"No, no, Galit, I'll take you."

"Are you sure, Max? There's going to be traffic..."

"Don't worry, I've got time. You're sure you don't want another coffee, Eyal?"

"I'll probably have another coffee with Jeff, assuming he won't make me drink whiskey, and then another coffee at home, and three more at the airport... Don't worry."

The three left Max's house together. Eyal and Galit kissed, and after hugging Max goodbye, Eyal sped along the highway toward the Dan Accadia Hotel, where he was in for a very frustrating experience. Jeff never showed up. Eyal walked in and went to sit by the pool, following Jessica's instructions. He waited, he had a cappuccino, enjoyed the sight of bikini-clad girls by the pool, and then came the call from Jessica who canceled the meeting and hung up without further explanation. When Eyal finally managed to contact Jeff, Jeff didn't seem to have any idea what he was talking about. He told him to talk to Jessica. What was that all about?! Maybe just stress. Everybody was stressing out about the trip to Italy. Eyal drove home, exceeding the speed limit the entire way. He was starting to feel the stress himself. He returned to an empty house, but he was okay with that since he had already managed to say a proper goodbye to his wife. He looked at the photos of Daniel and Meital, who were at their grandmother's. He'd see them in two days, not too horrible, he thought. But he already missed them. And he didn't get a chance to say goodbye to them. Oh well, better that way. The kids' tears was the hardest part of his job. He had to wean himself from this melancholic tendency of his, which was a substantial aspect of his personality—obviously not just some habit you could kick. He packed a small trolley for a few days. He was practiced. He had been on more of these short business trips than he could count, although this was certainly the shortest notice he had ever received. He took only the small suitcase, which he could carry with him onto the plane, and by doing so, spare himself the wait at the baggage claim. He made sure he had Max's USB, his laptop, and the USB with all the company's important presentations, since he wasn't sure what he would have to present. He also needed to print out his plane ticket and the voucher for the hotel. And where was his passport? Probably shoved inside one of the drawers in the den, between heaps of documents.

While searching for his passport, he fished an old photograph out of the drawer. Although it seemed at first like a photo of strangers, an entirely different world, after a longer look he recognized it and remembered the moment it was taken. It was a frisky photo he and Ranit took of themselves with a timer, kissing. A photo of a sexy young couple, a photo of a giant lie. What was it even doing there, and why did he come across it now, of all moments? On the back of the photo Ranit wrote—The sexiest man alive, May 1992. The word sexy was underlined, and two small hearts were drawn above it like tiny balloons on each side. Strange. It was like Ranit wanted to build a case, wanted to convince future generations of a fictitious history that was full of sex between them. Was it possible that with a little more pressure on his side he would have accomplished his goal? And why was he thinking about it now, when it bore no relevance to his current life? He looked at Ranit's round, pretty handwriting, with the small circle underneath the exclamation point and the cute hearts, and felt a twinge of regret. He wondered what happened to her, whether she was still religious, whether she was happy. He looked at his watch. The flight was in three hours and fifteen minutes. He didn't have much time, but he was dying for coffee and a quick shower. He sat in front of the computer, and printed out the electronic plane ticket and the hotel voucher. Cool, he was flying business! These days, with the money gone, they usually flew coach. Maybe the investor bought him the ticket? A ticket for business would save him at least half an hour at the check in line. He logged onto one of the news sites and saw a headline that reminded him of something—oh, of course, the murder Galit had told him about that very morning. Some girl murdered in her luxury apartment in north Tel Aviv. Eyal loved those definitions—luxury apartment in north Tel Aviv. It was probably some shitty one-bedroom pad off the highway. Had Galit really shown him the article only a few hours ago? There were days in which so much happened that it felt like their morning was last week. Now. What first—coffee or a shower? Despite the excellent coffee at Max's, he craved more caffeine. He made himself a hazelnut flavored coffee, a heaping tablespoon, because he was so tired and had to wake up. He opened the newspaper to the financial section, but then thought that he had better go back online and find more information about that Lombardia fund. But on second thought, the material from Yonit would have to do, because he simply had to rest for a minute and recharge his batteries. He cut a piece of the wonderful Bundt cake Galit had baked, and after reviewing a few financial statements from different high tech companies, and reading a few stories about corporate corruption, okay, now he really was out of time, the taxi was probably already... His cellphone rang, and indeed, it was the taxi driver downstairs.

He apologized and said he would be there in five minutes. After a two-minute shower, he got dressed, took his small suitcase and the backpack in which he carried the documents, checked once more that he hadn't forgotten to pack the hotel voucher, and left.

Eyal stood in line for the security check. Two religious Orthodox men were in front of him, and behind him a family with four kids who made a lot of noise, reminding him, not without some guilt, how much easier it was to travel alone, without Galit and the kids. Later he could go have a cappuccino and a pastry in peace over a newspaper.

"Excuse me, you dropped an envelope."

"Sorry?"

"This envelope, you dropped it."

He looked at the thick, elegant-looking envelope.

"That's not mine," he said, but he picked it up anyway, and on the side that had faced the floor a moment ago was written 'Eyal.' Where did that come from? He looked around, trying to see if there was anyone suspicious, someone who could have put it in his bag or dropped it next to him without him noticing, but he didn't notice anything. It was very odd. What was going on here? One moment he's on a regular business trip, and the next, he's in an episode of The X-Files.

"Did you happen to see…"

"What?"

"No, never mind, thank you, it really is mine." He wasn't supposed to ask that. If he explained to this woman that he didn't know where the envelope came from, she would ask, and rightfully so, if they shouldn't notify security. Or maybe she would just go to them herself, and they would open the envelope—to find what? Eyal wasn't sure, but the theory quickly forming in his mind was unnerving. He had to look into it. Right after check-in, he would do an internet search. Was it possible that the news about the murdered prostitute was much more relevant to his life than he had imagined? The cheerful mood he had enjoyed just a moment ago disappeared completely, and Eyal suddenly felt terribly anxious; his mouth was dry, and he wanted to get through with the check-in already. And maybe he actually should notify security? But he knew he wasn't going to. What if Galit had also received an envelope, and was going through a pile of photos that very moment? Eyal felt beads of sweat trickling down his forehead, and was short of breath. He couldn't wait even a moment longer, and took out his cellphone. After a few nerve-racking rings, he heard his beloved wife's voice, and immediately knew that everything was okay. She wouldn't have sounded so friendly with photos of him fucking Maria in her hands. She asked how he was, and he said that he was fine, and when she told him he didn't sound so great, he said that he was just tired, and that he loved her, and they started to say goodbye. But then she asked again if everything was okay, because Galit wasn't one to be easily fooled. But he told her that it was his turn at security, and he finally managed to dodge her interrogation, which now weighed very heavily on him. And yet he managed to slightly calm down. But what if she got the photos tomorrow, or even in half an hour? Enough, he had to stop with those silly thoughts. He didn't even know what was in the envelope yet! He decided to go to the lounge and open it there. Maybe it had nothing to do with that, maybe he was just making too many assumptions? Why was he so certain that the one time he cheated on Galit would come back to bite him in the ass? Since when did he believe in karma? Wasn't he a rational person? And yet, he had done something bad and was now awaiting his punishment. Who could have left him such a mysterious envelope with his name on it?

Eyal sat in the King David Lounge. He liked the new terminal, and was especially fond of the large, lavish lounge with the high ceilings and the gallery floor, the comfy armchairs and the cappuccinos he would probably have at least three of before the flight. But he found it difficult to enjoy himself now, and gazed at the envelope that was placed in front of him. He was sitting in the corner, where he felt less visible. But how, how could it be... The night he spent with Maria had taken place more than three years ago. But he still remembered the details. He reserved the room. Maria walked in, took a shower, they talked, they fucked... There was no way she had installed a hidden camera, and she didn't take any photos. And if she didn't, who did? The size and thickness of the envelope suggested it contained photos. Before opening it, he logged into the news site and searched again for the article Galit had read that morning. She told him there was a picture. He immediately found the article, and the girl was indeed very pretty, but it wasn't Maria. Eyal felt his breath starting to settle, but he still wasn't sure he was entirely out of the woods. The girl did look familiar. Could she have been one of Maria's colleagues? Eyal wanted to log into the escort agency's website, and although he was relatively secluded in the corner, he still feared someone would see him. Enough, he had to be sure. He typed in the website's name, but he didn't get anywhere. Maybe the site had crashed? Maybe the agency was closed? Who knew. It wasn't making him feel any calmer. If one of their girls was murdered, that would have been a very good reason to shut the place down. But it wasn't Maria, and most likely it had nothing to do with him. He needed to open the envelope. He did it slowly, and pulled a photo out of it, an inch at a time, ready to stick it back inside if there was anything incriminating. But it was just a photo of him and Galit in the car with Daniel. But suddenly he noticed that it was the car they had replaced over three years ago, and that Daniel, with his hands wrapped around Galit's neck, was much younger. Galit was already late in her pregnancy, probably about to deliver. Eyal felt the same pang in his heart that such photos always gave him. But who had taken the photo three years ago? At least it wasn't of him with Maria. But the photos in the envelope didn't have a particularly calming effect. There were about twenty inside, all of Eyal, either alone or with other people, mostly family. There was even one of him talking to Yonit. But there were also close ups of his neck, his ear, his eyes. It was so bizarre. What was he to make of it? Someone had been taking photos of him, probably stalking him, for years. Wonderful. The oldest photo was from three years ago. Around the same time Eyal had met Maria.

CHAPTER 8

Superintendent Andrey Friedman was having a hard time at the Israel Police Force. He had gotten used to the meager salary and the pathetic conditions long ago, but he still struggled with the attitude of the average Israeli toward his police officers. And the reason Andrey struggled was mostly because he knew the average Israeli wasn't entirely wrong. Andrey's cops were more or less good folks; they weren't corrupt, and they worked their asses off. But for the average Israeli the policeman was mainly someone who tried to screw him over for failing to come to a complete stop at an empty junction, when there wasn't another car to be seen for miles. Or someone who pulled him over when he was just slightly over the speed limit. Like everybody. Everybody exceeded the speed limit, so why did they stop him of all people? The Israeli police didn't return people's stolen cars, or their stolen property when their houses were burglarized. The cops did very important work, which for the most part Mr. Israeli never got to see. And they did it under shitty conditions. So when some asshole lawyer who brings home a hundred grand a month complained about the police, Andrey wanted to beat the shit out of him. He only wanted to, he never did. Andrey was against violence. The asshole lawyer could go wander the cold streets at night for ten grand a month instead of Andrey, and even that salary was only after a decade on the force. But Andrey also understood those who complained. And just now, he had an opportunity to perform a small public service, to prevent a disaster. A truck driver for a rather large company whose offices were located in the auto body shop area, drove a hundred mph on Highway Four. Got busted, his license suspended for a year, also because he behaved very badly toward the arresting police officer. And he got fired. Of course he got fired, what else can you do with an idiot who drives a hundred mph and loses the one thing he needs for his job? But he also behaved very badly toward his employer. Cursed. Threatened. So his employer decided to put a private detective on his tail, to see what he was up to. Obviously, they wouldn't be able to use the material the detective passed on to them as evidence, but it certainly made Andrey realize that the truck driver was up to no good. He had started surveilling his former boss's offices. He searched online for all kinds of flammable, arson-related material. He even purchased some of them. The detective was an acquaintance of Andrey's, and he passed on the information in the hope that Andrey would settle it quickly and quietly.

The truck driver was led into Andrey's small office and sat down in front of him. Andrey immediately recognized the type. An idiot. A small-time thug who couldn't control his temper. Like one of those little dogs who try biting you out of insecurity.

"I want to talk to my lawyer."

"Listen to me, you fucking idiot. If I let you talk to your lawyer then right after you're done I'm throwing you into a cell, and when you get out of there, I'll be able to shove a beer bottle up your ass without using lube, you get me?"

No comment. But Andrey saw that he was on the verge of crying.

Andrey would never have used such moronic threats had he not seen that this was a terrified idiot who only wanted to go home to his mommy. And that's exactly what Andrey wanted—for him to go back to his mom, without any more monkey business, and without wasting taxpayer money and resources by endless prison stints.

"Your other option is to have a friendly conversation with me, which might solve your problems without wasting any more of our time. What do you say?"

"Fine. Talk." He was trying to demonstrate control of the situation. Idiot.

"I have an offer. Forget about your boss. I know you've been surveilling his office. I know exactly what you bought, and what you're planning to do. If you even try to pull anything, even without succeeding, you'll spend the next ten years in prison. You're twenty-eight now. Even if they take off a third of your sentence for good behavior, you won't be out before your thirty-fifth birthday. You catch my drift?"

No comment.

"You spent the weekend in Eilat. Came back yesterday, am I right?"

The information was included in the private detective's report.

"Uh-huh."

"Went pretty well, didn't it?" What man would deny it? Especially a two-bit crook like him. The amusing report included an elaborate description of a blowjob he received from a stripper at the Gogo Club. He came after three seconds and left the club depressed. He also bragged to the stripper about the huge plans he had. Some people just don't know what they're in for, he told her, but didn't elaborate. The detective got those details from the stripper for four hundred shekels. Nothing else happened in the club. None of the girls even looked his way.

"Let's say I ain't complaining."

"You want to take more trips to Eilat, right? If you go to prison now for a few years, that'll all be over. No more hot Swedish girls on the beach. No more drinking and smoking with friends. And no more Friday night dinners at mom's. It will only be your ass, and the line waiting to enter it. Do you understand what I'm telling you? you could go home now, and stop with this bullshit, and we'll both forget this conversation ever happened. You could go back to your life, to your vacations in Eilat. All you have to do is be smart and forget about your boss. Sometimes life doesn't go the way you planned. But that's no reason to destroy it. But if something happens to him, so much as a flea bite, we'll be all over you like flies on a pile of shit. You catch my drift? I know you think you're a tough guy. Believe me, after one day in prison you won't feel so tough anymore. Don't go there. You'd be ruining your life, your mother's life, maybe even the lives of innocent people that might get caught in the crossfire if you succeed with your nonsense. Understand?"

It took him a moment, but finally he nodded.

"All the materials you bought, don't throw them in the garbage. I want them. I know exactly what you bought. Put everything in some old suitcase and bring it to me. And that's all. Tomorrow. Here's my phone number, call me. Don't worry. No one will bother you. Once we're done with this you'll be a free and happy man. You can go to Eilat straight from here. Okay?"

"Okay, okay."

"Good, so you can go now, and we'll meet tomorrow. And after that I hope we'll never meet again. Only on happier occasions."

"Fine." The truck driver got up and left with his head hung low. Andrey was pleased. He felt that it went well, although you could never be sure. If Andrey had the budget and manpower, he would have continued keeping tabs on the idiot, just in case. He thought it was a good idea to call the detective, to suggest the boss continue to use his services for a few more weeks.

His phone rang.

"Izzy?"

"Andrey, they found another one."

"Another what?"

"Escort girl, by the looks of it. Are you coming? I'm waiting for you downstairs."

"Okay."

Crossing the hotel hallway, quickly approaching the room, Andrey had a bad feeling. They already told him it wasn't a pretty sight, but now he was preparing himself for the worst. Hotels had always spiked his imagination. You walk down a hallway full of closed doors and don't know what's happening behind them. Wild sex? A spy preparing for a secret mission? Andrey saw that the room they were approaching had no door. Two cops were standing next to the gaping room, and soot marks spread from inside out into the hallway. The door was lying next to them. It was as if the room had tried to expel the horror from it. Andrey took a deep breath.

"This is going to be bad, Izzy."

"Yup."

Izzy was a small and angry man, built like a rock. He took out his rage on everything that smelled of elitism, high tech, trust fund kids, and actually, anything that had to do with big money, despite the fact that he himself obviously yearned for such money. Some were tempted to think that he was just a simpleton, one of those Israelis who didn't know anything apart from their own small corner of the country—Holon, in his case—and hated anything that was different. But Andrey knew that wasn't true. Izzy looked up to Andrey, who had grown up on the mean streets of Moscow. And Andrey appreciated Izzy—his attention to details that sometime went unnoticed by Andrey himself, and his combativeness was often very useful on the job. But he did think that Izzy's rage sometimes turned him into a narrow-minded person.

They walked into the room. Two officers were already waiting inside. Andrey wanted to be somewhere else. He usually loved his job, but there were cases that completely took the wind out of his sails, and he already knew this was going to be that kind of case. The entire room looked like a microwave in which a soufflé had exploded. Black marks dotted the wall, as well as weird looking sludge spread on it. Human material. Placed on the bed was something that looked as though it had once been a woman's body. Andrey sighed, trying to decipher what his eyes were seeing. Maybe he should just quit? There had to be easier jobs that paid a lot more. He had already been offered the position of head of security at some investment firm for four times the salary he had now. Four times the salary! Why didn't he just take it? When you looked at the net income, it was probably closer to two and a half times, he tried to console himself. Enough, there was work to be done! It looked a little like an unfinished puzzle. A neck, shoulders and part of a head were placed close to the headrest. The sight disoriented Andrey; he couldn't identify what part of the head was missing and what part was still there. He couldn't identify anything from the head, because there was no face left. Also very little hair—only one clump that oddly enough had retained its original, beautiful color, and was attached to a piece of white skin. A dark arm was attached to a shoulder, part of it missing. But from the remaining part of the detached hand, he could still see the Champagne-colored nail polish on her fingernails.

The stomach was one big mush. As was the pelvis. From about twenty centimeters above the hips and down to the feet, her legs were nearly intact. Long legs. An awful smell permeated the room, the smell of a mutilated human body which couldn't be described to someone who had never known such a smell before.

"Will you be able to identify anything out of this?" Andrey asked Shaul from the forensic division.

"I hope. We might be able to get a fingerprint off the hand. We already have a presumed identity. There's a bag. Here, take some gloves."

Andrey and Izzy put on the surgical gloves and went through the contents of the bag. The moment they came across the ID card, Izzy said: "It's Anna's friend. Anna, the girl who was murdered yesterday."

"You're right." In one of the drawers from the wooden dresser in Anna's lavish apartment, they had found a stack of photos of her with the most beautiful woman Andrey had ever seen. They started searching for her, and Andrey wondered what it would be like to meet such a girl—would he even be able to investigate her? So it seemed they had found her. From what was left of her, there was no way of telling whether she had been a top model or a gorilla.

"Maria Dubcek. Well, we still have to wait for confirmation that it's really her."

One of the pictures was of her with a child.

"Wow, there's a child, too. That's awful. I hope he never finds out how his mother died."

"Did you notice that there's no mention of a child on her ID card?"

"Really?" Andrey looked at the card again. "You're a hundred percent right, Izzy. Interesting. Well, maybe it's her nephew in the photo, who knows. And who do we have here?"

There was also a photo of a man in her wallet. A very handsome man, a real movie star.

"What do you say, boyfriend? We have to find him."

"Yes."

While going through the papers in her purse, Andrey couldn't help but glance every now and then at the horror that was resting on the bed and smudged on the walls. He kept looking up nervously, fearing some charred piece of flesh would fall on him from the ceiling.

"There are car documents here. Yuri, did they find a car?"

"No, that car isn't in the hotel parking lot."

"No car keys here either. Interesting. Maybe she didn't arrive with the car. There's also no phone. Weird. Did you guys find a phone?"

"There wasn't one."

"Okay, we have to find out what network she used. She must have had a phone. We have to find out if they can track the phone, or at least tell us where it was last used."

"I'll do it, Andrey."

"What's this? Nice, apartment keys. What's the address on her ID? De Haz Street, Tel Aviv. We need to go over there, maybe we'll find stuff we're missing here."

"Like what, her stomach?"

"Izzy, do me a favor." Sometimes Izzy's comments could drive Andrey crazy.

"Huh, what's this?"

There was a registered mail slip.

"Can you read what it says here?"

"No."

"It was sent today. Amazing, only a few hours ago she was standing at the post office on Ibn Gabirol Street to send registered mail. Izzy, call them, we might be able to intercept the letter. Then we can pass by the post office on the way to her apartment."

Maria's two-bedroom apartment was beautifully decorated. In the center of the living room stood a round glass table, a couch and elegant leather armchairs with beautiful, arched wooden backrests. There was also an open glass cabinet with vases and bowls, and on the center of the wall behind the couch hung a large oil painting of a desert landscape.

"She had good taste."

"Yes. Sometimes I really don't understand this world."

"Andrey, come look at this, the computer was removed."

"Yes, well, we'll have to wait for the forensic guys. Let's open this envelope. Addressed to Eyal and Galit Shiloh. I wonder if he's the man from the photo."

"Look, Andrey, some pictures were taken off the wall here, just like in Anna's apartment. I bet that in both apartments there were photos of the girls from all kind of trips around the world hanging on the walls."

"Maybe, you're probably right, Izzy. Someone tried to hide the connection between them, but whoever it was, they didn't do a very thorough job."

The apartment was spacious and airy, and a pleasant smell lingered in the living room. But Andrey was experiencing the occasional flashback to the smell of singed flesh, which made him sick every time. He could understand murder. A beautiful girl, maybe it was a crime of passion, maybe someone was just angry at her for being so pretty. And she was probably working as a call girl. He still didn't have any proof, but her friend Anna was definitely involved in the business, and his experience told him that her beautiful good friend was probably in the same shady industry. But why did they settle for a bullet in the head for Anna, and do this to Maria?

Andrey put on a pair of surgical gloves and opened the envelope Izzy had brought from the post office on Ibn Gabirol Street. The envelope contained many photos. The first was of a man. The same man whose photo they found in Maria's bag.

"Interesting. I wonder if this is Eyal Shiloh."

"You think me might have found our killer?"

"Not necessarily, I don't love it when evidence of a suspect just falls into our hands so conveniently. But who knows. We'll have to talk to the guy, that much is obvious."

"Wait, I'll try to locate him," Izzy said and called headquarters.

Andrey flipped through the photos. There were a lot of family ones with a kid, and then also with a little girl. In the photos with the little girl, the boy was older. And for each photo, there was one with another kid— the one who appeared in the photo they found in Maria's bag in the hotel room, the kid who may or may not have been hers.

"You know, this a very strange set of photos."

"What's so strange about it?" Izzy studied the photos.

"They stalked him for so many years?"

"Exactly. See how the kids look older in every photo? I'd say they stalked him for at least two years, maybe more."

"Seems so. Come see this, the guy has a pretty wife. I wonder if the murder victim was his mistress. Some people sure know how to live."

"Yes, Izzy, you might want to keep in mind that at this point he's barely a suspect. Even the hot wife, assuming it's him in the photos, is not exactly proof of guilt." Andrey was starting to suspect that Izzy was developing a certain hostility toward Eyal Shiloh.

"Believe it or not, Andrey, I am aware of that."

"Have you noticed how the pictures are paired up?"

"Oh, yeah. Eyal Shiloh and his family, if it's really him, and the kid who was in the photo with the murder victim."

"Yes. And that kid was the same age in every photo, which meant they were probably taken recently. Unlike the photos of Eyal Shiloh and his family, which were taken over several years. Something didn't smell right about it. And the weirdest thing was that in every pair of photos, Shiloh and the kid were photographed in nearly the exact same pose. And they certainly looked a lot alike. There were even a few photos that compared their ears and noses. As if the set of photos was meant to prove their resemblance."

"She was probably suing him for paternity or something, don't you think?"

"Maybe. It looks like someone was trying to build a case to prove how much this kid looks like this guy. And this guy's a family man, so the last thing he'd need is some call girl suing for paternity. But I told you, it just doesn't feel right. If it is Eyal Shiloh in the photos, then we already have a suspect and a motive, about two minutes into the investigation. It's too quick, too neat. And like you said, according to her ID she doesn't even have a kid. We have to find this character and talk to him, no doubt."

"We'll find him."

"And when they find the car, have them open it with a demolitions guy. After what they did to her body, we don't need to take any risks."

Izzy's phone rang. He talked for a moment and then said to Andrey, "Are you listening to this? Eyal Shiloh is out of the country. Flew to Italy. Maybe hasn't even landed yet."

"You don't say. Is there a return date?"

"Two days from now. Should we wait for him at the airport?"

"No, no need. We'll let him return quietly and then talk to him. If he isn't back by the original date of his return ticket, we'll assume he's fleeing and we'll alert Interpol."

"Whatever you say, Andrey."

"And we have to find out where this kid is. Does she even have a kid? Is he in the country? If she was raising this kid, there's a chance he's walking around somewhere without knowing where his mom is."

"We'll look into it, Andrey."

CHAPTER 9

Bellagio, the current residence of Simone Donadoni, is a resort town located on the coast of Lake Como, north of Milan. The beautiful town is situated on a mountainside that divides Lake Como in two—one arm stretching southwest, and the other southeast. Eyal was picked up at Milan–Malpensa Airport and brought to Bellagio by Philippe, a rather amiable driver. Philippe drove a BMW 760. Eyal was dropped off at a beautiful luxury hotel, a real enchanted castle, where a room with a balcony overlooking the lake awaited him. He ate a hearty breakfast of various French cheeses and Italian delicacies, and drank three cups of fine coffee. At ten a.m., Philippe came to take him to the fateful meeting. Everything was so opulent, so posh and so very wasted on Eyal, because he found it difficult to enjoy all that abundance just then. They drove along the lake for about ten minutes, exited Bellagio and finally, through a heavy electric gate, entered the grounds of an incredibly large villa. The mansion was almost the size of the hotel, three-stories high. The façade of the villa was covered with white bricks that sparkled with cleanliness. Atop the structure was a bell shaped-curve with a large round clock in the center. Stepping out of the car, Eyal saw the amazing gardens that sloped in the direction of the lake, and right in front of the house was a giant sundial whose hour lines were made of manicured poppy patches. Eyal gazed at the beautiful lake and all the splendor that surrounded him, and wondered what kind of life he could have had in a place like this. Maybe he was just living in the wrong place? Italy was simply a gorgeous country.

Every stretch of landscape Eyal had seen so far could have been framed and hung on a wall. Parked next to the villa were two other BMWs and a large black bus with tinted windows. A man in uniform—perhaps the head butler?—greeted him once Philippe had bid him goodbye and promised to pick him up at the end of the meeting. With much ceremony, Eyal was led into a large study which looked more like a library with a huge desk at the end. Every piece of furniture was made of heavy mahogany, and the ceiling was decorated with purple and gold hexagons. It was probably the most impressive room he had ever seen. Walking up to the huge desk, the butler bowed and retreated, leaving Eyal alone with Mister Donadoni. A huge but elegant man. His suit sat well on his frame, and he had very handsome features, bearded, Italian. There was something perhaps even calming about this man's soft eyes. He motioned toward the chair in front of him, and Eyal sat down. Mister Donadoni seemed pensive, and Eyal felt the need to say something, if only to alleviate his own anxiety.

"It's… very beautiful…"

Eyal didn't get to complete the compliment.

"Thank you. You can speak Hebrew." Eyal was shocked. Not only did Donadoni speak Hebrew, he spoke it with a completely Israeli accent.

"I surprised you, I see. I moved here twenty-five years ago, but it didn't ruin my Hebrew."

He got up with surprising ease, and now Eyal saw how truly large the man was, a real mammoth. Eyal wondered if a person of that size could even get into a BMW. Maybe the black bus parked outside was his town car.

"Yes, your Hebrew is perfect."

"Well, you never forget your native tongue. I was once a handsome young man like you. Now I can barely move with all this weight. You were in the paratroopers, weren't you?"

"Yes." Eyal's service in the brigade wasn't a big secret, but he started to suspect that Simone Donadoni knew almost everything about him.

"May I ask what your real name is? I mean, your Israeli name."

It was funny, but it seemed as though the world truly didn't know a thing about Mister Donadoni. The execs at Fugu and Sheringham didn't know that he was Israeli, or at least a former Israeli.

"The Italians know me as Simone Donadoni, but that you already know. You can call me Shimon, Shimon Dahan."

"No kidding." If he wasn't so tensed, it might have actually been amusing.

"Would you believe I used to be a commander in the Golani commando unit? You want to know how I found myself here?"

Eyal nodded, mostly because he felt as though he didn't have a choice.

"I did my stint as first company commander, first and last, I should say, it ended with a humiliating discharge, in a Golani training base. I commanded a rookie unit. Four days into boot camp, one of the recruit's guns accidently went off during shooting range practice. The bullet flew by the platoon commander's head, nearly killed him. I guess today they would have seriously investigated the accident, maybe called in the CID guys. But back in 1976 things were different. They brought him to trial. I saw that the guy was in serious shock. The platoon commander promised me he'd get him back into shape. I gave him three days in the slammer, and thought that would be it. After three days, on the day he was supposed to rejoin the unit, the rookie committed suicide. Three days, can you believe it? Three days."

"It's hard, I know. I was a platoon sergeant and I lost a soldier, it isn't easy."

"Yes, I know that Eyal. That's one of the reasons you spiked my interest." Of course he knew. He knew everything. Maybe that's the reason he had summoned Eyal and not someone else? His military past and the fact that he used to be a commander who had also lost a soldier?

"Do you have any idea why he killed himself?"

"It seemed that the prison guards had pushed him around and he couldn't take it. At first there were some suspicions of sexual abuse. But it wasn't that. Just the regular abuse, and it was too much for him. Between you and me, I guess that soldier should never have been recruited to

Golani. The paratroopers have one advantage. Golani recruits, for the most part, are good soldiers, real lions, but sometimes they get people who don't fit the bill at all, and shouldn't spend even a single day in the platoon. The paratroops have their own gruesome pre-training course that serves as a pretty good filter."

"So they blamed you for his suicide? You sent a soldier to prison, you weren't in charge of the guards' behavior. What else happened there? What you've told me so far doesn't explain your discharge."

"You're right, of course. After his suicide they had no choice, at that point they had to investigate. Turns out that the soldier, his name was Shimi Ben David, Shimi as in Shimon, we shared a first name, for some reason joined the unit a few days late, after the rest of the recruits already had some gun training. He arrived only one day before that fateful range practice. So basically, we sent a soldier who had never held a weapon before to the range. He barely knew which end of the gun fires, and we gave him a loaded weapon and told him to shoot."

"But usually something like that is the platoon commander's responsibility, isn't it? To know what goes on with every soldier, to make sure his soldiers have what they need, that they've been trained."

"True, but as you know, the company commander also has certain responsibility. I was complacent. I know that today people complain that the soldiers' mothers have the company commander's number on speed dial, and that is indeed taking it a step too far, but we were the opposite extreme. I was a living god to them, and I didn't even know most of their names. Certainly not on the fourth day of boot camp. I should have taken an interest, a new soldier joining late, I should have checked up on him, reminded the platoon commander that he has to see what the soldier needs."

"So you were expelled. Well, maybe it was justified. But something like that can happen to anyone. You just had bad luck."

"True. At least they didn't take my stripes. But I was removed from my post, and never got another commanding role. I was sent to waste time in the northern headquarters. But that's not the issue. I could have lived with that. The problem was that there was a dead man, a life that had ended over a stupid mistake. I went to see his mother. His father had passed away from cancer a few years before it happened. And there was a little sister. Sometimes I still have nightmares about Shimi Ben David's mother. About her crying. She told me about him. When you're a company commander and you have more than a hundred soldiers to think about, sometimes you forget they're people. They become a list of achievements and screw-ups. Apparently she had been nervous about his decision to join Golani. He was a sensitive boy, a violinist, a good one, apparently. There was even a possibility he could have received the status of gifted musician and get a post close to home, to allow him to continue to play and perform. But he wanted a combat unit. He also had outstanding grades. In a nutshell, the shining star of the family, the big hope of his widowed mother. He was also his sister's role model. So, maximal damage, if you follow. The death of a young man is always a tragedy, but sometimes his role in the family is so significant that it turns into a triple catastrophe. Ironically, I was furious at them. You know how you can get angry at the very people you've hurt? Suddenly they have the nerve to feel hurt by you, and ruin the wonderful image you have of yourself. I felt I had to escape. I don't know if it's the most noble of feelings. Certain people decide they want to dedicate their lives to helping others. I just wanted to run away. Two days after my discharge I just left without telling anyone. It took a long time before I even told my parents where I was. I don't know why I felt the need to do it that way, but that's how it was. At first I traveled to South America, and spent two years in Brazil. I met an Italian girl there, we were together for about three years, and then I went to Italy and stayed here even after we broke up, stayed to this very day, as you can see."

"Did you try to find out what happened to the soldier's mom and sister? Now that you're so rich you could probably help them out, right?"

"Yes, you could say I did that. They're taken care of. Their lives weren't ruined, as far as you can say that about someone who lost her child. Well, I guess you're anxious to know why I brought you here. You, of all people, huh?"

"Yeah I was wondering about that." Eyal suddenly felt a surge of anxiety regarding that very question.

"I must tell you how excited I am about your technology. I want to show you something, or more accurately, play you something. Come see, on the laptop. Come closer."

Eyal leaned over the table and Shimon turned the computer so they could both see the screen. The mouse cursor moved slowly across a list of files. It seemed as though Shimon was doing his best to build up the tension, like some movie director, and it was working. Eyal tried to make something out of the names of the files, but they meant nothing to him. Shimon double-clicked on one of them, an audio file. Eyal saw the familiar vibrating graph indicating sound waves, and then heard a female voice that for a split second he didn't recognize, because it was a woman he had met only once.

"Can I come in?"

"Yes, of course, forgive me, I know this will sound corny but you're just the most beautiful woman I've ever seen, I apologize."

"There's certainly no need to apologize. So, you're Yossi?"

"Indeed, Yossi, that's me."

Simone Donadoni stopped the recording, and Eyal thought he might have a heart attack. The minute he found those strange photos in the airport he knew something was wrong, should he have anticipated this? Eyal looked at Simone Donadoni, who was looking back at him with those same soft and soothing eyes. Only they weren't so soothing anymore. Maria's voice stirred many memories in Eyal. Even some form of nostalgia. Eyal remembered the guilt he felt at the time, and that feeling had never really subsided. While he hadn't cheated on Galit since, and truly believed he could maintain that record, he still felt guilty every time a beautiful girl looked his way. But apart from the guilt, he still had the sweet memory of an adventurous night, and now this man sitting in front of him could destroy his family life, maybe even his life altogether. Suddenly his life had turned into a big dirty rag. Shimon Dahan had heard their entire conversation, which meant he knew how many embarrassing things Maria told Eyal about him. Some people would kill for that alone. But how had he recorded this exactly? Did he record all of Maria's sessions? But how? Could Yermi have planted some device on him? Yermi. Every detail of that odd night now came back with vivid colors. The stack of papers! He had received a stack of blank papers to sign. Maybe Yermi hid a recording device between them? But Yermi worked for the escort agency, why would he give Shimon the tapes of Maria's sessions? It didn't seem likely at all. Maria would have never told Eyal so many embarrassing details about her husband, and then hand him the tape. It would have been suicide. Maybe everything she told him was a bunch of baloney? But Eyal believed with all his heart that she was being honest. Maybe while Eyal was in the lobby with Yermi someone else had gone into his room and planted the tape recorder? But that sounded so complicated, to produce such an operation for each session...

"I see you're trying to figure out how I recorded this. I advise you to save yourself the headache. It isn't important. The fact is, I have the recording of what seems to be the most significant fuck my wife ever had, a document with certain sentimental value, if you get what I mean."

"I think you're exaggerating a bit, I'm not that important."

"Oh, you'll see I'm not exaggerating at all."

"What are you planning to do with it?"

"Good question. I haven't decided yet. Let me tell you something interesting. Do you know what I did with this recording?"

"What?" Was it possible that the bastard had already sent it to Galit? What a disaster.

"It's not what you think. Your wife has no idea."

"What then?"

"Come on, Eyal, you're disappointing me. Think where you came from."

"You ran it on Fugu's technology."

"See? When you want to, you get there."

"Satisfied with ourselves, are we?"

"Forgive me, Eyal, I'm disrespecting you and you truly don't deserve it."

"Fine. So that's why you wanted Max's technology so urgently."

"Just a sample, a closed, protected code. You have nothing to worry about. Business-wise, I didn't get anything."

"Yes, I know what we give, more or less."

"Anyway, you know what conclusion I came to after analyzing the recording?"

"I have no idea."

"Maria told you the truth. She really wanted you, she actually enjoyed herself."

"Well, I kind of reached that conclusion myself after she turned down my money."

"She paid for you."

"Yes."

"And that rather offends me, as her husband. I'm sure you can understand."

"I don't want to offend you, especially when you're in a good position to hurt me. But I don't really understand this, what did you expect? What does it matter if she wanted me? If not me it would have been someone else. You know she was never really into you, you're too old for her. And a rich older man who marries a model twenty or thirty years his junior must be aware of this." Eyal wasn't sure whether he was pushing it with his honesty. After all, self-deception is a highly developed mechanism. He should know.

"Maybe. But you should keep in mind that I heard your conversation. The entire conversation. I heard everything she told you, and you now know way too much about me."

"Perhaps, but I have a wife and two small kids, do you really think I'm going to say anything to anyone? I'd be destroying my marriage."

"You'd still have a life. It might be difficult, if she leaves you, but you're young, you could still visit the kids on weekends, find a new wife, maybe start a new family."

"I don't want a new family."

"What I'm trying to explain is that unlike you, I don't really have anything to look forward to."

"You have Maria," Eyal said, and knew how phony it sounded.

"The day you met Maria was the day I lost her. Even though, as you were kind enough to mention, she was never truly mine, that day I lost what little of her I had. But today I no longer even have the privilege of deluding myself anymore. Maria was murdered."

"What?! Are you sure? There was an article this morning about a woman who was murdered, a very beautiful woman, but there was a photo, and it wasn't Maria. Are you certain Maria was murdered?"

"I don't know who else was murdered, Eyal, but I do know Maria was murdered."

"When?"

"I'm not sure yet. It could have even happened while you were still on the plane over here."

"That's unbelievable." Could it be true? Eyal couldn't decide whether it was more sad or scary. If Shimon was right, then it was too weird of a coincidence. On the very day of Eyal's visit with Shimon, someone decided to murder Maria? Maybe it was Shimon who had her murdered? Eyal didn't know what to think.

"My condolences. What is there to say? I know you loved Maria…"

"I *love* Maria."

"Love, yes, and now you've lost her, and I am very sorry. I just hope you'll agree with me that ruining my family won't bring Maria back. What would you get out if?"

"The satisfaction of revenge. You never wanted to get back at anyone? Even just some driver who cut you off, someone who cut in line in front of you at the supermarket, you never felt like chopping those people's balls off? Saw them to pieces? Burn them alive?"

"My revenge fantasies are not so grandiose, I'm afraid."

"And what does that tell you about me? You think you learned something about me now? Analyzed my fantasies and concluded that I'm a psychopath? Maybe it even leads you to the conclusion that I murdered my wife?"

"I don't know what it says about you, and I didn't say you murdered your wife."

"But the thought crossed your mind, right?"

"Sure it did, but that still doesn't mean you did it, does it? Anyway, maybe it's better you focus your revenge fantasies on the person who actually did kill your wife, I mean, you don't think I did it, right? You yourself said that I was on the plane when it happened."

"I said you might have been. But we'll revisit the subject later."

He made a phone call and blurted out something in Italian. Only then did it occur to Eyal that Maria might not have been aware of her husband's Israeli origins. He could have been sure to speak only Italian near her, and his Italian sounded completely authentic to Eyal. He recalled how, at first glance, this Shimon character had looked completely Italian to him.

"Can I ask you something?"

"Sure."

"Why did you reveal that you're Israeli? No one knows, right? No one at our company knows, so I guess it's something you've been hiding pretty well for all this time, and now you decide to tell me, of all people. Why? You would have still been Maria's Italian husband, I never would have guessed."

"You have a point. But I wanted to confront you, to talk to you. And I couldn't imagine the conversation in any other language but Hebrew. It's just so artificial, speaking to another Israeli in English. Pretending to speak English with an Italian accent, it doesn't seem ridiculous to you?"

"Yes, I guess you're right."

"This is an important conversation, I had to choose to conduct it in Hebrew, our native tongue. I want you to meet someone."

A moment later, a young boy entered the study dressed like a little lord, holding the hand of a woman Eyal assumed was his nanny. It felt like a scene from a movie about English Royalty.

They came closer, stopping approximately three meters from the large desk.

"Say hello to the gentleman," Shimon said in Italian.

The boy approached Eyal, almost touching him, and said hello with a slight accent. Eyal wasn't sure whether he spoke a word of Hebrew. Smiling at the boy, Eyal patted his head and said hello.

"Handsome boy."

It was the truth, the boy was beautiful. A toddler really, maybe three years old.

"Dino, sweetheart, you can go with Bianca, it's fine." The kid smiled at Eyal, and while walking away, holding his nanny's hand, he turned his head and continued to look at Eyal. There was something mesmerizing about his gaze, and it seemed as though he struggled to turn away. He kept staring until the nanny closed the door behind them.

"Dino Donadoni?"

"That's what Maria wanted. Shall we have a drink?"

"Sure, why not."

"Yes, and with our drinks we can cut straight to the chase, the reason I brought you here."

He took two glasses out of a beautiful wooden cabinet and poured a generous amount of Rémy Martin into each glass.

"Saluti." So, here it comes, Eyal thought. He felt a strange sense of tranquility instead of the tension he expected to feel. Up until that point he had been so nervous, and now that it was finally coming, he might as well relax. Life as he knew it was probably coming to an end, and there was nothing he could do about it.

"Thank you. I realize that my being here has nothing to do with your intention of investing in my company, huh?"

"I already told you I'm very serious about your company. It's true that it was you I looked for before I found out about the company, but I must say I'm full of admiration."

"Okay."

"Soon you'll find out why I admire your company so much."

"Right." His recording of Maria, it was obvious, but what had he gotten out of it? So he found out that Maria really wanted him, so what? Eyal tried to figure out what this Shimon guy could have learned from the tape that was valuable enough to make him want to invest in the company. Maybe he found out that despite Maria's desire for him, she had faked her orgasms?

"It was a long time ago, three years, right?"

"Yes, and I'm sorry if I somehow caused you any grief or embarrassment."

"You say you're sorry, but you're not really sorry, are you? Don't worry, I'm not holding you accountable. It was my decision to marry her, I knew what her job was, right?"

"Yes, I think so." They really were starting to repeat themselves. Where was he going with this?

"And yet, three years ago you made the decision to cheat on your wife. It might have been the first time you cheated, but nevertheless, sometimes the decisions we make have some strange repercussions, am I right?"

It was only then that the thought crossed Eyal's mind.

"I have to say, Eyal, you seem like an intelligent and nice guy. I think you're starting to realize something now, right?"

But how could it be?

"And you're asking yourself how this is possible, yes?"

Without a doubt, it was embarrassing to be so transparent.

"Yes, it is what I'm asking myself. As we both know, Maria made a living from sleeping with men. So you probably understand we used a condom. I'm married with kids, do you really think I'd put my wife at risk, my entire family, by sleeping with, forgive me, a prostitute, without a condom?"

"I know you used a condom. Well, I don't actually know for sure, I only have an audio recording and you two didn't discuss the issue, but I certainly believe you."

"So? What then? Am I not understanding you?"

"I think you are. You'll probably think I'm naïve, because it was only recently that I started thinking Dino might not be mine. It was after a pretty exhausting argument with Maria. We had many exhausting arguments, in which many unpleasant things were said. Very unpleasant. And in this particular argument, she told me exactly that. That I'm naïve. That I'm not as smart as I think. Maria told me a lot of things, but she never explicitly told me the kid wasn't mine, it was something in the way she said I was naïve that made me think she wasn't just saying that for no reason, that she was talking about something very specific. Something important. And suddenly it hit me. Maybe she was talking about Dino, maybe he wasn't mine. And maybe I even knew it all along. So I checked."

"You don't always want to go digging too deep."

"You're absolutely right, but I can see the same passion for knowing the truth in your eyes right now. I see it even though a kid from an affair is probably the last thing you need, right? Well, I wanted to know the truth too."

"So he's not yours."

"Correct."

"And how exactly did you reach the conclusion that he's mine?"

"You want to tell me you didn't notice the resemblance?"

"I guess there's something, but that's not exactly proof, you know. And there's the small issue of the condom."

"First of all, there's more than *something*, the kid looks just like you. Maybe next time you come I'll let you have some quality time with him and you'll start noticing the small details that make for this striking resemblance. And besides, I can even explain the condom. But how about I first explain how I got to you, what do you say?"

"Okay." This should be interesting, Eyal thought. What was going to happen to his comfortable life? That, too, was interesting.

"The father is one of the clients who slept with Maria three years and four months ago. Dino is two years and seven months old, so, simple math. I have the audio recordings of each one of Maria's sessions."

"Really? Do you have the recording of her last session? Because if you do, then you know who killed her, right?"

"Well, unfortunately I don't have that recording, even if there is one, it wasn't delivered to me yet. Like I told you, she was murdered today. But as far as I know, there's no recording. But I must say, you're quick."

Was it just his impression, or did he actually catch Shimon by surprise? He took a long pause before answering, and he even seemed a bit confused. And Shimon never even mentioned to Eyal that Maria was murdered in a session with a client, it was just a guess. Lucky guess, it seemed.

"And why would this be the one tape you wouldn't get?"

"It's just how it is. I understand your thought process, you think I don't have it because I, or someone on my behalf, killed her. But it's not true, you shouldn't think such things about me, please. Just accept the fact that there's no tape. I didn't actually record each and every session. There were certain ones I couldn't record for various reasons."

"Could there have been a tape but the killer took it?"

"Maybe, but let's move on for now. We listened to the tapes, my experts and I, and we reached the conclusion that you were the ideal candidate to be my son's father. Funny, isn't it? I mean, if you're his father, then obviously he's not my son, but sometimes the truth is hard to accept."

"You listened to the tapes, and from that you're basing this crazy hypothesis? Then let me suggest a different one."

"Go ahead."

"None of her clients is your kid's father, because in Israel, one hundred percent of the men who can afford a prostitute that charges ten grand a night wear a condom. Your wife had a lover. What do you say about that?"

"Maria didn't have a lover. Don't ask how, but I know for sure."

"I don't believe you can know for sure, but let's say you do for the sake of the argument."

"Like I told you, we analyzed the recording of your entire session with Maria with Fugu's technology. And I can tell you that the technology determined that Maria told you the truth, even when she spoke about her feelings toward you."

"From feelings you don't get pregnant, as far as I know."

"Fair enough. The software also states the level of statistical significance of the analyzed data."

"Yes, I know. So it stated a high level?"

"Almost the highest possible. While for the other potential fathers from Maria's sessions, about ten, it was obvious she didn't feel anything and lied about pretty much everything she told them. But in your session with Maria, there was one moment of complete dishonesty on her part. One moment. You don't know what I'm talking about?"

"I have no idea, but believe me, I'm curious to hear it."

"When you got out of the shower, you found her in a rather odd position. You asked her what she was doing and, and she told you... What did she tell you?"

"That she was doing exercises to release her stomach." Eyal suddenly felt his own stomach starting to hurt.

"Correct. And she had her legs folded up, right?"

"Right."

"I think she was doing what women do when they have sex with their husband and are trying to get pregnant. What do you think?"

Eyal felt the lightheadedness that usually preludes a panic attack. If Maria actually was trying to get pregnant, then her lie about releasing her stomach muscles was a highly charged statement, as Max would call it. The statement would receive an especially low level of credibility, i.e., a lie with high levels of significance. Eyal closed his eyes. He had a horrible headache. This couldn't be happening to him. He opened his eyes and looked at Shimon.

"I'll admit it's interesting, but it still doesn't prove I'm the father." Eyal's voice trembled.

"Yes, but I'll repeat, the moment Maria held her legs up and told you she was doing an exercise is the one moment in the entire session in which she wasn't honest with you. And between you and me, that's pretty amazing, since there are usually many moments of dishonesty when two people meet. She lied. The significance of her lie, according to the software, was through the roof. Come on, why would Maria lie to you about something as silly as an exercise to loosen her stomach muscles, when she was honest with you about the most intimate details of her life? I think the idea that she was trying to get pregnant is a very good explanation, I'm almost positive. Maria loved kids. She desperately wanted kids, even though she was scared, scared because of who she was, that she'd mess up the kid's life before he was even born. But then you came along, the perfect dad, and I guess she couldn't resist the temptation. Now to the issue of the condom. I know you took a shower right after you had sex. Three times that night, if memory serves me right. Not bad at all. What did you do with the condoms? Did you throw them in the garbage can? Did you check to see what happened to them? It's certainly possible that if you left one lying around, Maria took it and emptied it inside her. I know it sounds disgusting, but it's a possibility."

"It's only a possibility, it isn't a certainty. At least you admit it doesn't prove anything." Eyal knew he didn't sound convincing. He knew that he himself was almost convinced Shimon was right.

"Yes, you're certainly correct, and that's exactly why you're here! Well, not just for that, but for that too."

"You want me to take a DNA test, don't you? A paternity test."

"Yes."

"And what if I don't want to? Why would I want this problem now? Why would you even want it, care to explain that?"

"But, my dear, by admitting that it's a problem, you're also admitting you think there's a possibility I'm right. I'm not going to force you. I'm not going to bring in thugs to grab you and take a DNA sample. I admit I might be an oddball, but I don't do such things. But tell me the truth: you really want to tell me you're not interested in knowing? I've studied you, you could even say I started liking you even before we met, and I have to compliment you by saying that meeting you in person hasn't disappointed me. It's funny, or maybe sad, I don't know, but I understand Maria. I understand why she wanted you. You're not only handsome, Eyal, you're a good person. Like it or not, you are. That beautiful boy who hypnotized you with his gaze, who couldn't take his eyes off you, you don't want to know if he's yours?"

"Good question. I'm not sure. And if he is mine, then what?"

"We'll take it one step at a time. You don't have to give me an answer right now. Go back to the hotel, I'll give you my cell number, and you just think about it. Next week there's going to be announcement about Fugu's exit. It's going to be purchased by Fondo Lombardia for fifteen million dollars. Go back to Israel, take your time, but not too much time, and give me an answer."

"What did you just say? You already closed a deal with Sheringham to buy us? Fifteen million dollars?"

Eyal didn't know what to think. Under regular circumstances, it would have been great. Max would be a bit disappointed. He'd be making something like eight hundred thousand from the deal, maybe a bit more. And Max already had a lot more than that. Max was hoping that Fugu's technology would turn him into a giant like Mark Zuckerberg or Sergey Brin, if not in financial terms, than at least as a high-tech legend. His ideas might have been brilliant enough for it, but the company's business management, which Eyal couldn't deny being part of, turned Fugu into an esoteric company. And it was going to leave Max with a little under a million dollars for the company and perhaps an employment contract with a murderer who married a prostitute. Eyal would be getting about a quarter mill before taxes, which was a disappointing amount, but still substantial for him. But the bastard was trying to take over his life! And maybe even end it, who knows. It wasn't the exit Eyal had been hoping for. What would happen to Mandy? Fondo Lombarida would have no use for him. But he'd get his shares, Eyal was almost certain.

"I closed with Shringham, but as you know, Sheringham alone isn't enough because they don't own fifty percent. Your CEO will be getting the announcement in the mail soon enough."

"Yes, I imagined."

"Obviously I expect you and Max and the rest of the senior executives to stay in the company. I'm not interested in buying an empty shell. I'm going to want a written commitment from you and Max."

"From me? Why would you need me? You need Max, that's for sure, but me, there are a thousand others like me out there," Eyal said, but he knew Shimon wasn't interested in him because of his remarkable skills. Shimon didn't even bother to answer.

"I want to remind you of one thing. No one knows I'm Israeli."

"Yes, you already told me that. And I assume you'd like to keep them in the dark about it."

"Yes, I'm asking you to keep quiet."

Shimon used the word 'asking,' but it was clear to Eyal that this was no request. This man had enough information on him to destroy his marriage. It wouldn't survive even just the tape. Not to mention Shimon's tendency to murder people who irritated him, Eyal suspected.

"And I want you to understand that I truly didn't invite you here to ruin your life. It's just that… it's important for me to know."

"Okay, fine. I'll return to Israel and think about it."

"Good."

"So can I go back to the hotel now? You'll have to forgive me, I just need some air. You'll agree that was a lot of information for one day."

"Yes, of course you can. You came here with a lot of fears, you think I'm some kind of psychopath, huh? I'm not going to chop you into twelve pieces and mail them to every corner of the universe, you really have to relax. My wonderful Philippe will take you back to the hotel, okay? You're flying back to Israel tomorrow at noon, right? Philippe will pick you up in the morning and drive you to the airport. I suggest you spend the day strolling around Bellagio, it's a beautiful place. You can also do some mountain climbing here, if you feel like it, it's an opportunity you don't want to miss."

"Okay." Whatever you say, Eyal thought. He just wanted out of there. He wondered if he should pass on the wonderful Philippe's services and just walk, since it wasn't that far, but it didn't seem to matter now. It seemed as though Shimon Dahan wasn't interested in killing him, at least not for the moment, and Philippe's company actually put him at ease. And he certainly didn't know anyone in this enchanting town apart from Shimon and Philippe.

"You can leave. Philippe's waiting for you at the front door."

"Okay."

After Eyal left, Shimon opened a folder named M and started looking at photos of Maria with a mix of longing, rage and pain. Why did she have to be so stupid? They had a good thing going for them, why did she have to fuck up their lives and the lives of people who had nothing to do with them? Obviously, it wasn't the first time Maria had vexed him. She treated her clients a bit too affectionately. But something like this had never happened before. She told Eyal everything. When Shimon spoke to Eyal, he had to block out the fact that Eyal knew certain embarrassing things about him; it was just too awful. So why not just kill the motherfucker and be over with it? It was a question Shimon had asked himself hundreds if not thousands of times. There was one important fact that Eyal and even Maria didn't know about the escort agency. After Shimon met Maria and fell in love with her, and since she insisted on continuing to work in order to remain independent, he bought the agency. He gave the previous owner a fantastical sum, an offer he truly couldn't refuse. After purchasing the agency, he discovered there were certain unexpected advantages to it. He had made a lot of money from the agency. He did pretty well even from the daily profits, but the real money came from extorting clients. A few very big fish fell into his hands unexpectedly.

After each session, the girls would pass on all the information about the clients, everything they could get their hands on. There was always something, at least an identification document that enabled them to investigate the client. Most of them they didn't touch. Only the ones who were truly worth it. From the moment Shimon bought the agency, Maria became a very special employee, unbeknownst to her, and Shimon made sure to take further precautions when it came to her. He wasn't sure whether Maria's working there turned him on or drove him crazy. One way or another, he wanted to know everything.

Maria didn't know that her bosses were getting more than just the documentation of her clients, which she herself photographed during the sessions. They were also getting audio recordings. Had she known, she wouldn't have bothered blackmailing the poor Hezi, an endeavor that proved futile. When Maria was late in sending the client information to her boss, Boris, and then sent him the details of an old client, he became suspicious. Boris was the guy directly in charge of the Maria file. He never understood why his boss agreed to this strange arrangement, but he knew his boss wasn't the kind of man you wanted to cross. Simone paid him well, and Boris was completely loyal to him. Boris was obviously not allowed to listen to Maria's tapes, only his boss could. But he did advise him to compare the two recordings, the old and the new, which were supposed to be of the same client. The audio recordings proved beyond a doubt that Maria had lied. She had a new client whose details she didn't pass on, the photos of his ID card or credit cards. Listening to the tape shook Shimon to his core. The man knew intolerable, embarrassing things about him, worse than the information he used to extort his girls' clients. First they had to find him. It turned out the hotel didn't have any of his details. He had registered under the same fake name that Maria later provided them, which was very odd. Was it possible that he wasn't a client at all, but a lover Maria had been meeting in secret? Some clients did use aliases at hotels, but registering under the name of a former client of Maria's? That had to be coordinated with Maria in advance. Which meant they already knew each other. In fact, Maria's attempt to protect Eyal had actually placed him in greater danger. Shimon agreed to let Maria sleep with clients, but he wouldn't stand for real lovers. Eventually they succeeded in locating Eyal by tracing the computer with which he had logged into the agency's website. The natural thing to do would have been to get rid of Eyal, the sooner the better. As revenge for the passion he stirred within Maria, but also because he simply knew too much. But first Shimon wanted to know if Eyal really was Maria's lover, or just a regular client Maria happened to get excited about. He listened to the recording dozens of times, and it was rather obvious that it was Eyal and Maria's first meeting. But it was equally obvious that even if Eyal was a regular client, the relationship between them had turned into one of lovers during the session. So what difference did it make what they were before the session? But it mattered to him. Maybe if her crush on Eyal had developed during the session itself and not prior to it, it somehow would have minimized her betrayal, her lie. Shimon sent men to follow Maria and Eyal. He gave an order for the next session to include video as well as audio. In fact, Shimon was eager to see Eyal and Maria on videotape. But he couldn't document another session between them, no matter how hard he tried. The more he followed Eyal, the more he became interested in him. He wasn't sure why, but he knew he didn't want to kill him. At least not for the time being. He had all kinds of excuses. The need to find out whether he was still seeing Maria, for instance. And his company's technology; Fugu had started to interest Shimon at a certain point. But more than anything, he had simply developed a type of obsession about this man, and his relationship with Maria. Following them had become a central part of Shimon's life. And then one day, he was informed that Maria had decided to escape.

Maria wasn't sure when she realized she was being stalked. That she was a prisoner. And that even her shady workplace, which was supposed to grant her certain independence from her husband, was actually controlled by him. She suddenly realized that any wrong move she might make may lead to her death. It's not easy following a person for years without them noticing a thing. Once she even caught one of the men from the escort agency stalking her not far from her apartment. She put two and two together, and decided to make her escape. But how do you plan an escape when you know your every move is being watched? Nearly every vacation Maria took, mostly weekends in London, was with Anna. Escort girls usually find it difficult to develop friendships outside of work. There are many reasons for this: the shameful occupation, the inability to tell the truth about your life and your daily routine. She had a few childhood friends from Russia with whom she was still in touch. But Anna was her one true friend, her entire social life, in fact. When they started vacationing together in the Cayman Islands, Boris became suspicious, especially since they frequently visited the branch of a large bank near their hotel. At that point the boss ordered to increase the surveillance and tap their phones. The girls tried to be discreet, but they made mistakes, and eventually it became clear to Shimon that he was going to lose his beloved wife. That she had decided to run away from him.

Eyal left the enormous study, and while walking toward the front door he heard tiny steps behind him. The steps of a young child. He turned around and saw Dino running toward him with a plastic toy plane in one hand, and his nanny several feet behind, scolding him.

When the boy drew near, Eyal noticed how much he resembled Daniel, which wasn't very surprising considering they both looked like Eyal, who was probably the father of both boys. Four years ago, when Daniel was two years old, he had discovered the world of wheels and transportation. He would point at every bus, car or plane he saw and say 'wheels.' And Eyal would answer, Yes, sweetie, the plane has wheels. This child in front of him held the plane and made the childish sounds of an engine.

Eyal leaned forward, the child drew closer and Eyal patted his head. What a sweet child. Could he really let that psychopath be in charge of raising him?

The nanny picked him up despite his sounds of protest. She said something that sounded like an apology and they both retreated. The child started crying, and Eyal wanted to cry too, but he quickly advanced to the door instead. He heard the boy running behind him; he had freed himself from the nanny's embrace and was heading toward Eyal. Eyal lifted him and kissed him, and when he put him back down, the boy grabbed Eyal's hand and tried to pull him back into the house. The nanny reprimanded him, but he seemed unperturbed.

"I'm really sorry, I'm sure you are very busy, there's no need," she said with a heavy Italian accent.

"It's okay," Eyal said, and continued to walk with Dino hand in hand. They passed the lavish staircase and arrived to a giant playroom concealed behind it. At least in the toy department the kid wasn't exactly deprived.

Two large carpets stretched across the room. On one carpet were piles of Lego and toy cars of every type, and on the other was a model train, a giant set of tracks that occupied the entire carpet with tiny model houses, bridges and tunnels; it was clear that Shimon had brought in some serious experts to build this amazing set for his kid. Eyal wasn't sure how much time he spent in that room, maybe an hour, perhaps more. He laughed with Dino, hugged and kissed him as if he was his own child, since he probably was. Finally Philippe appeared and asked if he wanted to leave. The driver probably had other obligations and couldn't continue waiting. Eyal picked up the kid again, kissed him on his cheek and left with a strange feeling. He felt sorry for the kid and sorry for himself, for the decisions he would probably have to make very soon.

Eyal collapsed into the comfortable seat of the BMW, and apologized for the delay. He wished the drive weren't so short. Perhaps he should ask to return to Milan? But there was nothing waiting for him there. Shimon already had all the material he needed. Even if he recorded and videotaped him in the hotel room it wouldn't make any difference.

Eyal was simply overwhelmed by all the problems, and he was too tired to think about solutions. What was he going to say to the people at Fugu? Although it seemed that Shimon was going to solve that problem for him soon enough. Should he follow his instructions not to tell anyone about his Israeli origins? Yes, otherwise his marriage might end. Fuck Fugu. Should he tell everything to Galit? But how could he? Maybe he should just go to the police. But then Shimon would turn on him, and Galit would find out everything... What a mess. And what if the kid really was his? Could he hide it from Galit? When he was playing with Dino he felt absolutely confident that he was his. But now the doubts had returned. He was panicking, and he couldn't stop the thoughts from racing in his head in all directions.

Philippe dropped him off at his hotel, as promised. Eyal entered his room and stretched out on the soft bed. He wished Galit were there with him, in his arms; they would listen to the kids throw pillows at each other and giggle. Enough. He had to try to be constructive. Before Eyal returned to Israel, he followed Shimon's advice and took a stroll along the narrow alleyways of Bellagio, which was truly a beautiful city. He saw small ancient houses and went to a market that seemed mainly for tourists and was filled with wooden artwork and paintings. He strolled along the coast and gazed at the beautiful lake and the mansions built by Italy's richest, perhaps even tycoons from other countries, and had several cups of excellent Italian coffee in a few small cafes overlooking the lake. But of course, he didn't enjoy any of it. The sinking sensation in his chest wouldn't let up. He thought about going to the hotel's beautiful bar and downing a few shots of whiskey, but it felt too much like a cliché. He continued walking around town to exhaust himself, devoured a giant portion of lasagna, and finally managed to fall asleep. But his sleep was light and he woke up tired and irritated. After the hotel's rich breakfast, he checked out. The room was of course already paid for. Outside, the courteous Philippe awaited him, though on second thought, who could tell what that Philippe character really knew? Maybe he was a partner in his boss's crimes. Eyal didn't think it was likely, but he had seen stranger things before. Philippe drove him back to the

CHAPTER 10

When Eyal turned on his cellphone after landing at Ben Gurion Airport, he had fifty-three new messages. More than half of them were from Mandy. There were also a few from Max. And at least one from Jeff. Some were from friends, and even his dad, congratulating him on the exit. He didn't know whether he should laugh or cry. Was it possible that the official announcement had already been released, or did someone leak the rumor? While waiting at passport control, the inevitable phone call from Mandy came in.

"What's up, Mandy?"

"What's up? Shit. That's what's up. I want to tell you that I've often wondered what's hiding behind that pretty face and chummy attitude of yours, and now I know. I also want to tell you that you're a piece of shit, and I know that you're fucking Yonit. And the secretary from Delton X. The entire company knows."

It was the words of someone with nothing to lose, and it was strange. What could he possibly say? Delton X was a company that sat in their building compound, and the secretary was smoking hot. His relationship with her had never gone beyond a polite 'good morning.'.

"I never touched Yonit, or that secretary. And I had no idea the company was going to be sold to Shi... That Italian guy. Simone."

He almost said Shimon, and then remembered. Simone. Not Shimon. He couldn't afford to make that mistake, because he didn't know what the response would be. Mandy thought he had lost everything while Eyal somehow got the better end of the stick. How very wrong he was.

"You're so easy to read, Eyal. The two of you know each other so well that you actually call him by his first name, Simone, huh? I have to tell you that I'm impressed. The morning of the trip, when you said you didn't know anything, I actually believed you. I sure didn't give you the credit you deserved, you're worse than Jeff. Go fuck yourself."

"Mandy, excuse me but you're being a complete nut-job. No one can take away your shares, no one can fire you two seconds before the exit. No court in the world would let it happen. So you won't be CEO anymore, but you'll get your money."

"Screw you, Eyal."

And with that Mandy hung up. Eyal was so tired that a moment after Mandy hung up, he wondered if the conversation had actually taken place. It was a completely improbable conversation. He had to forget about Mandy. But the conversation did make him think. Eyal believed he was a good person. He knew there was something ridiculous about that thought, but he nonetheless believed it wholeheartedly. He was a good father, almost always a good husband, and in most cases, a good friend. Every word he said to Maria was true. He really was the good-looking guy who didn't screw around because his conscience wouldn't let him. He really did have a change of heart in deciding he wasn't going to sleep with Maria, but then she seduced him. But apparently not everyone viewed him the same way. He had never been so deluded as to believe the entire world loved him. But the whole 'stop playing nice guy and reveal your true and ugly face' was new to him. People never spoke to him like that. Maybe Shimon saw him the same way? Shimon had Fugu's software. He was supposed to be able to tell that Eyal was being truthful, that he was honest. But maybe Shimon didn't buy it. Maybe Shimon thought that was Eyal's game, to make up sob stories about how little he got laid in order to elicit sympathy from girls and seduce them, while making them believe they were seducing him. But it really didn't make much of a difference. Even if Shimon believed every word Eyal told him, he still had enough reasons to hate him. But maybe Eyal failed to understand the depth of Shimon's hatred toward him.

The next phone call was from Jeff.

"Eyal, how are you doing?"

"How am I doing? Don't ask. You really set me up for one hell of an experience. Maybe I shouldn't have been so surprised. After all, I knew you might be up to something. But you still managed to surprise me. Mandy just called me."

"I assume he was less than friendly."

"Indeed. He accused me of fucking more or less every woman within ten feet of the company."

"Are you serious? Well, I guess the man's falling apart. It's completely inappropriate, just another proof that he's not cut out to be a CEO."

"But by the way he went on about it, it seems like he's sure he won't get anything from the exit. You can't be planning something like that, Jeff, right?"

"Let's drop it for now. I wanted to apologize to you first. The company was already very close to shutting down. This Italian guy was your last chance. He told me you two knew each other from somewhere. I didn't know why it was so important to him, but he insisted on talking to you, and to be the one to tell you about the exit. I understand it put you in an awkward position, and I'm truly sorry about it, Eyal. I don't apologize often, so you can understand that this is important to me."

"You couldn't have at least told Mandy? You were the one who brought him in after you got rid of Itzik."

"I couldn't trust him. It's obvious that after losing his hold on the company, he had no reason to maintain the confidentiality clause the Italian demanded. Mandy was a mistake, I can admit that. I even had my doubts when we hired him."

"So you're really trying to take his shares? I think he'll sue you, and you'll lose. Forgive me, Jeff, I respect you, but that's what I think."

"Just leave that to me, okay, Eyal? It really isn't your problem. But you have to admit that Mandy tanked at his job."

"He failed, it's true, but sometimes I ask myself if anyone could have done better. Why did you even hire him?"

"Come on, Eyal, you know how hard it is to find a talented CEO. After we got rid of Itzik we were under a lot of pressure to find someone to replace him, and there were maybe three candidates we had to choose from. So we took the best, who was Mandy. Now I know that Mandy can't be a CEO, even though he seems intelligent enough, and organized. But he just doesn't know how to do business. He's not cool-headed, not ruthless enough, you might say. For instance, why is Boaz still an operations manager at the company, you have any idea?"

"It's a good question."

"A CEO needs to be able to cut people loose. You can't let a bad operations manager keep his position. But Mandy hesitated, he didn't want to be the bad guy, when it really has nothing to do with being bad. I once brought a development manager to a company that developed software for routers. We poached him from a competing company and he brought a lot of knowledge with him, and we could do it because of some loophole in his contract. They couldn't do anything to stop it. He rebuilt the entire product, all the development from scratch. Without stepping on any of the competition's patents. It was amazing. And after it was done and it was time to move on, it turned out that there was one thing he was really good at, and that was it. He wasn't development manager material. And obviously you can't demote him to a regular programmer."

"You fired him?"

"Of course. We gave him a very nice severance package, but he lost all his stock options along with his workplace. And he cried, he was furious, and believe me, it was bad. You used me, like some grilled chicken, you ate the flesh and now you're throwing the bones in the garbage, that's what he said to me. But I needed a development manager, and he couldn't deliver the goods. Nice CEOs might save a guy's job temporarily, but eventually the company will crash and then everyone loses their job. You understand? And besides, Mandy was never able to read your clients, which is even more important. He's a disaster at negotiations. For example, why did the GE deal fall through? It was a huge opportunity."

"We weren't familiar enough with their internal processes."

"Mandy wasn't familiar enough. It's nice of you to take part of the responsibility, but the truth is, it's not expected of you yet. You need to bring in new business opportunities, new clients, and you actually did that very well. But when it comes to closing the deals with their management, that's where a good CEO should shine. Mandy could never read the people in front of him, while everyone can read him like an open book."

"Look, I know Mandy's not an amazing CEO, but what... Oh, what's left to say..." Eyal was so exhausted he could feel himself slurring his words. And obviously he didn't want to share his personal mess with Jeff. Although maybe he should?

"I'm sorry if I caused you any grief. Forget about Mandy, okay? We need to meet. Talk to Jessica and schedule a lunch, okay? I'll put her on."

"Later, Jeff, I'm waiting at passport control and I'm dead tired. I'll call her."

"Fine."

"Wait, did Max know? He didn't know anything when I left, I'm sure of that."

"He didn't know."

"You can't force Max to work for the Italian."

"Of course not. Look, no official announcement has been made yet. The leak probably came from their side, I don't know why, but it's not a deal breaker. Obviously the Italian will have to talk to you and Max about your terms, so you're not actually in a bad position. Excuse me, I have another call waiting."

"Wait, wait, can you explain to me what happened two days ago, we were supposed to meet at the..." Eyal suddenly remembered the meeting that never took place at the Dan Accadia Hotel, but Jeff had already hung up. Well, what did it matter, his life was falling to pieces right in front of him, Jeff bailing from their meeting wasn't important now. In both conversations, with Jeff and with Mandy, he had a dazed feeling. Not only because he was so tired, but because those weren't actually important conversations, they had nothing to do with his real problems, but for some reason part of his brain still bothered to pretend that they were talking about the most important things in the world.

Eyal stood in the long line, surrounded by weary faces. His phone rang, a blocked number. Who could it be now? Maybe it was Jessica, wanting to schedule the lunch with Jeff.

"Hello?"

"Am I speaking with Eyal Shiloh?"

"Yes, who is this?"

"This is Superintended Andrey Friedman from the Tel Aviv central police unit. We need to talk."

"Can it wait till tomorrow? I'm simply exhausted. Spent."

"Okay, I'd like you to come over tomorrow at nine a.m."

"Sure."

Lovely. Maria's death would undoubtedly be the topic of conversation. At least this solved his dilemma about whether to go to the police. First thing when he got home was to see what they had written about it in the papers and on the internet. And he had to come clean to Galit. But he was just so worn-out that he wanted at least a few hours of sleep before the horrible confrontation that might end his life as he knew it. Which, who was he kidding, was already over.

The first thing Galit said to him after he kissed her and the kids and they managed to send the excited children to watch TV, was: "You look exhausted, it didn't go well? You look really awful, Eyal, there's no nice way of saying it."

"It was… it was…"

"It was what?"

"I'll tell you. You won't like this story. Just give me a few minutes to have coffee and take a shower."

"Sure, Gin, go take a shower, and don't worry, even if you screwed it up and no one will ever want to hire you again, I'll always love you."

Eyal knew that this declaration of loyalty warranted a small 'thank you,' maybe a kiss. But he also knew that in a few minutes Galit was going to want to skin him alive, and he was too tired to pretend. He went straight to the computer and started going through all the news sites to find out more about Maria's murder. There was a photo of Maria, so he could no longer doubt what Shimon had told him. They also mentioned her occupation, which pained Eyal. While there was no denying the truth, he never thought of Maria as a prostitute. At the end of the day, Shimon was right. Eyal was much more of a lover to Maria than Shimon ever was, even if only for a few brief hours. And then Eyal came across a detail that left him dumbstruck. Maria was murdered in the Dan Accadia Hotel in Herzliya. The same day he was there. Could it have been a coincidence? Impossible. Someone was trying to frame him. And that someone must be the charming Mister Shimon Dahan. Eyal looked for a mention of the approximate time of death, and found none. It was very likely that while Eyal was sitting at the pool, waiting for Jeff, Maria was murdered. No wonder he couldn't get anything out of Jeff about their meeting. Jeff didn't know what he was talking about. Maybe there had been some miscommunication, or he was too busy and didn't hear what Eyal had said. Eyal took his cellphone out and tried to reach Jeff. The line was busy, so Eyal left him a message. Suddenly he remembered that Shimon had said Maria might have been murdered while Eyal was on the plane to Italy. Shimon was in fact telling him that he could potentially provide him with an alibi. But Eyal was convinced beyond a doubt that Maria was murdered while he was at the hotel, and that Shimon was trying to frame him. He had to tell that to the cop tomorrow. Maybe they could track the location of the phone call from the woman who had imitated Jessica's voice and summoned him to the meeting at the hotel. There was no other explanation. But wait. Maybe the police didn't even know he was at the hotel? Why tell them? But it was obvious they'd find out at some point, and maybe it was better if he was the one who told them. Eyal heard Galit's footsteps and closed the computer, turning around in a panic. But why? He was going to have to tell her everything in a moment anyway. But he was too tired. He lay down on the bed. Maybe he wouldn't tell her the entire story? He wasn't sure if he should tell her about the kid. Was it really possible that he had a kid from Maria? Eyal had some time to think about it on the plane. Flights are a wonderful opportunity for serious contemplation. You're stuck on the plane for hours and can't do anything, even if your problems are especially pressing. All you can do is think. The entire theory about him being the father was based on Maria lying to him about the exercises to release her stomach muscles. Shimon's conclusion impressed Eyal with its sound logic. But he had nothing more than Shimon's word. Eyal didn't analyze the conversation on Fugu's technology himself, and Shimon might be making the whole thing up. Maybe Maria didn't lie to him. Maybe she was just lying on her back with her legs up because she really did have a cramp. But he saw the kid. He looked just like him. He couldn't deny it. And the kid cried his eyes out when Eyal left the game room in Shimon's mansion to go back to the hotel. Was he his son? Could he let Shimon raise his son? He wasn't just some eccentric man, Eyal was pretty sure he was a murderer who was trying to frame him. What kind of man would he turn his son into? And if Eyal raised the kid, would Galit agree to raise a child whose mother was a prostitute? Eyal felt that his mind was dangerously close to bursting. He had to calm down. Maybe it was best not to tell Galit about the kid for the time being. Not to overburden her. Even without knowing about the kid, she'd probably throw him out of the house after hearing about Maria. He might even have to spend that very night at a hotel. And with that thought, Eyal closed his eyes and finally fell asleep.

"Gin, baby, are you getting up? You have to get the kids to kindergarten, go to work... Time to land, you're not on the plane anymore." Galit kissed him and Eyal resisted the urge to hug her. He just felt that it wasn't right, why hug now? For every display of affection he would probably have to pay later. In some strange way he already missed the intimacy that supposedly still existed between them, but only as long as she was kept in the dark. Maybe he should have told her yesterday? But he had fallen asleep so fast. Galit took off his clothes and covered him with the blanket. When could he expect to be the object of her maternal instincts again? Maybe in the next lifetime. He'll go to work later. First he'll take the kids to kindergarten, return home, and tell Galit. And then she'll kick him out of the house straight to the police station, to superintendent what's-his-name. Andrey something. Great. He's going to have a great day. He had to do it now, the sooner the better. When Eyal dropped the kids off, he felt a certain foreboding. But at least he could still see the irony in his chronic melancholy. An idiot who always feels sorry for himself. Only now he knew he had some good reasons to feel the looming sense of tragedy. He kept imagining telling Galit the truth. He kept playing the scene over and over in his head. It always ended horribly. No matter how hard he tried, he couldn't imagine Galit reacting calmly. She'd kill him. Galit, there's something I have to tell you. Was that a reasonable opening? And what if he just dumped the truth on her straight away, unqualified? Galit, I cheated on you three years ago. Only once. It was nothing, completely meaningless. Yes, of course, my husband, you know I love you, just forget about it, why even bother telling me? As if. She would murder him. And maybe: Galit, I have something difficult to tell you, something awful— I burned the waffle! Ha ha! Eyal knew it didn't even matter. Even if he toiled forty days and forty nights he'd never find a version that would soften her response. He just had to do it and get it over with. Eyal never feared anything as much as he feared that moment, the moment after his first sentence, the moment when Galit would realize what he was saying to her. He parked the car. Entered the building. Waited for the elevator. Like a man on death row. But he wasn't a man on death row, was he? Or maybe he was. It wasn't just Galit, her response, and the future of their marriage. Even if he somehow managed to convince her not to tear their family apart over this betrayal, he still had Shimon the billionaire mur-derer to deal with. And the police. A real shit storm. The elevator door opened on their floor. When he entered the apartment, Galit was in the bathroom. Another minute to stretch the illusion of normalcy. He could make use of the time to drink a very quick cup of coffee. Or write a very short poem about the destruction of his life. Betty Botter bought a bit of butter. Eyal porked a porky prostitute. But Maria was far from porky.

Maybe—Eyal boned a banging babe? It was amazing—his and his wife's worlds were now so far apart. She was still living her normal married life, with normal people's problems. No. Choice. He'd soon have to burst her bubble. Upgrade her negativity, like some demented reserve soldier once said to him.

"So, my beloved husband, what did you want to talk to me about? You think you're going to get fired? Don't worry, we'll make do, and I'll love you even if it turns out you're not such a big catch after all," Galit said and smiled. The temptation to tell her she was right, that's what this was about, was enormous. To delay the real confrontation for a few more days. Maybe by then things would somehow work out by themselves?

"Eyal? I have to get going soon, so if it's not a good time for you we can talk this afternoon, or later tonight, if you want."

"No, take a seat and listen to me. This isn't great news, to say the least…"

"Huh? Why don't you just come out with it already, you're starting to worry me, what's going on? Did the shareholders decide to sue you personally?"

"A little over three years ago, I… I cheated on you. Only once. One night, three years ago."

Galit didn't say anything. She looked at Eyal with an expression he tried to decipher. It seemed as though she was in utter shock, completely dumbstruck. A few seconds later, she was on the floor. Eyal didn't understand how that had happened. She somehow fell. He drew near her and wanted to help her up.

"Don't touch me."

"Galit?"

"This wasn't supposed to happen to me! With you, this wasn't supposed to happen to me. I'm so stupid!" she said, and started to cry.

"Galit, I'm sorry."

"I want you out of here."

"I need to talk to you about…"

"Eyal, get the fuck out of here!" she said. She grabbed his briefcase, which was lying next to her on the floor, and hurled it at him. Eyal manage to duck in time.

"Galit, the kids are crying, I think you're overreacting a bit."

Eyal fled the room and went to check on his kids.

"Daniel? Meital?" Eyal looked at their empty room in a panic, and it took him a moment to remember that he had already dropped them off at kindergarten. Moron. Then what was that shout he heard? Maybe Rivka's kid from upstairs. He heard a knock on the door. Eyal wasn't in the mood for other people right now, but after a moment, the knocks grew louder, and he went to the door.

"Galit? Is everything alright?" He heard the neighbor from the other side of the door.

"Rivka. Everything's fine, don't worry, there's no problem," Eyal said with a trembling voice.

"Are you sure? I heard a lot of noise."

"I dropped something and Galit yelled at me, but no one died."

"Well, if you need anything, I'm right upstairs, okay?"

"Yes, thank you."

Obviously everything wasn't fine, but he had to calm the neighbor down. How powerful was that human instinct. Even if the house was on fire, the most important thing was that no one sees. Eyal went into their bedroom and sat on the bed. He had to get going, meet mister superintendent guy. His head was pounding. He knew that he was experiencing the most difficult time of his entire life, and that he had to stay strong. He was used to being strong with Galit, or maybe, in fact, he was just used to having her be strong for him. He was drained. He wanted to bury himself under the blanket and not see anyone. Too bad it wasn't an option.

Eyal heard footsteps, but he was too exhausted to pay any attention to them. The door opened.

"I thought I told you to get the hell out of here."

"Galit, it was just…"

A hard blow landed on his face. Eyal was a strong man, much stronger than Galit, but she had punched him in the nose and he felt the blood starting to pour onto the sheet. He held his nose with both hands and tried to stop the bleeding. After a moment, he heard Galit's voice.

"Here. Take this." She handed him a piece of cloth with ice cubes inside it. He pressed it against his nose, and felt her wiping his face. After the blood stopped gushing, he looked around him. The bed looked as though someone had slaughtered a cat on it.

"Okay, now that you showed me who wears the pants in this house, can we talk for a moment? I know you don't really want to listen to me right now, but there's something I have to tell you." Eyal knew that the punch he just got would at least enable Galit to conduct a conversation from a slightly better position. And it also got her out of the catatonic state she was in. A stronger punch could have sent him straight to the emergency room. Which annoyed him. He was much stronger than her, he could send her to the hospital, or somewhere much worse, with no problem. But if the tables were turned, and she had been the one who cheated, and he had reacted the way she had, he would have become a social pariah, if not a prisoner for a few years, so why was she allowed? There was no doubt, Galit's punch would become a legendary story of heroism among her and her friends.

"Eyal, I don't want to hear you right now, I want you out. I'm going to work, and I don't want to see you here when I'm back."

"Okay." Short and to the point.

Eyal remained alone on their marital bed. Or maybe it wasn't their marital bed anymore. He couldn't tell. He heard Galit gathering her things, and recalled the conversation they had when Eyal proposed to her. They were lying naked in bed in a small B&B in the Galilee. It was about two o'clock in the morning. Eyal had kept putting it off because he was nervous and scared, but finally he turned around, took the ring from the night stand and popped the question.

"Did you just pull that out of your ass?" she asked about the ring, and they both burst into laughter. Galit quickly apologized, because it really was the least romantic reaction to a marriage proposal in human history. But then she kissed him, held his hand and said: "I do want to marry you, very much. But there's an issue I have to raise first." She raised her finger like a student in class.

"Yes, I'm listening," Eyal said, and his heart was racing because he was no longer sure she was going to say yes.

"Every day I look at you, and I'm more and more impressed with how gorgeous you are. And you've never been with any other woman but me. Well, never slept with anyone else."

"I love you, I don't want anyone else." It was true. Eyal was crazy about her. It wasn't that he was oblivious to the fact that there were other beautiful women out there, but they didn't interest him anymore.

"And I'm flattered that you love me so much. What bothers me is that a few more years down the line, after you cool off from the achievement of scoring a goddess like me..."

"You really are a goddess," he interrupted her.

"Yes, Gin. So what scares me is that in five or ten years, suddenly you'll wake up and remember what a big fuckfest you missed out on, and you might feel the need to get some action on the side. I know it's a horrible thing to say now, but I'm being honest with you about what scares me."

"I won't want to get anything on the side."

"Let me tell you a little about Eric Roseman. I dated him for about a year, two years ago. We broke up a year before I met you, and he really hurt me. Eric was also a stud."

"Yes, I remember you dated Eric the stud."

"I didn't tell you everything. Anyway, he really was a stud, but not as handsome as you, and not as kind. He had a scar on his stomach, and he told me that he got it in some mission during his service. He was in an elite combat unit, like you, so I believed him. Until one of his friends laughed and said that it was the unit's janitor who stabbed him. And then I demanded to know the truth, and he told me his life story. From the age of fifteen to twenty, which was about two years before I met him, he had sex with about five hundred women. When he was fifteen he discovered he was a real stud and became addicted to sex, mostly with his friends' girlfriends, or the wives of his dad's friends and neighbors, or god knows. In the army, he had a friend he used to have these competitions with, who could score with more girls when they were on leave. They didn't have a lot of leaves, so they had to act fast, like in the unit, he said, try to do fuck at least two a night. Eric could walk into a bar and leave with a sure thing, almost always, which you could have done as well if you had tried, and it's pretty rare, I'll tell you that, these urban legends about how any guy in Tel Aviv can walk into a bar and leave with a girl have nothing to do with reality. Most of them walk in alone, and walk out with their dick in their hand."

"I'll remember that, it's a good line."

"I deserve the Bialik poetry award, don't you think? Anyway, he told me that his record was seven girls on a single Saturday. Seven! Good thing he didn't get many leaves, or he would have probably been counting into the thousands by then. And you have to understand, it's not that I thought he was a virgin when I met him, not at all. You'll forgive me, I hope..." She kissed him and continued. "But the mass of information caught me by surprise, as well as his special hobby of doing it with women who weren't single. And then one day, Musa, the subordinate janitor, brought his girl-friend to the base on Saturday, and I guess Eric thought she was too pretty to be a janitor's girlfriend. And Musa the janitor loved his girlfriend very much and was planning on marrying her. Eric told me a lot about him, because he became a central, even transformative figure in his life. Musa, for instance, loved the Scorpions, and was convinced that the song 'Still Loving You' was written especially for him. Everyone in the unit liked him. He was the kind of guy who always helped everyone. And obviously, dear Eric had to go and seduce Musa's girlfriend, and do it where everyone could hear. So the next day, after Musa's girlfriend returned home, Musa confronted Eric, screamed at him, and then just pulled out a knife. He tried to kill him, but it didn't go so well. He only gave him an ugly scar across the stomach, none of his internal organs were hurt. And then, as Eric described it, he had an awakening. Before that he was living in moral limbo, but afterward, he started thinking about what he was doing, about the implications his actions had on other people. He stopped chasing immediate gratification like a madman. For a few months after the incident, he didn't sleep with anyone, which for him was probably like a regular person going without water for two weeks. His friend, the one he used to have screwing competitions with, was really bummed out about it, and started giving him names of girls who were actually begging for dear Eric to nail them, and Eric told him that he was on a diet. And his friend said, even on a diet you have to eat. So Eric told him that he was fasting. He was very impressed with his witticisms during that important period, and of course, decided that he had to find the love of his life, and put that terrible time behind him. It doesn't matter, Gin, I won't keep you waiting, I'm going to marry you. The point is, that however amazing it sounds…"

Eyal felt his breath finally settling, and the choking feeling starting to slowly fade.

"A bona fide stud with a trauma that prevents him from screwing around behind his girlfriend's back… Sounds like a real bargain!"

"Funny, but after he told me all that I started noticing how he flirted with every pretty girl he saw, and how the instinct was still there, driving him crazy. And one night we were at a party, and so was that friend of his from the fucking competitions. They had broken off their relationship for about a year and then renewed it. I went to get a drink, and suddenly I saw him with his hand actually grabbing some girl's ass. And I screamed at him. Which was horrible, because I hate those kinds of scenes, but sometimes there's no choice. And he told me, You want me to live like some monk? And I just went ballistic. I yelled, What monk are you talking about, you have me! And his friend was standing there, laughing. I left the party outraged, and he ran after me, I could hear him yelling behind me that he was sorry, begging. He probably realized what he had said, because afterward there were endless phone calls and pleas for us to get back together. Because without me, he couldn't pretend he was a new person anymore. And even though I'm not sure whether he cheated on me or not, and you probably think I'm naïve just for entertaining the possibility that he didn't…"

"You remember the words of the Kurdish poet Azar Kamal el Erect?"

"Hmm… I forget."

"He said—your innocence has captivated my heart, young girl, as have your pink nipples."

"Is that from the Kurdish classics?"

"It's from a collection of toilet bowl poetry."

"You moron. Never mind, like I said, he might have cheated on me, I don't know, but even if he didn't screw anyone else when we were a couple, I knew beyond a doubt that if I built a future with that man, one day I'd wake up and find myself in a sea of shit. And I decided to leave before it was too late."

"So you're scared that one day I'll feel the need to fuck the five hundred women I didn't fuck when I was sixteen?"

"Yes. I told you. I love you and I'm going to marry you, but I have to warn you, you can't cheat on me. Ever. I don't care what you missed out on as a kid, or how much that girl, whatever her name was, screwed up your life. If you cheat on me, I'll cut your balls off."

"Ouch!"

"Exactly!"

And now Eyal was sitting alone on the bed, balls still attached, but he wanted so badly to go back in time to that moment when everything was so good, to go back to that intimacy and comfortable, silly banter. Or maybe go back to that stupid night with Maria and make a different decision. And he asked himself whether there was a chance that a woman like Galit would decide to forgive him for the most unforgivable thing.

CHAPTER 11

Before Eyal entered Superintendent Andrey Friedman's office he made another attempt to reach Max, but he didn't pick up. It was strange that Max hadn't called him. Was it possible that like Mandy, Max also suspected Eyal of some conspiracy? The idea of sharing with Max the whole story about Maria made Eyal's stomach twist, but he knew that Max was about to start negotiating his terms with Shimon, and he had to warn him. He had to let him know who he was dealing with. And who knew, Max might even have some good advice, not only about how to handle Shimon, but also about his predicament with Galit. Eyal always appreciated Max's opinion. Yes, he and Max should sit down over a glass of whisky and talk. But now he was about to talk to the police, and Eyal wasn't sure how that meeting would end. They might even send him straight to lock-up from here. Eyal knew he should at least try telling the truth to the cops, strange as the truth may be. His thoughts were all over the place, a complete mess, and if he lied, they would pick up on it in seconds.

With a heavy heart, Eyal walked into Superintendent Andrey Friedman's room. It was a rather ugly office; a peeling Formica desk, a scratched plastic computer screen that looked as if some cat had pummeled it. Superintendent Friedman appeared tough, but there was also something reassuring about his kind eyes, like the good hero of a western. Who knew, maybe after a few minutes with him, Eyal wouldn't think he was so nice anymore.

"Do you know why I wanted to talk to you?" He had a very slight Russian accent, but one that was still unmistakable. He had probably immigrated as a young boy like Max, Eyal thought.

"Maria's murder, obviously."

"Good, maybe this will be quick, no bullshit. What was your relationship with her?"

That question, predictable as it might be, sent Eyal back three years, to the one stupid decision that had brought him here.

"Eyal?"

"Sorry, what?"

"What was the nature of your relationship with Maria Dubcek?"

"Yes, sorry... Dubcek, you say? Maria was an escort girl. I met with her only once, a little over three years ago. Three and a half years, to be precise. We had one rather wild night together, and that was it."

"Your wife probably won't be happy to hear that."

"Oh, she's not happy, you could say that again. I told her this morning, and I got kicked out."

"Your wife's leaving you?"

"Sure looks like it." Eyal was hoping that wouldn't be the case, but he knew that hope didn't have much to do with reality.

"I'm sorry to hear, really. Good luck with that."

Andrey took notes with a simple pen on a yellow legal pad. Eyal tried to make out what he was writing.

"It's Cyrillic letters. You don't know Russian, do you?"

"No, no. Sorry."

"Let's continue. Tell me more about that wild night."

"We just hit it off from the very first second. Really good chemistry. Maria told me that night her entire life story, more or less. She was married to a rich Italian businessman, as you probably know..."

Andrey wrote something down again, and Eyal was almost convinced that he had managed to surprise him.

"You didn't know, did you? She's not registered as married?"

"Not in Israel anyway. It shouldn't be difficult to find out. If the Israeli wife of a major businessman from Italy was murdered, it's pretty surprising I don't know about it yet, don't you think? What's this businessman's name?"

"His name is Simone Donadoni. But he's actually a former Israeli, and his name used to be Shimon Dahan. He explicitly told me that he was hiding his Israeli identity from the world."

"And he told only you."

"He told me that it was important to him to talk to me in our native tongue. Hebrew."

Eyal listened to himself, and realized he had a problem.

"Listen, I know this doesn't sound too credible, but I know he's Israeli because the entire conversation took place in Hebrew, and he had a completely Israeli accent. He told me about his military service. Eyal told Andrey the story in a nutshell.

"That's very interesting."

Andrey made a brief phone call, spoke to someone in Russian, and returned to Eyal.

"Yes, let's continue. What kind of businessman marries a prostitute? Unless she's here and he's there and he doesn't know anything. But maybe you can enlighten me, since, as you said, she told you her entire life story."

"He knew everything. They had an arrangement. He would let her continue working, as long as she didn't have real affairs. Only clients."

"And this is a big businessman?"

"Very. He's about to buy the company where I work, for fifteen million dollars."

"Wait, so you knew his wife as a prostitute, or as the wife of your future boss?"

"Listen, this is turning into a giant mess. Can you let me talk a few moments without interrupting me?"

"Okay, Eyal. Shoot!"

"A little over three years ago, I made the very stupid decision to cheat on my wife. I don't know why, I just had that need. I hadn't done it before that and I haven't done it since."

"Okay."

"I called an escort agency for girls who cost ten thousand shekels a night."

"So you were realizing some kind of fantasy."

"You could say that. It was in a hotel in Haifa. We clicked like you wouldn't believe. She wouldn't even take my money. She showed me her ID and let me know her real name. She told me her strange story, including the part about the Italian husband who was totally nuts about her. She wouldn't stop working because she didn't want to be dependent on him. So they made that arrangement I told you about."

"Okay. It's a pretty crazy story, no doubt. Continue."

"Turns out he recorded audio tapes of all her sessions with clients. He told me that himself, and he even played me part of the recording of my session with Maria."

"He used to listen to tapes of his wife fucking her clients? That is an interesting story indeed, it was worth calling you over, Mister Shiloh."

"Anyway, he heard the tape of my session with Maria and went ballistic, because she was into me and told me a lot of intimate things about him. And then he decided to get back at me."

"By taking over the company you work for?"

"Also. But mostly, by killing his wife and trying to frame me."

"So now you'll have to explain to me how he's trying to frame you, because so far, from your very interesting story, there's no framing attempt. And obviously, you haven't explained to me his motive for killing her."

"Because she slept with me."

"But that was three years ago. Why now?"

"I don't know, maybe it took him some time to find me, and to orchestrate the entire set up. But it does sound a little problematic, I know."

"There are a lot of problems in this story. You don't have a shred of evidence that he was the one who actually murdered her, none. But let's put that aside for a moment, and get back to the question of how he's trying to frame you."

Eyal had already decided he couldn't lie. But once again, he hesitated. If he told him that he was at the Dan Accadia Hotel on the day of the murder, wouldn't he be burying himself? The problem was that the fake invitation from Jeff to meet at the hotel was the only evidence he had that Shimon was indeed trying to set him up. And of course, Eyal had no proof that a woman who sounded just like Jeff's secretary, Jessica, had called him. It seemed like Shimon's attempt to frame him was working great so far.

"Let me help you. It seems as though you were trying to tell the truth so far, as deranged as it sounds, so how about you continue?"

"Okay. The day I flew to Italy to meet Shimon, or Simone, our investor-murderer, I got a fake invitation from the secretary of our biggest investor, Jeff, to meet him at the Dan Accadia Hotel in Herzliya. I went to the hotel, and obviously Jeff never showed up, because he never actually invited me to the meeting."

"You were at the hotel on the day of the murder?" Andrey stared at him with astonishment.

"Unfortunately."

"Okay, this is very interesting information. Tell me, why do you think he went to all that trouble? Wouldn't it have been easier to just kill you? After all, you say he killed Maria. It would have been a lot simpler to take you out as well, don't you think?"

"Well, that's a good question. I thought about it. There's a pretty disgusting Holocaust joke that may explain it."

"Shoot."

"Why did Hitler commit suicide after murdering all the Jews?"

"Hitler didn't murder all the Jews, I think both of us are pretty good proof of that, no?"

"Come on, it doesn't matter, it's just a stupid joke."

"He got the gas bill."

"No, that's from a different joke."

"Okay, then why did Hitler commit suicide after murdering all the Jews?"

"Because he had no reason to live."

"Funny. So you're saying his hatred toward you is all he has left?"

"His obsession, in any event. Probably hatred as well. He killed his wife, I guess I'm all he had left of her."

"Okay, interesting. I want to show you a few photos, tell me if they mean anything to you."

Andrey handed Eyal a stack of photos of him, with photos of the kid attached to each one. Eyal looked at the photos with awe. He had seen some of the photos already, they were the ones he got in the airport. But this was the first time he saw the photos of Dino, the kid. The kid's resemblance to him in these photos was so obvious it was scary. Could he actually be the father after all?

"Yes, we're now at the part of the story I haven't told you yet," Eyal finally said.

"You're welcome to continue."

Eyal told him about the meeting with Shimon and the boy, and about the envelope with the photographs he received at the airport, with half of the photos identical to the stack now if front of him.

"Eyal, I have to tell you that every word of yours just blows my mind. So you're thinking about taking a DNA test?"

"I don't know. I suspect that this story with the kid is just another part of Shimon's attempt to frame me. It would be my motive, right? I'm married, she demanded I be a father to her kid and if I refused she'd talk to my wife, so I murdered her," Eyal said, and he could feel the knot in his stomach tighten as he said it. He felt as though he was betraying his son, despite his suspicion that he wasn't his son at all. But the brief meeting with him kept coming back to him in flashbacks.

"By the way, these photos rather support my claim that he's obsessed with me, don't you think? The man had me stalked for three years, he's been obsessed with me for quite a while."

"Maybe, but only if I agree with you that it's Simone Donadoni who's responsible for these photos and that he's even involved in all this, so it's not really evidence in your favor. Let's continue. I understand that in your company he's only known as Simone Donadoni, not as Shimon."

"Correct."

"Another thing. Do you remember the name of the escort agency?"

"It was a website called Filthy Rich. I spoke to a girl there, some secretary, and there was a pretty big guy who came to meet me at the hotel and vet me. But they shut down the website and there's no way of finding it, I checked."

"Okay, is there any chance you'd recognize the man who came to vet you?"

"Maybe if you show me photos."

"Yes, first we have to gather the relevant photos. I'll call you in."

"Okay, but know that I'm not so sure I'll be able to recognize him, a guy I met for five minutes more than three years ago."

"Okay. Look, Eyal, I'm not detaining you yet, but don't make me regret that decision. I want your passport. If you don't have it here with you, bring it in later. Under no circumstances are you to leave the country. Not even for a DNA test or anything else this Shimon tells you to do there. That's it, you can go for now."

"Okay, thanks. Here's the passport. I don't usually carry it with me, but it's still in my bag from my trip to Italy."

Eyal was fairly certain that Superintendent Friedman couldn't instruct him to remain in the country without a court order, but on the other hand, he could also arrest him right there and then, so Eyal didn't argue.

Andrey's phone rang and he took the call. He spoke Russian again, and then said to Eyal: "Interesting news. We managed to contact Mister Donadoni. He denies having anything to do with Israel apart from several business relationships. He says he's never been married. He also claims he has no kids."

"Really? Okay, I guess that means I don't have to take a DNA test. Amazing, he tried so hard to convince me that I was the father of his kid, and now he actually denies even having a kid, or having anything to do with the woman he claimed was the mother."

This obviously discredited Eyal's claims. His entire argument was based on Shimon's connection to Maria and his resentment toward Eyal.

"Okay, Eyal, go before I regret it."

"Yes, thank you."

As he left, a cop walked passed him and entered Superintendent Friedman's office. He was short and sturdy. He glared at Eyal, and Eyal felt as though he might jump on him and arrest him. He reminded Eyal of one his friends from the unit, one of those characters you want to have by your side, but if they turn against you, you start noticing they suffer from a complete inability to accept a different viewpoint.

Izzy, Andrey's deputy, walked into the room with an irritated expression, and Andrey told him about his meeting with Eyal.

"Are you sure about what you're doing, Andrey? You know I respect your instincts, but this time you're really walking the line. The guy has a motive, he admitted to having a romantic relationship with the victim, and according to his own admission, he was at the hotel at the time of the murder…"

"We still don't know if it really was the time of murder, we have to look into it, but you're right, he's in a pretty problematic position."

"Then why aren't you arresting him? Don't you think this story you just told me is the craziest thing we've both heard since we joined the force?"

Izzy couldn't stand still. He kept moving in front of Andrey, and at a certain point he jumped on the table and stood in front of him like a parakeet squatting with his legs on the edge of the table.

"Because I have a strange feeling about this case. Like I told you, the way we got to Mister Shiloh was too neat, too organized. Come on, take out the chess set and we'll play a round."

It was Andrey's regular joke. Izzy always carried a fancy, small set in his briefcase, but it was a backgammon set, not chess.

"The day you admit that it's backgammon will probably be the day you finally beat me, Andrey."

Izzy jumped off the table and took the set out of his briefcase. He patted it fondly. A good game of backgammon was one of the only things that made him sit still.

"It's pretty but it's a shame about the elephant they had to kill to carve it." Their backgammon conversations pretty much followed the same routine by now.

"If I could have saved the elephant, I'd be happy to throw the set away, but the elephant's already dead, Andrey."

"The elephant's dead, that's true."

Izzy set up the checkers. The game was also played as if according to a preexisting script. Andrey built towers. Izzy spread out the pawns, which Andrey gobbled up. It usually ended with Izzy winning with a gammon.

"You know what I think, Andrey? In life, the two of us are exactly the opposite of how we are in backgammon. In backgammon I've already given up on explaining to you that you have to take chances to win. I've already accepted you have some hang up in that area. But in life it's the exact opposite. I would have already thrown that high-tech guy in lock-up long ago. You're playing with fire here, Andrey, doesn't it make your stomach turn? Letting a guy with that much evidence against him walk?"

"You have a point. But it's not just that I don't like the evidence in this case. It's also… I have the feeling that something about the interaction between the characters in this case has to continue if we want to solve it. I don't know if I'm explaining myself well. I think that if we put him in lock-up, we'll be missing something critical here."

"A kind of 'let the young men now arise and play before us' type of thing?"

"Not crazy about the biblical phrasing, but yes, if you insist. Let the young men play before us."

"There, another gammon. Say, you want to play for money, Andrey?"

"Not at all. Tell me something, what about Maria's car? We haven't found it yet, right?"

"No, not yet. According to the cellphone company, her phone was last used in Herzliya, they couldn't get a more specific location. She probably took it with her to the hotel. But we didn't find it in the room. It might be in the car. Or maybe the murderer took it."

"You're probably right. We have to try to locate the escort agency. Two of their employees were murdered. According to Mister Shiloh, the agency's website disappeared off the face of the earth, and the girls' computers were taken, so I'm not sure how we're going to do it."

"We'll find a way. And you should know that I'm not buying this whole 'let the young men play before us' baloney, you're just a softy, Andrey."

"I just know what a disaster it is to arrest a decent man and place him in custody together with criminals. So if I'm right about him, I would like to avoid that scenario. But it's not only that. I really do believe that it's important for Eyal to roam the world freely and solve this case for us."

"I really hope you're not full of bullshit, Andrey, I do love working with you."

"Oh, yes, and another thing. We now know she had no kids in Israel, there's no documentation. But there's one thing that Eyal Shiloh said that rang true. He claimed that Maria had a husband in Italy—Simone Donadoni. She certainly had a lot of Italian stamps in her passport. We have to check if she had a kid in Italy, and if she did, then we have to find out who's the father."

"Sure, Andrey."

Andrey's phone rang again.

"Yes? Huh, really? Okay, good to know. Thank you."

"What is it?"

"There's a positive ID on the body, fingerprints and all."

"No shit, nice. Then everything's good."

"Always so sensitive, Izzy. I'm sure the girl whose body parts it just took more than two hours for the pathology guys to attach will be happy to hear that everything's good."

"Yes, I'm sure she'll be happy," Izzy said and smiled.

"And that's another thing that bothers me about this case. Why did they beat the shit out of her like that? Did it ever cross your mind that we now have no way of telling if she'd ever been pregnant? If she was more or less in one piece, it would have been easy to find out. But now we can't know, and for now there's no kid, which is pretty weird, isn't it? If someone's really trying to frame him, it makes perfect sense."

"Maybe. You said we might find the kid in Italy."

"It's a possibility. We have to look into it."

CHAPTER 12

Eyal once again tried to reach Max, but he still wasn't answering. He left Max a message, got into his car, and suddenly realized he wasn't sure where to go. Like a lost kid. He couldn't go home. Did 'home' still exist? He had never felt so abandoned and detached in his life. His instinct was to call Galit and consult with her. An option that no longer existed. But he had to talk to her, to let her know what they were facing, even if not together. There was no point going to Fugu, either. What would he do there? He had to find a hotel. Nothing too big, to minimize the chance of meeting acquaintances. There were a few nice, small hotels near the beach, on HaYarkon Street, maybe he'd try one of those.

After Eyal checked into one of the small, inconspicuous hotels on HaYarkon Street, he found out that apart from having a bed and a pillow to lay his head on, his situation hadn't improved much. He still didn't know what to do with himself. There were too many problems. He really wanted to solve the problems with Galit, but what chance did he have? She wanted to kill him. He had to call her and tell her the lovely tale of how Shimon Dahan had wriggled his way into their lives. It was an especially scary call to make. Truly terrifying. Later. He needed to give her more time to recover. Maybe he should wait a few more days with that phone call. But Eyal knew he couldn't wait that long, it had to be today. But later today. And what was he going to do about Shimon? And it wouldn't be long before he'd be arrested for Maria's murder. Too many problems. He was exhausted. Overwhelmed. Luckily he has a wife who's a therapist to provide the relevant terminology. Or rather, had a wife. But what do you do when you're overwhelmed? Call a psychologist. Ha ha. Eyal curled up in bed and fell asleep. He woke up two hours later with a headache. He got up, washed his face, took a shower and sat down on the bed. He looked at his watch. One thirty in the afternoon. He had to do something. It all led back to Shimon, right? Shimon had caused this colossal mess. Shimon murdered Maria. Shimon was trying to frame him. Shimon set him up. He had to attack the problem from that angle. But how? Reading about the murder on the internet proved useless. What did he need in order to prove to the world that Shimon was trying to screw him over? Suddenly it hit him, no one knew there was a Shimon. No one knew he was Israeli. So how does he find Shimon's connection to Israel? If he managed to peel off some of the mystery that engulfed that fat fuck, maybe it would make his life a bit easier. But how? What had Shimon told him about his life in Israel? Nothing. Wrong! There was the story about his military service. Eyal suddenly felt a surge of energy. First he had to write down every detail he could remember from the story Shimon had told him, before those details became one big mess in his head. Eyal took a little notepad from next to the TV and the pen that was attached to it, and started writing feverishly. There was a soldier, right? Yes, the one at range practice, who shot without prior training, and then committed suicide in the army slammer. And that was why Shimon Dahan, aka Simone Donadoni, was removed from his commanding position. What was that soldier's name? It was crucial! Eyal started to panic because he simply couldn't remember. It was on the tip of his tongue. But what was it? And then it flashed before him, Shimi. Of course. And his last name? Ben David! And all that went down in 1976. Eyal remembered that Shimon mentioned that unlike today, in 1976 they didn't really investigate those things. And what else did he say about Ben David? That he had killed himself because he was a sensitive guy! Yes, the hope of the family, the shining star, a gifted violinist, an honors student, but not the kind of soldier who should ever have been recruited to Golani. Suddenly he remembered every detail; the father who died from cancer, the mother who was torn to piece by her son's death, no surprise there, she cried to Shimon and gave him a hard time, and probably a heap of guilt.

And a sister who looked up to him. So he now had a name and a year, and he could go to some newspaper archive and search for stories about Shimi Ben David from 1976. After Eyal finished writing down everything he could remember about the story, he went down to the hotel business center. He preferred not to use his own computer. He searched Shimi Ben David and Shimon Dahan, and found nothing. He also tried archives on the internet and on news sites, as well as word combinations he thought might be relevant, but came up empty handed. There were only a few hits for Simone Donadoni, all relating to business. It was interesting that there were many references to Fondo Lombardia but with no mention of Shimon. A discreet man, to say the least. Maybe he should search the Italian press archives? But he was running out of patience, mostly because he had no idea how to go about it.

He wanted to call Galit, his number one consultant. But was that even an option? Would she be willing to talk to him? But he had to talk to her. He had to make her listen. She needed to hear the story about Shimon.

Eyal dialed the number, and she answered in such a cold tone that he nearly didn't recognize her voice.

"Galit, I have to tell you something. Something important. I know you want to kill me right now, but you have to listen, there's something dangerous here that can hurt all of us."

"Eyal, I really don't have the energy. Do you know how much you let me down? I just don't want to listen to you. Who was it? Your hot finance woman?"

"No, not at all."

"Not at all? Do you think there's an answer I'd prefer?"

"Probably not. It was an escort girl."

"A prostitute?"

"Yes."

"Why?"

"I don't know, I felt I had to sleep with another woman for just once. I... I hope you at least believe me that there hasn't been a day that's gone by that I haven't regretted it."

"Would you like to explain to me why I should believe one word that came out of your mouth in the last ten years? After all, you only told me that you cheated because you had to, right? Because it got you into some kind of trouble."

Eyal didn't know what to say. He was silent for a few moments, and then said:

"You have no reason to believe me, but it's the truth. It was only that one time, one night. There's been nothing else. I don't know if that helps right now, but it's the truth. I'm sorry."

"Great. Do you have any idea how exploitive that industry is? It would have been better if you had just fucked that finance manager. You really think women become prostitutes for fun? Because it's an interesting career? They're all exploited, a hundred percent of them, do you understand me? Even if they make tons of money. They're all girls who were raped and abused. How could you do something like that? It's disgusting."

"I'm sorry." Eyal knew that from the moment he told Maria he didn't want to have sex with her and they started talking, they stopped being a prostitute and a client, and became two people who found themselves in a hotel room together under unusual circumstances. He knew he didn't force Maria to sleep with him, it was her choice. He was sure of at least that much. But it didn't seem like a very smart idea to discuss with his wife the intimacy he and Maria had shared.

"You've said that already. It's not very convincing. Fine, what did you want to tell me? If I had to guess, you got into trouble with her husband, but prostitutes don't get married, so what is it?"

"This prostitute actually was married. But it's a long story. Give me a few minutes, please, it's important."

"I can't believe this shit. Fine, I'm listening."

Eyal told her almost everything, excluding the part about the kid and the request that he take a DNA test. He felt bad about it. Shimon, that nutcase, could decide to tell Galit about the kid himself. And if the kid really was his? Even though Shimon denied any connection to the kid, Eyal couldn't forget the way he looked at him. But he couldn't tell Galit about it, not before he decided what to do about it. Learning that he had cheated on her was enough, and it wasn't clear if their marriage was going to survive it.

"So you see, we have an investor who's not a real investor, who's mad at me because his wife liked me, and I'm afraid he might have been the one who murdered her. I'm actually convinced it was him. And now I'm afraid of what else he's planning, and I just don't know what to do, I'm at a loss."

"I don't know what to tell you, Eyal. I just can't believe this is happening, you've ruined our whole life. What can I tell you."

"I know you want to kill me, Galit, but I need your help."

"I really don't know how I can help you. You've given me a giant headache, I can't think of anything."

"Galit, you're the smartest person I know. And you're the only person I can talk to about this. Remember I'm still the father of your children, and that this mess can reach our doorstep. He took photos of us for three years."

"Fine. Maybe when I calm down I'll be able to think of something."

"Listen, I tried getting information about the murder, I searched online and read the papers, but I couldn't find anything useful and I have no clue how to investigate this. I have no leads. I tried going with the story about his military service. It felt like a pretty good place to start, to find his Israeli roots. But nothing comes up."

"Are you sure you even want to investigate this? Maybe you should leave the investigation to the police."

"I don't know, but I think I have to try to deal with him somehow and not leave it only in the police's hands. And I can't do that without having any information."

"Well, there is something. I can tell you that after listening to this story he told you, there's one thing that feels off."

"Only one thing?"

"No, I mean, his story about the soldier who committed suicide. It's… I don't know, it seems like a rather pointless story."

"What do you mean? It could have happened to him, life is a bit pointless sometimes, isn't it?"

"I mean, this particular story, it's the first thing he told you about himself, right?"

"Yes."

"And it sounds as though he holds you in some regard, or at least attributes a certain importance to you. I think this story is probably some kind of defining story in his life."

Galit was more relaxed now, and her voice sounded as if they were having a regular conversation like in the good old times. Eyal savored every moment.

"Okay, so if we believe him that this story made him leave the country and start a new life in Italy, it's a pretty defining story, isn't it?"

"Yes, but he didn't just start a new life someplace else, right? He murdered Maria and is now trying to frame you for it, so the man turned into some kind of monster, wouldn't you say?"

"I guess you could say that. Although, all that happened after my meeting with Maria. Maybe I was the defining event in his life?"

"What kind of man marries a prostitute, doesn't mind that she continues working as a prostitute, and records all of her sessions? No. I think he was probably a monster long before you met him. And I'm guessing that what's supposed to explain this transformation in his life is the story about Shimi, his soldier. And as a transformative event, which is supposed to explain to us why a person has become the person he is, something's missing here. It's a very unpleasant story, but frankly, it seems like the kind of story that explains why a person becomes a social worker, or something like that. He had a soldier who killed himself, and he struggled to cope with it. But as a story that explains why he turned into a murderer, something's missing. So, okay. He was angry at the family that might have accused him of their son's death. And he was discharged from his role as a commander. And maybe he was sick of this country. But what's missing is the element that's supposed to explain why he turned into this, this freak."

"And you're sure this element has to be in this particular story?"

"I'm not sure. But again, it's the first thing he told you. I think this story is supposed to explain a lot. And I'm missing something here. A motive. The thing that hurt him so deeply and changed his life so radically. I think he's hiding something from you. I have no idea what it is. I'm not much help, am I?"

"No, Galit, it's very helpful, I think I understand what you're saying. Maybe it's not much to go on now, but I think that when I know a bit more, it will help."

A long silence stretched over the phone. Eyal wanted to keep on talking about Shimon for another hour just to hear Galit's calm voice. But there was nothing left to say.

"So what's going to happen now, with us?"

"I don't know, Eyal. I don't know if I can live with you, if I can even be near you anymore. I need to think. I need to be alone."

"Okay. What are you going to tell the kids?"

"I don't know yet."

"I'll tell them that I have a lot of work so I won't be sleeping at home for the next few days, until you decide what you want to do. It'll be a natural continuation of my trip to Italy."

"Fine, tell then whatever you want." Wonderful.

"There's something else I have to tell you." They had been on the phone for more than an hour now, and throughout their conversation Eyal regretted not telling Galit the entire story. He was shaking just from the thought of how she would react if she found out from someone else. He had to tell her.

"What now? Don't tell me you had sex with her without a condom and now there's a kid in the picture. If there was any chance I could forgive you, and to be honest I really don't know if I could, even for the sake of our kids, I'd never be able forgive you for that, Eyal, never."

"I didn't sleep with her without a condom. Give me five minutes, listen to me, it's a little crazy, but you've heard a few crazy things today so listen to just one more."

With a trembling voice Eyal told her the story. At least he felt good with himself about finally making the right decision—to tell her about the kid.

"Oh, Eyal, oh god, what did you do to us?!"

Eyal was silent. He didn't know what to say. But after a few minutes, or maybe it was two hours, Galit said, "Well, at least there's some hope there, I don't buy that story one bit. It's very difficult to get pregnant that way. And there are spermicides, you know? You think this is his revenge, right? He murdered her and now he'll frame you for murder? So the son you supposedly fathered would be your motive, right? She sued you for paternity and you refused."

"Yes, that seems to be the case. This Shimon guy denied to the police having anything to do with this story, denied ever having a kid."

More silence.

"Can I come see the kids today?"

"Not today. Maybe tomorrow. We'll talk, Eyal, but for now I need some peace and quiet. I have to get going, I'm late."

"Okay, bye, Galit."

"Bye."

What to do now? He was cut off from his own life, no wife, no kids. Oh, how he longed to see the kids. Today he wouldn't be giving them a good night kiss. The thought alone made his stomach turn. And he didn't even have a workplace anymore.

Where hadn't he looked yet? Eyal suddenly remembered DEBKAfile, an Israeli military intelligence website; maybe they would have something interesting that the more conventional websites had missed? Sometimes DEBKA had good information you couldn't find anywhere else, as well as more bizarre articles. But there was also the possibility he would find out Maria had been abducted by aliens. He entered the news site and read an article about the murder that didn't reveal anything new to him almost until the last sentence: "The possibility that the murder was related to Satanists is being examined." Amazing! They were basing it on the fact that the murder had taken place in room 333 (half of the Satanic number 666). Eyal stared at the screen dumbstruck. There was his proof, if he needed any more proof that it was Shimon. The number three was Shimon's obsession, he remembered Maria telling him. It couldn't be a coincidence. But what could he do with that information? He doubted that anyone except for him and Maria, who was no longer alive, knew about his obsession. He should tell Andrey about it, even though it probably wouldn't help him. But who knows, they might locate some relative who would be able to tell them about Shimon's obsessions. But first he had to pin down Shimon's Israeli identity, and if he succeeded, it would probably solve a lot of other problems. Only he had no idea how, and he wasn't sure anyone even believed him. He needed to consult with Galit again, she might have an idea how to use that information. Eyal left the hotel business center and started walking along HaYarkon Street. He walked toward Atarim Square and paused in front of the sea, taking deep breaths. It almost felt like being single, he thought with a pinch in his heart. People around him were strolling along the boardwalk, some were jogging, beautiful girls passed him by, some looked at him with curiosity, and everyone seemed generally happier than him, people without problems. He wasn't accustomed to feeling that way. Eyal wasn't used to being jealous of random people on the street. He wandered around a bit, stopped to have coffee and a sandwich to fill the pit in his stomach, and continued to wander aimlessly. At about eight in the evening, he remembered he hadn't talked to Max yet. Max! He had to speak to him. He dialed, and this time Max answered.

"Max! How are you? Do you have a few minutes?"

"Can it wait a bit?" He sounded stressed. Eyal thought he heard a female voice in the background.

"Max, you're with someone…?"

"Yes."

"Okay, I won't bother you, just remember I have something important to tell you. We'll meet for whisky later, okay?"

"Okay, Eyal. Bye."

That naughty boy. Eyal couldn't deny the fact that he was a bit jealous of Max, being free and liberated. He was probably in for a hell of a night. Well, all the best to him. But actually, didn't they just make plans to meet later? Maybe Max wasn't very focused.

CHAPTER 13

Max stood on the corner of Maskit and Medinat Hayehudim Street in Herzliya and waited. He had a very strange day yesterday, a day of phone calls and rumors that quickly turned into certainties. The company was being sold. It was odd. Yesterday morning he arrived at work and there was no one there apart from management. Mandy called him and asked if he heard the rumor and knew anything. He also asked whether it was possible that Eyal had put on a poker face before his trip to Italy and was now going to screw them. Max replied that he found it a bit unlikely, since he had no motive to do that. Max also thought, but kept it to himself, that Eyal couldn't screw him over because no one could sell the company without him, Fugu without Max wasn't Fugu. But they could certainly give Mandy the boot without thinking twice, and Max didn't really care. Mandy said he could think of a million motives and a millions ways in which Eyal could screw the both of them, continuing to insist on placing them in the same boat. Max was a bit surprised. He knew Mandy wasn't Eyal's biggest fan, but he never thought he hated him that much. Max just assumed Eyal got along with everyone. Max told Mandy they would probably have to wait and see, and then felt bad about his answer—which was said mostly out of impatience with Mandy—since he should have been more collegial toward Eyal, a better friend. Max didn't have to wait very long. Soon after their conversation, the news appeared on Israel's leading financial website. He called Jeff, who seemed as surprised as he was and asked him to wait on the line. Jeff finally reemerged and told him that yes, it was true, they were going to sell. And no, Eyal didn't know about it before the trip, he learned about it from the buyer himself, and it was supposed to remain confidential, but if it was already leaked then Max had a right to know. The company was going to be sold. He's right, his technology was indeed worth more, but... You know how it is, Jeff told him. There are a million amazing ideas out there that never go anywhere for a thousand and one reasons. So this is where we are, it's now or never. Jeff also told Max to pressure the Italians into giving him a fat signing bonus and good terms. Now was the time. Without Max there was no company. Max knew that, but it felt good to hear Jeff say it. Nevertheless, it hurt. Until now he could have at least entertained the fantasy that the company would turn around and make it big. On the other hand, the company was in such a shitty place that Max was getting tired of it. Better to sell. It's interesting that Mandy doesn't know anything, Max commented. Life is interesting, Jeff said. If Mandy asks you again, tell him you still don't know a thing, okay? No problem, Max replied.

Max had been in contact with the Italians pretty much from the beginning, because they wanted to examine the technology from up close. In the past few days he had several conversations with Simone Donadoni. Donadoni turned out to be a fascinating man, a walking encyclopedia of Russian and Italian history as well as classical music, and Max was full of admiration. Of course there was also something strange and intimidating about him, but that was probably to be expected from a reclusive tycoon. Max's last conversation with Simone Donadoni was after his conversation with Jeff. Donadoni said he was certainly interested in hearing Max's terms. That he planned to be generous, very generous, within reason, of course. Then the conversation veered to a different subject—music. And then came the very strange invitation to meet with Mister Donadoni himself. It was a rather mysterious invitation. A little like that scene in The Matrix when Neo gets a special delivery—a FedEx envelope containing a cellphone. Well, Morpheus hadn't called just yet, but a delivery man did arrive. He informed Max that he was to wait on this corner for a car that would pick him up for the meeting with the big boss. It was rather late, why couldn't it wait until tomorrow? But Max didn't say anything.

He didn't even know that Donadoni was in the country. No one knew, and that was why they asked him to keep it a secret. That was why he was picked up from the street corner, and not from his house or in front of the company offices. That was probably also the reason for the mysterious delivery man. They were paranoid.

He was lost in thought when a Maserati suddenly pulled up in front of him. It was the executive model with four doors, and it looked a little like an intercontinental ballistic missile in a tuxedo. What a car, Jesus. The driver stepped out, a large man, but not the intimidating type. He was smiling.

"Please, get in." He opened the back door, and Max saw an amazing girl sitting there. She wore a long black evening dress with a generous cleavage, and what a rack, good lord, what the hell was this about? He entered the car and settled in next to her. Maybe the Lombardi people decided to give him his signing bonus at the beginning of the negotiations? Unlikely. But he also didn't think she was an executive in the fund. Not that there weren't some good looking senior execs, there certainly were, maybe even Yonit would be one in a few years. But he never saw any executive who looked like that, it was just too much, it was a woman whose goal was to... what? To soften him up, to motivate him, maybe to confuse him? If that was the case, he was ready to be confused. Just sitting next to her he already felt a bit disoriented. Her features were slightly masculine, a powerful jaw perhaps, but a very beautiful face nonetheless. Her hair was very short, her curvy body was mostly concealed by her long dress, even though it was black lace that wasn't completely opaque, and those breasts... big and gorgeous, paler than white, and also, Max thought, completely natural. He regarded himself as somewhat of an expert on the subject, even though he knew that some surgeons could perform miracles. This girl reminded him of one of his first projects during his freshman year at the Technion University, back when he was still more of a dreamer than an entrepreneur. Max read an article in some magazine that claimed the criteria for beauty are universal. A woman deemed beautiful by the Chinese would also be deemed beautiful by Africans, it had nothing to do with skin tone or the shape of the eyes, it had to do with the relation between the features and different body parts, the distance between the eyes in relation to their size, how prominent the cheek bones were, the ratio between the pelvis and the hips, and so on. It sounded logical to Max. He knew that to him, a beautiful woman was a beautiful woman no matter which part of the world she came from. He decided to take thousands of photos of beautiful women, models from all around the world and from every race, and analyze mathematically the topography of their faces and bodies. He wanted to produce the perfect woman. Analyzing large amounts of data quickly and effectively was always an important component in Max's projects. Even now, Fugu's software analyzed massive amounts of data, mostly the pronunciation and tone of thousands of words in the relevant language. After Max was done producing the image of the perfect woman, he planned to breathe virtual life into her. Who even needed movie stars anymore? In the future, Max thought, all the characters in movies would be the result of visualization. Max saw an entire virtual world in his imagination. Virtual stars living virtual lives, having virtual affairs. Maybe he wouldn't even let anyone know that the movie stars were his own virtual creation, maybe he'd let everyone believe they were real people. Obviously that dream never materialized. The algorithms Max had developed in order to produce computer animation were far from sufficient, and to be honest, far from what was already available on the market. And his perfect woman was rather disappointing. Just an image of another pretty woman. All his mathematical calculations brought him nowhere. And here, sitting next to him, was a woman who didn't meet many of those criteria. Her jaw was too heavy, the eyes a bit too small, the breasts probably too big for her frame. But she was amazing, oozing sex appeal in a way no computer would ever be able to decipher. Her presence was stupefying, she stunned Max, and he was aware of the dangerous effect and wasn't sure it was very helpful at the moment.

His phone rang. "Hello?" Max heard his own voice and knew he sounded stressed. But why? Because of this woman? Or maybe because he was about to meet Simone Donadoni in the flesh? There had been something very intriguing and a bit unnerving in his conversations with Donadoni.

"Max! How are you? Do you have a few minutes?" Eyal asked him.

"Can it wait a bit?"

"What is it, honey? Does this have to be now?" Did this woman just call him honey? Yes, it seems that she did.

"Max, you're with someone…?"

"Yes."

"Okay, I won't bother you, just remember I have something important to tell you. We'll meet for whisky later, okay?"

"Okay, Eyal. Bye." The very moment he hung up, Max already regretted it. Eyal had just returned from a meeting with Simone Donadoni, he probably wanted to tell him something about it, and Max was about to meet Donadoni himself. He should have probably listened to what Eyal had to say.

"Max, let me introduce myself. My name is Anita." So many thoughts were racing through Max's head that he hadn't even noticed they'd been riding in the car for several minutes and he hadn't said one word to her. He was wound up like a spring. She had a foreign accent but spoke excellent Hebrew. Maybe she was Dutch? Swedish? But she'd probably been in the country for many years. Then again, who knew.

"It's nice to meet you, Anita. I thought I was going to meet some men in suits and ties."

"Disappointed?"

"Not by a long shot."

"You have nothing to worry about, the suits and ties will be here soon. You're going to meet the big suit, as you probably know."

"Yes. Do you work for the Lombardy fund?"

"Yes, I'm one of the fund's representatives in Israel," she said, and Max wasn't sure he believed her. In fact, he was completely convinced it was lie, but what did it matter.

"You're certainly the prettiest venture capitalist I've ever seen."

"Thank you."

"When did Mister Donadoni land in Israel? Yesterday when I spoke to him he was still in Italy, right? Why was it so urgent that he meet me here?"

"Mister Donadoni took his private plane. Well, one of his planes. I'm sure you understand that he can decide to travel on a moment's notice. He just needs to drive to the airport and take off."

"So is he going to make me an offer today?" It was an idiotic question, but Max felt the need to say something, anything, because the woman's presence was making him nervous. She really was gorgeous, and she made sure to lightly brush up against him every now and then. Her perfume was driving him crazy. Indeed, a dangerous vixen.

"I think it would be best that you find out for yourself once you get there. You have nothing to worry about, the Dan Accadia is a very comfortable hotel."

Several minutes later, they arrived at the hotel. The driver dropped them off at the entrance and sped toward the parking lot. Anita took out her cellphone and said a few words that Max tried unsuccessfully to decipher.

"We need to wait a few more minutes, if you don't mind. We can go sit by the pool and have coffee if you want."

"Sounds great." In fact, it sounded rather flirtatious, and Max felt there was something affected about her attitude, as if she received instructions to be exceedingly nice to him. A lot of girls wanted Max. He was good looking, nearly no one knew how rich he was, a real millionaire, in fact, and not just on paper. And not from his salary from Fugu, of course. He was still receiving royalties from inventions he had developed, mostly from gaming companies, and there were other developments that earned him substantial sums. He rarely brought girls home, obviously. His shockingly messy home. He preferred taking his dates to fancy hotels. He was a rare combination of a successful businessman and a wild, messy anarchist. The ultimate tech entrepreneur—at least that's how he thought of himself, and there was some truth to it. And yet, his instinct told him that this woman didn't really want him, she was just putting on an act. But why worry? He knew from the first moment that she was there to butter him up, it was obvious she didn't want him, and equally obvious that she would be flirtatious. Maybe the thing that troubled him was that Max never started negotiations with investors like this. There were certainly many dinners in which the amounts of alcohol served could turn even the most resilient brain to mush, and there were also lavish functions with many gorgeous girls. But this was something new; her attempts to soften him up had been initiated rather quickly. They stretched out on the deck chairs in front of the pool, which felt rather odd in their elegant clothes. She looked into his eyes, and although they were in separate chairs, her cleavage was dangerously close to him, and as much as he tried to tell himself that this executive prostitute—or whatever she was—had no real interest in him, Anita was so sexy he couldn't remain indifferent.

"You're cute," she said, and caressed his cheek. Against his better judgment, he tried to gauge whether there was a chance of getting anywhere with this gorgeous woman. Suddenly they were kissing, and Max was already very aroused, but then her phone beeped with an incoming message. She took her phone and read the message.

"Okay, the big man's ready to see you."

"Really?" Max reprimanded himself for continuing to spew nonsense.

"He'll see you in his suite, if that's okay with you. You can be sure there'll be good cognac and cigars, and other nice goodies if you're in the mood."

"Great." He felt as though she just switched off that thing she had switched on a few moments ago and suddenly he felt depleted, left with some unsatisfied urge. Fuck her, what a manipulative woman. And what an idiot he was, god. Never mind. Cognac and cigars. He'd probably pass on the cigars, but fine cognac always made him feel better. And what were the other goodies she mentioned? A cheese platter? He only hoped they weren't going to serve him iguana steak or something weird like that. Max had already been forced to eat very weird things in meetings with big shot businessmen. It felt as though they were trying very hard to prove to everyone how special and different they were from the rest of the world.

166

They stood in the elevator, and once again Anita was inches from him, her perfume filling the cramped space, her breasts right under his eyes, starting to mess with his brain. She was a real snake, this girl, he had to be careful! They finally reached the right floor, walked out of the elevator and approached the room. She knocked on the door. It was all very strange, he was being led to a meeting with one of Italy's richest men as if he was some porn dealer. Anita's phone rang, she took a step back, and at that very moment she pushed him inside and disappeared. Max found himself staring at the barrel of a gun pointed at him by no other than their driver. How did he get here? It wasn't that impossible, actually. Anita, that whore, was stalling him downstairs while the driver parked the car, or maybe sank it in the sea, and managed to get to the room before them. The door slammed behind him. The girl was surprisingly strong, Max was a heavy fellow. This was an alarming situation. He remembered the assassination of Al-Mabhouh. Inside a closed hotel room you could do anything, interrogate a man, take him out, a long time would pass until anyone found him. No one would agree to sleep in a hotel room that had cameras installed on the ceiling. But what now? And what did they even want from him?

"So I gather the big boss isn't here?"

"Take out everything you have in your right pocket. No sudden movements."

Max took out some money, a credit card and his cellphone.

"Give me the phone, please."

His gun was less polite, and Max handed him the phone.

"Sit on the bed, please."

Max sat down. "Okay, what do you want from me exactly?" The man came from Russia, Max had no doubt, maybe even at an older age then he did.

"I don't want anything from you. My boss wants something from you, but I don't know what yet."

"I've had many conversations with your boss recently. We've had some differences, but I was under the impression we could solve them in a slightly more civilized manner than this."

"You're probably right."

There was something ridiculous and artificial about this conversation, a little like Anita's behavior toward him, and it made him feel uncomfortable. He didn't believe what his captor was telling him. And what was so urgent that they had to lock him inside a hotel room? There was nothing reassuring in the politeness of the man holding him at gun point. Was it possible they actually wanted to get rid of him? But why? Only yesterday he and Simone Donadoni had discussed his terms, numbers were tossed around and Max wanted higher figures, but surely that was no reason to kill him! Maybe this was just a means to apply pressure on him? If it was, it was certainly working. This guy looked pretty strong, but Max was no weakling, and suddenly Max was under the impression that the guy wasn't paying very close attention, and that if he caught him at the right moment, he could take him out and make a run for it. Because the more he thought about it, the more dangerous the situation seemed. These people seemed like real psychopaths. But Max's instinct was to keep talking to him, to have a calm and pleasant conversation, to ask him what he wanted, what orders he was waiting for, to make some kind of connection with him, to show him that he's a human being too, and after all, they had both spent their childhoods in Russia, so maybe there was a chance of getting some sympathy out of him? But a voice deep inside him told him that this man didn't have Max's best interest in mind, he was just waiting for orders. If the orders were to burn Max alive, he would do it without blinking. The hotel phone rang. The guy picked up, turning his profile to Max. He glanced at him every few seconds, but he seemed completely immersed in the conversation, and Max saw that the gun was pointing more at the bed's headrest than at him. Max was less than ten feet away from the man, maybe he could do it. Now the guy was looking at the window, shouting into the phone. He wasn't looking at Max at all. He was in another world, probably some trouble with his boss. What was he so angry about? Maybe his boss was ordering him to keep Max alive and it made him angry? And maybe it was just the opposite, maybe he felt some kind of Russian kinship and was refusing to kill him? Baloney, of course, pure horse manure.

But maybe they didn't want to kill him at all, maybe it was just Max's wild imagination, and the move he was planning to make would only put him in unnecessary danger. Maybe he should just wait for them to release him. The problem with that phone conversation was that Max couldn't understand anything, just a bunch of sentences that didn't make for a clear picture. 'I can't do that.' And a few times, 'That's unacceptable.' It was now or never, this opportunity wouldn't repeat itself. Quick. He had to try. Every muscle in his body tensed, his heart was racing, he felt his pulse in his temples, this is it, one, two, and he leaped from the bed without his captor noticing a thing. Amazing. Max was now close enough to touch him. He jumped on the man, who was still talking on the phone. The latter turned around with surprise and tried to punch Max, who pushed him with all his weight onto the carpet, but it was a mistake. The guy was on the carpet and could now shoot him. But when he tried to get up, he lost his balance and his gun fell toward Max. Ha! Max grabbed the gun and aimed at him. But what was he going to do? He obviously wasn't going to shoot anyone. The large man started running toward the door, and a second later he was no longer in the room. Max was overwhelmed with relief and pride. He felt a rush of adrenaline—he did it, he saved himself, he beat a professional criminal, he felt on top of the world. Today he would go out to a club and go home with the hottest girl there, maybe even two girls, after the whiskey with Eyal. He felt such a rush of self-confidence that he had no doubt he could do it. He checked the gun. Maybe he shouldn't have, because now he was covering it with his fingerprints, but what did it matter, no one was killed, no crime was committed there today, apart from Max being held against his will and threatened at gun point. And an attempted rape, he thought and laughed. He took out the magazine. It was empty. Interesting. A phone started ringing somewhere in the room. His phone! Max looked for his phone and found it on the floor next to the bed. He picked it up, and with it, for some reason, he lifted a pouch. It was the pouch the Russian was wearing earlier. Max hadn't seen him take it off. There was a small string attached to the pouch, and it was connected to his phone's USB port.

About two hours after his meeting with Eyal, Andrey received a phone call from Izzy.

"Andrey, we found it."

"Found what?"

"The car."

"No shit. Where was it?"

"Near the Yarkon Park, on Bnei Dan Street. It was parked in one of those grey, unrestricted spots, so there was no ticket. If a parking inspector had found it, we wouldn't have been looking for so long."

"Did we already search that area?"

"I guess we missed it. We also found the phone."

"Inside the car? Interesting. Stinks to high heaven if you ask me."

"Why?"

"She made the last call from the Dan Accadia area in Herzlyia, then the phone disappears from the network, like someone disconnected the SIM or something like that. And now suddenly we find the phone in the car, just like that. Too convenient."

"You're still liking the setup theory?"

"Yup."

"Wait till you see what's on the phone."

Eyal woke up in the hotel room, and it took him a moment to realize where he was. He went to wash his face, and tried to think what he was supposed to do today. Go to work? He had to call Max first. He had tried to reach him again last night, but Max was probably busy having fun. It was a shame. Eyal was looking forward to their meeting, it was supposed to be his bachelor-type fun during this forced separation. Whiskey with Max without having to report to anyone and without having to be home at a certain hour. An all-nighter with his friend. It didn't happen. He needed to call Galit. No, it could put her in a tough spot in front of the kids; he'd wait until she dropped them off at their kindergarten and then call her. Or maybe she was expecting him to make the drop off round? It was usually his job. Whatever. If she wanted him to do stuff around the house, she'd probably tell him. He'd call her later. Max. Eyal dialed Max's number, but there was no answer. He entered a news site on his phone. The war in Syria. Couldn't be bothered with that now. A bombing at the Dan Accadia Hotel. Unclear whether it was crime-related or a terrorist attack. Eyal's heart started pounding. The Dan Accadia. He tried reaching Max again, but to no avail. Galit called.

"Gin, are you okay?" She called him Gin. Eyal's heart leaped in his chest with joy.

"Yes, Galiti, I'm fine. What's up?"

"Haven't you heard? I saw on the internet, there was an article... It looks like Max was murdered."

The last shred of joy left his body. He felt weak, bludgeoned with exhaustion. He felt that if he didn't sit back on the bed he'd collapse on the floor.

"Gin, are you there?"

"Yes. I saw an article about the bombing at the hotel, I was a little scared, but I didn't see the article about Max. Fuck."

"Are you okay? Do you want to meet?"

"Yes, I'd love that."

"It's him, isn't it? That crazy Italian?"

"The crazy Israeli-Italian, yes, it's probably him."

"But why? Didn't you say he was buying the company? Then why would he murder Max?"

"That's a good question, I have no idea. You know what? Maybe... Remember when Max showed us that sophisticated phone that looked like just an old Nokia? Remember, when I explained to you our technology?"

"Yes, of course, it was only three days ago. Feels more like a year ago."

"Then maybe he was angry at Max for developing things outside of Fugu? I don't know, it's just a stupid idea. I really don't know, Galit."

"That is a stupid idea, but I'll tell you one thing. Everything leads back to you in this thing, right? Everything started with your meeting with his wife, right? It has nothing to do with Fugu's technology. Max was murdered because he knew something about you. Or about the Italian. Maybe the Italian was afraid that Max would tell you something he knew about him, and that's why he killed him. It has to be connected to you. The Italian's only interest in Fugu is because of you. Without you he wouldn't even know about Fugu, or about Max. It all starts with you."

"Yes, maybe you're right, it makes sense."

A horrible noise startled Eyal.

"Eyal Shiloh? Are you in there?"

Eyal approached the door.

"Yes, I'm here." Police, no doubt. He was being arrested. Fantastic.

"I'm being arrested, Galiti, call a lawyer."

The door was kicked in and a police officer stood in front of him with his weapon drawn.

"Turn around, hands on the wall, slowly."

"Can I at least say goodbye to my wife?"

"Toss the phone, we've already seen what you do with those."

"Okay, okay." Eyal followed the instructions, his phone was taken away, his empty pockets emptied. Then the cop handcuffed him, and it was very unpleasant. As a reserve soldier, Eyal had participated in a few arrests. They used to cuff the detainees with zip ties. Now Eyal realized how awful that method was. The touch of cold steel wasn't nice, but at least it didn't cut into the skin.

"You're under arrest for the murder of Maria Dubcek, you have the right to consult a lawyer..." The officer began to Mirandize him.

"Now walk out slowly through the door, we're going downstairs to the squad car, and I suggest you don't cause any problems."

"I have no intention of causing problems."

"Good."

Eyal was led out of the room and into the hallway, where three other cops were waiting for him. As if he was an important criminal. Some curious hotel guests stared. Eyal stared back at them with defiance, but he felt a wave of nausea slowly climbing up his throat, threatening to burst out. He took a deep breath, or at least tried to. They took the elevator, and downstairs things were much worse. The cute receptionist with whom

Eyal had already managed to develop a teasing sort of relationship looked at him with surprise, and Eyal tilted his head up in a gesture of 'what can you do, that's life.'

"Hang in there, Eyal, whatever it is, I know you didn't do it."

"Thanks, you are the best."

It gave him a good feeling. It was surprising how small, human gestures could change your mood. He already felt the wave of nausea fading and his breath settling.

"Be quiet," the arresting officer told her.

"You be quiet, this isn't your house," she replied, and Eyal wanted to clap his hands, which was a bit difficult with the handcuffs. But he knew that all of the receptionist's good intentions weren't going to help him now. They stepped out to HaYarkon Street, where two squad cars awaited him.

CHAPTER 14

Eyal was led into a room with bare concrete walls. There was a dinky desk in the room and one other chair besides the one he was sitting on. His handcuffs were removed, which was a huge relief, and he was given a glass of water. He wished he had time to have coffee before the cops showed up, but at least he managed to pee. But he knew his bladder would start bugging him soon. Would they let him out to go to the bathroom? Eyal decided he'd hold it in as long as he could. He didn't want to show weakness, but he felt very weak, and very sad. Why the hell would Shimon murder Max? It was absurd, he needed Max!

Eyal didn't have his watch on him, and his phone was taken, so he had no way of telling how long he had been waiting until inspector Izzy was kind enough to appear. With a stern expression, he sat in front of Eyal and launched his attack. "Why did you murder Max? We know exactly why you murdered Maria, you beat the living daylights out of her. But why Max?"

That was it. If he ever had even the smallest doubt, it had disappeared. His stupid night with Maria had cost Max's life as well. It was very depressing. He should have insisted, should have forced Max to talk to him. Eyal hoped Max at least had some serious fun with that girl.

"Cat got your tongue? No problem, we'll throw your ass in jail until you decide to talk."

"No, I'm going to talk. I didn't kill anyone. I know why Maria was murdered, but I don't know why Max was. It's a good question."

"Good question, huh? Let me remind you of the facts you yourself admitted. You, without being forced, in a nice, relaxed conversation with Superintendent Andrey over a cup of coffee. You were romantically involved with the murder victim. You were at the hotel at the time of her murder. We checked the tapes from the surveillance cameras. You walked in exactly ten minutes after her, and you were there for enough time to finish the job. We know you've met her kid. Your kid. We're pretty sure that was your motive to kill her. Quiet unpleasant, I imagine, having a wife and two kids, and suddenly this prostitute comes and wants you to be her baby daddy."

"I spent one night with her. I didn't hear from her or about her until I heard she was murdered. I was invited to the hotel with a fake phone call from an investor in my company."

"We checked that claim, it doesn't stand. There was no call made from him or his secretary to you."

"I told you it was a fake call. It wasn't really them."

"So you say, but you don't have a shred of evidence to support your story. Let's drop it for a minute. I want to show you some clips. Come see on the computer. Tell me what you think about it, when they were taken, if you can identify."

"Okay."

Inspector Izzy opened the first file. It was a clip of Eyal and the kid, Dino. They were sitting in the game room, toy cars, plastic soldiers and dice all around them. Eyal was building a tower with Dino. They were both laughing when it collapsed, and Eyal stroked his hair. At a certain point, the camera zoomed in on Eyal's face—a proud smile was stretched across it.

"When was this taken?"

"It was taken in Bellagio, Italy, in Shimon Dahan's house. Shimon Dahan who's also known as Simone Donadoni. It was in the game room he built for his son, or perhaps his fake son. It was taken three days ago, come to think of it. Feels more like two years ago."

"We found this on the victim's phone. It was taken two months ago. You know what I see when I look at you and this kid?"

"What do you see?"

"I see a father and son, that's what I see. There's another one, you want to see it?"

Izzy opened the second file. When Eyal looked at himself sitting with Dino next to the elaborate train set, he noticed a few staggering facts that had eluded him when he was inside the room. In the first clip, he now realized, only one half of the room was filmed, the half without the trains. The wall in that part of the room had a different color and there was a different carpet as well. Even the height of the ceiling on both sides of the room was slightly different. Eyal remembered that he actually did notice that odd detail about the ceiling when he was sitting there playing with Dino, but he didn't think anything of it. In the first clip, he was in his suit, and Dino also wore a fancy small jacket. Now Eyal remembered that the room suddenly became very hot, and Dino's nanny apologized for the old heating system, and both he and Dino gave her their jackets. Both clips, despite having been filmed on the same day, one after the other, looked as if they were taken in different rooms, in two different places. They wore different clothes in both clips, although the pants and shoes were identical. One clip looked as though it might have been taken in the summer or maybe the spring, and the other in the winter. It was one big nightmare.

"The second clip I just showed you was taken six months ago. It was also found on the victim's phone. Look how you're staring at the kid, how you're hugging him. You really think anyone is going to believe that you have no connection to this kid?"

Eyal said that both clips were taken three days ago, at the same place. Time stamps on phones could be doctored. He tried to explain, to point out the strange fact that in the first clip he looks like someone who just came out of a business meeting, but he knew he was grasping at straws. None of his explanations amounted to much. He had to give it to him, Shimon did a great job. A real masterpiece. Eyal suddenly realized something else.

Something truly amazing. The entire story Shimon told Eyal to convince him that he was the father, everything about Maria's stomach exercises and the analysis of his conversation with Maria through Fugu's technology—his entire trip to Italy!—was designed to get these two clips in which he did in fact look like the kid's father. The whole story was meant to elicit one hour of belief in his paternity. Soon after he left the mansion he already started doubting it, but it was too late, his belief that he was the father was already documented in a rather incriminating way. He didn't even bother sharing it with Izzy. How would it help him? He knew he had to make them investigate Shimon-Simone more thoroughly, to expose his Israeli past. It was the only thing that could help. But he didn't know how to do it, especially in his current position, detained, without any foreseeable chance of getting out in the near future. He was lost.

"How do you explain the uncanny resemblance between you and the kid? You admit sleeping with the mother, we have clips of you playing with the kid, and he looks just like you. You've already seen the photos comparing the two of you, right? You want to see them again?"

"I thought about it. First of all, I don't think Maria was even his mother. And all this fake documentation with the photos and movies just proves to me beyond doubt that I'm not the father. If I actually was the father, they wouldn't have to work that hard. When I first saw the photos, I also thought the kid might be mine. Now I'm sure he's not. Simone himself denied any connection to the kid or Maria, right? And I, my only connection to all this was my connection to Maria. So I thought about the stack of photos, which was meant to prove I'm the father, and I think it has another purpose."

"I'm listening."

"He used the photos to find a kid who looks just like me. The guy photographed every part of my face, from every angle, nose, ears, everything. And then searched for a kid who looks a lot like me. The kid's real parents probably don't know the whole point of this thing, I assume no sane parent would let his kid be part of a scheme to set someone up. Maybe they were told that he was going to act in a movie or something. You see, these photos weren't just meant to prove the resemblance, they were meant to create it. They used these photos for their search to find the closest looking kid."

"You know what amazes me? There's so much evidence against you. I haven't seen a homicide case backed by so much evidence in a long time. You slept with the murder victim. You were at the place of the murder, at the time of the murder. You have a well-documented motive. I'm listening to you and remember my childhood. Ever read The Bermuda Triangle? You're coming up with the most amazing plot here, I haven't seen anything this crazy in a spy movie, and you expect someone to believe it? Why don't you just confess and make both our lives easier? You will confess, eventually, you know. With this much evidence, even if you don't confess, any normal judge will throw you in jail for life. If you confess and express your remorse, you might save yourself a few years in jail. You might even get out in time to see your grandkids. I just don't understand how you can look at me with such indifference and give me that load of nonsense that a three-year-old might tell, not a grown up."

Eyal knew there was no way in hell that he'd confess to something he didn't do. But Izzy was completely wrong about his so-called indifference. Eyal was just exhausted. He wanted to go home. He wanted to hug Galit and kiss his kids. He wanted to have a good steak with Jeff, he even missed the smell of Jeff's cigar. But who knew, maybe if the interrogations went on for months, he actually would break down and give some cockamamie confession. If he was this tired after only a few hours, maybe after a few months he'd be willing to confess to anything just so they'd leave him alone.

"Let me help you a little, which brings us to another issue that's bothering us. Your theory that Maria never had a kid is baloney. She had a kid, there's documentation in Italy."

"Really? Who's the father?"

"You're the father, but obviously that's not mentioned anywhere. We found photos of her and the kid in her apartment."

"Shimon brought her to a photo-shoot, she probably even didn't know who she was taking pictures with."

"You have an answer for everything, don't you?"

"Who's raising him? Maria was living in Israel when she was murdered, right?"

"How about you leave the questions to me. The dates the clips were taken, the twenty-seventh of June and the first of March, you remember where you were on those dates?"

"Not really."

"Let me help you. Is it possible that at the beginning of March you were on a business trip in Brussels? Something about the European market, you had to get some kind of high tech grant for one of your projects. Right? The stamps are in your passport, there's no use denying it."

"If you say so. I remember the trip of course, I just don't remember the exact dates."

"And at the end of June, you were in... Lugano, Switzerland. You guys get around, don't you? You were close to the Italian border, something to do with some venture capital fund that was interested in your company, right?"

"I was."

"You know who else was in Belgium and Switzerland on those exact dates? You can probably guess. Maria."

"I met Maria once, one night, that was it."

"I don't think so. I think you had a little family vacation, you and your second family. And there's documentation, right here on the proud mom's phone. She took photos of the dad and their kid. You guys made a good looking family, you know? Almost everyone I know would die to have just one of your families, one of your two gorgeous women. I'd even be jealous myself, if I didn't know where you're headed from here."

"I don't have two families. Think about it for a moment, you actually think I have two giant game rooms, one in Lugano and one in Brussels? I should have thought about it myself!"

"I think you better save your sarcasm for the cell you're going to spend the rest of your life in, it might keep you warm on those cold nights."

Eyal knew that Izzy was right, and once again he found himself admiring Shimon and his men's thorough job. They probably brought Maria to Switzerland and Belgium on the exact dates Eyal was there, without her knowing why. And then they imprinted the dates on the video clips they took a few days ago, and planted them in Maria's phone. It was awful, how was he going to get out of this mess? He really was drowning in a sea of shit.

"Eyal, your lawyer is here, would you like to see him?"

"Yes."

The meeting with the lawyer was encouraging while it lasted. It was amazing how a few hours of interrogation made Eyal miss even the most modest display of sympathy. But all in all, the lawyer didn't bear much good news. He told Eyal, among other things, that he was going to spend the night in lock-up, which he probably should have guessed himself if he had time to think about it.

After the meeting with his lawyer, the interrogation proceeded for several more hours. Izzy kept asking him where the kid was. It was indeed interesting what Shimon had done with him, since the moment the police located the kid they would find out that Eyal was innocent, and Shimon's entire scheme would be exposed. Was it possible that one stupid night, could also claim the life of a three-year-old? Throughout the day, they had given him breaks to eat, drink and use the bathroom. But he was exhausted.

The cell Eyal was placed in reminded him a bit of a movie he once saw about a submarine, only that this submarine was made of ugly concrete, and there was no trace of camaraderie. Already five people were there, and one available steel cot at the end of the cell. There was a sink and a kind of military latrine. Eyal thought he recognized on the rim of the hole remnants that had missed their target, and obviously his cot was the closest to this health hazard. While passing by the five other detainees, he felt all ten eyes piercing him. Eyal wasn't sure what to expect. His burly physique usually prevented the need to actually confront anyone. But he was never in a position in which he had to confront any criminal characters, because all-in-all he was a good kid. Even in the military he never spent a day in the slammer. He had good friends who got short prison stints for disciplinary offences that weren't really serious. They were also good kids, the kind whose days in the slammer ended up being a source for campfire stories and not actual trouble. There were also more feeble ones, like Shimon's soldier, who probably suffered. But Eyal's friends mostly told stories about smuggling cigarettes, pot, and sometimes even girls into the military prison. It actually seemed as though their few days as detainees were a cheerful respite from the unit's difficult training regime. While Eyal didn't dare to actually stare at any of them, from what little he could pick up on, it didn't seem these guys were in the mood for good-spirited campfire stories. One of the guys there seemed particularly scary—the one sitting to the right of the door; his eyes were too close together and he had a low forehead, a real Neanderthal. Eyal sat down and had no clue what to do with himself. The rest of the detainees continued to stare at him, and Eyal was certain it was a good idea not to stare back. Each second felt like an eternity. Was he really going to spend the entire night there? It was simply horrible. How would he be able to stay awake in this place? Usually he had no problem staying awake even when he was completely exhausted. He had a lot of experience in that from the military. But he never felt this tired, and it wasn't only a physical thing, he felt hopeless, beaten, battling higher powers. Maybe the cell in the actual prison would be better, who knew. He focused on his breathing, trying to calm himself down. When Eyal had undergone particularly painful dental work, he found it useful to close his eyes and imagine that he was hugging Galit. Now he didn't think that daydreaming about his wife would help his predicament. It would only make him feel worse. He looked around carefully, trying not to seem frightened, but also trying not to stare. How was he going to pass the night? It felt as though time had stood still. After an hour in this place he'd probably go mad. I'm going to confess, Eyal thought. A few nights in this place, maybe even one night, and he'd tell them whatever they wanted to hear. He had to find something to think about. A challenge. What could he think about? He couldn't play chess in his head. He could barely play on a board. Eyal smiled, amusing himself. World capitals. Start with Europe. Ireland. Dublin. Britain. London. But what order should he choose, alphabetical or geographical? Geographical made more sense. West to East. Portugal, Lisbon. Spain, Madrid. Andorra. Does Andorra have a capital? He had to check. France, Paris. But now it got a bit more complicated, the geographical angle, what came next? Belgium and Holland, right? Brussels and Amsterdam. Which was more western, Ireland or France? In any event, Dublin. And London was Britain's, of course. And what about Andorra?

Eyal was standing on the deck of a boat. It wasn't a big boat, maybe fifty feet long. It was sailing across a river. It was the Mekong, he immediately recognized. Where was Galit? He had to get to Luang Prabang and find her. The river was vast, the banks far from the heart of the river, forested with spots of purple, yellow and orange. The current was fierce and greenish. All around him he saw small turbulences passing the boat, with twigs and leaves and odd plants spinning inside them and drowning after a struggle. Sometimes even human waste passed by. Plastic bottles, a car tire. Eyal wasn't sure how long he had been standing on the boat, watching the current and the river bank. Maybe five minutes. Maybe a year. Every now and then he saw villages, sometimes entire cities on the banks, towering skyscrapers that felt out of place. And suddenly the carcass of a duck floated past the boat, nearly bumping into it, and passing out of sight.

"Did you see that?"

"You probably wanted to say he's feeling a bit like a dead duck, huh?"

Max was standing next to him, looking very pleased with himself.

"It's very pretty here, but also terrifying."

"Did you hear about our new investor?"

"There's a new investor?" Fugu-related matters didn't feel relevant to Eyal on the boat.

"Rich as hell. He has a three-story apartment in Tel Aviv. And he also has a boat."

"A boat on the Mekong?"

"Could be."

"Say, you have any idea how to get off this boat?" Suddenly Eyal realized that he was a prisoner, that he had no way of escaping this boat that was sailing against the steam at an incredible speed, and it didn't seem there was any way of stopping it.

"Maybe you should jump?"

"In this current? I wouldn't make it to the bank, I'd drown."

"Why do you have to get off the boat?"

"You want to stay here your whole life?"

"I don't care. If I want to reach the investor, I have a special phone."

"And he'll come rescue us?"

"Why would he rescue us?"

"Eyal!"

"What?" Eyal was still half asleep, the views of the Mekong river blended with the unbearable stench of the real world. It took him a moment to realize where he was. When did he fall asleep? Eyal remembered that the idea of falling asleep in that cell had horrified him. But at some point he must have just run out of energy, and it seemed as though no particular disasters occurred while he was asleep.

"Eyal Shiloh, are you getting up or am I coming in to drag you out?"

"I'm up, I'm up."

They came to take him to another interrogation. Eyal looked at the sink near the military-like toilet, and decided to take a risk. He turned on the faucet and murky water gushed out. He washed his face, wiped it with his sleeve and was taken out of the room in handcuffs. He had been dreaming. Where was he a moment ago? He was in a whole different world. He wanted to meet Galit, in Luang Prabang. The Mekong! He was on a boat on the Mekong. And Max was there. It was amazing, the transition from sailing on the Mekong to this stinking cell. He would have been better off not waking up at all. But there was an eerie atmosphere in the dream. And what did Max say to him? Eyal didn't know how to get off the boat. He was in jail, no wonder he would have that dream. Eyal reminisced about the boat ride he and Galit took on the Mekong, sailing east from Luang Prabang. What was that Thai city in which they crossed the border? Chiang Khong. After that they traveled to Chiang Rai. Those were good times. But he felt as though Max had told him something important on the boat, something that could help him. What could it have been? They saw the carcass of a duck, and Max joked that he probably felt like a dead duck. Eyal suddenly found himself laughing, which surprised him, under the grim circumstances. Well, at least he was still able to make himself laugh.

"What it is?" one of the officers asked him.

"Nothing, just remembered a dream I had."

"Oh," the officer said.

But what else did Max say? The duck couldn't be much help, apart from temporarily lifting his spirits. There was something, something important that Max had told him in the dream. The moment Eyal woke up, he promised himself he wouldn't forget... But forget what, for fuck's sake? Eyal was led down a dank hallway. The place felt like the Dark Ages... He had to focus, what happened in that dream, he felt the memory fading, sinking in a thick fog of images and thoughts that couldn't be disentangled, and he knew he had to hang onto the memory with all his might, before it was lost forever. Skyscrapers. There were skyscrapers on the banks of the Mekong. Eyal felt as though he was regaining access to that world, Max on the boat, what did he say to him? That fucking duck again, but what else? A new investor in the company, Eyal suddenly remembered. He wanted to jump off the boat but the current was too strong. And Max told him... what did he say? That they didn't need to jump, because... because... he would talk to the new investor on the phone. But why was that even worth remembering, what new investor? The phone. Max said he had a special phone. Max's special phone!

Eyal smiled to himself with satisfaction.

CHAPTER 15

"Good morning." Izzy could make even a simple greeting sound snide. But Eyal knew what he had to do. There was a chance.

"Can I talk to Andrey?"

"Only if you're willing to give us a confession."

Eyal was so desperate that he actually considered telling Izzy he agreed to confess. When Andrey came, he'd explain the situation. But he decided against it. He wasn't really going to confess, and their response might be unpleasant, so he'd be better off not lying to them. He needed their trust.

"I'm not willing to confess because I haven't done anything, but I do have important information that pertains to the case."

"Important information? That you're willing to share only with Superintendent Friedman?"

"No, no. Of course not. Did you happen to find on Max's body an old Nokia phone?"

Izzy didn't bat an eyelash, but it seemed as though he was at least listening.

"If it wasn't on him, it might be in his apartment. That old phone is actually a sophisticated recording device. It records phone calls as well as anything else that happens within a radius of several feet, and then analyzes the speech through Fugu's software. It's a recording device and a portable polygraph. It might have recordings of part or even all of Max's conversations from the past few days, maybe even a recording of the murder."

It was only when the words actually left his mouth that he realized it was true, it wasn't only phone calls, it might have a recording of the

murder. It could save him! But the thought of a recording of the last minutes of Max's life made Eyal's stomach turn. He looked at Izzy nervously.
If this didn't impress him, it could be very bad.

"Tell me about Anna, Maria's friend."

"What?" And what if the phone was destroyed, or damaged beyond
repair? After all, there was an explosion, they killed Max with some kind
of bomb. Eyal felt his hope fading away.

"You couldn't have thought we'd miss the fact that Maria's best friend,
Anna Tarasova, was murdered two days before Maria. It's very convenient,
isn't it? Probably the only girl who could tell us anything about Maria suddenly disappears."

This was some unbelievable shit. Where was it coming from? He was
being accused of another murder?

"Sunday, I want you to tell me with as much detail what you did. When
did you wake up?"

Eyal racked his brains, but nothing came to him.

"Is there any chance of getting access to my phone? All of my meetings are listed there."

"No. For now you're going to try without the phone."

It went on like that the entire morning. Eyal was exhausted, he felt on
the verge of tears, which would have probably made Izzy very happy had he
known. But sometime around noon, Andrey entered the interrogation room.

"Good morning, Eyal."

Eyal almost cried from joy when hearing Andrey's pleasant voice, and
even his quiet gaze relaxed him somehow. Which was of course not only
naïve but completely idiotic, since who had ordered Izzy to interrogate
Eyal if not Andrey? But when Andrey took the old Nokia phone out of a
bag and placed in on the table, Eyal wanted to kiss him.

Judging by Izzy's look, he was obviously unpleased.

Now he only had to find out if it worked. Maybe the exterior had
survived the bombing, but not the technology? Eyal felt the knot in his
stomach tighten when he pictured the phone rubbing against Max's mutilated body.

"Did you find it on Max's body?"

They looked at him, and it was clear that he wasn't going to get an answer.

"Why don't you explain to us what this phone can do."

"Can I first wash my face?" Eyal was very tired. He had slept a few hours, but felt as though he didn't sleep a wink, and the sudden respite from the grueling interrogation only made him more aware of how exhausted he was. He could barely keep his eyes open.

"Okay, go to the bathroom and wash your face."

Izzy went with him, and when they returned, Eyal was feeling much better.

"Just to prove to you this phone is special, do you have a small Phillips screwdriver? If you open these four screws here, there's a USB port inside. I know a USB port is pretty standard, but not on such an old phone, this model here is more than ten years old, and it shouldn't have a port. Max built it there to upload files to the computer and analyze them with Fugu's full software. But you don't have to do that. There's a more limited version of the software on the phone itself, which provides a very adequate analysis, and obviously, you can listen to all the conversations he recorded, phone calls or conversations that took place near the phone." Eyal knew he was selling them a lot of things he wasn't sure of. He had no idea if the analysis was adequate. Hell, it was probably more than adequate, but who knew.

Andrey put on a pair of rubber gloves. He had a tester in his pocket, and he used it to remove the screws.

"You're right, interesting indeed. Okay, you've piqued my interest. How do you switch from recording a phone conversation to recording whatever's going on around you?"

"I think it's automatic. If a phone call comes in it will record it, and if there's no call, you press here and it records everything around."

"And if a phone call comes in when you're in the middle of recording a conversation in the room, what does it do? Is there a way to decide, or does it automatically switch to the phone call?"

"That's a good question, I haven't really thought about it…" Eyal considered adding that it was a shame they couldn't ask Max, but decided that it was probably a bad idea, given that they thought he was the one who had murdered him.

"Okay, Eyal, show us how you listen to what the phone recorded, and how you operate this software of yours."

"Okay, can you hand me the phone?"

They gave Eyal a pair of rubber gloves, and he turned on the phone, which immediately responded. Eyal felt his spirits lifting from one moment to the next…it was working, if the phone switched on, it had to work!

"Okay, let's enter the list of files."

"Give me the phone!" Eyal instantly handed the phone to Izzy, who glared at him.

"I wasn't going to delete any files."

"Okay, Eyal, just tell me how it's done."

Eyal hoped he still remembered how. Max had only showed him once.

"Yes, exactly, just press the scroll key down, that's it, now you choose the file with that button, simple. Oh, that's quite a lot of files. The last file is from two days ago, as you can see, the day Max died, I believe. You want to listen to it?"

"You're going to explain to us how to listen to it and how this polygraph software works, but you're not going to be listening to anything here."

"Fine, here, I'll explain it to you."

Eyal helped Andrey locate the small file Max had recorded of Galit, and explained to them how to listen to the rest of the files, and how to determine the speaker's level of credibility. Then they left him alone again, with a pitcher of water, a roll and some cheese.

Izzy was jumpy, and the moment they entered Andrey's office, he went on the attack.

"What exactly are you doing, Andrey? This is why we decided I'd do the interrogating, because you're all chummy with this guy, you've lost your objectivity. The guy was already going to break, I saw it on him, and then you come and talk to him like he's your friend, and a night's work goes down the drain."

"Izzy, let me remind you that our goal is to find the truth, not to break the suspect. This might be very important, we may have here a recording of what happened before the murder, maybe even phone calls Max had made. I understand why this is irritating you, but we have to look into it. If Eyal Shiloh is the actual murderer, this phone won't help him."

"And if it is such important evidence, then how could you let him anywhere near it? He could have deleted it all, and then, oops, didn't mean to."

"You're right, Izzy, it was a bad judgment call."

"Fine, whatever. This isn't for me to say, but it's almost like you're sabotaging the investigation."

"I hope I'm not. Come on, Izzy, it doesn't interest you to hear what's on this?"

They listened to the recordings, and were particularly eager to hear to the last one. It was rather disappointing, because it seemed that Max had stopped the recording rather abruptly, and it wasn't surprising.

"No shit, he sent a girl to seduce him."

"We're not sure it's him yet, Izzy."

"Andrey, you're driving me crazy! We're investigating a suspect that has a fucking mountain of evidence against him, I've never seen a case so documented, and you treat him like... I'm telling you, Andrey, I almost feel like I'm betraying my duty as an investigator by letting you stay here. Maybe you should just walk away from the case?"

"Have you noticed this? It's interesting. In this phone conversation between Max and Eyal, when Eyal asks Max if he's with a girl, his credibility is very high, which it is throughout the entire conversation, actually. If he sent the girl himself, the question wouldn't have been honest, and it would read on their software, wouldn't it?"

"What's with this bullshit? Do we even know anything about this software? You only have the suspect's word that that's what the phone does. These graphs might be describing the battery activity or something."

"You're right. For now let's go back to the earlier recordings. Let's see what we have there."

"You're going to trust these polygraph analyses?"

"We have to talk to this company, Izzy. I did some looking into it, and despite the stupid name, Fugu is a serious company, they have a strong reputation. We need to analyze these conversations on their software, the full version, and compare it to what we have on this phone. Obviously it won't be admissible evidence, but it might get us somewhere in the investigation. This phone may be a hidden treasure, so let's start investigating it."

"Yes, you're right, Andrey. I'll contact the company."

Eyal wasn't sure how long it had been before Izzy woke him up with a gentle tap on the shoulder. He seemed unusually calm, as if Andrey had given him a tranquilizer. But maybe this new, calmer demeanor wasn't a good sign. He seemed pretty satisfied. Maybe they didn't find anything on the phone? After all, Izzy was dying to see Eyal thrown into prison and rot there until he had grandkids. Izzy sat in front of him without saying a word. He seemed lost in thought. Lost in thought my ass, Eyal thought, he was dreaming about the moment he would get rid of Eyal and move on to the next case. Eyal could no longer stand the tension.

"Well... did you discover anything interesting?"

"A lot of interesting things, thank you, Eyal. You've given us some great material. But there's nothing there that can help you. From an initial examination, it seems the limited version of your software that was installed on the phone isn't worth much. Your trip to Italy and the meeting with Simone Donadoni, that's what I'd like to talk to you about, with your permission, of course."

Eyal had experienced many moments of despair in his life. In boot camp there were a few moments in which he thought he wouldn't make it. Now it was easy to look back at those moments with a smile, but at the time Eyal knew he felt true despair. And he came out of each such experience stronger. The moment after telling Galit that he had cheated on her was especially difficult, worse than anything he had known until then. But such complete hopelessness as he was now experiencing was new to him. Eyal felt that a great force was pulling him into a deep black abyss. On the edge of the abyss stood his wife and children, crying. He felt drained of life, defeated. He didn't care what Izzy would say next, he couldn't bare any more questions. He could barely breathe.

For the next two days, Izzy continued to wear Eyal down. Eyal didn't always notice what came out of his mouth. Izzy would say—so you admit you had other meetings with Maria, after the first meeting you told us about? And Eyal just couldn't remember how they got there, and what exchange had led Izzy to that conclusion. Every now and then Eyal tested himself— am I desperate enough to confess? But he was relieved to discover that the answer always remained 'not yet.' The notion of confessing and bringing an end to this nightmare appealed to him a great deal, but the thought that his kids would one day find out that their father had confessed to murder, even if it was a murder he hadn't committed, was unbearable. And then, on the morning after Eyal had told them about the phone, Andrey entered the room instead of Izzy. Andrey sat down in front of him with a solemn expression, but something about that expression told Eyal that despite everything there was still hope, and he sat on the edge of his seat.

"Things aren't looking too good for you, Eyal, as you probably know by now. I'm going to do a few things that an investigator isn't supposed to do. I'll do a lot of talking, I'll tell you a few things you aren't supposed to know. The reason I'm going to do this is because I have a feeling that we're missing something important here, and that you can help us. I wouldn't be doing my job as an investigator if I accepted the simple solution in front of me without questioning it. And I do question it. We followed your suggestion. The results weren't very impressive. First of all, I don't know if it's because of some malfunction or if it was Max's choice, but there are only recordings of phone calls, not of meetings or anything that happened around the phone. So our fantasy of getting a live recording of the murder didn't come true. The last conversation recorded is a very short one between you and Max, when he was on his way to the Dan Accadia. It could be viewed as evidence in your favor, but it isn't strong evidence and it's hardly worth mentioning compared to all the evidence against you. There's also no recording of the invitation to the fateful meeting. But that's not surprising. Obviously when someone's planning a murder, he doesn't want to leave a trail of evidence behind him. You should know that I've already told you much more than I should have. But it doesn't matter. If it helps me find out the truth, I've done good. If we've already discovered the truth and you actually are the killer, then these little details won't help you. The most interesting thing is the number of calls between Max and Simone Donadoni, or Shimon Dahan, if we decide we believe you. The last conversation is particularly interesting, and I'll tell you why. In that conversation, Max discussed his terms with his new boss. As Mister Donadoni explained to him, since he is the full owner of the fund, there would be no shares or stock options, and so they spoke of a very high salary, bonuses and so on. They had an entire conversation about it, which wasn't very interesting apart from how shocking it was to learn how miserable my salary is compared to what Max would have gotten there. With all the benefits, he would have been making in a single month more than I make in an entire year. A lot more. Then they moved on to other, unrelated subjects. Music. History. And then they went back to discussing Max's terms, in certain parts repeating almost word for word what they had already said in the beginning of the conversation. And here's the interesting thing. At the beginning of the conversation, Max's device attributed high levels of credibility to everything Mister Donadoni said. At some point, during the conversation about music and history, the credibility data is all over the place, a zigzagging graph. And then, when they repeat the things they said at the beginning of the conversation, the credibility attributed to the speaker stands at fifty percent and even lower, and deteriorates as the conversation progresses. At the beginning we thought maybe the device wasn't working properly, because what other explanation could there be for the fact that a person repeats the same thing twice during the conversation, and one time the device determines that he's being truthful, and the other time, that he's lying? We asked your people to analyze the conversation on the complete version of the software, and we received almost the same results we got from the phone. So I could come to the conclusion that this is all a bunch of hooey, but I developed a theory that should explain this, and maybe you can help me verify it. I think that maybe, and it's a big maybe, something happened during the conversation, something was said that completely eluded Izzy and me. Something that made Donadoni change his plan. Something that Max said, which would lead Donadoni to realize in the middle of the conversation, or at least suspect, that Max posed a risk to him. Hence the change. At the beginning of the conversation, Donadoni genuinely intends to hire Max, and discusses the terms he's willing to offer him with complete honesty. And then something is said that changes everything, and at that point Donadoni is confused, maybe he isn't sure what he's going to do with Max, and maybe he's even already considering taking him out. Which is why, when they discuss Max's terms again, during the second part of the conversation, Donadoni is no longer honest, or at least not sure what he wants. And that's what caused the shift in Donadoni's credibility levels, as opposed to some problem with the software."

"So are you going to let me listen to it, or at least show me the transcripts? Otherwise I have no way of finding out."

"Yes. You're the main suspect in a murder case. I'm going to show you evidence you're not supposed to see, certainly not at this stage. But it's essential for this final effort to make sure we didn't veer completely off course."

"Okay, thank you. I'm probably not supposed to say it, but whatever comes out of this, thank you."

"Sure. Here's the transcript of the conversation between Max and Donadoni."

Andrey gave Eyal a stack of no more than ten pages attached with a paper clip. Eyal started reading, and after the first page he got a headache. The back and forth about the amount of the bonuses wasn't going to help him. Nor was the argument whether Peter the Great was more barbaric or more great. Increasingly, Eyal was under the impression that this annoying documentation of the conversation that sealed Max's fate wasn't going to get him out of prison. Among all the technical business details and scholarly debates, how was he supposed to find whatever it was that had made Shimon decide that Max was endangering his business more than aiding it? It was probably something Max had said. About halfway into the conversation, they began talking about classical music, something about Khachaturian, some composer Shimon liked. There was even a bit that might have amused Eyal under different circumstances. Impressed with Max's musical knowledge, Shimon asked him if he had ever been part of a musical ensemble. Max tried to avoid answering, but finally had to admit that the only ensemble he had ever played in was a rock band he had formed as a teenager, The Marmites.

"That's pretty much the stage in which Simone's credibility levels start to plummet."

"After Max told him that he had played in a rock band called The Marmites?"

"Yes."

Eyal wanted to cry. He felt the new tiny glimmer of hope that had been flickering inside quickly abandoning him. But he knew he had to stay strong. He knew it wouldn't be easy. If Andrey had missed something that Eyal himself hadn't spotted yet, he had to be focused enough to detect it. But the more he read, the more his strength dwindled. Further along in the transcript, they revisited the issue of Max's bonuses. Max must have repeated it because he wasn't sure what they had agreed on, and Shimon explained the figures, only this time Shimon's explanation was apparently said without any intention of following through; he was being dishonest. But what made Shimon change his mind midway through the conversation? Maybe it wasn't in the transcript. Maybe one of Shimon's assistants walked into his office and whispered something in his ear, something that made Shimon suspect that Max was dangerous. Or maybe it was something Shimon remembered in the middle of the conversation. The fact that Shimon went from intending to hire Max to intending to murder him in the middle of a phone conversation might not have to be explained by something that was said during that conversation, it could have been something completely external. It would of course be very convenient to find the explanation in the conversation itself, but who could guarantee it was there? Enough, he had to stop with the useless thoughts, and just assume that the reason for Shimon's shift in attitude could be found in the transcripts, and that if he read closely enough, he'd pick up on it. There was just no other choice. Eyal tried to remember what Galit had told him. She said that everything led back to Eyal. Shimon found Fugu because of Eyal. Eyal was the reason for each of Shimon's moves. If he decided to kill Max, it was probably because he was afraid that Max had information that would find its way to Eyal. But what could it be? Eyal continued to read the transcript, and after another page about Max's bonuses, he suddenly felt dizzy. His breath caught in his chest. He knew he was panicking, but that knowledge didn't help him much.

"Are you okay? Come, sit on the floor, breathe slowly, in and out, in… out…"

Eyal focused on his breathing and after about a minute he started to feel better. He knew he had to sit up, and not give into the urge to fall asleep right there on the floor. At best he would wake up in some police infirmary, and he doubted they'd let him continue reading the transcripts there. Something Shimon was afraid Max would tell Eyal. Eyal had a sudden realization. If it was something Max had told Shimon during the conversation, then Shimon had no way of knowing whether Max had already shared that information with Eyal. Which meant that maybe killing Max didn't help him at all. On the other hand, if it was something Shimon blurted out by mistake during the conversation, something he didn't want Eyal to know, then he knew for sure that Max hadn't shared it with Eyal yet. He had to read what Shimon said to Max around the point in the conversation where his credibility levels started to zigzag.

"Do you want a glass of water?"

"Yes, thank you." Eyal was convinced that Andrey believed in his innocence. He was now behaving more like a merciful nurse than a murder investigator. This kind of opportunity wouldn't repeat itself. He had to pick himself up, read the entire document closely, and find the words that sealed Max's fate. Maybe not the entire document. Maybe he could start one page before the spiral in Shimon's credibility levels occurred. Eyal took a deep breath, picked up the transcript and opened it to the fifth page. There it was again, the part about Peter the Great. Apparently Shimon was a big fan. But as a murderer he didn't come close to the achievements of Peter the Great. And there was the bit about the Marmites. Why would Shimon care that Max played in a rock band? Oh, and there was another amusing fact, Eyal was so nervous, he had missed it the first time. Apparently Shimon had also played in a musical ensemble. Well, maybe that wasn't very surprising, he was a very educated man after all. And it was no rock band, of course, but a classical string quartet, all violins. Something rang a bell. Who played the violin? Of course, Shimon's soldier, the one who committed suicide. And now it turned out that Shimon himself played the violin. Did it mean anything? Something told Eyal that it did. What did Galit tell him? That the story about Shimon's soldier didn't make sense, that a person doesn't turn into a serial killer because his soldier committed suicide. It would make more sense if his soldier turned into a serial killer. But he committed suicide, so he didn't have the opportunity to excel in that area. Or maybe he did? Eyal had a eureka moment, and being a seasoned detective, Andrey noticed.

"What is it, Eyal? Looks like you're on to something."

"I think so. I think I know why Shimon decided in the middle of the conversation that Max was dangerous. But I don't know if it will help my case that much."

"Then why don't you tell me first, because I'm dying to know. Then I'll decide if it helps you or not."

"Okay. You remember Shimon's story about how he left the country, the one I told you? He was a company commander in Golani, his soldier accidently discharged his weapon and was sent to three days in the military prison, where he committed suicide. Shimon was removed from his post because it turned out that the soldier never had gun practice before the shooting range. I think Shimon said something like, the soldier barely knew which end of the gun fired. Shimon couldn't take it, and the moment he was discharged from the army, he disappeared in Brazil without telling anyone. The soldier was a gentle guy, smart, a gifted violinist who could have served close to home but chose to join Golani."

"And how does that help us exactly?"

"In their conversation, Shimon told Max that he used to play in a violin quartet. It took me a moment till the penny dropped. Shimon was never a company commander in Golani. He's a tough guy, no doubt, but he was never a company commander, I'm sure of that."

"So you're saying that Shimon is…?"

"Yes. Shimon was the soldier who got sent to prison. I don't know what kind of abuse he suffered there, but it was probably something that drove him insane. Obviously he didn't commit suicide, but it did make him leave the country without telling anyone, and it probably, to a certain extent, accounts for his charming personality today. You see, after he told Max that he played in a violin quartet, he panicked. He told me that his soldier was a violinist. He didn't tell me that he was the soldier, but he was afraid that I'd make the connection, that I'd understand who he was. The moment he accidently let this detail slip, he wasn't sure what do to with Max. And as the conversation advanced, he became more and more determined to kill Max as soon as possible, before Max blurted out that detail to me in some casual conversation, without even knowing it was important. But what can we do with this information?"

"Wait, don't give up so fast. When did you say this happened to him?"

"He said it was in 1976, I remember. Wait a minute…"

"What is it, Eyal?"

Eyal tried to remember.

"I met Maria in… 2009. And she was twenty-six at the time, I think. And she said Shimon was, how the fuck old was he?!"

"Is it important?"

"It might be. Oh, right, she said he was twenty-five years her senior, if I'm not mistaken. So in 2009, he should have been fifty-one, right? And that means that in 1976, he was… eighteen!"

"So you're saying that if everything you know about the dates and their ages is true, then there really is no way he could have been a commander, he was a rookie."

"Exactly! Although it may all be a bunch of baloney, what do I know."

"Okay, Eyal, it does make sense. So we're looking for a soldier named Shimon Dahan, or Simone, or something along those lines, who was a gifted violinist. Probably in a violin quartet before he was enlisted. He was offered a position close to home, but he chose to be a combat soldier in Golani. After a few days in boot camp he was sent to prison, and then? I assume that after the abuse he was discharged, or something like that."

"Maybe. You think you could really trace Shimon's Israeli roots this way? After so many years? And it's possible that some of the details aren't even true, right?"

"We have to try. I can't guarantee results, but I promise to try. You'll have to go back to lock-up, but I hope that in a few days we'll have some good news."

When Andrey found Izzy and explained the plan, Izzy felt as though he was going to explode. Andrey followed Izzy along the hallway, and felt that Izzy's nerves were making the floor shake. When they entered Andrey's office, Izzy's fancy backgammon set was placed at the edge of the table, and Izzy grabbed it and slammed it against the floor.

"Izzy, calm down."

Izzy stared at the scattered pieces on the floor with shock.

"I'm sorry, Andrey, that was uncalled for."

"It's fine, Izzy, let's pick it all up, you don't want to lose anything."

"Bummer. I hope nothing broke."

After a few moments of gathering the pieces, they sat down, took a few deep breaths and tried to calm down.

"Andrey, I really am sorry about before. But I have to say, again, that this is crazy, it's just crazy. We have a murder suspect with a mountain of evidence against him. If I brought the case right now to the district attorney's office, within a week this guy would be in court, and after maybe a month, he'd be in jail for life. And you want to let him order us around? Wasting our time looking for ghosts?"

"I'm not letting him order us around, there's no need to exaggerate. I got information from him, possible information, and I want to see if it leads anywhere. I think it might be important, even though I'm not sure what we'll be able to do with it."

"You think you got information. You've turned into his puppet, he's pulling your strings, it amazes me how sophisticated he is and how you… you're like some kind of guy in love! You can't entertain any bad thoughts about the object of your love."

"Izzy, do you remember Yaki Hagage?"

"You're going to throw Etti Hagage in my face again? So I made a mistake, the biggest mistake of my life, but you've made mistakes too, you're not as perfect as you think you are, Andrey. I told you to throw Eyal Shiloh in jail the moment we got him. You came with your theory about 'let the young men play before us,' and if you're actually right about him, and he had been in jail from the first moment, then we would have cleared his name by now, and if I'm right, which I'm pretty much sure I am, then Max would be in one piece right now."

"You're right, I was wrong about it, and I don't think I'm perfect. But I'm nearly positive I'm right about him. He didn't murder anyone."

Etti and Yaki Hagage were a happily married couple until one day poor Yaki was found dead in their bed—butchered like a lamb, his neck open and gushing like the Suez Canal, as Izzy so poetically described it. He was thirty, a year older than his wife, and they didn't have kids yet. It was one of those cases that any budding investigator would at least raise the possibility of the wife as a suspect. The beautiful Etti came from a low-income family. Yaki was the son of a major diamond dealer, and worked in the family business. The family had mountains of money. Etti and Yaki lived in a lavish villa in the suburbs of Tel Aviv, not far from Yaki's parents. They owned two cars; Yaki drove a BMW320, and his wife, a slightly more modest Ford. He also owned a stock portfolio worth several million. Most of their assets were under Yaki's name, and by law, were to become hers after his death. The murder weapon, which was found wrapped in a nearby dumpster, was a kitchen knife, from the set Etti often used. There were no fingerprints on it, but the handles of the garbage bag it was found in were covered in her prints. Thus, she had a motive, there was evidence pointing to her, and worst of all, she had no alibi.

According to Etti, that night Yaki had returned home earlier than usual. Etti was still at work. He called her and suggested that instead of her coming home, they would meet at the café at the marina in Herzliya. Eti arrived there straight from work. She was sure Yaki would already be waiting for her there, but he still hadn't shown up. She didn't feel like waiting alone in the café, so she went for a walk in the marina, looking at the restaurants and shops. When it got late and Yaki hadn't arrived yet, she called him, but he didn't answer. On her way home, she got a phone call from the police. It was a problematic story, because she hadn't sat down anywhere, hadn't entered any café or shop. There was no waiter who could have testified to seeing her, no acquaintance, she wasn't even picked up by any of the security cameras. Since she thought they were going to sit outside and enjoy the breeze, Etti had passed the time people-watching, and when she didn't see Yaki, she didn't bother to enter the café or talk to anyone, she just went for a stroll. The moment Izzy heard that story, he told Andrey he thought he didn't smell right. Andrey wasn't sure, but he was actually under the impression that the woman was telling the truth. Izzy decided to turn it into a challenge, and suggested to Andrey that they wager a month's salary. Andrey reluctantly accepted the bet. A few days later, they found a man who testified to seeing Etti entering her house around the time of the murder. He also swore he saw Etti taking out the garbage not long after returning home. Etti was arrested, and everyone was sure she was the murderer. Since Yaki Hagage was found dead in their bed, the assumption was that she butchered him in his sleep. That also would explain how a rather small and delicate woman like Etti had managed to overpower a big, burly man like Yaki. Izzy already told Andrey, with the graciousness of a winner, that he could keep his paycheck. The life of a cop is a financial struggle even without giving up an entire month's paycheck. Hold your horses, Andrey told him, you haven't won yet, don't give away what you haven't earned. Andrey was simply positive that Etti was telling the truth. He just couldn't imagine such a gentle and beautiful woman sneaking up on her sleeping husband and cleaving his throat like that. But he had no proof. Andrey went and spoke to the couple's friends and acquaintances. He talked to numerous people without knowing for sure what he was looking for. He found a few old albums with photos of Etti, the deceased Yaki, and their friends. In one of the albums he saw a photo of two people who looked familiar to him, although he didn't make the connection at first. The photo was perhaps ten years old, maybe more. One of the two people in the photo was their mysterious witness, the one who had seen Etti throwing out the garbage. He had a lot less hair now, went bald rather young, and he had also put on some weight, which made it difficult to identify him in the old photo at first glance, but it was him alright. And that was enough to raise Andrey's suspicion about his testimony. The witness hadn't mentioned his connection to the couple's social circle. The other man in the photo was a childhood friend of Yaki's who was now often seen beside Yaki's mourning parents, looking after them, taking care of all the arrangements no one wanted to make. Talking to Etti, Andrey learned that the childhood friend and Yaki had had a long, close relationship. But something happened in recent years that made them grow apart. Upon closer investigation, Andrey learned that there had been a real rift. The childhood friend wanted to found a joint business that Yaki was supposed to invest in, but Yaki didn't believe in his business plan. The business never materialized, and the childhood friend never forgave him. The childhood friend didn't come from a poor family, but he also didn't grow up rich like Yaki, and he had always envied his privileged childhood.

The childhood friend and the mysterious witness's plan was simple. They stalked Etti, and stole a garbage bag she had thrown into the dumpster the previous day. The childhood friend managed to steal a set of keys from Etti, so he had no problem getting into the house. Since Yaki was home, the alarm never went off. He murdered Yaki, placed the knife in Etti's garbage bag, and returned it to the dumpster. The witness testified to seeing Etti, and the damning evidence piled up against her. The only problem with the plan was that they had no way of ensuring they'd get a piece of the inheritance, despite how "lovingly" the friend looked after Yaki's parents, and after all, getting money out of the family was the whole point of their plan. While tending to them, he also made sure to present them with his old business plan, the one Yaki wouldn't invest in. He presented it as Yaki's final wish, and the parents believed their son's childhood friend, whom they had known since he was five years old. And they were indeed on their way to funding the business he wished to establish. The witness was supposed to join as a business partner, first as a silent partner and later, when they felt the case was over and no one was looking over their shoulder, as a full partner. They were both convicted and were serving a life sentence. Once they got the confessions out of both criminals, Andrey showed Izzy the same magnanimity and told him there was no need to make good on the bet. But Izzy was determined. He threatened Andrey that if he didn't accept the money, he'd just gamble it all away. In the past, Izzy had a gambling problem, and Andrey certainly didn't want to be responsible for Izzy going back to his evil ways. The following month, Andrey bought Izzy so many meals that it was no longer easy to determine who had lost more in the bet. It was obviously a case Izzy didn't like being reminded of.

"Izzy, let me look into it. We'll send him back to lock-up, give me at least three days. It shouldn't be that complicated, we'll talk to the military, they're supposed to keep that data in archives. We'll talk again tomorrow and see where we stand, okay? Don't be angry with me, Izzy, I'm just almost sure that Eyal Shiloh didn't kill anyone and that he's telling the truth, as sure as I was back then, and maybe even more."

"Okay, fine. Send him back to lock-up, and we'll see what we can find."

"Thanks, Izzy."

The phone call Shimon received from Israel at one p.m. alarmed him. He was used to getting his daily reports in the evening. Shimon held the phone in one hand, and a small fork in the other. He had just devoured a plate of fine tortellini, and now there was a plate of smelly French cheeses in front of him, some of which he ate with the small fork, and some that he smeared onto pieces of fresh baguette. It was horrible, he had completely lost any control he had on his appetite. It was as if the more his death grip on the miserable Israeli tightened, the more his crazy gluttony increased. He was hungry all the time. Maybe it's time my body becomes as disfigured as my soul, he thought.

"What's happening, are there any developments?"

The conversation was conducted in English, English with a heavy Italian accent on Shimon's part, of course. He still wasn't sure if any of his people had already figured out where he was born, but the consistency with which he concealed his Israeli identity was in his blood, it was one of his most important safety rules, and he always managed to maintain these rules, expect once.

"I'm not sure, but I think something happened there. He's in custody, but they haven't interrogated him in the past two days, and I think they're working a lead, I don't know what."

"You don't have any clues?"

"The chief investigator, Andrey, met with someone from the military. I think he's some old acquaintance of his, I don't know if it's important."

Shimon took another bite of cheese, put down the fork and sighed. Of course it was important.

"Get ready, we're probably going to have to execute plan B."

"You're serious?"

"I certainly am. I'll fly out to The Maria today."

"You spend most your life on that ship, don't you? Are you going to start sailing south?"

"Yes. Enough chitchat, get to work, there's no time to idle."

"Yes, sir."

Eyal was sent back to lock-up. He felt desperate. He was lucky that first night, he was so tired he couldn't remember falling asleep. The next few nights it took him much longer. He was wound up. On the one hand there seemed to be some hope. But that was based on a lot of assumptions which Eyal wasn't even sure were true. Maybe the year Shimon had given him was wrong. Or maybe it wasn't even his name, maybe it was Zalman or Eldad, or some other name. And maybe it was all one big nonsense. Maybe Shimon made up the entire story. Eyal thought that if it didn't work out, he wouldn't be able to take it anymore. If this last shred of hope shattered, it would only take a few days until he'd be willing to sign a confession. Anything to make them leave him alone. But two days later, he was led into Andrey's office.

"Eyal, I'm happy to inform you that we've tracked down Simone Donadoni's Israeli identity."

"Really?" While it was exactly what Eyal had been praying for, he found it hard to believe that salvation was near.

"Yes, his name is Shimon Ben Simon, rather surprisingly. He was discharged from the military after exactly a week and a half in the Golani Brigade, half of which he had spent in prison. He was abused there, probably sexual abuse, and discharged for good."

"So you've already made the connection to his Italian identity?"

"That will take a bit longer, but I don't think it will be a problem. We have photos and fingerprints. One of his guards in prison was murdered in South America about a year after his discharge. The case went cold, but there should be fingerprints of the murderer, and we'll compare them. Obviously it's not for sure yet, but the information you gave us might lead to closing a thirty-year-old murder case."

"So can I go?"

"Yes. I'm keeping your passport, don't even think about leaving the country. Between you and me, I'm convinced you had nothing to do with these crimes, and I'm shifting the focus of the investigation to Mister Shimon Ben Simon."

"Okay, thank you, Andrey, you were the kindest investigator I could have had. I'm sure that without you I would have been on the fast track to a life sentence. We'll be in touch."

"Eyal, there's something you need to know. Your friend, Max. He isn't dead."

"What?"

"You heard me. He's in a coma. The doctors aren't sure whether he's going to wake up, but they say there's a chance. The explosion didn't kill him."

"How?"

Eyal felt as though he was walking on clouds, and he didn't know whether it was because of the streak of good news or because he was just so incredibly tired. He felt dazed, exhausted and unable to distinguish between reality and fiction, between what had actually happened to him and what he had imagined.

"His phone was wired, the guy who tried to kill him attached the phone to a booby-trapped pouch. He left Max alone in the room and they called him on the rigged phone. Max was about to answer, and then realized just in time that it was a bomb. He stood beside the bed, threw the bomb and jumped to the other side of the room. So the bed shielded most of his body."

"Wow, that's unbelievable, you have no idea how happy I am to hear that."

"Yes, well, don't forget he's not out of the woods yet."

"Right. Okay, I'll get going."

They shook hands like old partners rather than investigator and suspect, and Eyal stepped out of the station and into the street, still finding it difficult to believe he was free.

CHAPTER 16

Eyal walked along the busy street searching for a taxi. His car was still parked in the underground parking lot, not far from his hotel. He wondered how much money he was going to have to pay there. He felt as though he was sleepwalking. He was so tired that everything around him seemed like part of a warped dream. He wasn't sure what made him happier, his near-final release from the nightmare of being accused of murder, or the fact that Max was still alive. In a coma, true, but it was still far better than being dead. He had to call Galit. Suddenly he felt that knot in his stomach again. There was one more very critical thing that no one could promise him—he didn't know whether Galit would stay with him, whether he'd still get to wake up his kids each morning. He turned on his phone and saw that it was already three in the afternoon. But what day was it? He'd been through too many twists and turns these past few days. His brain couldn't handle it, and he was completely disoriented. He dialed Galit's cell number, and after a nerve-racking wait that couldn't have lasted more than five seconds, he heard her voice. She sounded rather calm, not particularly angry. Her voice now sounded to him as pleasant as wind chimes.

"Gin?"

"Galiti? Is everything okay? I was released. It looks like they're not going to charge me with anything, they're shifting the focus of the investigation to our dear Italian-Israeli friend."

"Really? Ahh!" Galit sounded as if she was sobbing.

"Galit?"

"I'm here."

"And Max is alive, did you know?"

"They told you he was dead? Everyone knows he's alive, it was on the news, but he's in a coma, I think he hasn't woken up yet."

"They suspected I was the murderer, so obviously they didn't want me to know he was alive. And also, you told me he was dead, in our phone conversation before the arrest."

"Oh, I'm sorry, that was what they said on the internet at the beginning."

"It doesn't matter."

There was a silence that lasted for about a minute, a heavy, uncomfortable silence.

"Look, Eyal, I'm really happy to hear you're off the hook."

Eyal knew what she was going to say next, and it felt horrible. Could it be that at least in one sense, Shimon was going to win?

"Look, I knew this wouldn't solve anything between us…"

"I need to think, okay? What are you going to do now? Obviously you can come home at least for a shower and to get a few things… I'm sorry, I just need time to think."

"It's okay, Galit, take your time. I'll go to a hotel and get some sleep. I think that even if I go to sleep now I'll only wake up tomorrow morning, and then I'll come to say hi to the kids. Do they know what happened?"

"Not really, I don't think they really understand anything, I hope. Geez, I need to get going if I want to pick them up from kindergarten on time."

"Okay. Tell them that daddy's going to come see them very soon, okay? And that I love them. And I love you too. We'll talk tonight or tomorrow morning."

"Okay, Gin, bye."

"Bye, Galit."

A taxi pulled up next to Eyal.

"Where to?"

"Can you take me to Atarim Square?"

"Of course. Had a rough day, bro?" the driver asked Eyal after he buckled himself in.

"I've had a rough decade."

The driver laughed.

"Yeah, believe me, this government, all they want is to drag you down, I'm telling you..." And he started telling Eyal a story that Eyal didn't really listen to, a combination of his personal tribulations and national problems.

Eyal lowered the visor and looked at himself in the mirror, and while he didn't expect to see the most fresh-looking person, he was astonished by the image staring back at him. A person who had just gotten out of jail, tired, baggy eyes, unshaved. He wished he had stopped to wash his face at the station before leaving, but once Andrey told him he could go, all he wanted was to get out of that place.

"Just look at the ministers of finance here, one's in prison, another's from some other planet, thinks he's a philosopher."

"Yes. Well, he did study philosophy," Eyal said, and wasn't sure how long the driver had been talking to him, and if he had bothered to answer him until now.

"Exactly, you see?"

"Yeah, of course, what's there to say, you're right."

"That's exactly what I'm saying..."

They were on HaYarkon Street now.

"Stop at the corner of Ben Gurion, okay?"

"Sure, bro. Pleasure talking to someone who gets it."

"Yeah, sure. Thanks."

Eyal tipped the driver generously, although he wasn't sure why. Maybe he felt the need to compensate him for his inattentiveness, although it seemed the driver was very impressed with Eyal's listening skills. He walked the short distance to the decrepit square, and paused to look at the sea. But why did he stop there? For some reason he thought he had to take the car out of the parking lot, when in fact he had nowhere to drive to. And more than anything, he just needed to sleep now.

The breeze felt nice. Maybe instead of going to his hotel room he'd stretch out on a beach chair, even though the idea of sleeping outside like that, exposed to all types of dangers, seemed kind of scary. Eyal had certainly lost his trust in the world. His phone rang. Blocked number.

"Hello?"

"My dear Mister Shiloh."

"Shimon?" What did that mother fucker want from him now?!

"My people have your daughter. Listen to me closely…"

"Why? I'm probably going to spend the rest of my life in prison, what else do you want?"

Eyal searched for a place to sit, and when he couldn't find one, he simply collapsed on the floor. He couldn't bear any more of this.

"I don't know who you think you're fooling, Eyal. If you really were a suspect in a double homicide you wouldn't be out and about with your phone right now. I have eyes on you at all times. I don't know why exactly, but the police apparently decided to believe your dubious version. Go to the marina in Herzliya and wait for instructions. Remember, I'm following you, I know you're sitting at Atarim Square right now, that you took a taxi from the police station. Don't talk to anyone. Don't talk on your phone, either. I'm monitoring it. There's software that can monitor smartphones, as I'm sure you know. Your wife is going to call you in a minute, when she finds out that someone already picked up your precious daughter from kindergarten. You will not take her call. Under any circumstances. Your car is in Gan London parking lot, second floor, you'll pay at the machine and exit without talking to anyone. When you arrive at the marina, you'll have to pass their security guard to enter. Make it short and sweet. I'll have a person following you there, so no slipping any notes to the guard, no talking to him. Wait there in front of the boats. Someone will come get you."

"Okay." Wonderful. Eyal's head was busy coming up with a sentence he could have said to Shimon to express his state of mind. He wanted to murder the bastard. But he had Meital. Eyal knew he had to do something. But what? He barely had the strength to get up. He didn't know how he would get to his car and make it to the marina. And how the hell did the kindergarten teachers let this happen? Maybe someone got in, quickly grabbed her and ran off. It was impossible that Dikla the kindergarten teacher would just let some stranger take Meitali. How did this shit happen? He had to pull himself together.

"Sir, do you need some help?"

A cute teenager was standing above him, staring at him.

"What? No, I'm fine, thank you."

"You're sure we can't help you up?"

Now her friend was standing there as well. Both were very sweet, maybe fourteen.

"I think I might be a bit heavy for you girls."

"I don't think so!" one of them said, and they both reached out and grabbed Eyal, pulling him up and giggling. Eyal was up on his feet when his phone rang.

"Thank you, you two are very sweet." Good, he was suddenly feeling reenergized now. But of course nothing had changed, he was still drowning in a sea of shit, as Galit used to say so poetically.

"Shimon?"

"One more mistake, and your daughter's going to be the one who pays."

"Fine, fine, I'm heading toward the marina." He hung up.

"Fifty shekels for your bottle of water and cinnamon Danish," Eyal said. He took out a fifty-shekel bill and gave it to them.

"Why don't you just go to the shop?"

"I don't have time, I have to get out of here. Thanks, girls, you saved my life." He took the water and the Danish, which the girls had already bitten into, but he didn't care. He had to eat and drink some water, and wash his face. He went down to the parking lot, only to remember that his car wasn't there. Shimon told him it was in the Gan London parking lot, in front of Bugrashov Street. Eyal started walking along the boardwalk. He devoured the pastry in two seconds, drank half of the water and poured the other half on his face, then started running toward the parking lot. At least he was still in decent shape. He arrived at the parking lot panting. He paid and got into his car, and felt the exhaustion numb his body again. Was it even legal to drive when you're that tired? There were laws against drunk driving, but what about driving under extreme exhaustion? Was it possible that Shimon's men actually had Meital? Only now the true meaning of this started to sink in. Until now he was too busy getting himself on his feet and to the car. He drove up the spiral floors of the parking lot, which made him lightheaded. He almost drove into the barrier because he forgot he had to pay, but at least that woke him up a bit. Eyal sped past HaYarkon Street, turned onto the bridge above Namir Street, and was finally on North Ayalon Highway. His phone rang; it was Galit. He was about to answer, and just in time remembered what Shimon had told him. The phone slipped from his hand, he mumbled a curse, and noticed that the drivers behind were honking at him. The car was swerving and he was about to crash into the concrete wall, but he managed to gain control of the vehicle in time. Once again he was completely awake, but it was the nervous type of alertness of a man who wasn't in full control of his actions. Galit called again and again, the phone wouldn't stop ringing, and Eyal cursed again. Fucking piece of no balls shit, that Shimon. Eyal heard the sound of a helicopter above, and it immediately reminded him of Daniel, who always loved looking at helicopters and planes. The helicopter was flying very close above him, it was amazing, a blue executive helicopter with a darker blue stripe above the doors. This helicopter all but shouted 'I belong to a rich man.' Maybe it was Shimon's helicopter. Maybe it was part of the taskforce stalking him. It seemed that Shimon had men and gadgets everywhere. Eyal felt that he didn't stand a chance. The helicopter had passed Eyal twice already. By now he had no doubt. He had never seen such a helicopter in Israel before, and now he was seeing it twice in one day? But maybe he was imagining things. Maybe it didn't mean anything. He arrived at the entrance to Herzliya, and was suddenly gripped by real panic. Fucking idiot. He was so busy with his stupid theories, feeling sorry for himself, that he forgot the most important thing. How was he going to let someone know about his situation? There had to be a way. But how? Galit would only go to the police, if she hadn't already. But Eyal had to explain to them what this was all about. And he had to do it without this helicopter and god knows what other agents or robots following him finding out. The empty water bottle he had bought from the two girls was resting next to him, and he thought in despair, maybe he'd send a message in a bottle, like Sting. Yes! Eyal suddenly realized it wasn't such a terrible idea.

He stood at the traffic light of the first intersection in Herzliya and rummaged through his briefcase. He took out a pen and notepad and scribbled something under the wheel, so no one would see. He examined the result. Someone was honking behind him, the light had turned green. He drove ahead with screeching wheels. Shimon mustn't suspect, if he wasn't already suspicious. But so far Shimon hadn't called again. Then again, if Shimon decided to go through with his demonic scheme, maybe he wouldn't bother calling. But Shimon wanted Eyal, killing a little girl wasn't his plan. Eyal had to believe that. He had to believe he stood a chance.

Eyal rolled down the two front windows. Would that arouse suspicion? But he had no choice, if he wanted to pass the bottle to someone, he had to have his windows down. He crumpled the piece of paper and pushed it into the bottle. The bottle was empty but still damp inside, and he hoped it wouldn't smudge the writing. He screwed the cap back on. He was at the last traffic light before the marina. To his left stood a taxi with its window open. It was now or never. He threw the bottle into the taxi, and it hit the driver's face. Eyal yelled 'Sorry!' and sped off. He had just committed numerous traffic offenses—was it possible that Shimon didn't notice? But at least the helicopter was no longer hovering above him. It might have gone well. And it might not have. He had no way of knowing. It was possible that the angry driver tossed the bottle out of the window right after it hit him. Why did Eyal yell 'sorry'? What a moron. If he'd already taken the chance of saying something, he should have screamed 'help.' But it was done, no use thinking about it. The phone rang. It was Shimon.

"Yes?"

"Ten meters ahead you'll see a parking space. Park and walk straight to the marina."

"Okay."

"Are you sure it was a good idea to let him walk?" Izzy asked Andrey. They were sitting in Andrey's office.

"Izzy, if that guy murdered someone, I'll chop my dick off and eat it in a bun with ketchup."

"Come on, no need to go that far. I agree with you that there were some interesting developments in the past twenty-four hours. And I agree that most likely it isn't him, but I'm still not a hundred percent sure. Last time you let him go, you agreed with me it was a mistake."

"Did you ever wonder why they mutilated that poor woman's body like that? Maybe it was just so we wouldn't be able to know if she'd ever been pregnant. Thought about that?"

"You already told me that before, but then why is there a kid registered as hers in Italy?"

"I don't know. Maybe Shimon Ben Simon paid someone off to fake that registration. I can't believe any of the evidence we have against Eyal Shiloh anymore. I'm telling you, Izzy, it's all been forged. We've been trying to locate that kid for days, and there's no kid. It's pretty remarkable, isn't it? After all, this kid is supposed to be his motive, but there's no documentation of the kid anywhere."

"You're probably right, as always, Andrey the brilliant backgammon player. But I'm telling you, your kindness is going to be the end of you one day. Really, Andrey, I'm only saying this because I love you, there's no other reason."

"I love you too, Izzy. I've already called the Italians. Turns out they've been following this Donadoni for quite a while now, they like him for a lot crimes but can't pin anything on him."

"No shit. God, I'm dying to nail the bastard and move on, I'm sick of this case."

Andrey's phone rang.

"Andrey here."

"Am I talking to Superintendent Andrey Friedman?"

"That's me. How can I help you?"

"About five minutes ago I was standing at a traffic light in Herzliya with my window open, and suddenly someone threw a bottle at me from the parallel car. One of those plastic water bottles, you know? But without water."

"I'm sure there's a community police station somewhere near you, you can complain there if you want, I can give you the..."

"No, no, listen for a moment, this is important. You're Superintendent Friedman, right?"

"Yes, I've already told you I am." Andrey felt his patience running out.

"There was a note inside the bottle. A message for you. Are you listening?"

"Yes."

"My name is Eyal Shiloh. My daughter has been kidnapped. I'm on the way to the marina in Herzliya. I think Shimon is going to get me on a boat. I'm being followed and I'm not allowed to use my phone. Please forward this message to Superintendent Andrey Friedman at... Then he wrote down your number. Does this mean anything to you?"

Andrey covered the mouthpiece and said to Izzy, "This is some unbelievable shit."

"What is it?"

"You won't believe that you just said we should move on. Forget about it."

Andrey returned to the man on the phone. "Thank you very much, you're a good citizen. You have nothing to worry about, and I don't want to trouble you, but this is very important. I'm going to pass you on to someone who'll take your details. Again, you have nothing to worry about. You might even receive an award. But you will also be asked to go the police station near your house and hand in that bottle, okay? Thank you very much."

CHAPTER 17

At the marina, Eyal sat in front of the boats and waited. It was amazing how quickly he had returned to hell after a short departure from it. But there was no choice. He received an SMS, and assumed he was allowed to read messages. He opened it and saw a photo of Meital, looking scared in the back seat of a car. At least they put her in a booster seat. There was a small piece of paper next to her, reading—Hello Eyal. Motherfuckers. Eyal zoomed in on his daughter's face. She looked frightened but unharmed. At least that. He tried to zoom in on her surroundings, but apart from the fabric of the booster seat he couldn't make out anything else. Galit kept calling him, but obviously he couldn't answer. Eyal looked at the long rows of boats, most of them not particularly large, but there were a few pretty fancy yachts. Was he about to board one?

"Eyal?"

"Yes…"

Three men were approaching him. One was handsome and had a pleasant appearance, maybe a little insecure. The other, who was probably in charge, looked anything but pleasant. The third, who was the oldest—probably around fifty—seemed eager to get out of there, because his foot kept tapping the floor nervously.

"I just need your phone. Problems with the boat's navigation system. You'll get it back, don't worry."

"Fine." But why did they need it? They couldn't track the phone in the middle of the ocean. Once he drew away from the cell companies' antennas the phone would be useless. They actually should have taken his phone sooner, because now at least the police would be able to know that he made it to the marina in Herzliya. Maybe they wanted the phone to see who Eyal had called? Maybe Shimon was lying when he said he had software that could monitor the phone's activity. Now they were going to check if Eyal had made any calls since he was informed of Meital's kidnapping. He hadn't. But he tried to think if there was any important information on his phone, information he wouldn't want Shimon to have. Eyal mostly regretted the photo of Meital. And a million other photos he had taken and hadn't downloaded to the computer. But obviously he had no choice. If there were any other options apart from complete cooperation, he wouldn't have been there. He handed the phone to the older fellow, who immediately disappeared with it. That was probably the last time he'd see his phone, Eyal thought sadly.

"Okay, Gal, we're in your hands."

"Okay. Hi. I'm Gal, I'll be, your... chauffeur, I guess you could say."

Eyal wondered whether there was anything he could do expect board the boat. Was he actually going to step onto a boat that would take him to god knows where, without even trying to resist? Maybe these guys didn't know anything, maybe he could try talking to them. But eventually every idea he had hit the same obstacle—he was obligated to cooperate fully in order to protect his daughter, and any small mistake could place her in harm's way. His instincts told him that the chauffeur was just a clueless employee, his boss probably knew more, or at least saw himself as authorized to apply violence against Eyal. Maybe even to shoot him, who knew.

"Are we going on the boat?"

"Yes."

"Where are we sailing to?"

"To Mister Donadoni, of course."

"Where is he?"

"On his yacht. Mega yacht, actually. You'll be very impressed. You're lucky, not everyone gets to be invited there. Believe me, each girl on that yacht is a ten."

"I'm sure."

"Me and my big mouth."

"Don't worry, I won't tell anyone." There was something ridiculous about this conversation when the guard was walking three feet behind them. He didn't bother responding.

They boarded the boat, which was a rather standard motorboat. Thirty feet, maybe a bit longer, a small cabin for the captain, a tarp roof and two long wooden benches facing each other. Eyal and his guard sat in the back.

"Gal, we need a little privacy, okay?"

"Sure." Gal entered the cabin up front.

Once Gal disappeared and the boat began sailing, the guard whipped out a gun. No more pretending. He sat on the bench in front of him, maybe ten feet from Eyal.

"I'm not going to try anything, you have my daughter. If I thought I had other options I wouldn't have come here."

"Whatever you say, man." The gun remained pointing at him.

"I hope you remember that your boss wants me alive. With all the waves and rocking, the gun might go off by mistake."

"I don't make mistakes. The sea feels rather quiet, don't you think?" He seemed very pleased with himself. All that was left for Eyal was to try to believe him, look at the view, and forget about the gun. He didn't even know if Shimon actually did want him alive. But he did know that he could have killed him numerous times by now. Max was just lucky. And they probably wouldn't have this Gal character on board if they wanted to kill him. On the other hand, Eyal could easily identify this guy later, so why would he agree to expose himself like this? Maybe Shimon had promised him that Eyal wouldn't pose a problem after this little trip.

They started pulling away from Herzliya. Tel Aviv's skyline revealed itself before him, growing more and more distant, and there was a nice breeze. Eyal couldn't help thinking that he might be able to overpower his guard. It had to be difficult to remain alert with the lulling motion of the waves. And then what? Sneak onto Shimon's yacht and kill him? Obviously all these plans were useless. He didn't even know where they were keeping his daughter. He also didn't know where Shimon's yacht was. Eyal looked at the water and remembered a movie he once saw about an American girl who was attacked by a shark. She went speed-boating with her boyfriend, maybe twelve miles off shore, into the ocean. And then for some reason they decided it was safe enough for her to float on the water and sunbathe. Her boyfriend decided to film her, so there was also a rather rare documentation of the attack. Suddenly a great white shark emerged, the most horrible monster from the depths of the ocean. No blood was seen, only the massive white body and the huge triangular fin next to the screaming girl. Then the boyfriend stopped filming and tried to help her. The shark tore one of her legs off, and then, apparently deciding it didn't taste very good, he just disappeared. The girl was saved, but lost a leg.

"We're close."

Eyal lost all sense of time. How long had they been sailing? Maybe an hour? A long vessel appeared on the horizon, and as they drew closer, Eyal was under the impression that a giant missile lay in the water before them.

The closer they got the more details he could make out, and Eyal could now see how impressive the yacht was. He estimated its length at somewhere around three hundred feet. At the rear of the yacht, which was also its lowest point, stood a helicopter, painted entirely in a shiny blue. Mister Donadoni's private helicopter? Maybe it was part of an entire fleet. It must have been the helicopter that had followed him earlier. Everything was shiny. The body of the yacht was a mosaic of black and white. In the back was a series of leveled decks. They curved slightly in a kind of space-ship-like design, with arched windows. Up front the structure slanted in a way that reminded Eyal of a fighter jet, which gave the entire yacht a sort of high-techy look.

"What are you smiling about, anything funny?"

"No, not at all." The truth was that Eyal was smiling because he remembered the cliché about men buying big cars or big yachts or big dogs—anything big, really—to compensate for their small dick. What kind of normal person would even need such a boat? Was it possible that all those rich tycoons who bought yachts and planes were actually compensating for some insecurity? But Eyal had met some very rich businessmen throughout his career, and he knew that was nonsense. Most of them were very impressive people, and if there was some frightened little boy hiding inside them, he was hiding so deep that they had probably forgotten he ever existed. If anything characterized people who bought such yachts, it was a huge appetite for life, not insecurity. Shimon must also have had a big appetite, but it seemed to Eyal that there was something empty in it. Maybe because Eyal had the feeling that Shimon didn't actually enjoy his life. Eyal never saw in Shimon that sense of vitality that Jeff projected when biting into a good steak.

"We'll be there in a moment."

Eyal was awoken from his reveries and noticed a surprising detail, perhaps even creepy. The name of the yacht was The Maria. Could it be that here, on this lavish ship, his life was going to end? Better avoid such thoughts. He also couldn't afford to think about Meital now. He had to try to be positive. After all, he had been in dangerous situations before, stakeouts in Lebanon, for example, and he came out alive, so why not now? But he had never felt so alone as he did at this moment.

"Impressive, huh?" His guard, still pointing his gun at him, said in a tone that was almost friendly.

"Is it the biggest yacht in the world?"

"Not at all, not even in the top ten. The biggest yacht belongs to the ruler of Dubai. It's named Dubai, and I think it's about a hundred and fifty feet longer than The Maria."

If Eyal survived this event, this conversation would go down in his memory as the most macabre he'd ever had. This man was talking to him like a tour guide trying to impress a tourist with the marvel in front of him, all while pointing a gun to his head.

"Do you know why he called it The Maria?"

"No. Do you?"

Eyal remembered that Simone Donadoni had no official contact with Maria, nothing that was documented.

"No. How much does something like this cost?" Eyal tried to focus on the curiosity the ship stirred in him in order to forget about everything else. He was hoping that the rescue teams would be there soon. But then what? What would happen to Meital when they arrived? If they ever arrived. Maybe as soon as Shimon heard the police sirens he'd give the order. But what could Eyal do? Maybe it was a mistake to try to inform Andrey where he was. At least he knew that Andrey was no fool, he would surely understand the dangers involved. Maybe Andrey could locate Meital?

"I assume more than a hundred million dollars. Maybe a hundred and fifty?"

"It's amazing that I never saw Shimon's name on any of those billionaire lists."

"Shimon? You're talking about Simone Donadoni, I assume."

"Yes, I tend to think about people's names in their Hebrew versions."

"No kidding. Well, anyway, the guy doesn't like publicity, that's for sure."

They approached the boat, which now filled their entire field of vision. Luckily the sea was rather peaceful, but for some reason, even the modest rocking, especially as they approached the large vessel, almost made Eyal throw up. They clung to the side of the ship, and tied the small boat against it. Above them a type of accordion-like structure appeared and began to unfold into a staircase.

"Okay, you go up the stairs, they're waiting for you."

"Have a nice day," Eyal said, and the guard winked at him while pointing his gun at the staircase.

Eyal climbed onto the stern of the ship. The helicopter was now only a few feet away from him. It was a beautiful helicopter. Astonishing. But how could you enjoy it when you were that fat? He wondered what was happening with Meital. She was probably terrified. Eyal felt something he hadn't felt since he was a child. That wave that surges up the throat and threatens to burst out in the form of tears. He wanted to cry, but he knew he had to think about what he was going to do, and not about how miserable his daughter must be. Recently she had been having horrible tantrums. Eyal read that these tantrums, which start around the age of two, are an important part of a child's development. And yet it amazed him, the rage that was pent up in such a small and sweet girl. Meital, are you angry at the doll? Eyal would ask after yet another toy was thrown in rage. But he also sometimes lost his temper during these outbursts. He never raised a hand against Meital, but he had started to understand how people could lose control and do things that should never be done. And now Meital was with people who didn't care about her at all. People who had already committed murder. One order from Shimon and they might kill her too. And maybe they would abuse her without any orders. Just out of anger or boredom. He had to get her home. But how?

"Hello, Eyal. My name is Paulo. Welcome aboard The Maria." The man in front of him spoke English with an Italian accent.

"Thank you."

And what about this man? Eyal was inclined to think that most of these people didn't know. After all, Shimon had so many employees, probably only a very small group was in on his plans. Otherwise information would have been spilled. On the other hand, to carry out such complicated crimes you probably needed many people.

They climbed from the lower level where the helicopter was to the higher deck. Eyal saw a round pool with a diameter of about thirty feet. Two Asian girls were inside the pool, both incredibly attractive. A black man sat next to them, and three more girls and three men were sunbathing beside the pool. Everyone looked as though they had just stepped out of a fashion magazine. Several glasses of Champagne surrounded them, and a waiter arrived with a tray of finger sandwiches. It was amazing. He wondered if Maria was ever on this boat named after her by the very man who had her murdered. Why did Shimon need all this? Maybe it just made him feel good to be surrounded by beautiful people. Did he occasionally invite these girls to his room? Were they also familiar with his bizarre fetishes?

Eyal's pants were suddenly wet.

"Come on, baby, what are you waiting for?"

The girl who splashed water on him was studying him with mischievous eyes. She looked Chinese. She had long black hair all the way down to her ass, an amazing body in a tiny bikini and a wonderful smile. What did she know about the ship she was on? Probably nothing, just a pretty girl who was invited on a cruise. Maybe she had even been an escort girl in the former agency. Eyal tried to say something to her, but his voice wouldn't produce sound. He couldn't even manage to smile. This Chinese girl could be in for the shock of her life. All she wanted was her Champagne, she wasn't expecting police helicopters and coastguard boats. And maybe Eyal was just being delusional. Maybe there'd be no helicopters coming for him.

"Mister Donadoni asked me to make sure you take a shower."

"Really?"

They took the stairs to a higher deck and passed through a long hallway. Paulo opened a door. They walked into a room with mirrored walls. An elegant outfit hung on a hook by the door. The room was empty but for the clothes, a single chair and a pair of polished shoes. There was another door, which Eyal assumed led to the bathroom. Then he noticed there was also a clock on the wall.

"If you would kindly remove your clothes and give them to me. You have half an hour to shower, shave and get dressed."

"Take my clothes off now?"

"I hope you'll forgive me, but yes."

Eyal got undressed. He stood naked as a newborn next the embarrassed Paulo. Eyal didn't have enough energy to feel embarrassed.

"The watch, too. I'm sorry."

No gadgets in the meeting with Shimon. Was it possible that he knew about the special phone Max had on him?

"It was a gift from my wife, please try to take good care of it." Eyal remembered stories about watches that stopped ticking the moment their owner's heart stopped beating. He doubted this watch would honor him with such a noble gesture.

"Of course. I'll be waiting for you outside."

Eyal nodded. He took a deep breath and opened the door, which indeed led to the bathroom. It was a very elegant bathroom, befitting a five star hotel. And like in hotels, small soaps and toiletries stood by the sink. Eyal felt the exhaustion in his bones again. It was odd, as if it came in waves. Every time his body recovered, a worse wave came. Eyal wanted to fill the bathtub with bubble bath, lie down inside the warm water and never get out. Enough, he had to rush. If not to meet Shimon's schedule, then at least to keep himself awake. Eyal was afraid that if he surrendered to his exhaustion, no force would be strong enough to wake him up again. He shaved, took a quick a shower, used the aftershave by the sink—Fendi, which smelled better than anything he had ever used—and got dressed. It was incredible. The clothes fit him perfectly. Eyal felt the fabric of the suit and the tie, and knew that these were clothes of a quality he had never felt against his skin. The shoes were beautifully designed and also fit him perfectly. Galit would have been pleased. He looked at himself in the mirror. It was amazing. He had never looked so elegant in his life. And so ill. He looked tired, beat. The shave had only slightly improved his appearance. He approached the door and discovered, unsurprisingly, that it was locked. He knocked on it and it immediately opened.

"You're five minutes ahead of schedule. Mister Donadoni will be pleased."

"The commander likes meeting deadlines, huh?" Eyal said, and immediately regretted it. Shimon could be listening to every word that came out of his mouth, and he probably wouldn't like the sarcastic comment about his fictitious military past. Paulo didn't respond.

"Come with me, please."

Eyal entered a large room, Shimon's room, only this time two thugs entered with him. They didn't do anything, just stood at each side of the door and ordered Eyal to take a seat in front of Shimon. Shimon had gained weight, there was no doubt about it. No suit could conceal the horror now. He sat behind the large, elegant desk on a giant executive chair that must have been custom made for his new dimensions. The computer mouse was resting on a small tray attached to the desk with a mechanical arm, because Shimon's hands could no longer reach the desk. This room was obviously much smaller than the room in the mansion, but it was just as fancy—every corner was covered in expensive wood. Similar to his house in Bellagio, two stylish libraries stood against the long walls, one facing the other, brimming with books. Behind Shimon there was a window with a panoramic view of the stern and the sea behind it, and on the wall in front of the desk, between the two libraries, was a giant flat screen that displayed one of the rooms on the boat. There was an empty double bed inside the room, two bedside tables, and a bottle of Champagne resting inside an ice bucket.

"Welcome, Eyal, come, have a seat."

Shimon's politeness didn't surprise Eyal. It was much like last time, as if everything was just dandy between them.

"You kidnapped my daughter. You kidnapped me too, come to think of it. So why bother being so polite?"

"It's just more civilized this way, don't you think?"

"I think I want my daughter back. A three-year-old. You have no conscience."

"We'll see what we can do about that. Come, sit."

Eyal wanted to leap across the table and tear the motherfucker into pieces, or at least curse his fat ass, but he knew the best thing would be to try and have the polite conversation Shimon wanted, to drag things out, and maybe the rescue teams would arrive before Shimon threw him overboard, who knew. And of course, it was obvious the two thugs behind him would shoot him if he so much as tried anything. Eyal heard voices. He looked at the screen behind him and saw that the Chinese girl from the pool had entered the room with her African boyfriend.

"Sherri Han. Amazing girl, don't you think? I saw she was pretty into you. Once again you've proved your charm."

"Do they know they're being watched?"

"They're enjoying life. Here, we can have a glass of Champagne with them."

The African man poured two glasses of Champagne, and he and Sherri leaned back against the headrest and drank away. Eyal was horrified by the thought of what was about to happen. He really didn't want to see them fucking right now.

"You think I'm nuts, don't you?"

"After you kidnapped my daughter, you don't actually expect me to deny it, do you?"

"Your daughter is safe and sound."

Shimon had lied to Eyal more than once, and yet, it felt good to hear.

"Why can't you believe my love for Maria? Do you think I'm too fat to love someone?"

It was so bizarre that Eyal suspected his instincts were playing tricks on him. Was he really about to talk to Shimon about love?

"I think you need a shrink. If you let my daughter go, maybe my wife would be willing to treat you."

"And if it's your opinion I'm interested in, and not your wife's?"

Good god, it seemed that Eyal really was going to have to play the role of shrink. He had to do anything he could to pacify that fat bastard.

"I don't think this is about your weight. I just think that the kind of arrangement you had with Maria meant you had to sacrifice something."

"And yet. You know that Maria is something we both have in common."

"If you say so." The tiny fact that Shimon had Maria's bones crushed must have slipped his mind for a moment.

"It might sound odd to you that a husband could feel such kinship to the lover, but it's the truth, you're the only person other than me who truly loved Maria."

Interesting. He actually thought Shimon was being honest. Was that the reason he hadn't killed him so far? Eyal had assumed this entire time that his meeting with Maria was Shimon's ultimate reason to kill him, but perhaps it was also the reason he had kept him alive.

"What do you have to say about that? I'll tell you again, I love hearing your opinion."

"You really want to know?"

"I really do."

"There's something to what you're saying, but obviously you're romanticizing it. You weren't exactly her husband, not in the traditional sense of the word, and I wasn't exactly her lover."

"So, if we pursue that line of thought, you were much more a lover to her than I was a husband, right? A lover for a very short period, granted, but that night you were her lover in every way, and not a client, right?"

"Yes, that's true."

The fact that Eyal was conducting such a relaxed conversation with his daughter's captor was taking its toll on him. Despite the room smelling like a luxury lounge, his nostrils were filled with the smell of the ocean. He felt as though some kind of slippery sea creature was making its way up his throat, and he was afraid he might vomit any minute.

"He probably fucked and wrote at the same time, right?" Shimon said and laughed. "That's what I think." When Shimon laughed, his giant body shook.

"What?" Since he was so tired, Eyal wasn't sure if he had missed part of the conversation, or if Shimon had just gone completely crazy.

"Forgive me, this has been happening to me lately, I forget the world can't hear my thoughts. You see that elegant series of books over there?"

"Uh-huh."

"Georges Simenon. You like Georges Simenon, right?"

"How did you know?" Eyal was horrified. Maybe one of Shimon's men had broken into his apartment and scanned his bookshelves? But what did it really matter, the motherfucker had his daughter, nothing could be worse than that. Shimon ignored the question.

"They say he wrote four hundred books and slept with ten thousand women. Not bad, huh?"

"Uh-huuuh."

"I'm sorry. I guess I'm no longer fit for human interaction. But I'd like to show you what I can still do with people."

Eyal sneezed, hawking phlegm into his hand.

"Here, have a tissue." Amazing how polite that bastard was. He was just a lonely fat ass looking for a friend. Eyal took a big pile of tissues, turned around and tried to throw up into it, but only a little more phlegm came out. The huge screen was now in front of his face. The African man was hugging the Chinese woman's shoulder, and his hand strolled along the hem of her short nighty, gently lifting it up her thigh. She moaned softly. Eyal really didn't want to see this, but at least it alleviated his nausea for some reason.

"Would you mind changing stations? I really don't want to see them."

"Whatever you want! You see, when you ask politely, you get a polite response."

Now there was a picture of the pool, filled with all those good-looking people. At least it didn't seem like anyone there was about to fuck.

Shimon whispered something into the intercom and the butler arrived after a moment, the same butler from Bellagio. He was carrying several black bags.

Eyal looked at the bags with apprehension. What surprises were in them? So far all the surprises Shimon had arranged for him were bad ones, nothing nice.

"What do you think is in these bags?"

"I have no idea."

"How about we have a little quiz. Since you refused to take a DNA test, we'll have to take your word that you're not little Dino's father. So let's find the father."

"Huh?" It seemed that there was no point reminding Shimon that he had already denied any connection to the kid.

"Open the bags. It's essential if you want to succeed in your task. It's important to succeed in tasks, right, soldier?"

"Yes, sir." It was incredible how this frustrated Golani soldier, this violated soldier, liked to play mind games. It was amazing how full of shit he was. Eyal felt weary. He opened one of the bags, and the first thing he saw was a photo of a man. It was the first of a stack of large photos, approximately eight by twelve inches. The man in the first photo was very handsome, the photo showed in him full length, walking down a street in a fancy suit and an elegant briefcase in his hand. He was fair-skinned but with dark hair and large dark eyes, and the signs on the street seemed to be in Indian. The next photo was of Dino, the child who was supposed to be Maria's, in a similar pose, also in a suit. It was just like the set of photos he was shown, the one comparing the kid to Eyal. But while the kid looked like Eyal, he looked nothing like this man. No resemblance whatsoever. There were more photos comparing the kid to the man. Just like his set.

"Very nice, what exactly do you want me to do with this? Doesn't look much like his dad, huh?"

"Maybe not. We have many more bags here with clients of Maria from around the relevant period. Would you like to hear some information about this man?"

"I'm dying to. He's Indian, this guy?"

"Indeed, a Muslim Indian, from Tamil Nadu. His name is Ibrahim Amat."

"And he came to Israel and he was Maria's client?"

"Don't let your prejudices guide you. Did you know that before the British mandate, India was ruled by Muslim dynasties?"

"The Mogul Empire?"

"Right. It was a Muslim ruler that built the Taj Mahal, for instance."

"Well kudos to him."

"Don't underestimate it. Anyway, if we return to our matter, Ibrahim was a diamond dealer, which is why he frequently traveled to Israel. I assume you know that Israel is a very large diamond trade center."

"Was? He's no longer alive?"

"Listen to the story, it's an interesting one. Ibrahim had a big family, seven brothers and sisters. Among them, a younger, foolish brother named

Sharif. Sharif, the fool, was addicted to drugs. Since he was already well-known in India, and the police kept harassing him and he was tired of counting on his brothers and parents to pay the cops off every time he got into trouble, and since he really did come from a rich family and he could afford it, Sharif started traveling across Asia. He settled in Sihanoukville, a Cambodian beach town that has a lot of gambling and rather diverse sex services, as well as a nice amount of drugs—a match made in heaven for our friend Sharif. He stayed there for a while until he got into trouble with some local mobsters who claimed he owed them money for drugs, and he had to escape. He spent some time in Ho Chi Minh City, until he got himself into trouble again, this time with the authorities, and his family had to bribe local figures to get him out of there. Despite all their efforts to get him to come home and get him settled in a nice job in which he wouldn't have to do anything but would still get a fat paycheck, and they even arranged a pretty bride for him, he decided to go to China, to Shanghai, looking for more fun. Shanghai, as you probably know, is a huge city, about twenty million people. There's also a small community of people from Tamil Nadu, and it wasn't long before news about the wayward son's shenanigans made its way to his family. Now, China is a serious place. The Chinese execute drug dealers. Half of the countries in Asia do as well, but the Chinese don't fool around, and it was decided that the successful son, Ibrahim, would go get his stupid brother out of China before he got into some serious trouble. Unfortunately, Samir, a friend of Sharif who told Ibrahim he could help locate him, joined the trip. Ibrahim and his precious family didn't know that Samir himself was a walking disaster, a drug dealer who thought that Ibrahim's good reputation would help him get into China and make bucketloads of money over there. After all, Shanghai is where everything happens today. But of course, once they stepped foot in China, they were both arrested, and the police assumed that Ibrahim was Samir's partner, a drug dealer himself. Things went down so fast that even Ibrahim's well-connected family couldn't do a thing. He spent a week in a Chinese prison not far from Shanghai, and met his death in that same prison with Samir. They both got a bullet to the back of their heads. That's how the Chinese handle drug dealers, I've told you that, right? Anyway, Sharif made it home in time for his brother's funeral, alive and well, in case you were worried."

"Is that a real story?" Eyal was surprised by the level of interest the story managed to stir in him. His daughter was in the hands of this filthy fat fuck, god knows where he was keeping her, and he himself might be facing a fate similar to that of poor Ibrahim. And yet he still found himself full of sympathy toward the handsome young Indian, who might have been with Maria once, and met his death in such odd circumstances. Or maybe not? Maybe the man didn't even exist.

Eyal opened the second bag and found another stack of photos.

"Chinese? Maybe he executed Ibrahim?"

"Thai, actually. But Thai of Chinese descent, Aroon Suttirat."

"What's his story?" At least he was getting to hear some interesting stories, that was something.

"Ah, Aroon, his nickname was Kung, which means shrimp in Thai. The Thai have funny nicknames. Anyway, he was a contact guy for Western businessmen who came to Thailand. He'd help them with the authorities, sometimes help them find Thai businesses that were right for them, sometimes even arranged for them a nice girl, or boy, if they wanted. He spent five years in the States as a kid, and spoke English like a native as well as Thai, and pretty good Chinese as well. He was certainly a man of many talents."

"Is it just me or did you say *was* again?" Suddenly it hit him, and Eyal felt his breath catch in his chest, and knowing that the astute Shimon must have noticed only made things worse. Shimon told him he was going to show him what he did with people. So this must have become his hobby in recent years, arranging bizarre deaths for Maria's clients. He wondered what Ibrahim Amat's crime was? Did he make Maria come, heaven forbid? And what was he planning for Eyal? He could have killed him a long time ago, so maybe he had a different plan. Maybe Shimon was planning on keeping Eyal alive as a pet. When was the cavalry coming?! A dreadful image suddenly flashed before Eyal's eyes. He saw himself sitting in a room on Shimon's yacht. Three years had gone by, Eyal was wearing the fine suit Shimon had arranged for him and he was excited. Today Shimon was going to celebrate Eyal's fortieth birthday.

"Wait and hear, it's a fascinating story. Among the many companies he worked with, Mister Suttirat worked with Israeli high tech companies. There are quite a few companies in Thailand that manufacture relatively cheap computer chips. There were several Israeli companies that used his services, as well as businessmen who wanted to buy luxury apartments in Bangkok and Pattaya. He'd help them locate suitable assets. He used to come to Israel about once a year, and he was with Maria a few times."

"Okay, and how did he die?"

"I told you, it's a fascinating story. This Aroon character was born in Ubon Ratchathani, which is a province in Isan, the northeastern region of Thailand. It borders Laos and Cambodia, by the way. He came from a village that isn't far from the county town, which is also called Ubon. Like most Thai, he decided to go back home to celebrate the holidays with his family. He arrived at the big lavish house that he had built for him and his family in the village, and guess what he found there one day on the floor?"

"A poisonous snake?"

"Nice try, you're not that far off. He found something called the Asian Forest Centipede. It's a type of insect, something horrible. But usually not deadly. It's a kind of centipede that can reach ten inches, a monster the size of a croissant and, as fast as light. But our Aroon is no kid, he was born in the village. He trapped the creature in a bucket and planned to kill it. However, at that exact moment his sister came home, heard the story, and told him to wait. She said the insect had many advantages, and that drinking its poison was good for your joints. You know how you drink it?"

"Oh, believe me, I have no idea."

"You put the nasty motherfucker in a bottle of whiskey, Thai whiskey in this case, we're not talking about Jack Daniel's here. The creature drowns in the whiskey, flaps around till it dies while discharging its venom into the whiskey, and then you drink it."

"Lovely."

"Yes. Bottom line, our Shrimp found out too late that he was allergic."

"He drank it and died?"

"Pretty much, apparently it took him a few hours."

Was it possible that Shimon had organized an execution in China of some poor Indian and death by the poison of a centipede to a miserable Thai? How the fuck could he have pulled it off? On the other hand, Eyal had already learned that the ingenuity of Shimon and his men knew no limits. While his attempt to frame Eyal didn't succeed, it was nevertheless masterful.

"Well, Eyal, who's the father?"

"None of them, they look nothing like the kid. Come on, hand me another bag."

"I don't believe you. You don't even think you'll find the father in these bags, right? Then what's the point of playing the game?"

"You kidnapped my daughter, you piece of shit, you think this is a game?"

"Okay, Eyal, since you're refusing to continue playing the game, it's time to change the rules." Shimon blurted out some words in Italian to the two goons standing by the door in such perfect silence that Eyal had forgotten they were there.

"If you cooperate with them, there's no reason for this to end badly, I told them not to harm you needlessly."

"Wonderful."

The two large men who did not look nice at all waited for Eyal by the door, right next to the big screen that was still broadcasting the images of the beautiful people by the pool. Eyal exited the room with the two men following him closely. They went down the stairs, which led to an elegant white hallway with many doors on both sides. Maybe the Chinese girl and her African boyfriend were screwing behind one of those doors, Eyal thought, and hoped they weren't about to pay them a visit. Although it didn't seem that any better options awaited him. They paused in front of door number twenty-six, which opened for a split second.

"Daddy!" Eyal managed to catch a glimpse of Meital calling out before the door slammed shut. Eyal turned around to one of his two guards, a big blond guy with a long thin braid and an ugly scar on his left cheek. Eyal gave him the strongest right hook he had in him, straight to the face. He managed to surprise the burly guy, who cursed as he collapsed onto the floor. But his friend simply drew out his gun and pointed it at Eyal. Eyal knew it was a mistake, but he had to try. What would happen next? What happened next was that the guy Eyal had knocked down got up and dealt him a blow to the head. Eyal nearly fell back, but he hung on, his legs shaking and his nose starting to bleed.

"That's enough," his friend said, and signaled Eyal to keep walking. They continued for about another thirty feet, this time keeping their distance from Eyal. When he was about ten feet away from the next door, he heard one of them shout "Stop!" He paused. He had no intention of arguing with a gun pointing at him. The blond guy passed him and opened the door, and the other man motioned him into the room by waving his gun.

CHAPTER 18

Eyal slowly advanced toward room number thirty. He wasn't sure whether time was standing still or whether he had just stopped breathing. The door was open a crack and Eyal still couldn't really see or hear anything. He touched the door, more caressing it than actually trying to open it further, attempting to pick up sounds that would hint to what was waiting for him inside. The two Italians didn't rush him, and in fact, Eyal had once again forgotten about them. He pushed the door slowly until it was half-open, and he could see a table and someone sitting on a chair, but nothing else. At least the flames of hell didn't burst out of the room. Eyal pushed the door ajar, looked inside, and thought he was going to pass out. The blow he suffered to his head a few moments earlier didn't help his dizziness. He closed his eyes, opened them again, and the same sight was revealed before him. It wasn't a hallucination. A set table stood in the center of the room, with fancy china and filled wine glasses. There were also two beautiful silver candlesticks with two lit candles. At the center of the table was something that looked like a large slab of meat covered in a thick layer of gravy. The smell of the meat filled his nostrils and once again he felt a wave a nausea that he tried to suppress. There were also lavish bowls with vegetables and potatoes, two wine bottles and a bottle of Champagne. And at the head of the table sat Maria. Her head was resting in her right hand, and her expression was that of a captive animal that knows it will never be released. Her left hand, placed on the table, was bandaged. No, Eyal suddenly realized, there was no left hand. Her left hand was missing— the dressing was bandaged over a stump. The fingerprints, he suddenly realized. That's how they had identified the body. So who did they blow up in that hotel? Maybe another employee of the virtual escort agency. To Maria's left sat the boy, whom Eyal knew as Dino, although that was probably not his name.

On the wall behind Maria hung a large screen, on which Shimon's face suddenly appeared.

"Now you see why you needed a fine suit!"

"You're crazy."

"It's time for family dinner, Eyal."

"You sick fuck."

"Come now, you're forgetting you have very good reasons to behave yourself."

"You're bleeding."

"What?"

Maria was talking to him, and he was caught by surprise. He still hadn't come to terms with the fact that she was alive.

"Oh!" He took one of the satin napkins folded next to the plates, and dabbed his nose. He thought the bleeding wasn't so bad anymore, but when he looked at the napkin he saw that it was completely red.

"I'll just add it to the bill."

"What do you want from me?"

"I want you to live with your new family. I'll provide for you, everything you could possibly need. I apologize for Maria's hand, believe me, I'm the biggest victim of this business. It's a bit difficult stroking the cock and the balls at the same time with only one hand, I'm sure you understand. But now I'm passing her on to you, and I know you'll manage, even like this. Come on, eat and put the child to bed. Mommy and Daddy have to make time for adult things."

Eyal wanted to throw up. The large piece of meat seemed filthy now, even though he was sure it was probably the most expensive prime cut. Eyal was absolutely convinced he could see it stretch and shrink under the gravy like a giant worm. He knew he was hallucinating, but it didn't help. The blow to his head was probably partly responsible for the rising nausea.

He knew he had to stay focused. If the rescue teams arrived, he would have to get to Meital as quickly as possible. At least now he knew where she was and that she was unharmed. But he had no idea if he could even manage to get her as well as himself out of this place. How could you even leave this room? Eyal looked back and saw that the door was bolted shut, of course. Maria was alive. It was unfathomable. He looked at her. She didn't look well. No surprise there. Eyal remembered the color of her skin as one of the most beautiful things he ever saw, a kind of golden mocha. He had dreamt about her skin. Now she was paler than a ghost. And much thinner, although there was no lack of food in the place, that much was clear. She must have lost her appetite, for obvious reasons.

"What's your name?" Eyal asked the kid.

"Now now, Eyal, your and Maria's child is named Dino, as you know perfectly well."

Dino sat staring at his plate, full of untouched food. He completely ignored Eyal, even though only a few days ago they sat and played together for about an hour. No wonder.

"Okay, I see you're not very hungry, so time to send Dino to bed. Let's say goodnight to Dino, and give him a kiss."

Maria rose and gave the child a peck on the forehead. The kid remained with a frozen expression. When Maria approached the child, Eyal couldn't help but notice that her wonderful body was almost the same as he remembered it, only slightly thinner. How long had she been held captive here? Probably since her staged murder. No! That day she was already after her horrible surgery. Eyal wondered where the surgery was performed. On the ship? Maria looked at him and motioned with a nod for him to approach the boy. Eyal followed her instruction. Who knew what the punishment for insubordination was. And what would happen now? Would Shimon force him to cheat on his wife again, in front of cameras documenting the entire business? It was insane, but Eyal had no idea what he was supposed to do. In his meetings with Eyal, Shimon had always made sure to be courteous, almost stately. Their meetings were ridiculously polite. But now all boundaries had been crossed, and after the rivers of sewage Shimon spewed in front of him, he probably had no intention of ever meeting Eyal again. He would be too embarrassed. Eyal approached the boy, drew his mouth to his ear and whispered to him: "Don't worry, kid. We'll get you out of here."

The boy didn't react, and Eyal thought he probably didn't speak a word of English. But Eyal had no idea how to say this in Italian. What language had he spoken with the child in Bellagio? English. But they had communicated through the toys. And there, for that hour of play, Eyal was almost convinced the child was his. How surreal his life had become. He felt sorry for the kid. It was a heartrending sight, him sitting there with a blank expression, eyes focused on some imaginary spot on the wall. His parents must be gutted, crazy with worry. Like Eyal. Eyal tried to conjure up the storm of emotions and confusion the child's beautiful eyes had stirred within him less than a week ago. Now they were just two strangers. But what were they a week ago? Eyal's flurry of emotions must have frightened the boy. He probably thought Eyal was one of his captors. It was amazing how easy it was to deceive Eyal. An amoeba, Galit would often call him when laughing about the ignorance he displayed regarding other people's emotions. Galit would never have fallen for a stunt like that. He wondered how you prepare a three-year-old to play the role of a stranger's long-lost son. Only god knows. God and Shimon. The door behind them opened and the same nanny from Bellagio came to take the child away. The kid left quietly and Eyal remained with Maria next to the set table, laden with all the fine dishes he had no intention of eating.

"I don't know why you're not complimenting the chef, there are a few delicacies here you've never tried before. Have you ever eaten the trunk of an elephant, Eyal? It's right there in front of you on the table. I know it doesn't sound very nice, but it's the chef's specialty, very tasty, trust me."

Eyal eyed the long piece of meat covered in red gravy.

"The trunk is chopped off when the elephant is still alive. Keeps it juicy."

Eyal thought he was about to throw up.

"Fits you actually, you chop people's hands off, why not an elephant's trunk?"

"That's not nice, Eyal, I'm trying to accommodate your taste."

"Then bring me some fucking hummus."

"Not your taste in food, Eyal, in humor."

"What?"

"It was a joke you yourself could have told, I've studied you very thoroughly, Eyal."

Maria was staring into space, every now and then trying to look at Eyal with a sad smile that more than anything looked like a twitch of someone about to cry.

"Okay, I suggest you move on to more serious matters. I'm starting to get bored."

"And if we don't?"

Eyal recalled the thousands of times his son Daniel stomped his feet on the ground and refused to do what Eyal had asked or demanded of him. How many times he had faced the vexing truth that sometimes you simply couldn't force your will on a six-year-old. The difference was that Eyal had no desire to harm Daniel in the least. He never wanted to hit him, not even a little. And Shimon had the ability to force Eyal to do anything, if he really wanted to.

"Well, are you making your move, Eyal? I'm waiting!"

Eyal wasn't sure what to do. He knew that to ensure Meital's safety, he had better do something, buy more time, but he couldn't bring himself to get up and approach Maria. He simply couldn't do it.

"Fuck you, Shimon. It's you who can't perform, isn't it?"

Eyal instantly regretted his words. It was unnecessary. Why did he say that? Was it possible that Meital would pay the price for it? He looked at Maria, who closed her eyes and seemed frightened. There was some slight, annoying buzzing sound in the air, and the more the light dimmed the more the buzzing grew louder. It was an unbearable sound that kept intensifying, and Eyal covered his ears, but it was futile, there was nowhere to run. It felt as though someone were drilling in his ear, and Eyal thought his head was about to explode. He leaped off his chair, knocking it over, crawled under the table and curled up in a fetal position with both hands over his head, but it didn't help at all. He felt tears running down his cheeks, and just when he thought he couldn't take any more, the sound began to weaken and the light became brighter. Trembling, Eyal crawled out from under the table, a little embarrassed of himself for not being able to help Maria, but what could he have done? He saw that like him, Maria had hid under the table, and was now crawling out, trying to recover. How many tortures like this had she undergone? Maybe she had learned by now not to resist. Trained like an animal. It was horrible, absolutely horrible to know how easily his willpower could be broken, he knew he had to go to Maria and start... Start what? Kissing her? Ripping her clothes off?

"Eyal, I'm waiting. You can do it gently, if you want." Because of the buzzing and the shock he was in, it took Eyal a moment to realize that Shimon was talking to him, and to decipher what he was saying. He walked toward Maria and sat down, still maintaining a decent distance from her. Her being there still felt uncanny, too strange. He needed to talk to her without Shimon hearing.

"You know, my daughter is trapped here in the next room..." The buzzing was still driving him crazy, his head was pounding and he wasn't even sure if he was actually producing sound. Maria looked at him with anticipation, and Eyal cleared his throat and tried again. But Shimon started talking again.

"Eyal, get up this instant and sit two chairs from Maria. Now, or else I'll turn the siren back on."

Eyal got up and sat two chairs from her. There was no way out.

"Look what's become of us, Eyal. I actually appreciate you, even love you, you could say, almost as much as I love my wife. Why did it have to come to this?"

"I'm looking at your wife's hand, and it doesn't seem your love is such a great catch." The ringing in his ears reminded him that he shouldn't push it. He wasn't sure he would be able to stand another round.

"I'll ignore that comment, maybe just to remind you that I can be good too. I'm going to play a game with you. Ever play strip poker?"

There was a time, back when Eyal and Galit traveled together, that they had played a lot of strip poker. In musty rooms in guest houses in Laos and Thailand, and later in Cambodia and Vietnam, Galit almost always beat him on those pot-infused, arousing nights, after which came the best fucks he had every experienced, much better than his night with Maria. Without guilt, only pure pleasure.

"You want me to play strip poker with Maria?" The man was obviously bored. For how long did he think he could play games with Eyal and Maria? Or maybe he was planning on introducing new pawns? Shimon was an intelligent man, wasn't it clear to him that this could only end badly? The only problem was that Eyal wasn't at all convinced that he would get to see the end. He might not even get to see the next night. Suddenly Eyal understood that he didn't know what time it was, they had taken his phone and watch, and there was no clock on the wall. Could he trust Shimon to put Dino to bed here at a reasonable hour? And if that was the case, did that mean it was around nine o'clock?

"A special version of strip poker. You can consider it a continuation of our little quiz. For every answer you get wrong, someone has to take off an item of clothing, either you or Maria, it doesn't matter to me. And there's another special feature to our game, there has to be some kind of move, if you catch my drift. A kiss, to start with. After five wrong answers, I want to see a fuck."

"You don't say."

It was utter despair. Eyal looked around him again, locked in this cage. He couldn't break down the steel door. Shimon could do whatever he wanted with them. He could even kill them both and go on living to a ripe old age. No one would know. And what would he do with Meital after he killed him? If she lived, Eyal wouldn't get to see her grow up, he wouldn't be there to protect her, to comfort her in her difficult moments. Eyal knew he had to stop thinking that way. But how was he going to get out of this cage?

"Okay, let's hear your questions."

"I'll try to be fair, I'm going to ask about a geographical area significant to your personal history, Eyal."

"Huh?"

"You met your wife in Laos, right?"

"Indeed." At least that much he knew.

"Which language among the countries of the region is closest to the Lao language?"

It was complete insanity, he had turned into a contestant on Jeopardy. He would have laughed if it weren't so sad.

"Thai." He knew that too. The problem was that Mister Shimon was sitting there with his computer, he could ask anything he wanted. For instance, the length of the Mekong River. Or the total sum of Chinese investments in Laos over the past year. Shimon could accumulate Eyal's five wrong answers in no time. Not that it made much of a difference. Even if Eyal answered Shimon's next two hundred questions correctly, it wouldn't change his dire situation, he would still be a prisoner at sea.

"Ah, very nice. And what is the difference between the two languages?"

Here it comes, he was going to make his first mistake.

"There are probably a million differences between the two languages, and I don't speak either of them."

"Okay, I'll give you a clue. What's special about the Thai language? What makes it so difficult to learn?"

"What?" Eyal asked, but suddenly the answer came to him. He had once met a Thai student who tried to explain to him the musicality of the Thai language, the different tones. In Thai, the same word with the same vowels and consonants can have five different meanings. The difference was in the tone. Although it all sounded the same to Eyal.

"Tones. Thai is a tonal language. I guess Loa isn't."

"Very impressive, Eyal!"

It sounded as though Shimon was getting into the role of trivia show host. Maybe he had even forgotten for a second that his two contestants were his captives, that he had abducted Eyal's daughter and chopped off Maria's hand. Or maybe he had no intention of forgetting.

"What is the population of Laos?"

Of course he would ask something like that. Eyal had no clue. He remembered that Thailand had a population of about sixty million, maybe more. Vietnam had even more than Thailand. Laos and Cambodia less. Much less. But how much less? He didn't know, so he had to make a guess.

"Ten million?"

"Ahh, I'm sorry, first mistake, too far off, I can't accept that answer. Would you like to know the correct answer?"

"Dying to."

"According to the CIA World Factbook, Laos's population was estimated at about six million, six hundred fifty-eight thousand in 2012. I'm a little disappointed in you, Eyal."

"Okay."

"Now I'm waiting for your move."

Maria slipped her hand under her dress, and in about two seconds had her bra out.

"Catch the technique, Eyal? Good job! Now I'm waiting for you to take advantage of this new opportunity." Eyal suddenly realized why Shimon sounded so strange to him: his voice was almost completely neutral. Even when he said good job, or expressed disappointment in Eyal's mistake, his tone didn't change, and it only made the experience more surreal.

"Next time. I think Maria's move was certainly enough for one mistake."

"No no no, Eyal, you haven't listened to my rules. With every piece of clothing that comes off, one move has to be made. I assume there's no need to mention that I expect each move to be more interesting than the last."

Now his tone actually did seem to change, and it reminded Eyal of Daniel's whining when he felt his rights were being infringed upon.

Eyal approached Maria and kissed her on the cheek.

"Unacceptable."

Eyal wasn't sure what to do. He wanted to delay the inevitable, but was afraid that the horrible siren would go off again. Maria apparently had enough of the siren as well, and she got up and approached him. Eyal tried to avert his gaze from her awful stump and focus on her body and face. She still had an amazing body. He wondered if her hand could be reattached. Maria drew closer to Eyal, stood an inch away from him and then sat down on his lap, and Eyal was horrified to discover that his body was by no means indifferent to this, even as his daughter was being held captive in the next room, and despite the stump; despite everything, he was suddenly attracted to Maria.

"Ah! I see you're finally rediscovering each other, that's wonderful, I knew it would happen eventually. Don't worry, Eyal, even with one hand Maria can still work magic."

Maria smiled at him, kissed him on the cheek and slipped something into his pocket.

"Come on, Eyal, I want to see some action, don't be so passive! I heard your tapes from three years ago, as you probably remember. Even though I had only the audio version, I know you can do much better, now come on!"

"He completely lost it, huh? What did you put in my pocket, Maria?"

"It's a master key, it should unlock the door to this room as well as to your daughter's room, I hope," she whispered in his ear, while making sure to moan and press up against him so Shimon wouldn't realize what was really going on. But Eyal was shocked to realize how much this aroused him—it was truly insane!

"How did you get the key?"

"From all the times I had to fondle his balls," Maria said and smiled sadly.

"I don't know what will happen to you out there, or what he'll do to me, but it doesn't matter, we have to try, right?"

"What do you mean what will happen to me out there, you're coming with me, I won't leave you here. Come quick."

Despite all of Maria's efforts and Eyal's genuine arousal, it still seemed too obvious. Was Shimon actually buying this charade? Maybe he was just too engrossed to care about anything.

"The problem is that we're on a boat, like an island, you understand? Where is there to run to?"

"The cavalry could come any minute, I tried to notify the police."

"Really? Think you could bear one more kiss?" she whispered in his ear.

"Let's go for it."

They stood up and kissed.

"Now we're talking, I see what's going on in your pants there, Eyal, you're a real tiger!"

Maria pushed him against the door. Some distant corner of his mind was occupied with his guilt—was he cheating on Galit again? Did he have justification? He knew he did, but he also knew that his passion was all too real. Maria quickly pulled the key out of his pocket. Eyal held her tight while she had her stump against his back and her one hand busy with the key. The door opened behind them and they made a run for it.

CHAPTER 19

Eyal and Maria charged out with excitement only to realize they were now standing in front of the same two Italians with their drawn guns and their nasty smiles. Eyal looked at them with a surprise that was probably misplaced. What exactly did he expect? He felt drained of all energy.

"You're disappointing me, Eyal. That was your big plan?" He heard Shimon's mocking voice trailing after them from the screen inside the room. One of the Italians signaled to him with his gun, not back into the room, but to the hallway. Could this be it? Maybe the attempt to escape was a horrible mistake and now Shimon had decided to finally get rid of them? Eyal walked beside Maria and thought about holding her hand, but the arm next to him was the wrong one. When they passed by room number twenty-six, Eyal felt his stomach turn, but what could he do? They walked up the staircase. Now they could see the hallways that led to the upper deck, where Eyal was led into the lavish bathroom and then into Shimon's office. Where to next? Maybe they planned to force them into the helicopter and then push them out? Eyal looked back and saw that one of the Italians was pointing his gun to the left. They weren't going outside. They continued to walk several feet and were led into Shimon's elegant office. After they entered, the doors were shut with a strong clicking sound. The Italians didn't enter with them.

"Alone? You no longer feel you need protection?"

"Yes, you two sit on the couch over there and don't move, unless you want a bullet to the head. I'm aware of the fact that you managed to uncover my not-so-illustrious military past, don't think I don't know, but believe me, I know how to use a gun."

"I believe you, Shimon." Eyal tried to placate him. It seemed as though Shimon was genuinely worried that Eyal would try to make a quick move and attack him. But Shimon still had Meital, so what was he so worried about? And if he was truly scared of Eyal, then why keep the bodyguards outside and stay alone with him in the room? So far Eyal hadn't noticed a single crack in the loyalty of Shimon's men. But maybe Shimon was actually going to kill them now, and didn't want two witnesses?

Eyal and Maria sat down on the couch, which was soft and comfortable, too comfortable—Eyal felt as though his eyes might shut at any moment.

"How many books do you think are in this room, Eyal?" Shimon gestured with his hand at the bookshelves, a gesture that instead of emphasizing the impressive size of the library, mostly accentuated the shortness of his arm compared to his massive body.

"More riddles?" Okay, then maybe he wasn't going to kill them just yet, which was nice to learn.

"This time there's no price to pay for a wrong answer, just give a number."

"Ten thousand."

"Try harder. You'll soon find out that your answer is important. Maybe I was wrong when I said there's no punishment for failure. There's no immediate punishment, but in the long-run, you may want to give it a real effort."

What sick game was the motherfucker playing with them now? Eyal had enough experience to know that it would be very surprising, imaginative, and somewhere between unpleasant and deadly. His gaze scanned the two large bookcases. He estimated that they were forty feet long, two sides, eighty feet. And the average book was maybe an inch wide, maybe even a bit less. Which meant... He was too tired for calculations, but maybe he really should try. What a mess. So eighty feet, maybe fifteen books per feet, one thousand two hundred in one shelf. One thousand two hundred? How did he even reach that number? Never mind. There were six shelves. Seven thousand two hundred. But now Eyal studied the books closer, and many were wider than one inch. And there were also wooden partitions about every three feet.

"Six thousand?"

"A little disappointing, but no matter. I'll tell you. There are exactly five thousand and one books here."

"Five thousand and one, exactly?"

"Yes, if I bring a new book, I make sure to take one out. I don't throw it away, of course, everything goes to Bellagio."

"It's a great relief to hear that you're so considerate of your books."

"Eyal, you really ought to focus on our conversation and not your stupid sarcasm." Shimon waved the gun, and Eyal was scared it would accidently go off. He tried to focus on the conversation, but his mind was busy with the question of how he would get to Meital. The fact that his daughter was trapped maybe less than sixty feet away was driving him crazy. He had to get to her, he had to escape, but he was just so tired.

"Do you own a Kindle, Eyal?"

"An Amazon Kindle?" Eyal asked with surprise.

"Yes."

"I have an iPad. But the truth is I don't like reading on those things, I prefer books... from actual paper." The conversation was starting to get on Eyal's nerves, but Shimon had promised some sort of game and hinted to Eyal that he should pay attention to the details, and that seemed like the best option he had. But it was absolutely nerve-racking.

"I'm with you on that. The Kindle is a great device, but I hate it. You know that through the Kindle I now have access to more than half my books in Bellagio? It drives me crazy, there's just something about it... I don't know, it somehow took the fun out of my library, the fact that you can cram so many books into that tiny, uninspired device. Paper books offer something so... beautiful and dignified. But what's the point of having such a big library if you can upload all those titles into some silly little computer?"

"Yes, I understand that." And in fact, Eyal did agree with him, but this conversation about the wrongs of the digital age was exceedingly irrelevant to his life right now. Eyal wished the bastard would just say what was on his mind already.

"The point is that you're a bit like my Kindle."

"Excuse me?"

"With regard to Maria. Just as the Kindle took away the fun of owning a library, you… you could say that after you it was much harder for me to fool myself. You ruined my pleasure of life with Maria."

"Ohh."

Through the large window behind Shimon's desk, Eyal saw Shimon's state-of-the-art helicopter take off. It was perhaps midnight by now, but there was a full moon and the visibility was good.

"The rats abandoning? The ship's about to sink?"

"You have no idea how right you are."

"Why aren't you trying to escape?"

"You really see me escaping with all this weight? I don't think I'd make it very far. I'd rather have a heroic ending, maybe they'll write a book about me. Ah, there's an idea, if you survive, you can be the one to chronicle this story."

"What are you planning? To go down with the ship?"

"Indeed."

"My daughter's on board, you know. Maybe you could lower her into one of the small boats first? Also little Dino, come to think about it. I'm not sure the world would be very impressed with your heroism if you take two three-year-olds with you."

Maybe it was the complete exhaustion, but when Shimon replied that he might execute him and his daughter at the same time, Eyal couldn't feel anything but weariness and sorrow.

"But I'm leaving the matter to you. I'm going to ask you a riddle, and if you answer correctly, you'll have a chance of getting out of here alive."

"The final riddle?"

"Exactly. The ultimate game, the winner gets to live. I'll tell you something pathetic. The end is rather liberating, so I don't mind being pathetic. I don't enjoy Maria anymore. I haven't in a long time. Like I told you, it's hard to stroke the cock and the balls with one hand. She really is a magician, but I haven't enjoyed even these little pleasures for quite some time. It was difficult not to feel her resentment, in all sorts of small gestures. I assume you're not very sympathetic to my predicament right now, seeing how I was the one who handicapped her in order to convince the world she was dead. But I'm just telling it as it is. You, Eyal, it's the conversations with you that were the one remaining pleasure left in my life. So it's only fitting that I'm spending my last moments on earth talking to you. And that's also why I'm giving you one last chance. Let's be honest with each other. You ruined my life, even if it wasn't on purpose. I should have killed you, but you probably already understand that there's some part of me that doesn't want you dead. So now I'm going to give you a real gift, an opportunity. If you fail, you'll go down with me, like a captain. This ship is booby-trapped. In five minutes the helicopters of the glorified Israel Defense Forces will be here. The very army I was part of for a mere week and a half. I have no intention of meeting the soldiers. There's a huge amount of explosives underneath me. The bomb can't be defused. But the explosion can be delayed, to let you escape. In order to achieve this, you'll have to provide a password, to answer a riddle. I'll give you clues. Solving the riddle will allow you to escape this room. Right now it's sealed shut, even if you shoot the door you won't make it out. The windows were built to withstand a machine gun assault, so don't even try. You have only one chance. You two can figure out the answer together, and if you get it wrong, it's your problem."

"I'm all ears."

"Sherri Han, the gorgeous Chinese you saw in the pool. You know, there's something pretty incredible about the fact that this girl addressed you when you came on board, seems almost like destiny. Sherri Han is connected to you. You could say that solving the riddle is finding the connection between you and Sherri Han. And also, the answer has to do with something Sherri Han gave me, a gift, you could say."

"Okay," Eyal said, but he didn't really understand anything. What did he want from him?

"Go ahead, start asking questions."

"Does she have any connection to Laos or Thailand?" Eyal knew he was on the wrong track, but he just had no idea what Shimon was talking about.

"I can see on your face that you know you're talking nonsense." Eyal wanted to murder him, but he knew he had to think.

"You said you'll give me a gift, right? And after that you said Sherri Han gave you a gift. Are the gifts connected?"

"Now that's a good question, Eyal. The truth is there is a connection. In some sense, you could say that I'm passing on to you the gift she gave to me. If you solve the riddle, of course."

That was no help. What gift was he talking about?

"If you really want me to have a chance, you should give me better clues."

"Okay, that's reasonable. Remember that I told you earlier to pay attention to our conversation?"

"Kindle?"

"No, it's something else."

"Your library? The number of books in your library? The fact that you have five thousand books here?"

"Not five thousand. Five thousand and one."

"Five thousand and one can be divided by three, Eyal. Five thousand can't," Maria said to Eyal and he looked at her, how beautiful she still was, so quiet that Eyal had almost forgotten she was there. And how smart she was. Shimon's stupid obsession with the number three. But what was it connected to?

"Good job! See, Eyal? The hooker's smarter than you are."

"I think I'm starting to realize why you aren't so good with the ladies." Good grief, he thought, why couldn't he just keep his mouth shut?

"That's a very stupid remark, Eyal, but I'll forgive you, we won't let it interrupt our game."

"Okay, then I suggest you give me another clue, if you want this game to go anywhere."

"Fine, we'll attack the riddle from a different angle. When was the last fundraising round in your company?"

"Fugu's last fundraising? Let's see… it was about… maybe six months ago."

"And how much money came in?"

"A million dollars."

"Are you sure about that figure? Maybe it wasn't a million dollars that came in?"

"Of course it came in, otherwise the company would have gone bankrupt."

"Think hard, Eyal."

Eyal tried to think but his brain was just clogged, refused to work, maybe because of the stress and the fact that his daughter was trapped and he couldn't get to her, and there was a pretty good chance that she would die here at sea along with him and it would be his own fault, all because of one night of reckless passion three years ago. Or maybe it was just because he was tired, so utterly exhausted that after every sentence he wasn't sure it had been uttered or imagined. A helicopter crossed the sky, an IDF helicopter, he was sure of it.

"Listen, you have to enter a password on the computer here. A two-word password, four and five characters. Which makes a total of nine. A pretty fitting choice for a man who's nearly defined by the number three, don't you think? Now you see this? I have a syringe here that will put me under. A nice deep sleep. I don't know what I'll feel when all the explosives blow me up into a million pieces, the truth is, I'm rather curious. But…"

Eyal grabbed Maria with one arm and threw the both of them across the couch. He heard the gunshot even before he landed, and his hand felt as though it was on fire. It was just a superficial hit, the bullet merely singed his skin, but it hurt like crazy.

"I only want to kill the hooker!" Shimon yelled.

Eyal knew there was no time. The world was spinning around him. He was in horrible pain, but it was now or never. He quickly crawled from behind the couch to Shimon's desk, and another shot was fired. This time it didn't hit him, but he didn't know whether it had hit Maria. He hurled himself against the back of Shimon's chair and tried to push it, but the chair barely moved. The motherfucker must have weighed at least four hundred pounds. Eyal finally managed to spin the chair slightly toward him, and grabbed the syringe. He jabbed it into Shimon's neck. The effect was immediate; Eyal heard a loud thud and saw that Shimon's gun was on the floor. His head was leaning forward against his chest and his eyes were closed.

"Maria, are you okay?"

"Yes, yes, I'm here."

Maria stood beside him and they both looked at the computer. A minute and thirteen seconds were left. A cursor flickered next to two giant blank rectangles that occupied almost half the screen. It was the password field, a word for each rectangle, one four characters long, and one five. Below the rectangles was a clock, ticking away.

"What did he say at the end there, what was the last clue?" Eyal asked. His brain felt paralyzed and there was no time left, another minute and he would be blown to bits, evaporated, along with his baby girl. And it would all be his fault. But what could he do? He simply had no idea what Shimon was talking about.

"Eyal, he said something about money that was supposed to come into the company."

"Oh, right. The money from the last fundraising round. A million dollars. And he claimed that it wasn't actually a million dollars. What does that mean?"

"I don't know. It isn't very typical."

"What isn't typical?"

"Would the last thing he chose to tell us be a number that can't be divided by three? But I don't know, maybe he grew up a bit in those last moments. You remember, five thousand and one?"

"What are you talking about *grew up*, one of the last things he told us was that the number three defined him. But what can I do, it was a million dollars that came into the company, it had nothing to do with him."

Jesus, he was spending the last moments of his life analyzing the fucked-up personality of Shimon Ben Simon. A million. He had said it wasn't a million. That didn't mean anything. But suddenly Eyal had a flashback. He came into Yonit's office to check if the money had been transferred already, and what did she tell him?

Hey Yonit, are we still alive, is there money for paychecks, did they give us the million?

Yes, Eyal, you can calm down. The charming bastard even gave me a two-dollar tip.

"It was a million and two dollars that came in. Divides by three…"

"Are you serious?"

"But why the hell…" It wasn't Shimon who invested the money, it was Sheringham, Jeff Elroy. And Jeff wasn't obsessed with the number three, so why would he make sure the sum was divisible by three?

Eyal remembered the rest of his conversation with Yonit.

That's not nice, why are you calling him a bastard?

You're too kindhearted, Eyal, it's difficult for you to see meanness in others. It's true that Jeff is very professional, but I always get the feeling with him that he'd kill his own mother for a higher return.

Maybe Yonit was right? It was all coming back to him. The phone call in which Jessica, Jeff's secretary, summoned him to the meeting at Dan Accadia, the meeting that never took place. Maybe it actually *was* Jessica. What gift did Sherri Han give Shimon that he was now passing on to him?

"Eyal, quick, type something in, anything."

Eyal looked at the screen. Eight seconds left. Maria was right, of course, he had to try. Eyal typed 'Jeff Elroy' into the password field and pressed enter; immediately three more minutes were added to the clock.

"Well done!" Maria kissed him on the cheek. "Look!"

Eyal turned and looked through the window. An air force black hawk was landing on the deck.

"Come on, there's no time. You run with the master key to room twenty-six while I go get a soldier," Eyal said.

There was no time to relish this unexpected victory, no time at all! They ran to the door next to the giant screen, but it wouldn't open.

"Give me the gun… Ah, here, it's opening."

Eyal exited the room and took two left turns, ran across the hallway and climbed onto the upper deck of the pool. Apart from a few soldiers, no one else was there. The beautiful yacht and the helicopter, as well as two additional helicopters circling above them in the moonlight, seemed completely surreal to Eyal. He knew he had to break free of the dream-like feeling and exert himself, one more push, so he and his daughter wouldn't die there in two minutes. Eyal stood next to the pool, and on the other side a few soldiers were standing by.

"Hey, can you hear me?" he yelled over to them. "This ship is booby trapped, there are people trapped in a room and we have less than three minutes to get them out."

"Are you serious? Everyone back to the helicopter! I'm going with him. If we aren't back in two minutes, take off."

A lieutenant ran over to him and they rushed inside, down the stairs to the long hallway, and reached Maria, who was standing in front of room number twenty-six.

"The door won't open."

"Meital, honey, are you there?"

"Daddy?"

"Sweetie, can you hear me? Step away from the door, crawl under the bed and cover your ears."

There was no response, only the sound of crying.

"Meitali, sweetheart, can you hear me? Did you crawl under the bed?"

"There's no time, we'll all get blown to pieces."

The lieutenant waited a few seconds and then shot the lock.

They entered the room and found Meital and the Italian boy crying.

"Quick, there's no time."

Eyal picked up Meital, who hugged him, whimpered and buried her head in the crook of his neck. The lieutenant picked up the boy, and they all leaped out and ran as fast as they could. When they got to the upper deck, the helicopter had already taken off, hovering above them. It descended, they lifted the kids, and hands from inside the helicopter reached out to grab them; within moments they were all on the helicopter that began to fly away.

"Meitali, where are you?"

Meital was passed to Eyal and he hugged her. He covered her ears, and Maria covered the little boy's ears. Could it have all been a sham? No explosion, no nothing, just Shimon playing his usual games? But suddenly the entire helicopter shook, the noise was ear-splitting, and the ship disappeared behind a great wall of smoke.

"Wow, did you see that? Do you realize how many explosives he must have planted there?"

"He probably rigged the fuel pumps, otherwise it wouldn't have blown up like that. Jesus, did anyone get a picture of it? It could be a real hit on YouTube."

Eyal nuzzled his nose against Meital's, trying to get a smile out of her. His arm hurt, but he could take the pain now that he was sure the nightmare was over.

"Honey, do you want to tell Daddy something? When did you get to the boat? Who picked you up from kindergarten?"

"I want to go home," she kept whimpering.

"It's okay, sweetheart, we'll be home very soon. How did you get to the big boat? Did you get there on a little boat?"

"No, we were on a helicopter!" Meital said with pride; it was the first time that she looked at him and it seemed that the tears were subsiding.

"We were on a big helicopter!" Meital added and laughed, and Eyal kissed her cheek about twenty times.

"What a fun day, now we're on a helicopter again!"

"Does anyone here know where the blue helicopter escaped to?"

"They're being intercepted above Cyprus, they're not going anywhere."

"No kidding." Eyal smiled. He looked at the coastline of Tel Aviv and fell asleep.

CHAPTER 20

Eyal sat in Andrey's office with a cup of coffee in his hand. They had just finished a two-hour interrogation to tie up all the loose ends of the case. But it was a friendly discussion, by no means was it an interrogation under a bright light.

"Okay, Andrey, I can't believe I'm saying this after an interrogation, but it was truly a pleasure. Even the coffee was good. We're done here, right?"

"Yes, and believe me, I don't say this to many suspects, but if you ever want to meet for a whiskey, I'd be happy to."

"Sounds great, you can join me and Max. The wife lets me go out for a drink at least once a month."

One of the best pieces of news Eyal heard when he returned was that Max had woken up, and there were no signs of brain damage. Obviously, a long recovery was still ahead of him, but the doctors were very optimistic.

"Sure."

"There are a couple more things I have to ask you."

"Okay, what's on your mind?"

"Have you found photos of me with Maria? Or the recording of the session?"

"No. Surprisingly, one thing we haven't found is material pertaining to you and Maria. What we did find is an incredible amount of material that son of a bitch collected on many of their clients. Apparently these girls would gather information about their johns, and we have a pretty complete client list. Credit cards, photos of IDs, it's really amazing how careless these people were. There were even photos of some of these men with other people, important documents…"

"What are you going to do with all the material Shimon gathered?"

"We're going to destroy it all. We have no intention of continuing his blackmailing enterprise. But there are a couple of very serious cases of corruption we uncovered from the documents, cases we simply can't ignore, even if the source is so dubious."

"And did you happen to find photos of Jeff with Sherri Han?"

Andrey looked at him for a moment with what seemed like hesitation.

"Yes. It was only to be expected in light of what you told me happened on the boat, right?"

"Are you going to arrest him?"

"In the meantime we don't really have reasonable grounds. There are some suspicions, but it's hard to say we have solid evidence. I don't just go around arresting people without cause, as you probably noticed."

"Can't you get Sherri Han's testimony?"

"She's probably no goody two shoes, but I doubt she was involved in the details of the blackmail. And I'm not even sure we can interrogate her, she's in Cyprus right now and she may very well make it to Hong Kong soon and we'll never hear from her again."

"Okay, so be it. But what can I tell you, this Jeff character is a real piece of shit. The bastard preferred to send me straight into the lion's den than have his wife see some photo of him fucking someone else. And I was innocent enough to think they found someone to imitate Jessica. I'm such an idiot. I wonder if Jessica knew."

"I have no idea. It's very possible that Jeff also didn't know what he was sending you into."

"Jeff's no idiot. He knew something bad was going to happen to me, even if he didn't know exactly what. He just didn't care."

"I agree with you, but again, other than your own word, which I completely believe, we have no evidence of the phone conversation between you and Jessica. Even from Jessica herself we weren't really able to get very clear answers on the matter. What still interests me, Eyal, is why Shimon blackmailed Jeff in the first place. You see, the phone call summoning you to the Dan Accadia Hotel took place a few days ago. But they began blackmailing Jeff from the very beginning. There are photos of Jeff with Sherri Han from nearly three years ago. So what were they accomplishing by that?"

"Jeff controlled the company, so Shimon wanted to control Jeff in order to control me, it's pretty obvious, isn't it? And Jeff was a very important link in the attempt to frame me for Maria's murder."

"You're probably right. But there's something else you might be able to explain to me. I have a list here. You see this? They had a file on every man they blackmailed, and this paper here was in Jeff's file. There's a list of letters here, possibly initials? Do they mean anything to you?"

Eyal looked at the letters and immediately understood.

"That son of a bitch, this is just unbelievable. Thank you, Andrey."

Once again they sat in the same private room at Raphael, Jeff's favorite restaurant. As always, Jeff seemed very pleased with himself, a cigar in one hand and a glass of whiskey as an aperitif in the other. Eyal suddenly remembered that when he was in lock-up, one of the things he missed were his meals with Jeff at Raphael. He even managed to miss the smell of his cigar in that rancid cell. Had he known the truth back then, he probably wouldn't have missed it so much. The waiter had already taken their order, and Jeff was once again in the middle of an important conversation with the sommelier about matching the wines to the dishes they had selected, which Eyal was fairly sure were going to remain untouched.

"So, Eyal, I bet you can say you had an outer life experience over there, huh? Simply incredible. How's Max doing? You think he'll want to come back to work soon? I understand his condition has improved significantly. I didn't want to visit because, well, you know, we're not the closest. I thought the guy could probably do without my presence while recovering. I think he hasn't forgiven me yet for the whole business with Itzik."

Jeff took a sip of his whiskey and tore off a piece of the restaurant's wonderful hot Focaccia, looking, as always, like the most relaxed person in the world. Eyal drank a sip of his water. He made sure to steer clear of alcohol this time.

"If we're on the subject of Itzik, there's something I'm really curious about. When you saw that Itzik wasn't cut out for the job, you got rid of him quickly, as you no doubt should have. But Mandy, who's failed to close a single deal properly in three years, you always bust his balls but you don't actually do anything about it. For three years, you haven't done anything about him. You keep injecting money into this beaten-down company, but you accept its dud of a CEO as if you don't have the power to fire him. Why?"

"We've talked about that already, Eyal, good CEOs don't grow on trees."

"Oh, come on, I still remember, when Mandy came in I asked you if you're sure he'll do the job and you told me, maybe he will and maybe he won't, and if he won't, we'll replace him too."

"In hindsight, you're right. Let's just say that problem is going to be solved. We're going to replace Mandy, you can be sure of that."

"Do you even want to keep investing in the company? I remember you told me when I came back from Italy that it was the last chance. Now the Italian's dead and there's no more Fondo Lombardia. So what makes you suddenly think the company even stands a chance? After you've already told me that it's either selling to the Italians or shutting the company down. What changed?"

"We're going to replace the CEO."

"But you've had a good few years to replace him, you didn't need this catastrophic event in order to replace CEOs. So I'm asking again, what changed? Why do you suddenly think Fugu has a chance? Why all of a sudden do you want to put in more money? You know it's going to cost you a lot, the company's out of oxygen, as you're very much aware of, and there's not even one deal on the horizon that could produce new revenue."

"Is it just me, Eyal, or are you actually asking me to close the company? I thought, you know... after the difficult things you and Max went through..."

"You want to tell me you're going to keep Fugu alive as an act of charity toward Max and me? And that your partners will agree? I can't believe it's you I'm talking to, Jeff Elroy. You've never been this senti-mental about business. I even remember a few lectures you gave, whose motto was—in business there's no room for emotions, only cold, factual considerations."

"What do you want from me, Eyal? This whole affair did something to you, but maybe something good. You're asking me to close down Fugu."

"I'm asking you to sell Fugu to me and Max."

"Ahh! You managed to surprise me. But now at least I understand what you've been going on about. And how much money would you and Max be willing to pay for the company?"

"Max gave me a figure, believe it or not, the money is coming from him, as you probably understand."

"But you'd be a partner, I assume? And what's this magic figure?"

"Half a million dollars. Not a penny more."

"And why would you think we'd want to make such a deal?"

"You said it yourself, the company is worthless, the right thing would be to close it. You said you want to keep it alive as some kind of moral act toward Max and me, right? So here I am, sparing you the costs of that charity, and adding a bonus of half a mill. What do you say?"

"I'm not sure the partners at Sheringham will see it the same way. There are other investors, as you know."

"Then let me add some interesting information, maybe even informa-tion you already have. Who knows. Andrey, the investigator who worked on this case, shared with me some very surprising evidence about the con-nection between Shimon Ben Simon, also known as Simone Donadoni, and Fugu. A connection that apparently started long before I even knew Mister Simon existed. A relationship that's been going on for years."

"What are you talking about, Eyal?"

The main courses were already placed in front of them, but they were so focused on each other that they didn't take a single bite.

"They found among Shimon's possessions, I call him Shimon simply because that was his real name, a list of Fugu's deals. A list of deals he apparently managed to intercept."

"You're saying the reason that so many of Fugu's deals fell through is that Shimon screwed us?"

It was clear to Eyal that Jeff wasn't sure with which tone to react. After all, he wasn't actually surprised, given that he himself was Shimon's main pawn in the scheme to thwart the deals. But what reaction was Jeff supposed to fake? Surprise, or maybe distrust?

"He didn't just screw us over. They found material that has to do with some Chinese girl who was involved in this. Seems like they were blackmailing someone in our company, and used that same insider to botch the deals."

"You're telling me they blackmailed Mandy and made him botch all of Fugu's deals? That doesn't make sense to me. And why the hell would you think I already had this information?"

"First of all, I didn't say it was Mandy. I'm pretty sure it's not Mandy, because you have to be rather sophisticated to thwart deals without anybody figuring out what you're doing. A guy like that would have to be familiar with all the decision-making processes in each one of the companies, and I don't think Mandy has those skills. And why do I think that you already knew? Simple logic. Now you suddenly think it's a good idea to invest in Fugu. Maybe your renewed enthusiasm for the company has to do with the fact that you know that the person who impeded Fugu's success is out of the picture. No Shimon anymore, no more malicious insider botching deals, so maybe it's time to realize the company's potential. But of course, it's just wild speculation."

"I'm happy you're at least aware of the speculative aspect of your last statement."

"Yes. But here's the thing. The police has photos of this Chinese girl, who, and I don't know if you're aware of this, was on the very yacht I was brought to. The cops are going through all the material Shimon collected over the years at this very moment. It may very well be that the malicious insider is about to be exposed in a very unpleasant way, it's a criminal matter, of course, purposely botching your company's deals. It's very likely that the current investors won't want to be affiliated in any way with a company that has such a reputation, one that's involved with criminal acts and scams."

"That's what you think?"

"Yes. You see, Andrey, the investigator, hinted to me that if Fugu shut down, and even if it one day reopened in some different constellation, then maybe there wouldn't be any need for this investigation anymore. So maybe it's in everyone's best interest that you sell us the company for half a million dollars, and get rid of this burden. I thought you might want to introduce that approach to your partners."

"That's a very interesting thought, Eyal."

"Yes. You obviously don't have to give me an answer this minute, but I'd appreciate getting one as soon as possible," Eyal said and looked at his plate, still laden with food that had become cold by now, but still tasty. Loading a big piece of steak with mashed potatoes and pepper sauce onto his fork, he shot Jeff a piercing look.

"Yes, I'll certainly consider that interesting proposal. Well, you'll have to excuse me for not finishing the meal, but I'd like to get out of here to think about your idea."

"Certainly, Jeff." Eyal felt an adrenaline rush—could it have possibly worked? And what would they do if Jeff turned them down? Jeff rose from the table, and for the first time since Eyal had met him, it seemed as though he wasn't quite sure what to do with himself, how to straighten out his body. The napkin that had been resting on his lap fell to the floor, the chair screeched, and he looked at Eyal and mumbled something. He then put out his cigar in his still full wine glass, and left. Eyal felt something close to compassion toward this man, who had always made sure to project infinite self-confidence. He would probably bounce back. Eyal just hoped he wouldn't bounce back too quickly.

Eyal and Max thought long and hard about how to conduct the conversation with Jeff. Eyal had many difficult accusations he wanted to throw in Jeff's face. Jeff had been to Eyal's house at least twice. He kissed his children goodnight. And yet, when push came to shove, he preferred risking Eyal's life to confessing that he was being blackmailed by Shimon. He preferred to maintain his reputation. Eyal wanted to ask him what had crossed his mind when he told Jessica to schedule a meeting with him, knowing that he wouldn't appear. Did it ever occur to him that instead of him, a hitman would appear and try to take him out? But they arrived at the conclusion that a soft, insinuating approach would get better results. Eyal was terribly worried about using the false threat of the police launching an investigation against Jeff. If Andrey knew, he would be angry as hell, and might even accuse Eyal of committing a criminal offence. But they had to gain the upper hand somehow, and they knew that the information they possessed made the threat rather believable, and anyway, there was no way the content of the conversation between Eyal and Jeff would ever reach Andrey. And now Eyal hoped they were right, because otherwise, they were in for another difficult confrontation with Jeff. All that was left to do was wait.

CHAPTER 21

<u>Two Weeks Later</u>

Eyal and Galit were sitting on a large rock surrounded by bushes on Ha-Meri Street in Givatayim, gazing at the beautiful view of Tel Aviv's skyscrapers. It was one of the first places Galit brought Eyal to. She had grown up in Givatayim. It had been a long time since they sat together like this, and it gave Eyal that old feeling of time slipping through his fingers. It seemed that only a moment ago they were sitting here after returning from the Far East, right after his first meeting with Galit's parents, when in fact, that had been over fifteen years ago. He felt that in the blink of an eye they would be sitting here hand in hand after Daniel's wedding. Sometimes Eyal regretted not being more of a spiritual type. He understood people like Ranit and her father, Arieh, who had embraced religion.

They were holding hands, and Eyal looked at Galit and thought that despite the visible signs of aging, she was more beautiful now than at twenty-three, when he had first met her in Laos.

"I decided to forgive you. I want to forgive you, I really do, I know we still love each other and that there's hope for us yet. And that we have two children together. But you need to know that it's difficult for me."

"I do know."

"You don't know, forgiving you goes against everything I believe in, I'd be a complete sucker for doing it, because the only way to forgive you is to believe you that you'll never do it again. And I don't even know if you really did it only that one time, since you only told me about it three years later, when you had no other choice. There could have been ten other times."

"There weren't."

"I want to believe you, I even do, but I know I shouldn't. Why should I believe? In two weeks you and Max will fly to Korea or Japan, right? And I have no doubt you'll go out to have fun there. And it's so far away, it would be so easy to cheat, almost like cheating with an alien no one knew existed, so why wouldn't you?"

"I don't have a good answer, you're right. But if you're actually going to give me a chance, then it has to be a real one. If you're taking me back just to bust my balls, however justified it may be, nothing good can come out of it."

"Okay, my husband, what can I say, I'll try." Eyal knew he couldn't get more than that, but he was optimistic, and that was enough.

"What happened with that kid, Dino?"

"His name wasn't Dino, it's Adso, apparently. At first, Shimon's people told his parents he was going to star in some TV show. And they paid them accordingly. Later they just kidnapped him. He's been returned to his parents, and I think he's all right. I hope. He's probably still in total shock."

"And how's Maria doing? I can't believe I actually care about her, but the truth is she does kind of deserve it, after all, she did pretty much save your life over there, right?"

"Yes, she rocked it. I'm trying to organize some kind of group support for her. I spoke to Andrey and Max, they both grew up in Russia, and there's a chance they might be able to introduce her to their social circles, at least help her meet new people."

"Well, I hope it works out. Can't be easy with everything she went through, and no left hand, that's a hard life."

"Yes, I hope she'll be okay."

Eyal even had the brilliant idea of suggesting to Galit that they invite Maria over to dinner sometime. He wasn't thinking about anything salacious, it didn't even cross his mind that something would happen between him and Maria, he was just feeling guilty. And Maria indeed helped him on that boat, and now he also knew that back then, after their session, she tried to protect him from Shimon, not that it helped much. But when he told Max about his idea, Max whacked him on the head.

"Say, are you some kind of idiot? Would you have been able to forgive Galit if she was the one who cheated on you? You should kiss the ground she walks on for even agreeing to stay with you. You still dream about her, don't you? Would you want to host for Friday night dinner the guy who fucked Galit three years ago, the guy she still dreams about at night?" It was a winning argument, no doubt. The mere fact that Max was alive was a cause of great joy in Eyal's life. He had even gotten into the habit of kissing Max on the forehead, until Max told him he couldn't take anymore. The company they were planning to found on the ruins of Fugu would, at least at the beginning, be funded exclusively by Max. They agreed that Eyal would get twenty percent of the shares. Max would get sixty-five, and the rest they would divide between the new employees. Eyal managed to convince Max to give Mandy two percent of the company, even though they had no intention of using his services. Even if he wasn't to blame for most of Fugu's problems, they wanted a fresh start, and so it was decided that in the meantime Eyal would serve as CEO, and if it outgrew him, they'd look for a replacement. Eyal was worried. He had never held the position of CEO before and it was certainly scary, but he also knew that even with the best of intentions, it was human nature to want to keep your chair. He knew that when the time came, it would be difficult for him to give up the position. He kept thinking of the Itzik precedent, and whether it was smart to start a new company with the same old mistakes? But Max was completely confident in Eyal's managerial skills as well as his ability to one day step down as CEO if the need arose. And truth be told, Eyal didn't really need that much convincing. It was a very tempting opportunity. From the old company, they took Yonit as well as a few programmers who were more than happy to work for Max.

"Come on, Gin, are you coming to see if my parents managed to put the little monsters to bed yet?"

"They were almost asleep when we left the house, I think we can have a bit more fun."

"What, are you thinking about drinks at that sports bar on Katzenelson Street?"

"We could. Or maybe you're in the mood to eat an elephant trunk?"

"What??" Galit asked and laughed. "Gin, I see your sense of humor has really become more refined over the years."

"Why? Ohhh, no, no, I really didn't mean that! Didn't I tell you about it? What I meant was…" Eyal told Galit the last joke Shimon told him.

"That's the last thing the guy did before he died? Tried to imitate your sense of humor?"

"You see, there's still someone out there who appreciates my attempts to be funny."

"Yeah, a serial killer who chops ladies' hands off."

"And elephant trunks."

"You know what? On second thought, I think I will go for the elephant trunk." Galit kissed Eyal.

"You think it'll become part of our official terminology?"

"No freaking way, I don't want to be reminded of everything that happened whenever we have sex."

"As always, you make an excellent point."

"The trunk of an elephant, but the tongue of a scaredy cat."

"Yes, my love."

They got up and with their arms around each other, quietly snuck back to her parents' house.

Made in the USA
Coppell, TX
01 July 2020